Dear Reader,

This month I'm delighted to include another book by Kay Gregory, whose first *Scarlet* novel, *Marry Me Stranger* was such a hit with you all. You can also enjoy the second book in Liz Fielding's intriguing 'Beaumont Brides' trilogy.' Then we have another romance from talented author Maxine Barry. *Destinies* is a complete novel in itself, but we're sure you'll want to read *Resolutions* next month to find out 'what happens next!' And finally, we're very pleased to bring you another new author – Laura Bradley has produced an exciting and page-turning story.

Do let me know, won't you, what you think of the titles we've chosen for you this month? Do *you* enjoy linked books and books with a touch of mystery or do you like your romance uncluttered by other elements?

By the way, thank you if you've already written to me. I promise I *shall* answer your letter as soon as I can. Your comments will certainly help me plan our list over the coming months.

Till next month,

Sally Cooper

SALLY COOPER,
Editor – *Scarlet*

About the Author

Laura Bradley lives in San Antonio, USA, with her husband and three daughters. In 1990 she began to pursue her writing career full time and is delighted to have had *Wicked Liasions* accepted by *Scarlet*. When she isn't working on her novels, Laura writes non-fiction articles and is a regular contributor to many American periodicals.

After working her way through University as a television and radio reporter, Laura graduated in 1986. The ABC television affiliate in Honolulu hired her as a weekend news producer and she was quickly promoted to the weekday ten o'clock news. A year and a half later, Laura was KITV's senior producer, a position she held for another two years.

In her spare time, Laura enjoys riding and training horses, hiking, water skiing and reading (of course!)

Other *Scarlet* titles available this month:

THE SHERRABY BRIDES by Kay Gregory
DESTINIES by Maxine Barry
WILD LADY by Liz Fielding

LAURA BRADLEY

WICKED LIAISONS

SCARLET

Enquiries to:
Robinson Publishing Ltd
7 Kensington Church Court
London W8 4SP

First published in the UK by Scarlet, 1997

A copy of the British Library Cataloguing in
Publication data is available from the British Library

ISBN 1–85487–711-9

Printed and bound in the EC

10 9 8 7 6 5 4 3 2 1

To my mother who always knew it was 'when', not 'if',
and
To my husband who made the 'when' possible

When we are in love, we often doubt that which we most believe.

La Rochefoucauld

PROLOGUE

Miranda had never thought of her C-cups as business assets before. But looking up at the tall tree now, she had to admit her bra size was about to come in very handy for this job. Tucking her heavy Nikon camera snugly into her cleavage, she shinned up the trunk. The tree's rough bark snagged at her brand-new Levi's. As she leaned down to free a piece of denim, her cotton T-shirt got hung up on a limb which ripped a hole in her right sleeve.

'Damn,' Miranda muttered. 'I'm going to have to ask for a clothes allowance.'

Just as she reached the limb she'd scouted out as the best vantage point, the door to the condominium creaked open. Miranda's heart jumped. She strained to blend into the foliage, wishing the live oak's tiny leaves were thicker and fuller, a little more like a magnolia's maybe. But no, she thought, then I'd have a helluva time getting a shot of the bedroom, wouldn't I?

Anxiety silenced Miranda's inner debate as a man's head peeked around the corner. Her subject. Or one of them, anyway.

'Can't be too careful, Pumpkin,' he called back toward the doorway, which was out of Miranda's view. 'Thought I heard somethin' out here. Since we have all afternoon, you know I don't want any interruptions.'

Miranda heard a breathy giggle. Her other subject. The man reviewed his reflection in the window and ran a hand over his silver hair before he disappeared without looking

1

up into the tree. Thank God for mid-life-crisis male vanity. Miranda let out the breath she'd been holding.

Settling herself in her hiding place, Miranda extracted her camera. At least that had come through the climb unscathed. Unlike the rest of her, she thought, as she ruefully examined the scrapes on the insides of her forearms. She scooted further down the branch to get an unimpeded view of the bedroom.

She waited.

And waited.

Suddenly it occurred to Miranda that the pair might never even get to the bedroom. If that was the case, she was lost.

'I'm not cut out for this business,' she whispered to herself, actually looking forward to giving up on the stakeout that was now into its eighth hour.

Just then the couple inched, lip-locked, into the bedroom. Miranda focused her camera and began shooting.

Click. Click.

Suddenly the woman pushed him away impatiently. Miranda tried to read their lips but could only make out what looked like 'vaudeville' but must have really been 'vodka' because the man hurried over to a cabinet that doubled as a wet bar, complete with mini-refrigerator.

Miranda pursed her lips in a silent whistle. 'This dude is prepared.'

Click. Click.

She took some shots of him, thinking her client would be interested in how well he kept his lover's nook stocked with a variety of liquor, from Glenlivet to Ouzo. It certainly implied a variety of guests with expensive tastes.

While Loverboy busied himself making drinks, Miranda got her first good look at the girl he'd called 'Pumpkin'. She was at least thirty years his junior, young enough to be his daughter had he not married so late in life. Her straight, bleached-blonde hair hung in a sheet to her waist. She peeled off her skin-tight tank-top, leaving her bare breasts loose above her micro-mini skirt.

2

He grabbed a bottle of chilled Stolichanaya from the refrigerator and poured their drinks into gold-rimmed highball glasses. Handing one to her, he ran the beading glass across her nipples. After downing half of her Stoli in one swallow, Pumpkin put the glass down and planted her hands on her hips. She was certainly agitated about something. Her mouth moved in a persimmon-colored blur. Miranda prayed for a sudden ability to lip-read.

Click. Click.

She also prayed they wouldn't close the curtains.

Loverboy tipped his head back and downed his vodka, then reached into his pants pocket and pulled out a black velveteen jewelry case. Pumpkin snatched it from his hands and Miranda swore when she couldn't see what was inside. Whatever it was must have been good because Pumpkin threw herself on her lover, burying his face in her high breasts. Surely artificial, Miranda told herself as she watched Loverboy (who didn't care if they were artificial or not) revel in his thank you for a while. Finally, he pushed her away. She did a sensuous strip-tease. Miranda's camera began to rewind its roll of film.

'Damn,' she whispered.

Quickly, she reloaded, just as the man put his gift on the nude woman, a stunning sapphire and diamond necklace. Miranda gasped at the brilliance she could appreciate even through the lens. Then the blonde undressed him, her mouth on him and his on her. Miranda felt her face growing flush with embarrassment. She'd been told it would get easier. It would get to be routine, her colleagues and boss promised. But it wasn't yet. She still felt like a voyeur. She still regretted the invasion of privacy.

Click. Click.

Miranda's stomach turned as she thought of his wife and two young kids at home. They thought he was hard at work right now. Well, he *was* hard at work. It just wasn't business he was working on. Miranda shook her head to the sick sense of humor she was developing.

Loverboy shoved Pumpkin up on the dresser, which,

3

because he faced the mirror, ironically gave Miranda a great shot of both his face and that of his young lover's.

Click. Click.

Her legs wrapped around his bare buttocks, her long polished nails dug into his shoulder. His face – tattooed with persimmon-tinted lip marks – shone with sweat and was contorted with lust. Pumpkin looked bored. The dresser shook with such force, the lamp crashed to the floor. He was too far gone, but Pumpkin looked toward the broken glass which also happened to be near the window. Her eyes widened as she caught sight of Miranda, and realization dawned.

Miranda didn't wait. She stuffed the camera back into her cleavage and slid back down the tree, doubletime. She could see and hear her frenzied shouts over his groans as Pumpkin tried to get her lover's attention.

Miranda jogged halfway across the lawn before she heard a man shouting at her. Looking back, she saw Loverboy pulling on his pants as he ran.

'Stop, bitch, or I'm gonna call the cops.'

Time to crank it up, Miranda thought.

Running now at full speed, Miranda gave thanks that he was fifty instead of thirty and that his orgasm had given her a headstart. As she reached the spot where the condominium complex ended and the woods began, she glanced back to see that the old dude was flagging. Slowing her pace somewhat, she was just about to duck into the woods when she heard the pop and a branch next to her head splintered.

Before her mind could make sense of it, her body responded by diving into a bush. Miranda peeked through to see Pumpkin holding a revolver. Apparently she'd surprised Loverboy too, because he'd turned around and was making a beeline back to Pumpkin.

'Oh hell. You just don't know who's going to be shooting at you these days.' The Governor of Texas had signed a concealed weapon bill into law earlier in the year. Miranda had backed it wholeheartedly. The close

4

encounter with the bullet made her reconsider her position.

The complex's uniformed security guard appeared, gun drawn, and he looked all too eager to use it. Miranda didn't want to give him the chance. She headed deep into the underbrush, snaking her way in between trees and through a gully in case anyone was still following her. When she decided they had given up, she slowed to a walk and caught her breath.

'I need to look on the bright side,' Miranda told herself. 'How many people can get a workout and do their job at the same time? I can give up my health club membership. Think of all the time and money I'll save.'

Turning in the direction of her car, she tried not to think about how shaken she was, not from the chase and not from the shot, but from the intimate scene she had witnessed and recorded. Maybe it was time to think about another line of work.

CHAPTER 1

'Hey, babe, let's work a deal. I get you in the door and you be my woman for the night. I hear babes hit their sexual peak at thirty and I'm eighteen. It'd be bitchin'.'

Miranda stared into the acne-riddled face and wished she'd brought her gun. Not that she'd shoot him. Just letting him know she had it would be pleasure enough. Or would it? she considered wryly. After all, he had thought she was thirty and she was still a few years shy of that. Maybe raging hormones were clouding his vision. Or maybe she needed to invest in some cold cream.

Plucking the boy's hand off her hip, Miranda graced him with a rare smile. Thinking she was about to acquiesce, his leer broadened and he bobbed his head up and down as his buddies elbowed him.

'If you are eighteen, you can't get into this place,' Miranda pointed out loud enough for the bouncer at the door to hear. 'So I guess you can't hold up your part of the bargain.'

The bouncer, whose carved muscles and stillness could have made him a perfect body double for a statue, proved he was alive and moved away from the neon 'Electric Blues' sign. With astonishing speed, he wove through the line of people and grabbed Miranda's would-be paramour by the collar. Giving a grunt, the bouncer propelled the youth to the Paseo Del Rio, the walkway that bordered the San Antonio River. The boy's three buddies followed, muttering obscenities.

7

Miranda thought they'd do some macho posturing and then leave with their pride intact. But, instead, one of them shoved the bouncer in the back. Mistake. With one sweep of his arm, and no change of expression, the bouncer sent all four of them into the water.

A few in the queue gasped and rushed to help (obviously tourists who didn't know the river was only waist deep). But the dripping boys stood and waded to the other bank, clambering out and heading down the flagstone sidewalk as fast as they could. The line of people parted to let the bouncer back through. Miranda grabbed his arm as he passed. Blinking once, he turned to her with a stony glance.

'Look, I was headed up to you when that cretin stopped me,' Miranda began. He gave no response, so she continued. 'Wayne Lambert is expecting me. I'm Miranda Randolph.'

He looked her up and down and nodded once, then inclined his head toward the door. He obviously expected her to follow him. Maybe he was mute, Miranda thought as she elbowed her way past those at the head of the line. He certainly was immune to the gorgeous women whispering all sorts of offers if he'd let them in the club early.

It took a moment for Miranda to realize some of the whispers were directed at her:

'Just another Lambert Lamb.'

'Wayne had a little lamb, little lamb, little lamb.'

'Is what you gotta do for Lambert worth jumping the line, babe?'

Miranda felt the heat on her cheeks at their insinuations. She wasn't even guilty of what they were suggesting, yet her psyche was responding as if she was. Figure that one out, Dr Freud.

Making note of her new client's apparently famous promiscuity, Miranda ducked under the arm of the bouncer. He held the door open just enough to let her squeeze through. She felt pressure on her back as a few others tried to slip in with her. They didn't make it and the door swished closed behind her.

8

She paused at the vacant hostess stand and caught her breath. The air inside the nightclub was charged with excitement. Taped blues music floated down from ceiling speakers, serving as a harmony for the chattering of customers who were just getting settled in their seats. The interior was lit with an odd combination of neon signs and recessed lights. It was at once inviting and electric. Aha, Miranda thought to herself, hence the name of the club: Electric Blues. She'd have to ask who came up with such a fitting moniker.

Gradually, she came to recognize the prickly feeling of being watched. Casting her eyes about the entry way Miranda could see it wasn't any of the customers milling around. Her visual tour came to rest on a poster on an easel nearly beside her. She met the eyes she'd felt on her. Twinkling, teasing eyes that made her face feel flush. Blushing over a poster? What was happening to her?

'Cole Taylor and His Baby Blues' the poster proclaimed in big blue letters. The eyes belonged to a guy who might have stepped straight out of the fifties: he wore tight, faded blue jeans, a white T-shirt and slicked-back dark blond hair. With a raised left eyebrow and quirky grin, he looked like James Dean with a sense of humor.

Just then a harried waitress carrying a tray full of glasses of frothing beer bustled up to her. 'You better grab a seat before he lets any more in here. They're going fast.'

'I'm here to see Mr Lambert.'

The waitress lifted both eyebrows and gave Miranda a quick once-over before pointing. 'Wayne's at the bar.'

Miranda bit her lip on the explanation that rose in her throat. It wasn't anybody's business why she was there. They could think whatever they wanted to think. Still, she reached up and closed another button on the long-sleeved silk shirt she wore with her matching black skirt. Then she turned toward the bar.

She saw a middle-aged man in black Levi's a size too small, brown hair a shade too dark and inch too long and a laugh a decibel too loud. He was fifty trying to be thirty-five and failing miserably.

9

'He's just too-too,' Miranda said under her breath.

'He is that,' the waitress chuckled, surprising Miranda who didn't realize she'd spoken loud enough to be heard.

As she watched, Wayne left the woman he'd been talking to at the bar and swaggered over to two giggling blonde co-eds sitting at a table in the middle of the club. Miranda thought he must have a great view of a mile or two of cleavage, considering his vantage point and their choice of fashion. She guessed these two 'lambs' didn't have to wait in line.

Wayne put his hand on the taller one's shoulder and let his thumb trail to the bare skin below her collarbone. Miranda thought about what her boss had said about Wayne Lambert, a gigolo who'd married a wealthy widow twenty years his senior. Victoria Rickover Lambert was one of the most prominent philanthropists in the city. She'd bankrolled him in a half-dozen different businesses over the years. They'd all gone belly-up. Miranda wondered if Victoria knew how 'friendly' Wayne was with other women and if that was the reason he'd had to come up with his own financing for Electric Blues.

Now Wayne thought he was being blackmailed, which was why he called Miranda's boss, Doug Sanders. But Doug thought Wayne was just being paranoid which was why Miranda was meeting with Wayne now. She was at the bottom of a very tall totem pole at the largest private investigative firm in San Antonio.

She was probably wasting her time with this loser, Miranda admitted to herself. But if she was going to make it in her new career, she was going to have to do more than be a Peeping Tom. Or would it be Peeping Thomasina? Anyway, she had to start somewhere. Although, watching Wayne slobbering on the Busty Bunnies, she doubted that this was her big break. As she stood mired in inertia, Wayne caught sight of her and rushed over without a goodbye to the bewildered girls.

Miranda reached out for a handshake. Wayne clutched her hand, but used it to pull her to him where he planted a quick kiss on her cheek. She recoiled. Her burning nose told her he was well into a bottle of scotch. Great, she thought, a lecher and a drunk. This blackmail case is going to be a real step-up from all that tawdry divorce surveillance, after all.

'I'm Miranda Randolph. Wayne Lambert?' Miranda hoped he'd mistaken her for someone else.

'Of course you are, and of course I am. Guess we should have introduced ourselves before we got intimate. Ha!' Wayne got lost in his own hilarity and laughed until tears were forming in the corners of his eyes.

Miranda failed to see the humor but admitted that she might after a fifth of Chivas Regal. Wayne was still guffawing as he grabbed Miranda around the waist with his right arm and guided her to the only empty table, at the right side of the stage.

For the sake of the job, Miranda fought off the urge to slap Wayne and reluctantly yielded enough to make the transition graceful for the casual observer, which is what Cole Taylor was.

Making last minute adjustments to equipment on stage, Cole had caught sight of the lithe beauty with the porcelain skin and cascading auburn hair. It had been a long time since a woman in the audience had caught more than his passing notice. But this woman was different.

Cole leaned over a speaker and watched the woman through the hair that fell down across his forehead. Her hair drew his attention. It wasn't auburn, he decided. It was red. No, it was brunette. It was indescribable and it was incredible. Cole ached to reach out and touch it. He frowned as Wayne put his hand on her thigh. Disappointed, Cole was ready to dismiss her as another 'lamb' until he saw her back stiffen and her hand reach down and firmly place Wayne's groping appendage back on the table between them.

'Any problem?' asked Trent Simon, the band's lead guitar, and one of Cole's best friends.

'No problem,' Cole straightened up. 'We're ready to roll.'

'I meant with you, guy. Any problem with you? You've been pretty distracted tonight.'

'No,' Cole paused. He shook his head and then let out a breath. 'Well . . . I've decided to break it off with Sable. I've been trying to work out the best way to tell her.'

'It's about time.' Trent smiled and slapped Cole on the back. 'I never did see what kept you two together. Except it was convenient. But that ain't enough, man. I guess you've figured that out.'

Cole nodded. 'Yeah. I suppose I've always known it wasn't enough, in the back of my mind anyway. And, now that we've brought the band back home to San Anton, I can feel the lack. You know, I'd like to have somebody to really care about.'

'You mean somebody to love. It's not a bad word, Cole,' Trent teased.

'Easy for you to say. You are in love.'

'It's an easy thing to do. Just let your heart lead your head for a change.'

'Yeah,' Cole allowed as he let his eyes drift back to the mysterious redhead with Wayne. 'Maybe I'll do that.'

'I'm being blackmailed.'

Wayne issued his declaration in a stage whisper across the table at Miranda. She fought to keep her face impassive.

'I know,' she whispered back, just as dramatically. 'You told me over the phone.'

Wayne's florid face colored a deeper red. 'Oh, yeah.'

So much for melodrama, Miranda thought. Wayne looked as if he didn't know how to go about explaining now that his shock value was down to zero.

'Is there more, or am I going to have to guess?' Miranda couldn't help the sarcasm. Wayne just seemed to invite it.

His eyes narrowed. 'You got a smart mouth for such a bodacious babe.'

Miranda didn't know whether to laugh or spit in his eye. Much to the disappointment of her impulses, she chose a

12

higher road. 'Look, Wayne, you may have "babes", as you call them, lined up for two blocks wanting to partake of your numerous charms. However, I'm not one of them. I'm not here to have you rate my body or criticise my speech. I'm here to solve a problem for you. That is, if you really have a problem.'

''A course I've a Goddamn problem,' Wayne asserted as he reached into his red western-cut jacket and handed her a manila envelope. 'Lambert' was written in roman type in the upper right corner. Miranda knew Wayne had handled the envelope extensively without using gloves, so any fingerprints that might have been there had probably already been obliterated. Still, she slid the contents out carefully with her fingertips. On the top was a note written in the same type that appeared on the envelope:

Copies of these will be sent to your wife unless you comply with the demands that will follow in a future package. If you think the photos are hot, wait till you see the video.

Miranda thought the note sounded more like an advertisement than a threat and it must have shown in her face because Wayne barked out defensively, 'What? What's so funny?'

Miranda ignored him, which was getting easier to do, and set the letter carefully aside. The five photographs, eight-by-ten glossies, were explicit and Miranda felt her face growing hot with embarrassment. They showed Wayne and a younger woman in what Miranda considered exotic sexual encounters, all apparently inside Electric Blues. In most they were both naked, on the bar, on the stage, on a table. Ropes, whips and other equipment Miranda could not identify were being used in various combinations. In one shot, both were clothed, Wayne's pants around his knees, his shirt ripped. His hips had the mini-skirted woman pinned against the wall.

Miranda wondered what the customers would think if they knew what had happened where they put their glasses and elbows. She briefly raised her eyes to see that next to the neon sign on the far wall, a man was tipped back in his chair with his head leaned against the spot where Wayne's companion had been caught in a, well, compromising position.

Letting out a long breath, Miranda put the pictures on the table. Wayne covered them with the envelope before they were even out of her hand.

'Who is she, Wayne?'

Just then, the crowd roared and Miranda had the answer to her question. Cole Taylor and His Baby Blues came on stage. Wayne was having an affair with a Baby Blue. She looked about thirty years old – splitting the difference between an eighteen-year-old body and a forty-year-old face. The signs of hard living more than wrinkles belied her age. Her olive skin stretched tight over high cheekbones that framed deep-set dark eyes. Miranda knew from the photographs as well as the skin-tight blue leather jumpsuit she wore now that her body was as hard as her face. As she moved across the stage Miranda noticed there was something serpentine about her. She exuded sex.

'Her name is Sable Diamonte,' Wayne said reverently. 'I met her two months ago when Cole bought into the place with me and brought his band in for a run. What a lay . . .'

Wayne's crudeness was really making Miranda uncomfortable, but she was determined not to let him know. He was perverse enough to enjoy watching her squirm.

'So your affair started right after you met?'

'A couple of days later. We couldn't keep our hands off each other. Still can't.'

'How often do you meet?'

'Whenever one of us has a hard-on. Ha!'

Miranda decided Wayne's short, barking laugh was a nervous habit.

'Which is how often? Once a week? Every day?

Do I really want to know this? Miranda asked herself.

'Sometimes twice a day,' Wayne answered with a braggart's grin. Miranda felt like she was in the men's

14

locker room at the health club. Who said divorce surveillance was tawdry? Her skin was beginning to crawl.

'So when were these taken?' Miranda waved toward the photos that were still hidden under the envelope.

'How would I know? I di'n't take 'em,' Wayne paused. 'I do recollect the one against the wall, though. She ripped my shirt. Wild. That was . . . uh . . . last Wednesday. In the afternoon.'

The band started playing, putting a stop to their conversation. Miranda was relieved. Dealing with Wayne took all her concentration. Now she'd have time to sift through what little he'd told her. She also wanted to get a handle on the Diamonte woman. What kept her involved with Wayne? He certainly wasn't an irresistible physical specimen. And his personality was offensive. Not to mention his breath. Maybe it was the sex. It was Wayne's singular motivation. But Miranda suspected Sable Diamonte had more on her agenda. Women usually did.

Miranda had her back to the stage so she turned her chair around to face the band just as Cole Taylor started singing the lyrics to the first song. She felt like the oxygen had suddenly been sucked out of her lungs. She gasped for air in quick breaths, hoping no one would notice her hyperventilating.

His eyes had made her blush, but his voice was doing unspeakable things to her body.

The very cute, very slow button-nosed waitress stepped into Miranda's line of sight. She plopped the wineglass in front of Miranda. Grateful for the distraction, Miranda took a swallow instead of a sip.

'Better slow down, or you'll end up like me. Ha!' Wayne yelled across the table, waving his Chivas on the rocks.

Turning back to the stage as she crossed her legs, Miranda met Cole's eyes and his smoldering look sent her heart out of control. It was as if he burned a path straight into her soul. Miranda didn't look away and wasn't sure she wanted to. The lyrics he sang didn't register in Miranda's mind, but the way he sang them did. His voice was both raw and sensual, mischievious and mysterious. It was Cole who finally looked away, to other members of his audience. But he kept glancing back at Miranda, and when he did, she felt as if they were the only two in the room.

Miranda didn't know much about music, except what she liked. And she liked Cole Taylor and His Baby Blues. A country and blues fan, she couldn't fit his music into either category neatly, although it carried the flavor of each along with a dash of jazz. With the self-deprecating humor of country, he sang about losing his dog, his woman and his job 'in the same day, in the same way'. Then he'd remind Miranda of Al Jarreau as his voice traveled octaves telling of the exuberance of falling in love. The next song was a wild duel of electric guitar and husky voice as Cole recounted a telephone conversation with 'his baby'. The last song in the set told a ribald tale of a girlfriend. It was sexy and funny and Miranda found herself wondering if it was true. She guessed it was and, inexplicably, felt jealous.

Cole thanked his audience in a low-key murmur into the microphone and the band split up for a short break. His clothes might have looked sloppy on someone else, but on Cole they came off as casual chic – the sleeves of his T-shirt too small across the biceps, his Levi's faded in a custom-made way that only comes from lots of wear from the right body, and black ostrich boots scuffed enough to show they were old favorites. He wore no jewelry save a piece of brown suede leather knotted around his wrist.

Miranda was unnerved by his effect on her. She was afraid if he got any closer his touch would erase her judgement, his breath would make her senses melt. She couldn't let that happen again. The disaster with Rick nearly destroyed her. Panic welled up in her chest.

As she always did with her life, Miranda tried to analyze her feelings. What is it about Cole Taylor that is so compelling? she asked herself.

His hair was slicked back, revealing a soft widow's peak. But it was so thick and unruly that his hand often had to

16

run through it to brush back errant strands that fell down over his forehead. Miranda decided that mannerism was what made him seem vulnerable. Nothing else about him was, though. His eyes seemed to laugh at the world with a knowledge of all the ironies life dished up. But underneath all that those eyes were honest and that made them incredibly magnetic. He was a man comfortable in his own skin, unapologetic and unbroken.

The hand waved in front of her face gave Miranda a start.

'Earth to Miranda!' Wayne bellowed. 'What orbit are you in?'

'What?' Miranda hadn't realized she was so lost in thought. How long had Wayne been looking at her like that? Could he guess what she was thinking?

'I'm sorry. I was just running through a few things in my head.'

'Yeah. Like I was saying, Vicki just can't find out about this. So, no cops, no reporters. You ain't gonna call any of your friends at the TV station, are ya?'

Usually Wayne's crass comment would have upset Miranda. The way she was ousted from the news business was still painful, but she was so distracted by Cole's presence that she barely noticed the twinge in her stomach.

'I don't have that many friends at the station anymore, so don't worry about it.'

She glanced over at the stage and saw Cole crouched down, his elbows resting on his thighs, talking to the Busty Bunnies who leaned invitingly against the stage. Those two sure get around, Miranda thought. Cole laughed. Miranda wrenched her eyes away to look at Wayne, who was blathering with embarrassment.

'Oh yeah. Sorry about that. Hated to see them give you the boot. Sure do miss you on the tube.'

The guy spouted so many cliches, if you banned them from his vocabulary he wouldn't have anything to say. Miranda held her tongue in deference to her better judgement.

17

'You look different, in person, I gotta say,' Wayne looked at her closely. 'It's the hair I think. It's longer. And it never looked this red to me. You get a dye-job or somethin'?'

Miranda sighed. Television did tend to distort people's looks. People, in the flesh, rarely looked exactly like they did when transferred through the little screen. It uniformly added weight and emphasized certain features, making some more attractive, others less so. But in this case Miranda had to admit her appearance had changed.

'It's the other way around. I used to color my hair. My news director thought the auburn was too distracting so I had to keep a brown rinse on it. And I had it cut in a short bob then too.'

'I like this a helluva lot better, that's for damn sure,' Wayne enthused as he eyeballed her hair that grazed the bottom of her shoulder blades.

Uncomfortable talking about her appearance, Miranda got back to the case.

'Wayne, tell me why you don't want any police involved.'

'Well, uh,' Wayne's eyes shifted around the bar. Then his gaze sharpened as it settled back on Miranda. 'Hey, that's right. You used to be the police reporter, di'n't you? You know all those pigs. You might tell them about this.'

'If you're not going to trust me, then I shouldn't be working for you,' Miranda challenged, as she reached for her bag in a move to leave.

Wayne reached over and put a damp, restraining hand on her arm.

'Now don't go gettin' your panties in a wad. I'm just tryin' to be circumspent.'

Miranda ignored his mispronunciation. She suspected he was trying to impress her with a big vocabulary he obviously didn't have. Fortifying herself with a sip of wine, Miranda got back to business.

'Wayne, who knows about your affair?'

'With Sable, y'mean?'

18

'Are there others?' This was going to be harder than she thought.

'Well, a couple,' Wayne hedged.

'Now? Recently?'

'Not now, that's for sure. Sable keeps my motor primed all by herself. Ha!'

'Would any of your former, ah, girlfriends be particularly jealous?'

'Why? Are they suspects?' Wayne wiped the beading sweat off his forehead with the back of his hand.

'That first note was so vague that anyone who can work a camera or could hire someone to use one is a suspect.'

'Well,' Wayne began reluctantly. 'One moved to Seattle. One got married and she wouldn't be a problem anyway. Then, Roxanne told me –'

Miranda put a hand up to stop him. 'Let's do this. Let's wait until the next note is delivered and we'll see if that doesn't eliminate them as suspects. It may get more specific and help us narrow this down. We still don't know what the blackmailer wants. That will be the most telling.'

The band was gathering again on stage and the Busty Bunnies reluctantly drifted back to their table, batting eyelashes over their shoulders at Cole. The denim-clad waiters and waitresses hurried drink orders to the restless customers.

Button-nose bounced back with another Merlot for Miranda and Wayne's third and fourth double Chivas. She brought him two at a time.

'So, back to my first question,' Miranda continued after Button-nose had flounced off. 'Who knows about you and Sable?'

'No one. I told ya why I have to keep a lid on it. To tell ya the truth, Sable made a point of keeping it hush-hush, because she said it wouldn't look too good for the boss to be hosing the help. As if it was the first time. Ha! 'Scuse my French.'

'You were so discreet that no one knew or even sus-

19

pected anything was going on?' Miranda was dubious. 'Where do you meet?'

'Here, almost always. A few times I get a nice hotel room, y'know.'

'Never at her place?'

'I ain't got any idea where her place is. I guess it's in the computer, but I ain't thought to look it up. What would I want it for?' Wayne sounded incredulous.

Miranda tempered her amazement. He was sleeping with Sable but didn't care where she lived?

'Okay. So, no one ever caught you two here. Well . . . obviously someone did.' Miranda inclined her head toward the hidden photographs. 'But no one you know of?'

'Nope.'

'No current or former employees who might have a grudge against you?'

'Nope.'

Miranda's eyes were drawn like a magnet to the stage, where Cole was leaning over an amplifier, the seat of his jeans stretching tightly at the pockets leaving an outline of the bunched muscles underneath.

'You said earlier that Cole owns a share of the club?'

'Yep, he's got forty and I got sixty. Percent, that is.'

'You've told him about the threat?'

'Hell, no,' Wayne yelped.

Once again the volume of the music stopped their conversation. Cole jumped into the second set with a teasing tale of a bachelor on the prowl with women his willing prey. Miranda didn't doubt that this was the story of his life. With his pure animal magnetism and naughty little-boy looks, she was sure he had his pick of women, and then some.

Still, Cole didn't appear to take himself too seriously. For all the arrogance of his song, he seemed to be laughing at himself. Suddenly, Cole jumped off the stage and Miranda's heart jumped with him. He landed like a tomcat on the floor next to her table. Miranda gasped and prayed fervently that he wouldn't catch her eye now. Not while he was close enough to touch.

She didn't know whether she was relieved or disappointed when he ignored her.

Cole went on the prowl like the man in his song, from woman to woman, teasing and tempting them. He bent down to blow in the petite Busty Bunny's ear. She giggled and blushed a babydoll pink. Miranda felt as if his lips were on her ear and she felt herself growing hot. All over.

Then Cole turned back toward the stage and looked straight at Miranda. She stiffened while her heart beat wildly. She didn't trust herself to move. What would her body do if he touched her? Implode, melting like a nuclear reactor, she decided. His casual, jaunty stride brought him to her table and she went deaf. He was singing, but Miranda couldn't hear the words. Their eyes carried on a conversation. Miranda felt simultaneously disoriented and focused. Why did his proximity drown out some of her senses while it brought others to new levels of sensitivity?

The intimacy of their look began to embarrass Miranda. She knew she should put on a superficial smile to break the spell, but her lips would not obey her mind. Then he was gone. Leaping back on stage, Cole finished his song and within seconds it was as if the moment between them had never happened. Maybe for him it hadn't, Miranda admitted to herself as she watched Cole through the rest of the set. He flirted unmercifully with every female in Electric Blues.

As Cole and Sable eased into a sexy duet, Wayne leaned over to yell in Miranda's ear. He had to talk to the bartender. Miranda nodded stiffly as she shoved his hand off her upper thigh. She wondered if his exit was a coincidence or whether it was because he hated to see anyone touch his mistress. Wayne didn't seem the sentimental or even the jealous type, though. Miranda guessed he would perceive attentions paid to his lovers as justification of his own good taste and sexual prowess.

Actually, Miranda found her own stomach clutching at the sight of the pair on stage. She averted her eyes, but

21

found them drawn magnetically back to Sable whose deep, smooth olive skin, short-cropped hair and incredibly toned body invited sex just standing still. Cole's hand traveled down the blue leather that molded to Sable's skin, while she wrapped her serpentine body around his.

Miranda jumped up to escape into the ladies' room but, just then, Cole shook himself loose and ended the song a little abruptly. Even the guitarist in the corner looked surprised.

The Baby Blues were already into their next song before Miranda could figure out what had happened, if anything. Had Sable taken the performance a little too far for Cole's taste? Maybe his girlfriend (or wife?) was in the audience and Cole didn't want her getting the wrong impression. Miranda shook her head impatiently. Why should she care whether or not he was involved with anyone? She couldn't imagine how it could have any bearing on the blackmail case. And that was the only reason she was there.

All at once, Miranda felt worn out. Maybe two wines were her limit. After all, she rarely drank anymore. It was too easy to blame the alcohol, though. Her muddled mind could more likely be traced to the attraction she felt for Cole. It had been so long since she'd been interested in any man that she was probably letting a look from a sexy singer go to her head.

By the time Wayne returned to the table she had talked herself out of an attraction to Cole Taylor and was ready to wrap up business and call it a night.

'Let me know when you get the next note.' Miranda slid the photographs back into the manila envelope. 'I'm going to take this stuff with me.'

'You have to take them?' Wayne whined.

'Well, Wayne, if you want me to find out who's doing it and why, I do need the evidence. If you've changed your mind and would rather have someone else do it, that's fine, too.'

Miranda made it sound like an invitation. She was ready to get out of this case. For a lot of reasons.

'No! No! No!' Wayne barked hysterically. 'I want you to handle it.'

The second set ended and customers started to mill around and talk. Miranda kept her eyes away from the stage as she gathered her purse and put the envelope inside. She pushed her chair back.

'Aren't you going to introduce me to your lovely companion?' asked a voice from behind Miranda. It was lazy and deep. There was a teasing grin behind the words. She didn't have to look to see who it was. Her treacherous body told her.

'Oh, uh, sure,' Wayne finally untied his tongue enough to continue. 'Cole Taylor, entertainer extraordinaire, this is Miranda Randolph.'

Miranda knew she had to turn around and face him, common courtesy demanded that. But she was afraid. Afraid that her hand might reach out and touch the hard line of his jaw, the dimple that was losing itself in a five o'clock shadow, the chest hair that just peeked out the top of his T-shirt.

She swiveled around and stood up all in one fluid motion.

'It's a pleasure to meet you,' Miranda intoned in a way that sounded stiff even to her own ears. She extended her hand.

'Oh my, a real lady.' Cole gave a wicked chuckle while casually brushing his lips across the top of Miranda's hand. She hoped he couldn't feel the shivers it sent to every erogenous zone in her body.

'This surprises me, Wayne. Not your style at all. In wives, yes. In dates, no.'

Miranda narrowed her eyes at Cole while Wayne sputtered, casting his eyes nervously about the room.

'Watch it, Taylor.'

'Are you afraid that I've offended your guest, or that I'll give away the worst-kept secret in San Antonio?'

'Miz Randolph is not my date, okay?' Wayne said in his stage whisper.

Miranda raised her eyebrows at the formal reference

that was anything but Wayne's oratorical style. Why did talking to Cole put him so on edge?

'It's not pleasure. Hmm. Then it must be business.' Cole sounded bored, as if he were killing time. His eyes drifted slowly down Miranda's body and back up again. 'What are you? A scotch saleswoman? Or maybe a city tax auditor? Really, Wayne, as part-owner of this joint I ought to be apprised of these official visits.'

Irritation was fast replacing her attraction to him. Miranda was itching to slap his cocky face, but before she had the chance to, Wayne rose to the bait.

'I am still majority owner and manager. I make the damned decisions. My voice carries the most weight.'

'Calm yourself, Wayne. I do have a right to be involved in the decision-making, but you are the manager and so far we've been working it out fine.' The sparkle in Cole's gray eyes clouded over as he studied Wayne's sweaty face. 'This is really serious?'

'It's serious as a heart attack, but it's personal. So get lost, Buttinsky.'

'A serious, personal, business discussion that you are having in a crowded, loud club instead of at your quiet, discreet home with your wife. Hmmm.'

Miranda noticed that Cole had recovered his biting tongue quickly. She couldn't tell whether he really cared what Wayne was up to or whether he just enjoyed antagonizing him. Despite her irritation with Cole, she couldn't blame him for wanting to do the latter.

Cole leaned against their table and ran his hands through hair that refused to stay slicked back. Miranda wondered idly what his hair felt like, what it smelled like. Then those gray eyes, lit up again by that lazy grin, turned back on her.

'Not a tax collector . . .' Cole slipped his fingers through his hair. 'You must be Wayne's divorce lawyer. That would explain why he's so jumpy.'

'What makes you think I need a divorce lawyer?' Wayne bristled.

'It's only a matter of time before Victoria gets tired of her charity work,' Cole pointed out, eyebrow cocked.

'What in the hell are you talkin' about?' Wayne cast about in confusion. 'Vicki's devoted to the Children's Safehouse and all those retarded groups.'

Miranda shook her head. If Wayne only could hear himself.

'Subtleties escape you, Wayne,' Cole shook his head too, giving up the game.

Miranda was tired of both of them, and made a move toward the door. 'Get back to me tomorrow, Wayne.'

'Not leaving so soon, are you? Not on my account, I hope,' Cole said with exaggerated sincerity.

'Not at all,' Miranda refused to let him see that he had any effect on her. 'I was on my way out when you walked up.'

Wayne followed her halfway to the door, leaving Cole behind. He watched them, leaning against the table, his arms crossed over his chest, his legs crossed at the ankle. Miranda felt inexplicably self-conscious.

'I really appreciate your help,' Wayne breathed hot, sour scotch fumes into her ear.

Miranda nodded once and was gone.

Wayne walked back to the table. 'Why are you busting my balls tonight, Taylor?'

'Who is she, Wayne?' Cole demanded, his grin gone.

'I told you. Miranda –'

'I heard her name. That doesn't tell me much. What is she doing for you?'

'You don't recognize her from the boob tube? Oh, I guess she got canned right about the time you rode back into town.'

'TV? What did she do on TV?'

'She was a reporter for KATX. Channel Ten. She was a tough-as-nails reporter. Pulled down the pants of the bigwigs at Ravalo Oil and some state politicos with a bribery story. Pissed off folks in Austin and she got the boot. Square in the ass. Not fair really. Her story was right on the money from what I hear.'

25

'Okay,' Cole mused. 'But that still doesn't tell me what she's doing here. Talking to you.'

'You're a stubborn son-of-a-bitch. She's a private eye now. That's all I'm sayin'.'

Trent beckoned Cole for the start of the last set. He left Wayne and leaped back up on stage. His interest was piqued. Miranda Randolph was gorgeous and snotty. An ice queen. But he had pushed her far enough to see something hot flash under that glacial exterior. Fire and ice. He wanted to see a meltdown.

The last set was usually his best. But not tonight. Every time Cole glanced over to Miranda's empty chair, expecting to see those unusual turquoise eyes, he felt disappointed. He realized he had to see her again. Cole finished the show in auto-pilot, his heart and mind on something else.

Outside Electric Blues, Miranda paused to take a deep breath of the early fall air. It was mid-November, but it usually took that long for autumn to reach South Texas and the city was feeling the first cold snap of the season. The dropping temperatures invigorated the crowd that snaked along the flagstone-lined riverwalk. They walked a little faster, laughed a little louder and rubbed bare arms with chilled hands.

It was easy for Miranda to blame her racing blood on the weather. But the seductive music that drifted out of the club mocked her.

She strode off, headed back to her car, cursing her decision to park on St Mary's Street. Miranda reminded herself that she had parked so far away so she could enjoy the glittering water of the river. It had been a mistake because now it was so late that the only people on the romantic Paseo Del Rio were couples. Couples walking arm-in-arm.

Couples laughing. Couples kissing. Couples teasing. Miranda even looked with envy at the man and woman arguing. She felt silly and sentimental. And she felt lonely.

CHAPTER 2

'That was the weirdest show we've ever done,' Trent commented as he packed away his guitar after the last set.

Cole stopped testing chords on his guitar to look at his longtime friend.

'Weird? What was weird?'

'You. Something is going on with you, man. More than just worry about how to break it to Sable. When you want to talk about it, I'm ready to hear it.'

'Oh, it's just something going down with Wayne. I'm trying to figure out what it is. He's not talking.'

'I bet I know what's going down. I saw that lamb he had with him tonight,' Trent laughed.

Cole looked up sharply. 'It's not like that.'

Trent took a step back and waved a hand in surrender. 'Okay, okay. Whatever you say.'

The two men stood in an awkward silence for a beat.

'Well, I'm taking off,' Trent piped up. 'Coming?'

'Nah. I think I'll stay and work on some new songs I'm putting together.' Cole plucked at the guitar strings with little enthusiasm.

'I get first pick then,' Trent called over his shoulder.

Cole smiled at their old private joke that referred to the groupies who waited sometimes for hours outside the clubs where they played. But that's all it was for Trent. A joke. He was happily married with a new baby boy, and if he'd ever taken a groupie to bed Cole didn't know about it.

When he first started performing, Cole thought he'd struck gold with the choice of women willing – some begging – to go to bed with him. It had worn thin fast. Cole admitted to himself that that was one reason he'd stayed with Sable for so long. Being with her gave him an excuse to keep away from the cheap one-night-stands.

'But why did I need an excuse?' Cole asked himself out loud.

'Who are you talking to?'

Sable came from the small dressing room in the back of the club, her eyes darting around. She'd changed into black leather pants and a halter top that showed two inches of rock-hard abdomen and her well-muscled back.

'Myself,' Cole answered shortly.

Sable glanced around furtively as if to satisfy herself that he was indeed alone.

'Well, you don't have to talk to yourself anymore,' she stated as she walked up onto the stage behind him.

Cole didn't turn around, but in a second he could smell her scent. It wasn't a fragrance, it was pure pheromones. A blatant advertisement of sex. As his body responded to that, Cole felt a familiar hand come from behind, settle on his chest and slide slowly down to the zipper of his Levi's. He steeled himself against the inevitable seduction. Sable's voice vibrated against his right ear.

'You were waiting here for me.'

It was a statement, not a question. Sable was nothing if not confident, Cole observed wryly.

'No, I was just brainstorming.'

'Something tells me you need a break.' Her fingers squeezed on his hardening crotch.

Cole stood and turned around, plucking her fingers from his zipper. He despised his weakness and her power over him.

'It's good you're here, Sable. We need to talk,' Cole struggled for the right words, the right tone. He wanted this to be easy, yet knew it couldn't be.

'Okay, talk. Tell me where you want it, how you want

28

it.' Sable's hard, wet mouth affixed itself to his, her words blowing straight into his throat. Her sinewy legs were wrapping around his calves. Her hands rubbed with increasing pace and pressure over the hardness that betrayed what his body wanted, even if his mind didn't.

Cole pushed her away, a little rougher than he meant to, hoping physical distance would help establish a psychological one. She stumbled backwards, grabbing at the guitar amplifier to regain her balance. She shook with anger at his rejection – her sparse lips drawn now into a thin line, her black eyes shining like wet stones.

Cole opened his mouth to apologize, but stopped himself. He wanted to get this over with as quickly as possible. He spoke matter-of-factly.

'It's over. Us, together. It just isn't going to work anymore.'

Sable drew back in a way that made Cole think of a coiling snake.

After a few moments of tense silence, she spat out her words. 'You decided. Of course. You're the boss. Throw me out with the garbage.'

Her harsh laugh made Cole's stomach tighten. 'I never made any promises to you. We never talked about love or –'

'Love? Who said our rutting around had anything to do with love?'

'I just thought . . .' Her sharp look stopped him in mid-sentence. He changed gears. 'I certainly understand if you want to leave the band.'

'Understand! You don't even understand yourself!' Sable sucked in a breath through clenched teeth, then flashed a cold smile. Her voice was tight, but calm. 'Oh no, I think we can continue to work together. You know my music is damn good. You couldn't get on without it.'

Her mercurial change caught Cole off-guard. This wasn't what he'd expected. Not even close.

'Yes,' he admitted. 'Your music is better than it's ever been.'

29

'Good. Then I'll stay on and we won't talk about this again.'

She spun around on the heel of her lace-up black boots and was gone. Cole was left standing in the middle of the stage, staring at the rows of empty tables and chairs.

He blinked twice and shook his head. He realized he didn't know Sable any better now than when she had first latched onto him when the band stopped for a run at the Underground in Austin. A groupie with raw musical talent, she had seduced Cole, then talked him into honing her skills on the bass guitar. Six months later, Sable was good – on the instrument and in bed. Then Greg Pittman, the band's bass guitarist, disappeared without a word and Cole let Sable take over.

Two years of sharing work and sex and still she was an enigma. Cole had tried that first year to unravel the mystery, to see inside her soul. But that soul was surrounded by an impenetrable wall, if she possessed one at all, and Cole eventually stopped trying. For the last year a relationship based on lust had turned into one of mere convenience.

He saw this now in retrospect, for, at the time, he'd been too busy to notice what their relationship had become. Ever since his graduation from college six years before, the band had toured dingy bars across the United States, mostly in the southwest and midwest, with brief trips through the Mexican Riveria. They had picked up Sable along the way and kept on moving. It was rarely glamorous, but always exciting. That excitement and Cole's ability to do something he loved for a living had camouflaged his homesickness and an undefined lack in his life.

Actually, Sable had been the one to encourage him to come back to his hometown. She'd said they needed a place to settle in for a while, build a name for themselves. Cole felt the need too, but when he suggested Austin, Sable insisted on San Antonio. But home was full of bittersweet memories, memories he'd spent his whole adult life running from. Maybe, he conceded, it was time to learn to live with them instead.

30

When Cole not only landed the headline act at Electric Blues, but also the right to buy into the club, he felt his homecoming was meant to be. Suddenly, Cole saw with great clarity that he was at a crossroads of not only his career but of his personal life. Ironically, the woman who brought him home was not the woman he wanted to share it with. With Sable he got sex – whenever, wherever and however he wanted it. Good mechanics. No emotion. It amazed Cole that he hadn't seen it before.

A door slammed down the hall. Cole jumped. Was Sable back? Heavy, uneven steps thumped down the hall where the offices and dressing rooms were located. Wayne's bulky outline appeared, backlit by the hall light.

For a moment, Cole stood frozen, wondering if Wayne had overheard his argument with Sable. Wayne hadn't known he and Sable were involved and Cole wanted to keep it that way. One look at Wayne's alcohol-dilated pupils as he stumbled toward the stage told Cole he had nothing to worry about.

'Just finished checking tonight's ring,' Wayne slurred. 'Good for a Sunday. Sixty-five hun'red. I'm goin' home. Be back in the mornin' to fin'sh the books.'

'Let me drive you.' Cole didn't want Wayne behind the wheel. He could barely stand.

'Nah. I called Paul. He should be outside.'

Victoria's chauffeur didn't get much sleep, Cole decided, with Wayne's late nights and Victoria's early mornings.

Finally alone, Cole sighed and sat down on the stage with his legs dangling over the edge. Knowing he should go home, Cole still couldn't bring himself to. His apartment would be empty. He told himself it wasn't the loss of Sable, who'd never lived with him. What was making him feel so alone tonight, then? Could it be Wayne's pretty private eye was having an effect on him? Cole laughed at the fairy tale his imagination conjured up.

Maybe he should bring Reggie to live in town with him. But it really wouldn't be fair to the Golden Retriever who

31

was happy running free on the ranch. Happy, that is, when Sable wasn't there. Cole's dog had never failed to bark and growl at Sable, so unlike his usual easy-going nature. Cole remarked once that Reggie was just jealous, only to have Trent point out rather wickedly that dogs were good judges of character.

Cole found himself wondering if Reggie would like Miranda. Despite the icy reception he got, there was a softness and vulnerability to her that was lacking in Sable. Cole's laugh sounded loud in the deserted room.

'Most people wonder how their parents will like their girlfriends. I'm hoping mine would pass muster with my dog.' The irony had a bitter ring of truth. Cole knew Reggie would care a helluva lot more about his love interests than his parents would. Hell, it'd been ten years since they'd last seen him, why would they care about any of his friends?

'Well,' Cole found himself again talking to the empty chairs. 'If I'm going to wallow in self-pity tonight, might as well make something of it.'

Cole picked up his old hollow-core guitar, the one he'd had since he was ten years old. His older brother had given it to him for Christmas, after teasing him mercilessly about the songs he made up while the two of them worked cattle on the ranch. Crayne never would have guessed that his gift would inspire Cole to turn a dream into reality.

Not that the dream had come completely true. While Cole was doing what he loved most in the world, he was still unsigned. A few record companies had shown interest, but nothing had ever materialized. He knew he should get an agent, but the ones he'd met were so unsavory, Cole never had the stomach to put his career in their hands. Except for one. Jared Williams. He seemed both interested and ethical. Despite his promises, though, he never got back to Cole. And Cole, afraid of rejection, had never pursued Williams. Now that he'd settled in one place for a while, Cole promised himself he'd get serious about taking the next step in his career.

32

Caressing the familiar wood of the guitar, Cole started to play. After sitting there ruminating for almost an hour, the melody and lyrics suddenly began flowing as if the stopper had been pulled out. It was a song about a man with true friends, good looks, a successful career and his pick of women. A man who had long sensed something was missing, but was just now understanding what that something was. It was a song about himself.

By the time Cole finished revising the new ballad to his satisfaction, it was five in the morning. He wasn't surprised when he looked down at his watch. He often did his best work in the early morning hours.

'The Riverwalk will continue to be one of the safest places in the city of San Antonio. This rape is an isolated incident. We've ordered beefed-up patrols, although I'm sure police will have the perpetrator behind bars by nightfall.'

Coffee sloshed onto the bathroom counter as Miranda set her cup down with a clank. She'd missed the first part of the story while she was in the kitchen. She reached over and turned the volume up on the radio. The mayor's voice was replaced by that of the news anchor.

'Police say they have no suspects in the case at this time. Now turning to news of the state . . .'

Retrieving her coffee cup, Miranda quickly made her way to the television set in the living room. She glanced at the clock as she sank into the butternut suede easy chair. It was 7.25, nearly time for the local newsbreak. The rape story intrigued her because there was rarely any crime on the Riverwalk. The police and hotel security kept it well patrolled without an obvious uniformed presence and a fleet of bicycle cops kept the labyrinth of streets and alleys downtown under a tight rein.

Miranda realized that part of her fascination was natural human curiosity – the reason most drivers slow down to look at an accident on the side of the road. She had been down on the river last night. She could've been the one the media was buzzing about this morning. She could have been the victim. She could have passed the rapist. Remembering the dark walk alone to her car, she shivered involuntarily.

Sherry Silverman replaced the national news anchors on the screen. Miranda sat up.

'San Antonio police detectives this morning are searching for a suspect who is accused of raping a woman near the Riverwalk in the pre-dawn hours. Police reports say the attack occurred in an alley between two buildings. The suspect is described as a Caucasian man in his late twenties to early thirties, six-feet-tall. He was reported to be wearing a black coat or cape over a white T-shirt and faded blue jeans. Anyone with information is asked to call the sex crimes division of the San Antonio Police Department.'

The anchorwoman went on to repeat the mayor's statement. Miranda punched the remote control. Sherry Silverman was replaced by a black screen. Miranda took a gulp of her coffee and choked it down. It was cold. She got up to pour some fresh java into her cup and reached for the phone. Intuition told her to find out more about this case.

Picking up the phone, she punched in speed dial number two.

'KATX,' a voice barked.

No matter what time of day, the news staff were too busy for niceties. They left that up to the receptionist and she wasn't in yet.

'Tanya Friesenhahn, please,' Miranda was answered with a click that indicated she was put on hold. It made her wonder if she was this abrupt when she worked in the newsroom. Probably, she decided.

'Friesenhahn, here.'

'Wouldn't it be easier if you just said Tanya?' Miranda joked with her friend and the best news producer in San Antonio.

'Miranda! How have you been? Aren't you up kinda early for a woman who can keep her own hours?'

'You're just jealous.'

'You bet your booty. You got a gift when you got your ticket outta this joint.' Tanya softened her voice, 'We really miss you around here, y'know.'

'I miss you. Daniel, Marcia, Sherry and Jamie, too. But mostly you.'

'Spoken like a true asskisser. What d'ya want, you leech-of-information.'

Tanya's tough guy act didn't intimidate Miranda, although it used to until she figured out that it was nothing more than an act. It was Tanya's way of surviving in a business of warring monster egos.

'Now that you ask, I do have a favor to ask.'

'Surprise, surprise. Get on with it. I don't have all day.'

'Do you have any unairable stuff on the Riverwalk rape?'

'I might,' Tanya hedged.

'Can you share it with me?'

'I dunno. It was given to me off-the-record,' Tanya wavered. 'Why do you want it anyway?'

'I think it might have something to do with a case I'm working on.'

'Uh-huh. Okay, but if you spill where you got this I'll tan your hide. The victim is a sophomore at the UTSA. She's shook but will be okay. Physically anyway. She spent the evening at a club on the river, told the cops she was waiting outside with her girlfriend after it closed. They wanted to talk to some guy who sang there. Wanted to get picked up if you ask me. Still, it's no excuse for what happened to her.

'Anyway, the friend saw an old boyfriend on the River-walk and went off with him. About a half-hour later, the victim gets tired of waiting and takes off back to her car that was parked in the city lot. She felt like she was being followed and hurried but he caught up with her, hustled her into an alley and did it. What's weird, though, is she said he was so polite. Kept apologizing to her in this gravelly voice, like he was trying to disguise it. She said he wasn't really rough – the doc says there's no bruising –

35

pretty unusual. But she says after it was over he just let her go. The weirdest is, the doc tried to get a sample of sperm to DNA and there was none.'

The cold coffee in her stomach lurched sickeningly. She didn't want to ask anymore questions, but she knew she had to. 'What was the name of the club?'

'You don't want much, do you?' Tanya complained. 'Hold on. Let me look at my notes.' Pause. 'It's called Electric Blues. Ever heard of it?'

'Maybe,' Miranda tried to sound casual. 'What does the victim look like?'

'Hey, you're not talking to God here. I don't know everything. Go ask the cops.'

Through the receiver Miranda heard the police scanner announce to the newsroom the city's latest crime.

'Speak of the devil. Gotta go. Hope that helped.'

'Thanks Tanya. We have to . . .' But Tanya had already hung up. Distracted, Miranda sipped her coffee and spat it back in the cup. She had let it get ice-cold again. Setting the phone down on the counter, she walked back to the kitchen, poured the cupful out and refilled it with fresh. The mundane routine was somehow comforting. It helped her get a grip on her queasiness.

The phone rang. Miranda reached for it. Tanya must have forgotten to tell her something.

'Yeah? What 'cha got?'

'Well, that's a new one. Definitely a warmer and more hip greeting than I got the last time I called, if a bit eccentric. Don't tell me. I know, I know. You're doing a Dan Rather, but instead of sign-offs, you're trying out salutations.'

It was her boss, Doug, in rare form.

Miranda started to explain herself, but stopped. Silence stretched out through the phone lines.

'Hello. Hello. Calling for Miranda Randolph, PI. Know her?'

Doug's jocularity seemed strained and Miranda didn't help put him at ease. Doug was a chauvanist, though he'd be the last to admit it. Miranda would bet in his decades as a cop and gumshoe, he'd never worked alongside any woman who wasn't a secretary.

'I'm here, just waiting to hear the reason for this pleasant interruption of my morning.' Miranda took a sip of her coffee. Hot. Finally. Now maybe her day could get a decent start.

'My, my. Now polite as the Queen Mother. I can't keep up with you. That's good, I guess. Maybe the bad guys won't be able to either.'

Miranda rolled her eyes up to the ceiling at Doug's jibe. Having to deal with both Wayne and Doug might turn her into one of the bad guys. Or a saint.

'Did you forget to give Wayne your pager number?' Doug sounded slightly accusatory.

'I guess I did forget.' She'd been in such a hurry to get away from that cocky Cole Taylor before she did something she would regret. Like kiss him.

'Well, he called here a few minutes ago looking for you. Wouldn't even tell me what it was about. He doesn't want you to call either. He just told me to tell you to meet him at Electric Blues. ASAP.'

'Okay.'

'You certainly aren't very forthcoming. How was your first meet?'

Miranda's reticence was obviously irritating Doug. Good, thought Miranda, let him stew.

'There isn't much to come forth with. The meet was fine. I have the evidence, some background. There's a threat, no conditions yet. Maybe that's why Wayne called this morning.'

'He didn't put the moves on you, did he?'

'The moves?' Miranda chuckled. 'Doug, sometimes you are positively groovy. The fatherly concern is touching, though. You do care.'

'Alright,' Doug grumped. 'I get the message. You can take care of yourself. I guess I know that since I wouldn't have hired you if I didn't think you could.'

'Right,' Miranda answered non-committally. She had few illusions as to why Doug hired her. Free PR. Her investigative reports on the news were popular and her firing was well publicized. With forty percent of all private investigators now women. Doug was under pressure to add one to his all-male firm. She fit the bill.

Miranda promised to check back in with Doug when she needed staff support. She knew she would have to get the photographs and the note analyzed. And if Doug's team of specialists couldn't do it, they knew who could.

'Are you the first one to get here every day?'

Standing in the doorway of Electric Blues, Miranda looked at the note and videotape as Wayne showed her where he found them. They had been propped against the front door of the club.

'Hell, no! I try to stay in bed 'til noon whenever I can. No use being rich if you can't enjoy it. Ha!' His exclamation shot a bit of spittle out of his mouth.

Dodging it tactfully, Miranda took a deep breath and realized she should have had another cup of coffee before braving Wayne this early in the morning.

'So how do you happen to be here so early today?'

'Well, with this blackmail stuff going on, I don't want someone else finding anything lying around here for me.' Wayne glanced anxiously to the now deserted Riverwalk as he ushered her in and closed the door. 'I mean anyone could have seen this and picked it up. God knows what's on it.'

'Do you have a VCR here?'

'Nope.'

'I have one back at the office. We can go –'

'No!' Wayne screeched. 'I mean, I don't want to be seen at your office. I don't even want to see the tape. You watch it. You let me know.'

'I may need for you to see it eventually.' Miranda was relieved. The thought of sitting through a most likely pornographic tape with Wayne was nauseating.

38

'Okay, if I have to.'

'What does the note say?' Miranda asked as she reached into the envelope. It looked identical to the first one. Wayne's name written in the same corner, with the same type.

'He spells out what he wants.' Wayne sounded glum.

'Good. Now we'll have more to go on.'

Miranda read the note out loud:

'*If you got a hard-on from those pictures wait, 'til you see this tape. Hot! Unless you want your wife to enjoy it too, let's make a deal. You sign over your interest in the club. All of it. A contract will arrive soon. You continue to manage the club, only if you follow orders sent to you thru the mail.*'

'What the hell am I gonna do?' Wayne's voice bordered on hysteria, he flung his arms around wildly as if trying to grasp an answer out of thin air.

'Don't panic yet. At least now we have the motive and we have some time. I seriously doubt this contract will appear tomorrow. It takes some time to find a completely unethical attorney. Or at least one that won't ask a lot of questions.

'Plus I think this guy likes jacking around with you. Part of what he's getting out of this is pleasure at watching you sweat it out. So, he'll risk a couple of extra days to keep you miserable.'

Miranda pulled the wooden chair off the table and sat down across from Wayne. Beads of sweat ran from his receding hairline into his furry eyebrows. His shaking hands lifted a steaming mug to his quivering lips. A small belch told Miranda his coffee was spiked.

'You mentioned Cole Taylor owns part of the club. How much?'

'Oh, just forty percent. Plus, he gets a percentage of the daily ring as salary for performing.'

'Does anyone else share an interest?'

'Nah, just me and Cole. So far.'

Miranda caught his implication. 'So there have been offers from others?'

'Well, my lawyer has fielded a few calls once word got around about Cole's show. But clubs are risky investments and I guess I was asking too much for the ten percent I was willing to sell. Cole wouldn't budge with his, and even made me an offer. Wasn't good enough, though. I think he'd rather not have a partner.'

'He said that?' Miranda asked sharply.

'Oh no. Just the vibes I get.'

'Is he a problem to work with?' Miranda remembered their argument last night.

'No, can't say that he is.' Wayne looked like he was thinking hard to find some fault with Cole. 'Except for that smart mouth of his.'

'Did your attorney get the names of those interested in the club?

'Yeah, except one. Wanted to remain anonymous.'

'I need those names. Can you have your attorney forward them to my office?'

'Sure.'

'I'm going to have to take the notes to our analyst. Probably the pictures and video too.'

'No! Nobody but you sees those!' Wayne panicked.

'Wayne,' Miranda was struggling to be patient. 'Doug has been running the most reputable investigation firm in San Antonio for twenty years. Client confidentiality is virtually unbreachable. If you want me to catch whomever is blackmailing you, we have to use all the resources we can. Or, as I said last night, you can look up another firm.'

'Okay, okay,' Wayne held his hands up in surrender. 'Vicki just can't find out about this.'

Miranda accepted that without comment, then changed the subject. 'I need to talk to Cole Taylor tonight.'

'You're not going to tell him why you're working for me, are you?'

'No. I don't think that's a good idea. But from my questions he will probably guess you are being black-mailed. I'll tell him that, but not why.'

'Yeah,' Wayne brightened. 'He'll think it's Vicki finally

crawling up my ass. He's been waiting for the day since he got here. He thinks she's too good for me. Ha!'

'What time does he get here, usually?'

It depends. Sometimes he comes in and looks over the books during the day. He and the band set up rehearsals some afternoons, but they never let me in on it. Come to think of it, though, they probably won't meet today because Cole was here late working on some music.'

'That caught Miranda's attention. 'How late?'

Wayne looked curious. 'I left about 2.30 and he was still here, by himself, don't know when he left. Why?'

'I think I'll wait and talk to him tonight,' Miranda dodged Wayne's question. 'I'd rather make it appear casual than set up a formal appointment. That would have him too tense and I wouldn't get much out of him. I'll talk to Sable too.'

Miranda made it a statement, not a question. She'd be damned if she'd let Wayne's hysterics bully her into changing the way she conducted her investigation. But to Miranda's surprise, Wayne just shrugged.

'Same rules apply to her.'

'Can I tell her about the photos and the video?'

'No way.' Wayne obviously didn't trust his ladylove.

'I can't tell her she's blackmail bait? Doesn't she have the right to know? Maybe she'd be as anxious as you are about the pictures going public?' Miranda stopped. She knew Doug would be disappointed by her line of questioning. He cautioned against imposing morals on the client.

'Not Sable,' Wayne gave a mirthless laugh. 'If she knew about the tape, she'd probably make copies and sell them hoping for a hit. Sable wants to be a star. Porn star, music star, I don't think it matters to her.'

Miranda attributed his bitterness to the end of the affair. Maybe it was messy.

'She didn't take it well, huh?' Miranda was sympathetic.

'What?'

'When you told her it was over.'

41

'Over? What's over? She screwed my lights out in the office last night after the show. With Cole sittin' right out here. Ha!'

Miranda was incredulous. She couldn't speak.

'Oh, did I offend you?' Wayne sounded gleeful.

'I'm offended by your idiocy.' Miranda was furious, nothing would hold her back now. 'You're paranoid that I will do something to jeopardize your marriage, yet you continue to flirt with disaster. At least if you get caught in all this blackmail mess, you could argue that you ended the affair. Instead you're putting the noose around your own neck. That creep is probably still out there taping and photographing you. If you keep on providing the juicy evidence, who says he'll stop at getting the club? Your actions are beyond my comprehension.'

Wayne said nothing. His doughy face was blank. Miranda expected a flip remark, an angry explosion or maybe a simple 'you're fired'. What she got was a pitiful admission.

'I can't help myself. I'm addicted.'

Miranda couldn't get out of there fast enough. She didn't know whether to comfort Wayne or shake some sense into him. Instead she left him sitting there, a pitiful middle-aged man who was an alcoholic in denial. A has-been who had convinced himself he was a nymphomaniac, which was no more than an excuse for his lifestyle.

Miranda had to remind herself she was not his therapist – although he needed one – she was his investigator and her job was to find a blackmailer. But she had always had a weakness, even while reporting, for getting too wrapped up in the lives of the people involved. Her news director said she cared too much. For a long time, Miranda wondered why that was a bad thing. For it had been a criticism, not a compliment.

She learned, the hard way, that caring too much cost her her perspective in reporting. Caring too much left her emotionally drained. Caring too much let her get her heart broken. Miranda thought she had turned it off – the

42

caring. But she didn't want to become one of those callous reporters who pushes microphones in the faces of mothers who come to plane crash sites to find what's left of their sons, or one of those burned-out cops who make jokes over bodies. What she hadn't learned yet was a happy medium – how to care, but not too much. Miranda sighed. She knew she should be disgusted with Wayne and leave it at that. But she found herself feeling sorry for him too.

Miranda had parked her car in the street near the club. She got in the gray Ford Taurus and made her way through downtown's maze of one-way streets to her office. Her choice of car was an unlikely one. In fact, it was not her choice at all. When Doug hired her, Miranda owned a red Miata that she had bought when she first moved to San Antonio. Doug said it was too flashy for a private eye and instructed her to trade it for a sedan in light blue or gray. It was hard to tail someone when yours is the first car they noticed. Miranda recognized the reasoning, but it didn't make parting with her little sportscar any easier.

The traffic wasn't bad, being in the time pocket between morning rush hour and lunchtime. Miranda pulled into her parking place in three-and-a-half minutes. The Tower Life Building, where Sandborn Services was headquartered, was a historical landmark. Built in 1929, it boasted being the tallest high-rise west of the Mississippi River until the 1950s. The pinnacle-shaped structure sat along the San Antonio River, just above the Paseo Del Rio, and had once been home to Dwight D Eisenhower and his Third US Army. The legend of the building, as told by riverboat tour operators, was the man who built it went bust in the stock market crash and jumped from the top. That explains why, they say, the gargoyles that decorate the building are grimacing on the side of the building that he jumped from, and are smiling on the other.

Though pure fantasy, Miranda thought the tale gave the building a sense of romantic history. She had to admit that was at least a small part of the reason, when the job offers came rolling in after she was fired, she said yes to Doug. She loved this building.

Miranda rode the elevator up to the ninth floor and pushed open the heavy wood door to the office. She waved at Marjorie before she realized that it was just her mini-skirt-encased hips and a lot of thigh visible over the receptionist desk. Shaking her head at the flamboyant woman who was old enough to be her mother, Miranda headed back to her knothole. A tiny desk, computer, two chairs and small file cabinet filled the small rectangular space, leaving barely enough room to turn around. But it met Miranda's sole requirement. It had a window.

She had resolved to bring in a plant too. Corn plant or ficus, some fluorescent-light and air-conditioning survivor. She kept forgetting, though, until she walked in the door, and then it was too late. She wrote 'remember plant!' on her new personalized notepad and stuck it in her purse. It was really a combination of a purse and a briefcase. Her sister had bought it for her years before while on a business trip in London. She knew Miranda hated carrying both a purse and a briefcase and when she did she usually forgot one or the other, so Melly found this Cordovan leather bag, tailored on the outside to look like a large, conservative, rather nondescript purse. Inside it held compartments for files, pens, calculators, even for the manila envelopes it carried now. It was convenient while Miranda was a reporter and now even worked as part of her 'cover' as a PI.

The intercom on her desk buzzed. 'Sleeping Beauty has arrived. You must have been kissed. How are you and Prince Wayne Charming getting along?'

Fresh from her repulsive conversation with Wayne, no thought could have nauseated her more.

'Ugh,' was all she could muster.

'Ah, I see. Would you like reassignment?'

'No!' Miranda was surprised by her own vehemence. What was with her? One minute she's begging Wayne to fire her, the next she's fighting to keep the case.

44

'Oh-Kay,' Doug stretched out the vowels sarcastically. 'Time for a short chat this morning?'

'I have to drop something off for analysis. Then I'll stop by.'

Plucking the envelope out of her case, Miranda headed down the hall. Tony Garza headed the analysis division. He'd worked with the SAPD for twenty years before Doug finally lured him into 'retirement'. It must have been an attractive lure. San Antonio police had the best pay and benefits package in the state. Operatives brought their evidence to Tony, and he dispersed each piece to the required resident expert. Sometimes he went 'out-of-house' to consultants that no one at Sandborn's knew, except Tony. He dealt with a lot of talented people, on both the right and wrong sides of the law.

Miranda was relieved his door was open. No one touched Tony's door when it was closed. It was an unwritten, unspoken rule. And one of the first things she learned when she started work there.

'Hey, Tony.' Miranda knocked on the open door as she spoke. His head of thick salt-and-pepper hair was bent over a page of what looked like newsprint glued on typing paper. He held a magnifying glass in a hand deceptively large for a man so short. There was nothing small about Tony, Miranda conceded. He was burly, stocky and strong and always reminded Miranda of a bulldog. While he spent most of his time on the phone or behind a desk now, the stories about his brute force and the occasions that demanded he use it were legion at the SAPD.

'*Mi bonita*, come in.'

For some reason, Tony's flattery always made her blush. A gentleman, he stood. Miranda slid into the leather wingbacked chair opposite his desk. Tony sat back down.

'I need your guys to look at these. Blackmail. One received this morning.' Miranda placed one envelope and note on his desk, then the other next to it, handling both at the edges. 'And this one received yesterday morning.'

'Police?' Tony spoke in shorthand when it came to business.

'No.'

'Should we fingerprint?'

'I suppose so, although the client's are probably all you'll find.'

Tony nodded. Then he broke into a wide smile. It warmed his face in a way that might lull some into thinking he was easy-going. Tony was anything but easy-going. But that smile he often used as a business asset. Miranda had seen him use it while making a threat to another operative in the office. It was more powerful than a scowl. This time, though, it went all the way to his eyes. Miranda relaxed. For some reason Tony liked her, and for that she was infinitely grateful.

'It's a pleasure as always, *mi bonita*.' He stood.

'Thanks, Tony.'

Miranda walked back down the hall and passed her office on the way to Doug's. His office took up the east corner of the floor and was, naturally, the largest. Miranda guessed it was at least fifteen times the size of hers. The space didn't make her envious, the four windows did.

Doug, like Tony, had worked for the SAPD. But it had taken him only ten years to decide that he wanted to keep doing what he loved, investigation, but work for himself. It had been a good decision. He'd tired of playing politics on the police department's terms. Now, he still played politics, but the rules were his own. Sandborn Services was a respected, successful business that begged to be expanded. But Doug resisted. He liked to keep a close watch on every case, and he knew he couldn't do that if he hired a dozen more operatives or opened another office in Laredo or Austin.

Doug was on the phone when Miranda appeared at his door. She hesitated, but he waved her in.

'I'm sorry, Peter. You'll just have to tell her that we won't be bribed into bending our rules for her.' Pause. Miranda could hear Peter continuing his argument on the other end of the line.

'She doesn't have to take an ad out in the paper. She can either call me, or come in, or write a letter if she's so afraid of bugs and tails. And it can be talked about in general terms. I don't have to necessarily hear specifics from her. That's your job. But, yes, she has to contact me before we can accept the case.'

Peter started up again. Doug was losing his patience.

'Fine, fine, Peter. Tell her I'm paranoid. Good idea.'

Doug hung up, with Peter still yammering. Miranda had talked to Peter a couple of times since coming to work with Sandborn. He brought to mind a Californian surfer boy: energetic to the point to hyperactivity and a bit immature. Miranda had mentioned her impression to Marjorie who'd quickly assured her that Peter was a fearless investigator. Miranda thought he just charmed Marjorie, which was pretty easy to do.

'Sorry to keep you waiting.'

'No problem. It was very enlightening.'

Doug raised his eyebrows, but said nothing. He did not tolerate gossip among his employees.

'Just seeing the rules you taught me put into practice,' Miranda continued.

'Ah.' Doug was caught without a rejoinder.

Touche, Miranda thought, suppressing a self-satisfied chuckle. It was fun to outwit Doug.

'So, Lambert is being difficult.'

'Well, I think he's being himself, which just happens to be difficult.'

'Do you need some mace? Or is your thirty-eight enough?'

'Gee, I didn't think of waving my gun at him. I'll try that next time. But I think he got the message today.'

'Today? You've already seen him this morning?' Doug's eyebrows lifted quickly before dropping back down into position over his hazel eyes.

'He got a second note, with terms, when he got to the club this morning. It was on the doorstep.'

'What's the bait?'

47

'Photos of Wayne's latest affair in action. There's a video too. In fact, I have to get home and watch it.' Miranda started to rise.

'Let's just see it here.' Doug pushed a button at his desk and a door slid open on the bookcase on the opposite wall to reveal a television and VCR.

'No. Wayne didn't want anyone but me to see the tape. I promised him I'd take it home.'

Doug nodded. Once he accepted a case, he gave the operative a lot of leeway and privacy with the client, although he kept track of the progress. He wasn't big on written reports, except the final one given to the client, but he talked with his investigators about each case every day. Miranda could sense he was having a hard time keeping his rules consistent with her. He was itching to get a hand in. Either because she was a woman or a rookie, she couldn't be sure.

'You gave Tony what? The notes and photos?'

'Just the notes. I wanted to keep the photos to compare with the video. Get angle and perspective to see if I can figure out where and how this creep is shooting.'

'The terms?'

'Wayne's ownership of the club.'

Doug's bushy eyebrows shot up again. Higher this time. They were getting a workout, Miranda thought.

'Time frame?'

'No, a contract and deadline are promised in the next delivery.

'Are you considering any suspects yet?'

'Well, I still haven't talked to the major players yet.'

Doug was quiet for a moment, while he openly studied Miranda. She withstood the scrutiny, holding her breath. She wanted to keep this case, and she didn't want to show her whole hand now or it might be taken from her.

'Okay, okay. I know I'm riding you hard. You've had all of twenty-four hours to work the case. It's a lot of legwork, though. You need help? I can spring Phil.'

'No thanks.' Phil was Doug's most trusted and best

operative. He'd been with Army CID before he joined Doug fifteen years ago. The bossman must be worried.

'I have it under control.'

Miranda walked out of the office, trying not to show how offended she was. Doug had tried to come across with casual confidence but it was obvious he would prefer someone else on the case. She'd show him. If she could do this, maybe divorce surveillance would be history.

Getting into her car, Miranda was surprised to notice it was nearly noon.

'Time flies,' she said to herself. 'Ugh, Wayne's cliches are beginning to rub off on me.'

Miranda had to inch her sedan into the street. Traffic was heavy now and she was forced to crawl to Interstate 10. It gave her the chance to think about her conversation with Doug. As always his razor-sharp instincts had picked up on her hesitancy to formulate a list of suspects.

She knew Cole Taylor would have to head the list. As part-owner of the club, with an expressed desire (according to Wayne, anyway) to control more, he was the obvious choice. He was well acquainted with Wayne's infidelities and Miranda had to believe he knew about the affair going on between a member of his band and the owner of the club. He had access, too.

But, to Miranda, it was just too pat. Too perfect. And Miranda knew cases like this rarely were. Or was that damned attraction clouding her judgement? Someone that great looking, that talented, that sexy couldn't be a criminal. Or so her subconscious was telling her. She knew it was ridiculous. She resolved to force her mind to overcome her body's reaction to Cole when she questioned him that night.

Victoria Lambert would also have to be on the shortlist. She might have hired someone to follow Wayne and get the pictures. The blackmail threat might be a way to throw him off the trail, teach him a lesson and emasculate him by giving power to Victoria, the anonymous order-giver.

49

It would be a sick, secretive game, but Miranda wouldn't rule it out. Infidelity twisted people when they found their trust and love so thoughtlessly violated. Miranda had first-hand experience with that. Some lashed out from the pain. Others, like Miranda, lashed inward, blaming themselves, then building walls around themselves so they couldn't be hurt again.

Miranda pulled into her subdivision. Hunter's Bend was an affluent neighborhood on the north side of town. A few garden homes were hidden among the larger residences owned by doctors, dentists and lawyers. Miranda had been lucky enough to find a foreclosed garden home for a bargain. It had needed some work – a coat of paint, new flooring, landscaping – but Miranda enjoyed doing that herself. Plus, it kept her busy on nights and weekends, giving her an excuse to avoid the social life she was afraid to start again.

Miranda unlocked the door and disarmed the security system. She felt a familiar furry body rubbing her ankles and reached down to pick up her two-year-old Himalayan. She was the only good thing that had come of her relationship with Rick. Sheba had been his last birthday present to Miranda.

'Let's watch a movie,' she said as she nuzzled the cat's soft gray fur.

Miranda put the tape in the VCR, but before she turned it on she went back into the kitchen to grab some tuna salad out of the refrigerator. Sheba sniffed the air and mewed to remind her mistress of her prediliction for what was now being dished onto a lettuce leaf.

'You can share, piggo.'

Miranda eased into the butternut chair and turned the tape on with the remote control. Sheba jumped in her lap and licked tuna off Miranda's index finger. Miranda took a bite, her first and last. For, just then, the tape began and she lost her appetite, relinquishing the rest of her lunch to Sheba.

Wayne's white, overweight, underexercised body was

completely naked. It shone a sickening green in the neon lights of the club, and clashed almost comically with Sable's olive-skinned, muscled nakedness.

They were coupling with loud abandon on the unlit stage. Sheba looked up from her tuna at the animal-like sounds coming from the TV screen. Miranda was repulsed and embarrassed by this violation of privacy. She wished she didn't have to watch it all, but she knew she did. The tape displayed the date, for which Miranda was grateful, because Wayne would not have to see the tape to tell her when it was made. The camera distance and angle never changed, as if it had been set up and left unattended. Maybe the photographer got as nauseated by the scene as Miranda was now.

When their grotesque coupling finally came to an end, Sable got up, pushing Wayne away. He scrambled up awkwardly, his suddenly flacid genitals waggling as he followed her, begging her to stay. She barked a 'no', picked her clothes up off a table and stalked off-camera. He sat down next to his sad heap of clothes and downed the drink on the table.

Miranda fast-forwarded through the rest of the tape. Wayne, still naked, grabbed a third-full bottle of Chivas and drank it all before the tape finally ran out.

How depressing. Maybe divorce cases weren't so bad, Miranda reconsidered.

She rewound the tape so that she could look at the camera perspective again. She decided it was set up somewhere near the hall that led to the restrooms and office. She didn't remember any windows on that side of the building.

The tape had paused on Sable. Miranda had to marvel at her body. There really seemed to be no fat on it, except maybe at her small rounded breasts, and not even much there. Sable made Miranda feel lumpy. With a figure-eight shape that, despite regular visits to the health club, would never straighten out, Miranda had a body that one college boyfriend described as luscious. But next to that sleek sex machine on the screen, she felt more Ruben-esque.

Her beeper buzzed at her side, interrupting her contemplation.

Not recognizing the number left as a message, she dialed.

'Electric Blues.' That voice: deep, a hint of a drawl, sensuous. 'Hello, Electric Blues.'

Miranda suddenly realized she hadn't spoken when he'd answered the first time.

'Oh, uh, Wayne Lambert, please.'

'Certainly, *Miz* Randolph, just a moment.'

There was a teasing grin in his voice. Miranda must have sounded as dumb as she felt. And how did he know she was on the line anyway?

'Yeah?'

'Wayne, this is Miranda Randolph. You know, it is not a good idea to call from the club.'

'I got the feeling you thought I was bein' paranoid about that.'

Maybe she was underestimating Wayne. She didn't argue with him. 'Maybe I'm changing my mind. What did you want?'

'You saw the tape?'

'Yes.'

'And?'

'And, it's what we expected.'

'Like the pictures, then? That horny?'

'With the addition of sound and movement, I would have to say more so, Wayne.'

'Really, hot, huh?' Now Wayne was starting to sound perversely pleased, as if he were getting some kind of review.

'No, really sordid and sick,' Miranda snapped, wanting to change the course of the conversation. 'The tape recorded the date, but I want to double-check.'

Miranda glanced at the calendar on the kitchen wall.

'Do you remember last Monday night?'

52

'Refresh my memory.'

'On the stage. You finished a bottle of scotch afterward.' The latter he probably did every night, Miranda admitted.

'Yeah, Monday's right. It was probably eleven o'clock or so.'

'Fine. See you tonight,' Miranda hung up. She grabbed the envelope with the photographs and brought it back to the living room. Comparing the photos and the freeze-frame on the tape, she could see they had been taken at the same spot in the club. But while the videotape remained at a set distance, the photos differed. Some were close ups, others farther away. Yet, Miranda reminded herself, they were obviously taken on various days. The camera could have been set up on a tripod, with the zoom set differently, depending on where Wayne and Sable ended up. Miranda couldn't get the notion out of her head that the cameras had been set up and left. But how would the photographer know where the action would take place? And, if he set up after the action started, how could he have gotten out unnoticed?

The VCR automatically clicked the tape off of pause and it rolled forward again. Wayne's pitiful begging began again. Sable walked beyond the camera, hissing something under her breath. Miranda turned it off. She headed for the shower. She felt dirty.

CHAPTER 3

Cole knew he was a cop the moment the guy walked in the door. He exuded a tangible force of one who had the power behind a gun and the authority to throw anyone in jail. He didn't need a uniform to command respect. He did it in plainclothes with an attitude. Cole knew the type and despised him on sight.

Wayne hurried out from behind the bar, looking around to the band on stage as if to say 'Who let this guy in?' It was late-afternoon and the club wouldn't be open for a couple of hours.

'Sorry, we ain't open yet. You gotta leave.'

'I apologize. I had to let myself in. Apparently no one heard my knock on the door over the music.' He said the word with a flicker of distaste as if The Baby Blues weren't making his definition of music. 'Lieutenant Rick Milano, SAPD.'

'Oh, oh, oh, are we in some kind of trouble?' Wayne had gone pale and was fumbling around nervously for his drink – what looked like a soda, but really was a Coke and Chivas.

'Not yet. I'm just here to ask you some questions regarding a crime that took place last night.'

'Crime? Crime?' Wayne sounded like a hysterical parrot. 'There wasn't no crime here last night, right guys?'

Wayne looked to the stage for reassurance. Cole looked at Rick, their mutual dislike palpable.

'Not that we know of, anyway,' Cole finally answered.

'A woman who says she spent the evening here watching your show was raped early this morning in an alley off the Riverwalk.'

Cole thought of Miranda and his heart jumped a moment, until he remembered he'd heard her voice on the phone and she'd sounded fine. Her snooty self.

Rick was watching them all closely, especially Cole.

'Wh . . . uh . . . well, what does that have to do with us?' Wayne sputtered.

'Right now, it means you were some of the last people to see her before the attack. It may mean more than that after I talk to you.' The implicit threat hung heavy in the air.

'We'll do anything we can to help, right? Right, Taylor?' Wayne stopped his nervous pacing long enough to glare at Cole, who ignored him.

'And you are?' Rick reached into the pocket of his mohair blazer for his notepad as he eyed Wayne.

'Oh, uh, Wayne Lambert. Owner, uh . . .' he glanced at Cole before correcting himself. 'Majority owner, of the club.'

'I'll talk to you first.' Rick cast a stern look at the stage. 'The rest of you, hang around for a while.'

Rick led Wayne to a table at the far end of the room. Cole stalked around the stage, annoyed that Milano had ordered them around and more annoyed that he let it get to him. They tried to get back into the song that was interrupted, but everyone was distracted, so Cole called a break.

Sable lit a cigarette and sidled up to Cole.

'When do you want me to move my things out of your place?'

Cole turned a wary eye on Sable. But she was calm. Dead calm.

'There's not much there. What do you want, your toothbrush?'

Sable narrowed her eyes at Cole. 'I left all that crappy jewelry you bought me there. You can throw that away. But I want my lambskin jacket.'

55

'Go right now and take it all.' Cole turned his back so the cop couldn't see them and dropped the keys into Sable's hand.

Cole reflected that though Sable kept a few clothes at his apartment, she never lived there. She'd never even spent a whole night. Never in those two years had they woken up together. Her decision. Cole had asked her to move in with him when they first started to get serious. She had refused without an explanation. He never asked again, somehow relieved by her answer. While on the road she even kept her own hotel room. The only thing they really shared was the music and sex.

'The cop told us not to leave,' she took another drag on her cigarette.

'What? Are you worried he's going to arrest you?' Cole snickered and Sable shot him a sharp look. He shrugged. 'So, go after you talk to him.'

Cole walked away without looking back at her. He noticed Milano had been observing their exchange from the other end of the room. Nosy bastard. Cole smiled and flipped him a wave. Rick turned back to Wayne.

'You do recognize this woman, then?'

'Oh yeah, she and her friend are real cutie pies. They've come in about two or three times. I always find them a good table. Up front and in the middle. It's good for business, y'know, to have such great-looking centerpieces. Ha!'

'So you think other customers in the club noticed them?'

'Wouldn't you, with those headlights tucked into a tight sweater?'

Wayne was losing some of his nervousness in talking about one of his favorite subjects. Rick was not amused.

'Mr Lambert, I'll remind you that we are discussing the victim of a sex crime here. You could be considered a suspect.'

'I'm a suspect?' Wayne's voice rose an octave, hovering near the hysterical range.

'No, I'm saying watch your language or you could be.'

'Sorry,' Wayne mumbled.

'So, did you notice anyone paying special attention to the victim?'

'Well, I saw Cole talking to them during one of the breaks.'

Rick was instantly alert. 'Cole Taylor, your singer. He went up to their table?'

'No. They went up to the stage.'

'Was their conversation heated? Intimate? Did you hear what was said?'

Wayne shook his head, throwing a bead of sweat on his silk shirt. 'Just looked like Cole was playin' nice-nice with 'em.'

'Okay. Anything else about these girls you remember?'

'The one in the picture. She asked if she and her friend could wait inside the club for Cole after the show. That's against club policy, so I told them to beat it. They left. When I left about an hour later, she was outside the back door. I offered to give her a lift home. She said she'd wait for Cole.'

'What time was that?'

'About 2.30.'

'Why was she waiting for Cole? Did they have a date?'

'Doubt it. That guy gets more offers in one week than we would get in a year. Ha! He always has chicks waiting for him. He ignores most of 'em, far as I can tell. A damned waste.'

'So Cole was here when you left? Was he alone?'

'No,' Wayne started fidgeting. 'Sable, the chick in the band, was here.'

'Just one more question for now. Does Cole have a wife, girlfriends?'

'No wife, no steady chicks that I know of.'

'Okay. That's Sable? Tell her to come here.'

Wayne beckoned Sable. She stubbed out her cigarette, only half smoked, and slunk over to Rick. Wayne hovered.

'Now it's your turn to "beat it",' Rick threw over his

shoulder to Wayne as Sable slid into the chair and put her high-heeled boots up on the windowsill.

Rick's order seemed to amuse Sable, who was already lighting another cigarette. Rick felt his groin tighten as he watched her tongue taste and tease her cigarette. He knew what she was doing and was glad his involuntary reaction was hidden under the table.

'Your name?'

'Sable Diamonte.'

'That your real name?'

'Is Rick yours? Or is it Dick?'

Squeezing his jaws together in an effort to maintain his temper, Rick took a deep breath.

'How long have you been with Cole's band?'

'How long since you've had a good lay?'

Rick's eyes narrowed. 'Longer than you, I'm sure.'

It was almost incredible the way she smelled of sex. It penetrated his mind and went straight for his hormones. He resisted and wondered what she was trying to hide. She was the kind of woman who used sex to get what she wanted. Maybe simply for an orgasm. Or money. Or murder. Rick had seen her kind do it for all three reasons.

Sable took a long draw, sizing Rick up, planning which tack to take. What he'd said was inviting, his eyes were not. When he spoke again his voice was low and hard.

'You're going to answer my questions, you slut. Now.'

Sable's body had gone still. Rick couldn't even see her breathing. Not calm, just energy under tight control. She looked out the window.

'Two years.'

'Does he have a girlfriend?' Rick asked cocking his head toward the stage.

'Who? Wayne?'

Rick was puzzled. 'No . . .' He answered slowly. 'Cole Taylor.'

'No.' She answered on an exhale, smoke wafting around her face. Rick wondered why she sounded relieved.

'Does he usually pick up anyone during or after shows?'

'If he does, he doesn't tell me.'

'Are you sleeping with him?'

'No,' her obsidian eyes examined her cigarette, then shifted to the window. 'What does this have to do with a rape?'

Rick ignored her question and pushed the photograph toward Sable.

'Do you recognize this girl?'

She barely glanced at the face before looking out the window again.

'She was here last night, all creamy over Cole.'

'And he was after her?'

'I wouldn't say that. He talked to her and her bimbo friend a couple of times.'

'When?'

'When they came up to the stage.'

'Cole seemed interested?'

'I guess. Aren't all men interested in an easy lay?'

Rick let her crudity pass without acknowledgement. 'Did they talk about plans for meeting later?'

'Don't ask me. He was here working on some songs when I left about 2.30 this morning. I don't know what he did after that. And I don't care.'

'Did you see the victim outside the club when you left?'

'I went out the back door. If she was there, I didn't notice her.'

'You leave before or after Wayne?'

Sable looked him in the eye for the first time since he got tough with her. Her eyes searched for something. 'After.'

'I'm done with you.' Rick stood up.

Sable's lips curled up at the edges in a semblance of a smile. 'If you'd done me you wouldn't be able to walk, cop.' Her black eyes drifted down to just below his belt buckle. 'I see you might have trouble walking anyway. So, either way, you're screwed!' She let out a barking laugh.

Rick resisted the urge to cover the growing mound at his fly. He waited until her eyes met his. 'You want trouble, bitch?'

59

Sable threw her head back, exposing six inches of corded neck. Slowly, she exhaled, letting the smoke settle around her face. 'How'd you guess, copper? Trouble really turns me on.'

'I'd guess you're turned on all the time.'

Rick ignored Sable's low whistle as he turned his back and walked over to Cole, who was going over some sheet music with Trent.

'You're next.' Rick motioned Cole toward the back of the club.

'We can talk right here.' Cole's eyes challenged the investigator.

'I don't think so,' Rick said looking at Trent.

'No problem. I'm outta here.' Trent picked up his guitar and jumped off the stage.

'You remember this girl?' Rick flung the photograph on top of the sheet music Cole had in front of him.

'Oh God,' Cole paled.

Great acting, Rick thought. 'Well?'

'Yeah, she was here with her friend last night.' Cole's voice was quiet.

'That's it? They didn't make an impression?' Rick sounded sarcastic.

'What do you want me to say? They were giggly college girls who seemed a little starstruck. I talked to them a little and that was it.' Cole couldn't figure out what the cop was after.

'Oh, excuse me. I didn't realize you were such a big star.'

Oh, excuse me. I didn't realize you were such a big prick, Cole thought, but kept his mouth shut. He flashed a roguish smile at Milano, figuring it would irritate him more than an argument. He was right.

Frustrated, Rick feigned looking for another pen in the inside pocket of his jacket, thus exposing his nine-milli-meter Glock. He knew Cole was screwing with him and he wanted him to know who was boss.

'So, what did you talk about?'

60

'Mostly small talk. They asked about some of the songs. They told me about some of the music classes they're taking.'

'Did you arrange to meet the victim later?'

'No. Why?' Cole's brows drew together. 'Did she say that?'

'I can't reveal whether she did or didn't. Did you know she was waiting for you outside the club?'

'When? Last night?'

'After the show, until about three a.m. When did you leave?'

'It was about five o'clock, I guess.'

'You guess. You were here alone; could it have been more like three o'clock?'

Cole was beginning to feel like a hunted animal. 'So I'm a suspect.'

'A lot of people are suspects.'

'Well, if you're asking whether I have anyone who can corroborate the fact that I left at five, the answer is no. I did not see her or anyone except one pre-dawn jogger.'

'What did you do when you left?'

'I went home and went to bed.'

'And home would be your apartment in the Majestic Tower?'

Taken aback that the cop knew where he lived, Cole nodded hesitantly.

'And, no one was there to meet you at home?'

'I live alone.'

'That's not what I asked,' Rick shot back. Cole's eyes narrowed as the two men challenged each other wordlessly.

'I slept alone. Is that what you were asking?' Cole finally spoke in a voice teeming with hostility.

Rick slid his notepad back inside his blazer and started toward the door.

'Don't leave town,' he called without looking back.

'Is she going to be okay?'

Rick stopped and turned around. After a long pause, he said: 'She'll be able to testify.' And he was gone.

Cole fought the urge to chase the cop and knock that self-satisfied look right off of his face. But he felt like he'd been punched in the gut and couldn't catch his breath. A suspect in a rape? He strained to remember the night before. He'd only given half an ear to the girls while he kept an eye on Wayne and Miranda.

Damn! Maybe they'd said something about meeting him later and he'd agreed. Or, had something he said or did seemed like an invitation in itself?

No! He had to stop second-guessing himself. It would drive him crazy, and that is exactly what the cop wanted him to do. He wouldn't give the jerk the satisfaction. Every week women waited, hoping to see him after the show. He did nothing to encourage them. Wincing, he remembered blowing in the girl's ear. Damnit, he was paid to perform and flirting was part of it. Still, Cole wished he'd picked someone else last night. It was a terrible coincidence. Wasn't it? He wondered what it was about the rapist that made the cop think the attacker might be Cole.

Miranda looked at her reflection in the glass of a riverside cafe and adjusted the neckline of her ivory angora sweater. Chastizing herself, she walked on. It had taken her more than an hour to get ready, after changing a half dozen times. It was as if she was going on a date instead of going to work, Miranda thought with contempt.

Nearing Electric Blues, she noticed with relief that there was no line tonight. She paused under a bridge to take a deep breath to calm her nerves. Miranda climbed the stone steps and, with a smile, nodded at Mr Statue standing guard at the door. Without acknowledging her, he leaned a shoulder into the heavy door and stepped back to let her pass.

'Nice to see you again, too,' Miranda offered as she stepped into the club. She nearly jumped out of her skin when she was grabbed from behind. What? Had the guy changed his mind about letting her in?

62

But the scotch fumes wafting past her nose told her who had her by the shoulders.

'I'm so glad you're here,' Wayne said.

Miranda shrank away from his grip as he hustled her to the office. 'What is it, Wayne, did you get another note?'

'No, no. The cops came here this afternoon.'

'The cops? But . . .'

'It's not what you're thinkin'. Not about the notes. It was because of some girl who was raped last night. She was here for the show, then waited for Cole afterwards. The cop was nosing around to see if we knew anything.'

Miranda didn't let on that she knew Electric Blues was named in the police report. 'And? Who was the girl, did you remember her?'

'Yeah, she was one of the cutesy pies who was talking to Cole during the breaks. Remember?'

Miranda did. The Busty Bunnies.

'Who was the cop?'

'Oh, I don't remember his name. He really didn't ask very many questions. Talked to Cole the longest, I guess.'

Wayne was sitting behind the desk, but she could see his right leg nervously bouncing up and down. It was clear he wanted Miranda to stay and reassure him everything was going to be okay. But she didn't have time to play babysitter.

'Are Cole and Sable here? I need to talk to them before the show.' Miranda stood up.

'Oh, yeah, yeah. Around somewhere.'

Miranda walked out of the office and nearly ran into Cole. He grabbed her to stop the collision and it was as if they received an electrical shock. They both jumped away from each other.

'I'm sorry,' Miranda mumbled.

'I'm not sure I am.' A lazy grin spread across Cole's face as he stared into her eyes stretched wide with surprise.

Miranda composed herself instantly and dove back into business. 'If you have the time now, I'd like to talk with you.'

63

Something that looked like hope crossed Cole's eyes for a split second before Wayne spoke up from the office. Miranda had forgotten he was there.

'It's that confidential thing we talked about last night, Cole. Try to cooperate and not get too nosy.'

'Oh, of course.' He answered with a voice dripping with sarcasm. His eyes teased her. 'Where shall we *talk*?'

Miranda bristled at the emphasis he put on that last word. Her nerves felt raw. She forced herself to be detached and professional.

'What's that room there?' She pointed at an unmarked door down the hall.

'Dressing room, lounge, general purpose space.'

'How big is it?'

'Oh, big enough for us to fit in. We probably wouldn't even have to touch each other, if you stood at one end and I stood at the other.'

'That's not what I was worried about.' Miranda tried to cover. Was she that transparent?

Cole's left eyebrow arched, Miranda's heart lurched. How could that small movement cause her insides to contort?

'What was it you were worried about then?'

'Oh, I just wanted to make sure we wouldn't inconvenience other members of the band who might need to get in there. How much time do we have before the show?'

Cole glanced at his digital sports watch, the face of which was worn on the inside of his wrist. 'A little less than an hour.'

'Let's get started then.'

Miranda moved to the closed door while Cole followed behind. He had to admire the grace of her gait. She didn't go places, she flowed to them.

But somehow Cole sensed the calm waters on the surface of Miranda Randolph disguised the strong current underneath. He antagonized her and he couldn't help himself. He wanted to see that current of emotion whether it be anger or passion.

64

Miranda had perched herself on the edge of the dressing table, her back to the mirror. That left Cole to stand or sit on the deep-cushioned leather couch. He sat, leaned back and set his booted feet on the dressing table chair.

Miranda felt her breath coming quicker. Being in a closed room alone was nearly overwhelming – for her, anyway. Cole seemed cool and unaffected, with that air of self-righteous amusement.

'All I can tell you is that Wayne is under surveillance. I am to find out who is doing it, how and why.'

'How long has this been going on?'

'For the last few weeks. Have you noticed anything unusual in that time? Anyone hanging around the club at off-hours, any repairmen who return repeatedly, any new employees?'

'No.' Cole dragged his attention away from the rich red-gold-brown hair that cascaded down the back of her soft sweater. 'All the employees have been with us for months, since we opened.'

'Any of them acting nervous, edgy?'

'No one but Wayne.'

'How long has he been jumpy?'

'About a month. It has to be a new girlfriend. He can barely function he gets so scared Victoria will catch him. Why I don't know. His many exploits are well known around town. Looks like she's after him this time, though. Good for her.'

Miranda ignored his baiting comment. Something else he said caught her attention.

'You don't know Wayne's new mistress?'

'So, he is into it again.' Cole nodded smugly. Miranda could not believe he was unaware a member of his band was Wayne's bed partner. Or stage partner, as the case may be, Miranda thought ruefully.

Then again, he could be trying to throw her off-track, sending her after Victoria while he was the blackmailer. Miranda put her defenses back up. She had to be more careful around him.

Cole watched with fascination the play of emotions in her eyes. Suddenly they iced over again.

'Wayne tells me you are interested in owning more of the club?'

Cole's brow furrowed at the sudden change in the direction of their conversation. 'What does this have to do with the surveillance case?'

'Maybe nothing. Just answer the question.'

'Well, sure. Why not. It's making money, my band is the headliner. Wayne's not a bad partner, but whenever he feels threatened he throws his majority ownership down like a gauntlet,' Cole sounded wary.

'So you'd like to buy him out?'

'I couldn't buy him out, but I could afford a bigger interest.'

Realization dawned on Cole. He stood up suddenly and in a short stride was standing between Miranda's feet, his face inches from hers.

'You're doing more than just a little surveillance, aren't you? Are there threats? Blackmail?'

Miranda was mute. His sudden, simmering anger paralyzed her. What she'd said had lit a fire in him that had merely begun to smolder, but was not yet blazing. She fought to find the right thing to say. She didn't want to give anything away. Not the case. Not her feelings. She wrenched her eyes from his.

'There's my answer isn't it?' His voice was hot and bitter. 'I'm a suspect. For the second time today. Well, I at least deserve to hear what I'm accused of doing.'

'You aren't accused of anything.' Miranda's voice sounded weak to her.

His hand reached up and roughly turned her face back to him. His touch sent a tremor down her neck to her breasts. His look sent the tremor down further, down the tender center of her abdomen, to the now throbbing center of her sex, confined in tight acid-washed jeans. She could feel the hard ridge of the seam and almost unconsciously rubbed her pubic bone against it.

66

Cole saw her squirm and thought she was just trying to wriggle away from the truth. 'At least that arrogant ass of a cop was honest. You can't even be that.'

The air was so thick with emotion that neither one was sure if it was anger or arousal, fear or passion. Then his mouth was on hers, crushing. His tongue attacked as if searching for the truth. His groin pushed between her legs, into her throbbing heat. Her protest was drowned into a moan of submission.

'Well, excuse me,' came the cool voice from the door. Neither Cole nor Miranda had heard it open.

Cole reluctantly withdrew from his assault and turned toward the door. It was Sable. Without a word he walked out, shoving Sable against the door jam. She stared after him without expression. Miranda, feeling disheveled and unsatisfied, pushed herself off the dresser and paced the tiny room.

Sable turned her flat black eyes on Miranda.

'What are you doing in here?'

'Wayne has hired me to do some investigation for him.'

'Investigate what? The inside of Cole's mouth?'

'Someone has Wayne under surveillance and I am to find out why and who. That's all I can tell you. My name is Miranda Randolph.' She held her hand out to Sable, who glanced at it and lit a cigarette before dropping into the couch. Unnerved, Miranda let her hand drop.

'So . . . I'm you're next victim. Hope you don't try to tongue-lash me. You're not my type.' Sable's voice held no humor as her eyes appraised Miranda's body. Miranda was repulsed, although it didn't surprise her that Sable might swing both ways.

'How long have you and Wayne been having an affair?'

'I've been sleeping with him a couple of months.' Miranda picked up on the correction. To Sable, calling what she and Wayne did an affair was glorifying it. Miranda silently agreed.

Suddenly, Sable sat up and glared at Miranda.

'Hey you didn't ask Cole about me and Wayne, did you?'

'No.'

'He doesn't know, does he?' Sable's anxiety struck Miranda as being out of character.

'I think your job is safe,' Miranda responded bitterly.

Sable's face twisted into a smile as that answer seemed to both satisfy and amuse her. Miranda had never before seen anyone who became less attractive with a smile.

'Have you noticed anything unusual since you and Wayne started, ah, seeing each other? Anyone following you? Anyone hanging around the club? Any employees acting strangely?'

'No. Been too busy trying to keep track of Wayne's hard-ons.'

At least they had something else in common besides the sex, Miranda mused as she tried to overlook Sable's crudity.

'You know, you're just wasting your time,' Sable said between draws on her cigarette. 'Wayne's paranoid. He's always seeing boogymen. He's afraid his wife's gonna divorce him. He's afraid Cole's either gonna pull the band from the club or take it over.'

'Has Cole threatened to do that?'

Sable shrugged, then leapt up and started peeling her clothes off. Miranda was embarrassed and turned away as that muscled olive skin was revealed. Sable slid into a blue leather outfit, different from the night before. She tugged up the zipper that ran from crotch to her chin. She wore no underwear.

'Has he?' Miranda was still after her answer.

Sable peered in the mirror, slapped more mousse on her short spiked dark hair, stubbed out her cigarette, lit another, grabbed her guitar and was out the door. That all elapsed in no more than ninety seconds. Miranda was still standing there as if a tornado had blown through, when Sable grabbed the threshold door and stuck her head back in.

'You better keep away from Cole. You'll get hurt.'

Was it a warning or a threat? Miranda couldn't tell. It

was said in that same flat cold tone of voice Sable seemed to use for everything. Somehow, Miranda didn't believe Sable would issue friendly advice to help her avoid heartbreak. Sable only did and said things that helped Sable. How would she benefit if I kept clear of Cole? Miranda was perplexed.

The bigger mystery, Miranda had to admit, was why she was sleeping with Wayne. Sable showed no passion or even lust for Wayne. In the tape and talking about him, the only emotion she'd displayed was scorn. Miranda knew Sable had to be sleeping with him to get something. But what did Wayne have that Sable wanted?

Miranda considered the possibility that Sable was involved in the blackmail somehow. Maybe the blackmailer was using Sable to frame Wayne, for a price. Maybe she could be bought. That theory didn't sit quite right with Miranda, though. Sable looked like a woman who liked to make the rules, not live by them. But if she were in financial straits, she might compromise. Miranda mulled it over.

'How'd it go?' Wayne, who appeared with a Chivas in hand, was already slurring his words.

'Horrible. Sable told me nothing. Cole was,' Miranda paused and involuntarily touched her bruised lips. She could still feel his pressure between her legs, his hands in her hair. 'He was not helpful, either.'

'Damn. I'll talk to him.'

'No!' Miranda was more vehement than she'd meant to be, startling Wayne. 'He seems to have gotten the idea that he is a suspect. He's ticked. Just give him some space for a while. Don't pick a fight. Let's just see if these questions will stir up something.'

'Okay.' Wayne was leery. 'But I just hope it's not my wife who gets stirred up.'

Miranda walked down the hall with Wayne tagging along behind. 'I saved a table.'

'Fine.' Miranda didn't want to stay for the show. She didn't trust herself to be around Cole, even with a room full of people. But she had to finish this case and soon. Not only for her career, but for her sanity. Sable's warning echoed in her subconscious. Cole would be another Rick and end up hurting her.

Miranda knew she must find out where the tape and photos were taken, tonight. And she needed to watch Sable. Intuition told her she had a lot more to do with this blackmail threat than just being an innocent pawn.

Wayne had reserved a table on the opposite side of the stage from where they had sat the night before. Miranda gave him credit for sharp thinking. Sitting at the same table with the same woman two nights in a row would draw unwanted notice. Wayne led her to the table, offered to get her a drink, which she refused. Then he left and stood guard behind the bar.

Miranda should have been relieved. Instead, she was terrified. Tonight, she wanted Wayne's inane small talk to distract her from the stage, to give her an excuse to look away if Cole's attention came her way.

The band jumped into its first set with a romping, stomping country blues tune. Miranda couldn't keep her toes from tapping. In that second she was sorry that what had happened in the dressing room would keep her from coming back to hear His Baby Blues after the case was wrapped up. This music was fun.

But that kiss was . . . unforgettable. And it couldn't happen again. Miranda felt a wet heat develop again as she watched his lips rest softly on the microphone and thought about how hard they had crushed her mouth. She re-crossed her legs and shifted her eyes from Cole to Sable.

Their eyes met. Sable had been watching Miranda watch Cole. The expression in her flat, dark eyes was unreadable and after a moment her gaze moved back to the rest of the crowd. It left Miranda unsettled. She got up and walked to the bar, ordering a club soda. Her senses were in enough of a jumble without alcohol.

Wayne was dressed tonight in designer jeans, suede vest and handstitched western shirt. His clothes always seemed brand-new and made for someone else. Not like Cole,

70

Miranda thought, who wore his faded jeans and old T-shirts as if they lived for him. Wayne was busy on the other end of the bar with a couple he seemed to know. He ignored Miranda.

Feeling at loose ends, she walked to the front window. Looking out toward the river, she noticed a plainclothes cop hanging around the entrance to the club. There was probably another one inside. Miranda knew she'd been putting off talking to the cops about the rape, because of Rick. But, she told herself now, the police force was huge. She hadn't talked to Rick for two years and for all she knew he could have been transferred out of sex crimes by now. Or could have given up the force altogether. To-morrow, she would find the investigator in charge and find out how deeply the police believed Electric Blues figured in the rape.

Miranda heard the first set ending and congratulated herself on getting this far without having any uncomfort-able encounter with Cole. She sipped her club soda and, staring out the window, contemplated the case.

Ever since the set ended, Cole had been looking for her. He sensed her restlessness and saw her leave her table. Though he'd tried to catch her eye all night, she'd studiously avoided his. Oh God, how he wanted to kiss her again. He wanted her, all of her, to be his. He wanted to become part of her, to know what she wasn't telling him. Because he knew she was lying, not by what she said, but by what she wasn't saying. She thought he was guilty. But guilty of what?

Cole told himself he should turn his back on her and not look back. Distrust and secrets were hallmarks of his relationship with Sable and look what he was begging to get into again. But something was different this time. When he'd kissed her, so angry and frustrated, there was a connection. A passion that went beyond his wrath and her outrage. A passion that begged to be explored.

'Whoa. Are you hot tonight,' Trent broke into Cole's reverie.

71

'Yeah?' Cole sounded only politely interested as he scanned the milling crowd.

'Yeah! This is the show we should be taping for our demo. I don't know what's gotten into you but you oughtta plug into it every night.'

'Nothing out of the ordinary, except being questioned by a conceited cop for a rape and a some gorgeous gumshoe for blackmail. Maybe being a wanted man turns me on.' Cole let out a bitter laugh.

Trent's eyes widened. 'Blackmail? Wanted man? You lost me, bro.'

Cole waved him off. 'It's nothing. That babe Wayne hired to look into surveillance he's been under was asking a lot of questions before the show. I guess it has me spooked.'

'She has you something, but it's not spooked,' Trent gave Cole a knowing smile and walked off.

And then he saw her, standing in the shadows, gazing out the window. He felt a strange tightening in his chest. She looked so lonely and vulnerable. He saw a pair on the roam approach her and without thinking he took steps toward them. But with a charming smile she gave them an undeniable dismissal. Cole changed his direction. Not so vulnerable, he decided with a twinge of satisfaction. The ice queen chilled them out.

It was almost time for the second set and Cole headed back to the stage. A young woman who had been sitting at a front table jumped up to flirt with Cole while her date was at the bar. Cole was polite, but extracted himself as soon as he could. He usually enjoyed the verbal play – the little coquettes were so fun to tease. But the rape investigation had him gunshy and Miranda kept him distracted.

Miranda pulled a camera out of her case and headed to the far corner of the club, near the hall. This was the angle from which the tape and photos were taken. Unobserved, she snapped a few pictures standing, then crouched down. No, she decided, they hadn't been taken from under or

72

hiding behind a table. It was impossible. She looked over the corner, then the walls. They were adorned with an eclectic mix of art – modern sculptures, neon lights, 1950s photos of San Antonio, Impressionist and Mexican-American paintings. It was a crazy collection that worked. She wondered who thought it up. Probably the same person who named the club. Somehow she couldn't believe it was crass old Wayne.

The strains of Cole's guitar spread through the club again and the crowd started to quiet. Miranda turned around and met gray eyes. How long had he been staring at her? His look was penetrating. It unstripped her to her soul. Miranda felt desire banging on the door of her resolve and she spun back around and almost ran to the restroom. Passing a pair of middle-aged beauties who were talking about their ex-husbands while they touched up their make-up, Miranda locked herself in a stall and caught her breath.

She waited until they left, then she opened the door and came out. She looked at her reflection in the mirror.

'What am I afraid of?' she asked.

Miranda knew the answer. This case had developed into a proving ground, personally and professionally. And she didn't trust herself – to have good judgement about a relationship, to keep her perspective about the case, to stop herself if he touched her again.

Then something about the mirror caught Miranda's attention. It was different than the other three. They were glued to the wall, over the sinks. The one at the end hung loosely from a hook, above empty wall.

'That has to be it,' Miranda said under her breath.

She was about to reach over and see what was behind the mirror when three drunks meandered loudly into the restroom. She couldn't help eavesdropping as they stood only an arm's length away, debating an age-old dilemma.

'I'm telling you Brenda, he's a stud-and-a-half,' slurred one woman whose mascara was smeared across her cheek.

'You should give him another chance. You'll forget he ever dumped you for that other gal.'

'She's right, Bren,' the second woman agreed. 'If he wants to get back with you, take him back. He realizes his mistake and he'll be good to you.'

Out of the corner of her eye, Miranda could see Brenda wavering. Then, unexpectedly, the small blonde turned to Miranda.

'What do you think? Should I let him move back in?'

Miranda spoke without thinking. 'Never. You might be able to live with him, but you won't be able to live with yourself.'

Blinking rapidly, the trio stared at her as if she'd grown a horn. Then they turned away and continued their debate. Miranda tuned them out, not wanting the memories Brenda's plight invoked. The mirror drew her attention again. She was itching to confirm her suspicion. So, she loitered a little – brushing her hair, washing her hands – to see if she could outlast them. But when one launched into an empty stall with grotesque choking sounds, Miranda decided she couldn't stand it. Once outside the restroom, she hurried down the hall.

Entering the bar area, she studied the wall. The bathroom would be on the other side. She estimated the location of the mysterious mirror. A large, framed photo was hung on the bar side.

Bingo, Miranda thought.

Miranda made her way slowly back to her table. The seductive strains of Cole's music enveloped her and she dreaded the slow torture it would be to have to sit through another set. She would force herself, though. She had to see what was behind that mirror, and it would have to wait until after the show.

Finally, Cole announced his last song. It jolted Miranda back to reality. Somewhere, in the battle between her mind and body, a truce was called and for the last forty-five minutes, she'd sat back and lost herself in the music. She watched the dance of emotions across his face, his eyes alive, as the songs seemed to pour from his soul. Cole didn't feel the music; he was the music.

At times, she felt he was singing just to her. Those moments were more intimate than when they had kissed. But now it was over. The sudden void of sound was filled with the hum of talking as the lights went up.

A petite girl, who looked barely twenty-one, raced up to the stage to talk to Cole, leaving her date, sulking, at their table. It gave Miranda her escape. She headed back to the bar.

'Wayne,' she called after she was sure his friends had gone out the front door. 'I'm going to stay for a while.'

'I can't hang around. Vicki called, and I have to get home.'

'I won't be long,' Miranda said with some trepidation. She wanted to get it done and get out of there before she saw Cole again. She asked the bartender, Trey, a few casual questions about the case while waiting for the last of the barflies to leave. The trio who had interrupted Miranda in the restroom earlier emerged. Miranda wondered if they had been in there for the last hour.

Peeking into the restroom, she found it deserted. Hurrying over to the mirror, she tried to pull it out enough to see behind it, but it was wedged too tightly on the hook. She reached up and gently eased it off and to the floor. There, just as she guessed was a small hole. She pulled her camera out of her case and compared the size of the lens to the opening. It was a little larger than it needed to be for a camera, just big enough for a videocamera.

Miranda heard steps on the hardwood floor of the hall. She quickly grabbed the mirror and put it back as the restroom door squeaked open. Cole stood in the doorway. A thin current of fear ran through her.

'Excuse me, isn't this the women's restroom?' Miranda tried to sound politely offended as her heartbeat thundered in her ears.

'Excuse me, but isn't this my club, and isn't it closed?' His smoky eyes teased as his lazy voice challenged.

75

'I have permission from the majority owner to stay and look around.' If he was going to throw his weight around, she could too.

'So, you're checking to see if the restroom is bugged. Good strategy.'

Her blood raced at his sarcasm and arrogance. She opened her mouth for a smart retort then snapped it shut. The longer she parried with him the more she risked that he would guess why she was really in there. Steeling herself, she grabbed her case and tried to brush past him.

Cole caught her arm as she made it into the deserted hall. 'Don't we need to talk?'

'About what?' Miranda, her face averted, strained against his grasp.

'About what you're investigating for Wayne, about what you think I have to do with it,' Cole's voice grew husky. 'And why you are so damned irresistible.'

Shocked, Miranda turned to look at him. It was a mistake. Their eyes locked. Like magnets, their lips drew together, violently. His strong hand released her arm, claimed the small of her back and pulled her against him. She could feel him already hot and hard against her abdomen. His hand slid down to cup her buttocks, while the other hand buried itself in her hair.

Her mouth was eager and pliant, but the rest of her body resisted. Miranda pressed her hands onto his chest and told herself to push him away. Her body didn't listen. Cole pulled her head back, exposing her creamy throat, and with his lips and tongue nibbled a trail from her jaw to her cleavage. Once there, his mouth formed over each nipple, blowing his hot breath through the softness of her sweater.

Miranda's low, agonized moan signaled her surrender. Her arms wrapped around his neck. She felt weak with wanting. Her reaction was like blowing on Cole's already smoldering fire. Wild with desire, he picked her up. His mouth never leaving hers, he carried her to the dressing room and laid her on the couch.

76

In one swift movement, his shirt was over his head and on the floor, exposing a chest so masculine, Miranda sucked in a breath. Golden brown hair curled over his pectorals, diminishing into a line that disappeared invitingly behind the top button of his jeans. His upper body had the slightly tanned and well-toned look of someone who works outside in the elements.

Their physical separation lasted only a few moments before Cole was kissing her again, his hands tracing every curve of her body. As he reached back to free her breasts, Miranda ran her hands down his back. This time it was his turn to moan. He tested the weight of her breasts under her sweater, and kneaded them gently first, then harder. His hips strained toward hers urgently. In answer, hers pressed to meet his.

His hands slid down her trim abdomen, sending shivers through her body, and began to release the button of her jeans. Then, the sound of glass crashing to the floor and voices on the other side of the door shot like a bright light through the haze of her desire. She pushed at Cole and tried to sit up.

'Who . . . what . . . was that?' Her voice sounded like a stranger's.

'Who cares?' Cole's face was buried in her unbound hair as he breathed an answer onto her neck. He wasn't giving up.

'What am I doing?' Miranda struggled to break free from Cole, as she began to realize how deep she'd fallen out of her job and into desire.

'You sure are good at it for not knowing what you are doing,' Cole teased playfully.

The slap seemed to come from nowhere and surprised both of them. It shattered their brief connection.

Miranda, who radiated a tangible sensuality just moments earlier, now shook with an anger just as tangible. She was angry with herself, for giving into her longing, for getting involved with probably the chief suspect in her investigation, but most of all for making herself vulnerable

77

to another heartbreak. Cole's words, sounding smug and cocky to her ears, touched a chord. She lashed out at him instead of at herself.

Miranda tried to maintain her indignation as she awkwardly put her clothes back in order. Cole leaned up against the dressing table with a half-smile on his face. Miranda couldn't take her eyes off his strong, muscled back reflected in the mirror. He's probably reveling in his latest conquest. The thought made Miranda's blood boil.

Cole tried to shake off the haze of lust that had enveloped him for the last ten minutes, or was it hours? Miranda Randolph made him lose track of time, space, judgement. He struggled to think of what had set her off. It had to be more than just the crash from the bar. He knew she wanted him as much as he wanted her. What had stopped her?

Finally pulled together, Miranda almost ran to the door.

'Where are you going?'

'Away from here.'

'Where are you parked?'

'None of your business.' Her hand turned the knob.

'Well, you can't walk out there alone.' He crossed his corded arms across his chest.

'I suppose you have to be a gentleman and accompany me to my car. And then you wouldn't be able to let me drive home alone. Then, I couldn't walk in my house alone. Then I couldn't sleep alone. All in the name of chivalry, of course.' Miranda spit out sarcastically.

Cole laughed with that one eyebrow arched. 'Sounds like a good idea, wish I'd thought of it myself.'

'As if you didn't. Goodbye.'

Suddenly Cole was in front of her, barring the door, his hand over hers. Shocked that he'd moved so quickly, Miranda didn't move for a moment. Then she pulled her hand from his as if burned.

'Look,' Cole's eyes were shadowed and his voice soft. 'There may be a rapist out there. You can't walk alone.'

'And who says you aren't the rapist?'

Stunned, Cole stared at Miranda. She slipped out the door around him and rushed down the hall. Trey was behind the bar, sweeping up the glass. Sable perched on a barstool watching him.

'Everything okay?' Sable asked knowingly. Miranda felt as if she was walking by naked.

She couldn't begin to answer Sable's question, so she didn't, and left without a word.

CHAPTER 4

Miranda got in her car, shut the door and laid her head on the steering wheel before even trying to get the key in the ignition. It had been a rough night. She'd gotten maybe three hours of sleep in bits and pieces. Her body was frustrated and her mind was discontented.

She had tried to call Melanie early this morning, on the pretense of discussing Thanksgiving plans, but there had been no answer, even though it had been six a.m. in Boston. Miranda had to smile. She hoped her ultra-responsible, workaholic older sister was finally allowing herself to be romanced. It was either that or she had taken to getting to the office before dawn. Miranda had to admit the latter was more likely.

Miranda sipped at the coffee she'd brought with her. She hated drinking her favorite beverage out of styrofoam, but it was the only way she was going to get through the morning. She had changed her plans for the day eight times over the course of her restless night and finally decided to drive by the Lambert home in prestigious Olmos Park on her way to the office. She didn't know what exactly she was looking for, but at least it would make her feel like she was doing something other than thinking about Cole Taylor.

Finally starting the car, Miranda switched her radio to one of the all-news stations. Usually she listened to radio or TV while getting ready but this morning she had not wanted the noise.

The sports was just wrapping up. The Spurs won on the road at Phoenix.

'Great!' Miranda said aloud. She was a big basketball fan and missed the tickets she had often been given when she worked at the TV station. She missed a lot about working at the station, but she tried not to think about that now.

'Now, our top story,' the anchor announced. 'For the second night in a row, there's been a sexual assault near the Riverwalk. Police believe the suspect is the same man who raped a young woman the night before. He's described as a Caucasian, six-feet tall, 200 pounds, in his thirties, wearing jeans, a T-shirt and boots. He wears a dark, hooded cloak. Police say both victims, women in their early twenties, had spent the evening at the Electric Blues nightclub and were walking back to their cars alone when the attacks occurred.'

'Damn,' Miranda had hoped the cops would keep the club's name out of the media. Usually they tried to, so there wasn't a panic and so the business wouldn't be destroyed. Someone at the club must have pissed off the investigating officer. Cole, probably. Miranda had the feeling he didn't cotton to authority figures.

'The mayor is assuring tourists the Riverwalk is safe. At least a dozen hotels have beefed up their private security forces after dark, and the police chief announced a dozen officers would be put on overtime to patrol downtown and the Riverwalk at night until the suspect is caught.'

Miranda pulled over to the side of the road. The description of the suspect still rattled around in her mind. It could be Cole. It could be her brother for that matter, or at least three TV reporters she knew, or thousands of other San Antonians. If it was Cole, why would he be so obvious, targeting women that had been to his club? He wasn't that stupid. But was he that arrogant, to think he wouldn't get caught? Miranda decided he was, but arrogance didn't automatically make one a rapist.

She had left him obviously frustrated last night. Did

81

that have anything to do with it? No, no, Miranda told herself. Rape was a crime of violence, not sex. Last night he'd been passionate, not violent. Or maybe that's because she had wanted him. It changes one's perspective. But he couldn't be a criminal; not with those eyes, that smile. Remember Ted Bundy or Jack the Ripper, she told herself.

She had accused him of being the rapist last night. She'd felt guilty about that all night. It had been a low blow she'd dealt in defense, to put distance between them, to make it easier for her to walk away. He had looked so shocked, so hurt, so disbelieving. Was it an act? Or was he just shocked that she could guess the truth?

What about the other possibility – that he was being set up? But why? The husband or boyfriend of a woman with whom Cole had a one-night-stand might want revenge. It seemed an elaborate and dangerous scheme just for revenge, though. Maybe Wayne orchestrated it to get Cole out of the picture, giving him sole ownership of the club. But that would be shooting himself in the foot. Cole was making him money, and the bad publicity could close down the club forever.

What about one of the people interested in buying into the club? He could be getting Cole in trouble with the law, which would throw the club into disrepute. Then he could buy it at a firesale, opening it up under new ownership. If that was the case, the blackmail could be tied in with the rapes. Channeling her sudden urgency into action, Miranda got back on the road, headed now for the police headquarters downtown.

Miranda felt like someone who has worked hard to break an old habit then easily falls back into it. She used to come down here several times a day when she first went to work for KATX as the police reporter. That's where she met Rick, and after being transferred off the beat, she'd come here to meet him for lunch or dinner. It had been two years, though, that she had avoided this place. She felt a

82

tremor as she climbed the steps to the front door, but reminded herself that out of the thousands on the police force the likelihood of seeing Rick was slim.

Unfortunately, the desk sergeant was the same. Fred Vandiver was probably a year away from retirement. Five years before, his wife had issued an ultimatum: get in another patrol car and he'd be single. She wanted him around to enjoy the fruits of working for the department for thirty-five years.

'Oh, ho, what do we have here? The prodigal reporter?'

'Ex-reporter to you,' Miranda shot back in good humor.

'Hey, that was a bum rap. Those TV execs are a bunch of ass kissers to corporate America.'

'I don't know if I agree with you, but I appreciate you being in my corner.'

'So what you up to now, working with another station?'

'No. I gave up the glamor world for the underworld. I'm a PI.'

'Geez, around here that's worse.'

'Don't I know it.'

'So, did you just come here cuz you missed me?'

'Of course,' she said indulgently. 'But while I'm here, might as well earn my keep too.'

'Then, go ahead and ask the man who knows everything.'

'Who's on the Riverwalk rapes?'

'Who isn't?' Suddenly his grin faded. 'Is that the case you're working?'

'No. I'm on something else for a Riverwalk business. I wanted to touch base with the detective working the rapes to make sure I don't have something you guys might need.'

'Sure, sure,' Vandiver dismissed her explanation. 'But you may change your mind.'

'Why?'

Fred didn't have a chance to answer her question before a hand wound around her waist from behind and lips lightly caressed her neck. Miranda spun around, but she

83

didn't need to see to know who it was. As always, his overpowering cologne gave him away.

'Watch it, I'll have you arrested for sexual harrassment,' Miranda glared at her ex-lover.

The two plainclothes cops with Rick let loose with some locker-room laughs. Rick, looking like a cat eyeing a wounded bird, was triumphant.

'Oh, I guess I'd better arrest myself then.'

Miranda cast a confused look at Fred, who shrugged apologetically. 'Rick's heading up Sex Crimes now, Miranda.'

'My day gets better and better,' Miranda muttered under her breath as she turned to face Rick and his flunkies.

She remembered them now. They'd latched onto Rick way back when he was a mere investigator, thinking he was a promising rung in the ladder of police department politics. Miranda never trusted them. Turns out they were all right: they about Rick and she about them. After the fact, they went out of their way to boast they knew Rick was two-timing her with Sheila. They probably helped plan the wedding, Miranda thought bitterly.

'Well, Lieutenant,' Miranda emphasized his title so he'd understand that her visit was purely professional. 'It's you I need to talk to then.'

'About your sexual harrassment case?' Rick asked, deadpan.

'No. About the Riverwalk rapes.'

The mood changed abruptly. The tension was palpable and Miranda suspected the pressure on this case was intense, from the chief and from city hall.

Rick dismissed the goons, who took off on a coffee break. Fred Vandiver was still watching the show, probably the most exciting thing he'd seen all week. Miranda thanked him and turned back to Rick, who took her arm and propelled her toward his office.

Miranda tried to be nonchalant as she extracted her arm. She didn't want to make a scene, enough people were staring already. Their affair was well known at the time.

Miranda, the TV reporter, dating Rick, the rising star of the department. Occasionally, they had been written up in the local newspaper gossip column as 'San Antonio's answer to the Perfect Couple.' The irony of that statement came later. Sheila had known Rick and Miranda were lovers. Miranda was the only one involved the lover's triangle who didn't even know there was a lover's triangle.

By the time Miranda found out, Rick and Sheila were married. The only thing Rick loved more than power was money. Sheila had the ability to give him both. Heir to the richest car dealer in San Antonio, she was also goddaughter to one of the state's US Senators.

Miranda was hurt, but philosophical at first. She thought she had loved him. He seemed the ideal boyfriend: drop-dead gorgeous, intelligent, generous, attentive, ambitious and a lusty lover. But once he'd taken himself out of her life she realized he was also deceitful, shallow and self-absorbed. A week after his marriage, Miranda was still bitter, but she also had decided Rick had done her a favor.

Then, one night she came home after work to find him on her couch, sipping Dom Perignon, holding a dozen long-stemmed red roses. It hadn't occurred to her that he still had the key to her house. He said he was sorry about marrying Sheila; it was a spur-of-the-moment thing that he now regretted. He was going to get out of it as soon as he could. He missed Miranda, couldn't they keep their affair going in secret while he filed for divorce?

Miranda was aghast. She stood paralyzed, speechless. Rick poured her a glass of champagne, probably lifted from his new wife's mansion, and carried it to her, his free hand taking the chance to caress her breasts.

His touch tripped the powerkeg of emotions inside Miranda. She knocked the glass out of his hand, crashing it against the fireplace. She felt like both throwing up and beating him up. His proposition disgusted and infuriated her.

'How stupid do you think I am? Or is your ego so

monstrous that you think I couldn't possibly live without you in my bed?' Miranda stared at Rick with hate blazing in her eyes.

'Get out!' she commanded through a choked throat.

That was the last time she had seen him. She had read not long ago that Sheila had run off with her personal trainer, a Nordic bodybuilder, but she wasn't really sure whether they were separated or divorced. And she told herself that she didn't care. He must have gotten a good settlement, though, Miranda thought now as she eyed his Armani suit. He had always dressed well; now he dressed like a millionaire.

Miranda was honest enough with herself to admit the sexual attraction was still there. His touch did raise her body temperature a few degrees. Casting a sidelong glance at his muscled body she could see he still spent as much time at the gym as he did when they dated. She was reminded of the many long hot nights they spent wrapped in each other's arms. It had been satisfying physically, if not spiritually.

Rick stepped into his office and closed the door behind Miranda. He shut the blinds on curious eyes and moved behind his desk.

'So, what did you need to talk to me about?' His dark eyes appraised her, comparing reality to memory. The comparison was more than favorable. She was more mature, and, if it was possible, more sensual.

'I'm a private eye now,' Miranda began in explanation.

'I know.'

Miranda was surprised. 'How did you know?'

'I was told you got your license. Anyway, it was in the paper. And Sandborn's making sure it's not a secret.'

'Oh,' Miranda said to fill the silence.

'I've always kept up with you,' Rick's voice grew husky.

Miranda didn't like the tack the conversation was taking. 'Are you saying you've been spying on me?'

Rick ignored her question. He shifted some reports on his desk. 'Sheila and I divorced.'

86

'Good for her.'

Rick's eyes narrowed. 'Are you still mad at me?'

Miranda had to laugh, he was so out of touch. Mad didn't begin to describe what she had felt. 'No. I'm not mad.'

Smiling at her lightened mood, Rick walked around to the front of the desk and leaned on it, inches from her. He was getting too friendly for Miranda.

'I need some information about the Riverwalk rapes.'

The deep olive skin on Rick's face tightened. 'What do you have for me?'

Miranda could see he meant information and was relieved he'd dropped his personal pursuit.

'I can't tell you much. Client confidentiality.'

Rick scoffed, and motioned her to continue.

'Off the record?'

'Off the record.'

'I've been hired by Wayne Lambert, owner of Electric Blues, to investigate some threats.'

Rick stood up, muscles bunching. 'Threats? Someone threatening to rape his customers? Why didn't he come to police?'

'No, nothing like that. Rapes aren't even remotely alluded to in the notes, which by the way are very specific. In fact, I don't know that the two cases are even related.'

'Something makes you think they are. What?'

'It just struck me as a strange coincidence that this new club would be involved in two investigations at once.'

'Why didn't Lambert want to take these threats to the police?'

'He doesn't want his wife to know,' Miranda said simply.

'Why? Is she threatened with harm in these notes?'

'No physical harm.'

'I see,' Rick scoffed. 'Lambert's bedding one of his lambs. He's being blackmailed.'

'I cannot confirm or deny.' Miranda should have known

better. Rick could read between the lines better than anyone she'd ever known. Except when his own desires became involved. They tended to dull his razor-sharp deduction.

'What does the blackmailer want?'

Miranda gave him her best poker-face look. After a few minutes, Rick held up his hands, breaking the standoff.

'Okay. I'll give. A little.' Rick stood up and began pacing his small office. It was obvious this case had him deeply agitated. 'How much do you know?'

'What's been in the media, plus,' Miranda hesitated, uncomfortable with what she was about to say, then plunged forward in a rush. 'The rapist, with the first victim, was not as abusive and rough as most rapists. And that he apparently did not leave any sperm in the victim.'

'You always did have good sources,' Rick said with open admiration.

'I know people with good sources,' Miranda returned, not willing to accept the compliment.

'Well, the sources are right. However, tests did show a spermicide, the same type, in both women. We are assuming he used a condom, although neither victim can confirm that. He entered them from behind.'

'Isn't that unusual?' Miranda remembered a court case that wrapped up in Austin recently. The victim had begged the rapist to use a condom. The defense tried to assert that her request constituted acquiescence of the act. The jury didn't buy it and the man was convicted.

'What? Entering from behind?' His eyes burned into hers as the words slipped off a silky smooth tongue.

Miranda took an uneven breath. He was testing her. 'No. Using a condom.'

Rick paused, giving her another hot look before answering. 'Extremely. Our psychologists are working up a profile now. But preliminary theories are that he either is using one so his DNA can't be traced for trial or he's a head case.'

'Or he could be worried about AIDS,' Miranda added.

'Maybe. Most rapists aren't.'

'So, what else do you have?'

'You sure are greedy. You're lucky I gave you that much,' Rick said, eyeing her. He was not an investigator who put much stock in symbiotic working relationships, and Miranda had heard talk that most private eyes found him a hard-ass to work with.

She sat stubbornly silent, waiting.

'Okay,' Rick said with poorly feigned reluctance. 'The rapist repeated the lyrics to songs while he assaulted both women.' He wasn't about to tell her he also carved the letter 'C' into their shoulders with a knife. That was evidence the chief had put a tight lid on.

'He *sang* to them?' Miranda was incredulous.

'No, he hummed a tune. The tune to a song both women remember Cole Taylor singing in the performance they saw before they were raped.'

Miranda's heart tightened. She felt like she couldn't get enough air in her lungs. She forced her next question from numb lips.

'Are you saying Cole Taylor is a suspect?'

'I'm saying Cole Taylor is *the* suspect.'

Miranda struggled to remain outwardly nonchalant.

'What makes you zero in on him, besides the tune? Anyone at the club could have heard and repeated that.'

'The suspect wore a white T-shirt and jeans. Taylor's trademark. He fits the physical description of the suspect.'

'So do thousands of other men in San Antonio,' Miranda became animated in Cole's defense. 'And doesn't this all seem too pat? It could be a set-up.'

'What's the motive?' Rick pressed, his eyes narrowed.

'I don't know,' Miranda admitted.

'Ah.'

Miranda didn't let Rick's self-righteousness stop her. 'If you're so sure, why don't you just arrest him?'

'Would that screw up your investigation?' Rick asked.

Miranda eyed Rick suspiciously. 'Since when do you

care about a dick's investigation when you're ready to make an arrest?'

'Well, you caught me.' He threw his hands up. Miranda couldn't help but notice his biceps as they strained the sleeves of his coat. 'I have my suspicion, but not quite enough evidence. Although I will soon.'

Rick was watching her carefully, but Miranda pretended not to notice.

She stood and thought about extending her hand, but decided against it. The animosity that had begun to dissipate in the middle of their conversation had grown back up again. Instead she reached for the door.

'Rick, I appreciate your cooperation.'

'Miranda,' his voice had changed from business to bedroom. She turned around, even though she didn't want to. She had to face her ghosts and put them to rest.

Desire blazed in Rick's eyes. 'I still want you.'

'Too bad I don't.' Miranda closed the door in his face as he crossed the room to her.

Rick opened the blinds and watched as she glided through the bullpen, her head held high, her back straight. A model's posture. He recalled how she used to melt in his arms. Just then Miranda glanced back. Their eyes met and held for a half second. Hers were as hard and ungiving as the turquoise pendant around her neck. Rick wondered if she'd changed. He was going to find out.

Some hastily manufactured conversations sprung up as Miranda walked through the bullpen. No one would meet her eyes, and just as well. She hoped she did not look as rattled as she felt. Hearing Cole officially named as a suspect had sent her reeling. A still strong attraction to a man she no longer respected or loved confused her even more.

An officer she knew from her reporter days walked past and Miranda had enough presence of mind to inquire about his wife and kids. Then she beat a quick exit, making sure Fred Vandiver saw her leave with a smile and a wave. He might be fond of her, but he certainly wasn't beyond furthering department gossip.

Once inside her sedan, Miranda wound her way through the maze of one-way streets that led to her office. She didn't know which of her personal and professional problems to mull over first, although she had a feeling they were all intertwined, and that solving one may lead to a solution for all of them.

'But which one?' she asked herself.

As usual, she decided to tackle the case first, setting her feelings aside. Talking to Rick hadn't shed much light on the blackmail case, except maybe to reinforce her idea that Cole was being framed. At least that's what she wanted to believe. The alternative was too ugly.

Miranda breezed past the empty reception desk and headed to her cubbyhole to call Wayne Lambert at the club. It was time to talk to his wife. Hopefully, Wayne could help her plan an 'accidental' meeting with Victoria.

'Miranda! Miranda Randolph!' A voice rang from somewhere down the hall.

Looking back, Miranda saw Marjorie chasing her in unique gum-cracking, hip-swishing way. A smile tickling the corners of her mouth, Miranda stamped down the urge to call out: 'Va-va-va-voom'.

The forty-five-year-old receptionist was a package of contradictory stereotypes. Her ultra-teased, bleached-blonde beehive circa 1960 was perched atop the body of Betty Grable, legs and all. Sitting down she looked like someone's mother. When she stood up, she looked like the other woman which, according to rumor, she had been several times.

'There's a message for you,' Marjorie paused to pop her gum. 'He said it was urgent.'

Miranda's stomach took a leap. Cole, she thought. Maybe he called to talk about last night. She took the note from Marjorie's hand. It only had the number of Electric Blues written down.

'He wouldn't leave his name. Just said you'd know who it was.' Marjorie cracked her gum.

'Was it a young guy, sexy voice?'

'Honey, that's redundant. All guys have sexy voices.' With a wink, Marjorie sashayed into Peter's office. Dictation on his lap, no doubt.

Chuckling, Miranda continued on into her office. Marjorie was a character, but extremely efficient at her job, which is why Doug had put up with her antics for twenty years.

Setting down her bag, she stared at the phone as if it was about to reach up and grab her around the neck. It might as well and put me out of my misery, Miranda thought. If I hear Cole's voice, I'll dissolve into a pool of desire. I need time. Time to solve the case. Time to steel myself against his powers of seduction. Time to get away from trouble.

Dialing the number quickly, she sucked in a deep breath.

'Electric Blues.' His voice. Her heart went wild.

'This is Miranda Randolph.' She said it too loudly, too quickly. She sounded nervous to her own ears.

'Yes?'

'Didn't you, um, I got, ah, someone there left a message at my office.'

'I see, so you didn't just call to accuse me of yet another crime. Maybe last night's rape?' Cole's voice bit with sarcasm.

'No.' It was breathed more than said.

'I'm sure it was Wayne who called you. Who else here would?' He added cruelly. Then he put her on hold and she heard his voice again, this time in songs piped through the phone. Mercifully, Wayne came on within seconds.

'I'm so glad you called back right away,' Wayne began in a rush. 'You have to do me a huge favor. Vicki is running this fundraiser bash tonight and talked me into buying a whole table for Electric Blues. Sable was supposed to be there. But now, with all this going on, there's no way in hell she can go. I'm giving Vicki some excuse like she's sick, or PMS or somethin'.'

'Knowing Sable, that excuse could work all month long,' Miranda pointed out snidely.

'You're right. Ha! Anyway, I need you to go in her place. I called all the waitresses and they all have class or dates or some such bullshit. You gotta go.'

Miranda wanted to tell Wayne to stuff it. Some high society dinner was the last place she wanted to be tonight. But it would give her the chance to see and talk to Victoria and her friends. It would tell her a lot more about Wayne's wife than watching her briefly across a tearoom or through her living room window.

'Okay. What time and where?'

'Oh, I forgot one thing. This is a couples-only deal, which is a good thing since we need an excuse to explain why you're there anyway. You're going as Cole's date. He's picking you up at 6.30.'

'What?' Miranda was aghast. She remembered Cole's thinly veiled hostility on the phone earlier. 'He knows this already?'

'Nope. I'm just about to tell him about it.'

'He won't do it.'

'Yes, he will,' Wayne assured her. 'Vicki talked him into singing so he has to go and he has to have a date. I know you two aren't getting along like scotch and water, but it's not like you have to spend the whole evening sucking face or anything. You have to sit with him at the table and maybe a few bump-and-grinds, just enough so's Vicki believes you're his honey for the night. She's a romantic, so it won't be too damn hard.'

'You want me to dance with him?' Miranda said dumbly. The day had turned into a nightmare and it wasn't over yet.

'Doesn't Cole have to perform tonight?' Miranda suggested brightly. Maybe she could get rid of him early.

'It's Tuesday. We're closed.'

Miranda knew she didn't have any choice. She gave Wayne her address then hung up.

Miranda didn't know how long she sat there, trying to understand how her life had turned so upside-down, when suddenly a head peeked around the corner. It was Doug.

'So, the eagle has landed. Caught your prey yet?'

'Doug, what is it with you lately? Yesterday I was a Disney character now I'm some critter out of a Jack Higgins novel.'

'Been reading a lot, I guess,' he admitted sheepishly as he stepped into her office.

Miranda knew the answer was more than that, though. He still didn't know how to treat her. Whether to come in hitting hard on the case, to comment on the way she was dressed or to talk about the weather. Maybe one day he'd learn to treat her like any other investigator. Instead of like an attractive female rookie investigator.

'Well, it's gotten a little complicated,' Miranda began. 'With these rapes.'

'I heard. Is there a connection? Or is it just coincidence?'

'My instincts tell me there's a connection.'

Doug nodded. 'Do the cops have any suspects?'

Miranda shot a sharp look at Doug. So he either assumed she'd already talked to the cops, or one of his spies down there told him about her visit. News travels fast, she thought wryly.

'Yes.'

'Anyone on your shortlist?'

'Yes.'

'Want to kick theories around a little?'

'No.'

Doug sighed and looked out the window. 'Look, Miranda, I know you want to do this yourself. But asking for help does not mean you've failed. It's a big case, getting bigger, apparently, and if I put another operative on the case, you would still be in charge.'

Yeah, sure, in name only, Miranda thought. She couldn't really put a finger on why she didn't want Phil to join the investigation. Part of it was her pride, she knew. The rest had to do with Cole. If there was another investigator, he'd undoubtedly come between her and the chief suspect. That would make it easier to deny her craving body. Which she was intent on doing. Or was she? If she had help they might be able to solve the case sooner. That was her goal, wasn't it?

Miranda became so lost in her self-analysis that she forgot where their conversation had gone. Doug watched her at war with herself and tried to press his advantage.

'So, should I call Phil in?'

Miranda decided to throw Doug a bone, thinking it might placate him. 'No, I'd really rather brainstorm with you for a while.'

Doug took what he could get. 'Shoot.'

Miranda outlined the case vaguely for Doug, omitting her weak moment with Cole the night before.

'The sense I have is that this Taylor fellow has the best motive and access, but you don't think he did it. Sable is suspicious, but with no obvious motive, except maybe cash in an accomplice situation. The 'anonymous share inquirer' would have motive, to gain the club, or at least part of it, but who is he? And Victoria might have hatched a convoluted plan to punish her husband. Does that about sum it up?'

'That's it.' Almost.

'Have you met Victoria?'

'I meet her tonight at the Children's Safehouse Gala.'

'Ah, rubbing elbows with the rich and famous. But I guess you are one of the famous.' Doug looked contemplative. 'It's couples-only. Who's your escort?'

'Cole Taylor.' Doug raised his eyebrows at that. Miranda added hastily: 'Wayne arranged it.'

'You be careful. Carry your piece,' Doug warned, then left.

Miranda eased back into her chair in relief. Doug had let her off the hook about the partner, for today anyway. But he'd made it clear the clock was ticking. The next time he brought it up it would be an order, not a suggestion.

CHAPTER 5

The phone rang. Miranda glanced at it in irritation, at the mirror and back to the phone as it rang again. She was frozen there in her black lace bra and panties, with Teasing Taupe liner on only one eyelid.

Another ring. She was already running late. Maybe she'd just let her machine pick up.

Finally, after four rings, she gave in. 'Hello.'

'Hey, little sis, what's up?'

'Melly!' Miranda never realized how much she missed being near her sister until she heard her voice. That's probably why they didn't call more often. It was just too hard.

'I got your message. I miss you.'

'Me too,' Understatement of the year, Miranda thought. 'I just called to see if we could spend some of the holidays together.'

'I'm so swamped at work. Thanksgiving is out of the question. I will definitely make time at Christmas though.'

'Can you come here?' Miranda asked hesitantly.

'Let me talk to Mark and see what's best for him. Have you heard from him lately?'

'Not since he took that group white water rafting on the Colorado River.'

'Well, let's see. When I called him last he was taking off for some kind of alligator hunt in the Everglades.'

They both erupted into laughter. Mark was their little brother. Miranda always thought of Melly as the epitome of responsibility and Mark as the polar opposite. He graduated from college with the smallest margin in the school's history, then turned playing into a profession. He was a thrill guide. His specialties were daring and dangerous. Miranda had to admire him, he made a good living talking people into risking their lives, making them pay for it, then having them believe they enjoyed it. Or at least that's the way Miranda saw it. She knew she wasn't much of a risk-taker, neither was Melly. They often joked that Mark got their share of the 'risk' genes.

'Shall we invite the Flavor of the Week?' Another inside joke. The one thing in life Mark wouldn't risk was a serious relationship, so he had never been seen with one woman for more than a week. With a muscular, six-foot-two-inch body, wavy hair, Miranda's turquoise eyes, and the charm to go with his looks, Mark usually had a waiting list of women who wanted to be the next 'flavor'.

'Why bother? He'll bring her whether there's an invitation or not,' Miranda pointed out.

'True,' agreed Melanie, still chuckling.

'Oh, it feels good to laugh,' Miranda grew misty.

'Randi, what's wrong? I could hear it in your voice on my machine.'

Miranda admitted to herself that the real reason she called Melly was to talk, to have someone hear about her dilemma with Cole. But now that Melly had asked, Miranda wasn't sure if she should even put what she'd been feeling into words.

'Oh, I don't know.' Miranda hated it when she heard herself sniffling.

'Do you want me to fly down there this weekend?'

'Melly, you just said you were swamped at work,' Miranda protested.

'You're more important any day. If you need me, I'll be there.'

Then Miranda really started to cry. That's what real love is, she thought, when you need someone and they come, no matter what. Miranda indulged her tears for a minute or so,

Melly listening quietly on the other end. It wasn't the first time Melly had provided the shoulder and it wasn't the first time Miranda had felt guilty about using it.

At sixteen, Melly had become the parent to her two younger siblings when their mother died in a car wreck. Their father withdrew emotionally and was now so far removed they didn't even know where he lived anymore. Miranda was a young woman before she appreciated what Melly had sacrificed to raise them. Her own youth.

Finally getting a grip on herself, Miranda wiped her eyes with a pillowcase, stifling the leftover sobs.

'Melly, you are the best sister and friend ever. I'm so lucky.'

'I'm coming Friday.'

'No, no. I'm okay. I just needed to talk.'

'Is it work? Do you miss reporting?'

'Sometimes. But my new job is exciting, at least this case I'm working on now is. Blackmail.'

'Good for you. I know you can handle it.'

'I'm not so confident. If it were only business, maybe, but . . .'

'It's a man.' Melly knew her sister so well.

'Well, it's really two men,' Miranda admitted. She went on to explain most of what was going on – about her attraction to Cole, how Rick was involved in the rape investigation, how he wanted her back.

'How do you feel about Rick?'

'He's the same old operator, sexy and good looking. I don't respect him, personally anyway, and I don't trust him, but there's no denying we have this . . . connection. With him at least I know what I'd be getting.'

'How about this singer?'

'My thoughts about him are all jumbled up. One minute I hate him and can't stand the sight of him, and next thing I know he's the most irresistible thing on earth. He's sensual and antagonistic and talented and witty. When we . . . last night, I lost track of everything, myself, where I was, what I was doing. It's like I'm under some kind of spell.'

98

'You said he was a suspect in both the blackmail and the rape?'

'One of the suspects in both, yes.'

'You think he's guilty?'

'I don't know. His eyes seem so honest. I'd like to trust my intuition, which tells me no. But I know there are wives of rapists who never know what their husbands are capable of, so how can I make that kind of judgement after knowing him only two days? And he certainly would have a motive in the blackmail case. My feelings for him are distorting the case. Do you think I ought to turn it over to someone else in the office? Doug is pressuring me to accept a partner, and would be thrilled if I gave it up altogether.'

'You can't do that, you said yourself this was a proving ground in your boss's eyes. Personal feelings are often a part of work, we all have to learn to accommodate them. We are people, not robots. You haven't made any ethical or moral violations. Stick with it. But be careful.'

Miranda felt better. She'd drawn strength from her sister's confidence in her.

'But the most important thing I have to tell you is this: don't be afraid to take risks with someone you might be attracted to. Mom's dying and Dad's leaving us without any support left all three of us unable to make emotional commitments. We're afraid of being abandoned again. What Rick did to you just confirmed your fears. That's not always going to happen, Randi. You have to risk something to get something. It's how people get rich, with money and with love. Think about it, will you?'

'What makes you so philosophical?' Miranda asked playfully, a little embarrassed by her sister's accurate intuition.

'Maybe I have some personal experience,' she answered coyly.

'Out with it. Who is he?'

'He's great, but we can't get into that now. Didn't you say you were going to some hifalutin' dinner?' Miranda laughed at Melanie's colloquialism and thought of the saying: you can take the girl out of Texas but you can't take Texas out the girl. Melanie had tamed most of her accent and colorful language now that she lived in Boston, but every now and then it crept back in.

Miranda admitted she had to go. In fact, she thought she had heard the door open, and decided it was her overactive imagination. Glancing at the clock she noticed with minor panic that it was already time for Cole to pick her up. He was even a little late, which didn't surprise her. She reassured Melanie that she would be alright and promised to call soon.

Miranda had indeed heard the door open. Cole had stood outside for a few moments after knocking at the door. But receiving no answer and refusing to use the doorbell, which he considered technological nonsense, he opened the door and called out in a low voice. He hoped this was the right townhouse, or he'd be in more trouble than he was already. Then he heard Miranda's voice, apparently in conversation on the phone, and he relaxed. He heard her laugh, deep and sexy, and realized with wonder it was the first time he'd heard her laugh.

Her intimate tone lured him to her bedroom. He couldn't hear what she said, just how she said it. He wondered if she was talking to a boyfriend. Despite his best intentions, he peeked in. His hormones reacted to what he saw before his mind did. Her bare back faced the door and her curves were clad in nothing but black lace underwear.

Cole sucked in a silent breath. Her body was as indescribable as her hair. An amazing, alluring combination of soft and hard, of curve and line. Skin the color of fresh cream.

He carefully withdrew and sneaked back out the door. Shaking his leg to make his tightening pants more comfortable, Cole struggled to get his libido under control. He didn't know how he was going to make it through the evening without embarrassing himself.

'Damn,' Cole muttered. He had to appreciate the cruel irony. Never before had a woman had such power over him – that a mere glance at her, clothed or not, sent him to near climax. But she was also a woman who suspected him of being a blackmailer, and maybe even a rapist. That thought cooled Cole off considerably and with a charming wink at a nosy neighbor who was making a show of watering her plants across the street, he settled back against the courtyard wall to wait.

Assessing herself in the bathroom mirror, Miranda decided to forgo eyeshadow, making do with only some mascara and a balancing smudge of eyeliner. With no time to curl her hair, she twisted it up in a half-messy chignon instead. She was just pulling on her black hose when she heard a loud knock on the door. Her heart thudded in her ears.

'How glamorous can you get?' she said to herself in disgust, knowing most of the women at the dinner would have gone to their high-dollar salons to have their hair and make-up done.

She called out: 'I'll be right there.'

Miranda wiggled into her black silk sheath dress, smoothing it down her slick thighs as she walked to the door. She made her steps slow, deliberate, reminding herself with each that this was business, business, business.

'You're late,' she said as coldly as possible, for he looked hot. He wore a gray double-breasted suit of obvious elegant tailoring, a starched white shirt and a vivid tie on the wild side. She was sure he would be one of only a few men at the gala not in a tuxedo, but she admitted he couldn't have looked any better than he did right now.

'So are you, apparently,' Cole shot back with a questioning glance at her stockinged feet and earrings in her hand.

'Come in. I'm almost ready.' Miranda gestured to her living room, then disappeared back into the bedroom.

Cole went straight for her small bar and poured himself a gin and tonic. He needed something to do with his hands. He didn't think it possible that she could look even sexier

101

with more clothes on, but that dress did it. The silk rode her skin like a whisper, hinting of promises that lay underneath.

Downing his drink in one gulp, Cole fixed another. Miranda walked in with fresh lipstick, diamond earrings in place, and black suede pumps on her feet. A single teardrop diamond hung between her breasts on an almost invisible gold chain. Cole wanted to put his lips where the pendant lay so brazenly. He ached to free her hair and bury his face into it. He lived for one more peek at the black lace underwear. Instead, he gulped at his drink.

'Why don't you drink straight out of the bottle? It won't offend me,' Miranda said with emphasized disdain.

'Oh yes, then I can add alcoholism to the rest of my vices. Blackmail and sexual assault.' The words tasted bitter on his tongue.

'And insolence,' Miranda added, still standing. She didn't want to get comfortable with him, especially not in her home.

Cole bit back his rejoinder, though several came to mind, and instead eyed her warily as he finished his drink.

'Can we go now?' Miranda finally asked to break the tense silence.

'Aren't you going to get an overcoat?'

'You don't have one.'

Cole's eyes moved slowly from her bare neck, to the tops of her pale breasts, down her torso to her sleek legs and ankles and four-inch heels. Miranda felt a slow burn build between her thighs.

'I have more on than you do,' he pointed out in a thickening voice.

With an exaggerated sigh of exasperation, Miranda stomped to the coat closet and threw on a black all-weather coat.

'No fur? I would think someone as famous as you are would have two or three minks,' he said, baiting her.

'Fame is an illusion. Besides, I'm no longer famous, if I ever was.'

Cole looked at Miranda sharply. Her usually honeyed voice had turned sour. Her job as a reporter must have ended painfully. He softened.

'I'm sorry.'

'Don't be,' she shot back. Her turquoise eyes flashed at his pity. 'I'm much better off. Now I get the chance to put bad guys behind bars.' She punctuated her last comment with a pointed look at Cole.

Anger welled up from the pit of his stomach and Miranda saw his jaw tighten. His gray eyes darkened to thunderclouds. His biceps tensed under his suit coat and his knuckles whitened as he squeezed the keys in his hand. She had seen him look this way in the dressing room the night before and it frightened her. It made her wonder what he might be capable of with such a powerful rage kept under strong control. Did it escape, taking innocent victims? Suddenly, Miranda didn't want to be alone with him and she rushed out the door.

Cole stood alone in the foyer for several moments. He hadn't felt such frustration and fury since he'd fought with his father over his career choice, and that had been more than ten years ago. His father was insensitive, obstinate and selfish. What was it about this woman that could provoke him to such emotion? Maybe the same things, he decided. She was out for herself, to solve her case, maybe to get him for the rapes, too, and make even bigger headlines for herself. She obviously missed the lime-light. Cole braced himself for a treacherous evening. God only knew what she would try.

The ride downtown was mostly silent and uncomfortable. Miranda had been shocked to walk out of her house and see a black Miata waiting in the driveway. Save for the color, it could have been her old car, and she felt a pang. Not allowing herself to be nostalgic, or to wonder why this probable felon would choose the same car as she did, she climbed inside and immediately honked the horn. Cole emerged a few minutes later, brooding.

The only time he spoke was to ask what music she would like to listen to. When she flipped her hand as if to say she didn't care, he rattled noisily through his compact discs. Though pretending not to look, Miranda peeked at his collection. It was an eclectic mix of blues, jazz, country, crooner, big band, a few rock artists and, she noticed with shock, classical. Miranda looked hastily back out the window. She would have bet her last dollar that he would not have Bach in his car. Cole was full of surprises, and that's what scared her.

The romantic voice of Frank Sinatra replaced the silence in the small car. There again, Miranda had been wrong in second-guessing him. She'd expected some loud, lively music to counteract the tension between them. That's what she would have chosen. Instead he put on amorous lyrics and sentimental melodies, which served to only accentuate the emotional distance between them.

It was music that made you want to bury your head in a strong, masculine chest. Music that begged for two to blend into each other and sway as one. Music that invited soft words and stroking hands. Music that resurrected the memory of Cole's hands, on her face, in her hair, on her breasts. They had been smooth and strong, but they hadn't stroked. They'd searched, impassioned and demanding. Suddenly, the memory made her restless and she scooted closer to the window.

Two songs later and despite herself, Miranda began to relax. The aesthetics of the evening demanded it. The purr of the engine lulled her body. The new stars and cherry indigo of the twilight eased her mind. The soft music caressed her soul, and she let it, resolving to put her guard back up as soon as they left the car. She seemed safe enough, for now. Giving Cole a sideways glance, she saw he too had lost his brooding look.

Feeling her eyes on him, he turned to look at Miranda. Through the half-light of the car's dashboard, their eyes met and connected. Their gaze held for maybe a second until it was broken by a braking car ahead that demanded

Cole's attention. It was over so quickly that Miranda was left to wonder, again, if it had truly happened, or whether she had imagined it. And if it had, what was it?

Cole was intense behind the wheel now, shifting gears, weaving the black jet in and out of traffic. He hadn't been driving like a madman before, and they certainly weren't in a hurry, so Miranda surmised that Cole was tying to keep himself occupied on purpose. But why? Had the look they'd shared disturbed him as much as it had Miranda? Had it embarrassed him? Or was the psychic connection they made nothing more than Miranda's imagination?

She could see his eyes, so soft and gray, like the fur of her childhood cat. It was an odd comparison, Miranda knew. But that cat had been her lifeline when she was a teenager.

With her mother dead, her father absent, and her sister taking the reins of the family, Miranda had no one to confide in. Melanie encouraged her to talk, but Miranda felt her older sister had enough of a burden to carry, without having to hear all of Miranda's problems. The fresh boys, pre-prom pimples, backbiting girlfriends, a growing sense of isolation were problems that Miranda thought her big sister would see as trivial, problems that made her teenage years hell.

So, it was Scorpio who heard all of Miranda's heart-breaks and heartaches. When a friend since second grade stole her boyfriend, he was there, on her bed waiting, his soft gray fur ready to make the ultimate sacrifice and absorb a night-long stream of tears. She remembered with a smile that he used his rough salmon tongue to wash himself of the salty residue for days after that. When she was down, he could sense it and would jump in her lap, onto her pile of school books, and just be there for her, purring at the smile and caress he could evoke.

Scorpio represented trustworthiness to Miranda. Did the memory Cole's eyes recalled mean he too was worthy of her trust or was it just evidence of a master manipulator?

At that moment the man in question was trying to keep his attention on the road. The questioning look that had been in her unique, changeable eyes a few minutes before had reached in and grabbed his heart. It had been full of hope and wonder and vulnerability. It asked him a question he couldn't hear, and maybe didn't know the answer to anyway. It made him believe that the woman he thought of as hot or cold, either or, had more dimension than he'd given her credit for. There was something more there he wanted to know, more than just her erogenous zones.

The beautifully lit Tower of the Americas loomed larger as they neared downtown. Miranda always thought of the thirty-year-old spire built for the Hemisfair as the signature of the San Antonio skyline. From the top, on a clear night like this, you could see the lights of Austin, a hundred miles away.

As Miranda watched the glass elevator rise to the top, she suddenly realized she didn't know where the evening's gala was taking place. She considered asking, but the silence, drawn on so long, seemed inpenetrable. She was mentally ticking a list of probables, mostly newer ritzy hotels that boast big ballrooms, when Cole whipped the car into the Menger Hotel.

Next door to the Alamo, the Menger was the oldest first-class hotel in a city. Steeped in rich history and legend, Miranda thought of it as having the most character as well. The bar was where, in 1898, Teddy Roosevelt recruited his Rough Riders, the first US Volunteer Cavalry. A host of other Presidents and movie stars, including Joan Crawford, John Wayne, Jimmy Stewart and Roy Rogers, chose the Menger during their stays in San Antonio. She knew other contemporary stars stayed there as well, but it was these who made an impression. A sucker for an old film, Miranda would rather sit through *It's a Wonderful Life* for the twentieth time than see the new Christmas offering out of Hollywood.

The valet opened her door, offering a hand. She took it

and stood, expecting Cole to come around the car and walk with her. Instead, he breezed straight through the glass doors without looking back. Fuming, Miranda followed, but forced herself into a leisurely pace. She'd be damned if she'd rush to catch up with him.

Determined to keep her mind off the man in front of her, Miranda mentally reviewed the history she'd learned while doing a news story on the hotel years before. Her favorite tidbit was that just after the turn of the century, alligators lived on the patio. Might restrict a midnight stroll, but somehow she wished the reptiles were still there. Something that was still there was a host of tunnels snaking under the building. According to legend, they were used as an escape route during the fall of the Alamo. Unfortunately, the truth was not so romantic. The Menger was built as a brewery, twenty-three years after the fall of the fort. Most believe the tunnels were used to house beer.

The sounds of tinkling glass and animated conversation drifted out into the mahogany-paneled hall to greet them. Cole finally stopped to let her catch up with him.

'I see breeding will out,' Miranda said.

'Well, then, I guess you were bred from a sloth because I don't think I've seen anyone walk so slowly,' Cole returned.

Miranda bit her tongue for fear she would say something that sounded even more supercilious than her last comment. She was acting like a stranger. What was it about him?

Turning her attention away from his mocking grin, Miranda could see the flashes of a rainbow of sequins from the well-dressed and the over-dressed inside the ballroom. She breathed a silent sigh of relief. For once Miranda, not much of a partygoer, was looking forward to socializing. It would provide distraction from a man who had become too tempting, too dangerous, too confusing.

Miranda began reassessing her eagerness for company almost immediately as the first distraction walked toward them. Launched or bounded were probably better words.

Miranda marveled at how the woman could move so fast in such a skin-tight dress. Lena Howland-Hansen was San Antonio's foremost gossip columnist. And she was out for tomorrow's ink.

'Miranda! It's so nice to see you back part of Life again!'

Lena's every sentence was punctuated by an exclamation point. Her wildly flying hands were so laden with shimmering stones that one couldn't tell where hands ended and jewels began. The light playing off her jewelry combined with her nonstop sequins made it so bright Miranda couldn't blame Cole for shielding his eyes, although she gave him a stern look to show Lena she disapproved of his action.

Better stay safe, Miranda told herself. Lena was deadly when crossed.

'Lena, it's been ages,' Miranda agreed, playing the game. She leaned into the older woman as they touched cheeks in that false high-bred way that Miranda despised.

Lena stood back to give Miranda and Cole the once-over. She was an attractive brunette of around forty who'd already had at least one facelift, one collagen lip injection and two liposuction treatments. She never failed to over-dress. It was her trademark. And all her jewels were real. She had been married for ten years to an oil heir, who was refreshingly around her age and who conveniently brought two sons from a previous marriage into theirs, which relieved Lena from having to disturb her career and her figure with pregnancy. No one could claim Lena had bought her way into the paper's most visible job for she had established her brand of delicious nastiness long before she met Howard Hansen.

At the moment she was openly surveying Cole, nearly licking her lips with anticipation of a fresh target.

'Miranda, hon,' she asked, still looking at Cole. 'Who is this? Your brother?'

Miranda relaxed when she realized Lena was out to flirt with Cole not turn him or, worse yet, her into tomorrow's news.

108

'Lena, this is Cole Taylor. Cole, this is Lena Howland-Hansen.'

'Miz Hansen, so pleased to make your acquaintance, ma'am.'

Miranda had to catch her mouth from dropping open as she glanced at Cole for she'd never heard him sound so polite, nearly humble. But one look at his rascally, dancing eyes told her he was just toying with the poor woman.

'Oh dear, Miranda, and I'd heard you were getting back together with Rick.' Lena sighed in overly dramatic distress. 'I guess my sources are not what they used to be.' She clucked loudly.

Stiffening at the sound of her ex-lover's name, Miranda felt the color drain from her face. Damn, she should have expected this. Cops had to be the biggest gossips in town. Rick had made such a big deal of escorting her through headquarters, so that the greatest number of people in the building would see them.

Cole had turned in question to Miranda, but she couldn't look him in the eye. She didn't know what to say and both of them were staring at her. Why couldn't Cole be a gentleman and rescue her from such embarrassment?

'Cole is the headliner in the hottest club in town. You must have heard of Electric Blues. Lena, you really should talk to him.' That'll serve you right, Miranda smiled snidely at Cole.

'You're kidding! I have your club on my calendar for next week. It's all anyone can talk about! You are hot, hon! So, you are the "Baby Blues"?'

'That's just the name of my band, ma'am' Cole answered with a desperate look Miranda's way. She ignored him.

While she had the chance, Miranda made her escape before Lena could interrogate her any further. That shot about Rick had really floored her and she needed time to recover. She hoped Cole would forget to ask her about Rick, because if they got into that it might open up more than her old romance. The whole situation was all getting too complicated, and Miranda felt the walls closing in.

'Does the lady need a drink?'

Miranda knew without looking who it was. Probably the most recognized voice in town and one of Miranda's favorite people, Daniel Cox.

'You've always had excellent timing,' Miranda admitted as she leaned over to embrace him. Daniel gave her a loud kiss on the cheek, which drew a dozen stares from other galagoers.

Miranda owed many of the opportunities she had got in her television career to Daniel. The main anchor at the most-watched television news department in San Antonio for over fifteen years, Daniel had loved Miranda's work from the moment he'd seen her resume tape. He'd campaigned to get her hired. He'd campaigned to get her transferred from the police beat to investigation. He'd campaigned to keep her on the air when the big brass at the station were being pressured to fire her for her expose. He was about to put his own job on the line for her when Miranda begged him to stay out of it. Always willing to help her find ways to improve her work and always ready with a compliment when her reports deserved it, Daniel was a rarity in a world of egomaniacs – someone who cared about boosting someone else's career, instead of destroying it.

Although Miranda had a tremendous admiration for Dan's work, what she most admired about him was his relationship with his wife. Married for twenty-four years with two daughters in college, they were still in love and proud to show it. Miranda didn't realize until Rick betrayed her that the Cox marriage had become her model.

She had been too young when her mother died to remember much about her parents' relationship, although by Melanie's account they were a happy couple. But when she reached the age that marriage began to really mean something to Miranda, there were Dan and Cindy to show her what to aspire to. They respected and trusted each other, that was the key, Miranda told herself. And, of course, they were still passionate about each other.

Miranda allowed a private smile as Cindy Cox slid an arm around her husband's waist from behind. He responded with a tender kiss on her proferred cheek. Miranda felt a pang of envy.

'I have missed you so much, Miranda.' Cindy Cox greeted her with an earnest look in her brown eyes. 'I have no excuse. I should have called you to see if we could do one of our tearoom lunches. How could I let one of my favorite people slip away?' She shook her smooth, strawberry-blonde head with self-reproach.

Miranda had always adored Daniel's wife. And if she had seen any of her friends in the past few months, Cindy would have been one of the first. Born into money as the daughter of a West Texas communications mogul and marrying Dan after he'd already become a success, she was the antithesis of a stuck-up rich girl. She was truly interested in people and cared more than anyone Miranda had ever known.

'It's my fault more than yours. I've become sort of a hermit, coming out to do necessary work, then retreating back into my cave. But I think I'm about ready to move on now. I'm getting into the swing of things at the agency and feeling more comfortable.'

Dan had kept a watchful eye on Miranda and now carefully asked a question, a light voice in a serious face.

'So, you're enjoying the business?'

Miranda knew what her old friend and mentor was after. She smiled at him in affection.

'I do miss reporting sometimes, I probably always will a little. But I seem to be catching on to this private eye biz, making the clients happy anyway. And I guess that's the goal.'

Daniel looked unconvinced, but let it drop. Cindy apparently found it a romantic line of work, for she kept after Miranda with twinkling eyes.

'Have you done any exciting or dangerous cases?'

'Well, up to now, not really. But I'm working on something now that could end up being both.' Perhaps the Coxs saw the apprehension in Miranda's eyes when she said that for they changed the subject gracefully and spent the next five minutes in some enjoyable small talk, catching up on the time they hadn't been in touch.

'Does Sandborn have a table tonight, or are you on the job?' Daniel asked, glancing around casually.

Miranda hated to, but knew she had to be cagey. 'Neither. I'm doing a client a favor.' Which told them nothing.

While Cindy looked intrigued, Dan accepted her answer wordlessly. He wasn't sure he liked the new mystery Miranda lived under now. In the time he'd known her, she'd been a self-assured woman with an air of – what? – optimism, he decided. A rare ray of sunshine in a career of cynical malcontents. But tonight she seemed more pessimistic and inexplicably restless. She was as beautiful as ever, maybe more so with this new aura of mystery, but obviously troubled as well.

Rick was partially responsible for the change in Miranda. But even after he'd hurt her so terribly, she had bounced back with just a few scars. Of course, after that she resisted getting involved in any relationship with a man, but her attitude did not affect her work or the rest of her life.

When she uncovered a sordid trail of graft and bribery between some vice presidents at the largest oil company in the city and two state Senators and a state Representative, it was a brilliant piece of work. Her mistake had been taking it public before she had enough facts to prosecute, even though that was not her job. Her story had tipped off the guilty parties and sent paper shredders at Ravalo Oil and the state capitol into overdrive. It tipped the authorities off too, but too late. By the time investigators got there most of the evidence, that Miranda didn't have already, was gone forever.

The bad publicity forced the vice presidents out of their

jobs, although one was actually promoted onto the board of directors. The politicians, with million-dollar public relations campaigns, tried to take the heat off of themselves by turning it on Miranda and the television station. In the media, advertisements and news stories, she was depicted as a capricious, overly ambitious young woman out to further her own career at the expense of some valuable public servants. The station was called irresponsible for letting her do it.

The accused used Miranda's second mistake to build their case. She had uncovered an affair between the wife of one of the oil company vice presidents and the legislator. Attracted to state Representative Garrett Giles, Gina Langstrom slept with him after one capitol party. She then began regular rendez vous with him. Her husband found out, but kept quiet until he could blackmail his wife's lover into dropping the favor money he was charging Ravalo Oil.

The vice president's wife became an unwitting pawn and she was devastated when, several months later, she overheard a telephone conversation between her husband and her lover. She discovered she had become, in effect, a whore. Or, more accurately, as Miranda pointed out to her later, her husband had become a pimp.

Gina Langstrom became one of Miranda's best sources for the story and Miranda had grown fond of her. Usually unyielding in her aversion to adultery, Miranda made an exception this once. Trapped in an unhappy marriage with a selfish, cruel and unethical man, Gina was looking for a little human warmth when she turned to Garrett, his smiling charm beguiling her.

Miranda had this information about the vice president in effect prostituting his own wife, but chose not to use it. She rationalized that it wasn't necessary to make her case, not necessary enough to destroy Gina Langstrom's life anymore than it already had been destroyed. It proved to be the mistake that cost her career.

Miranda warned Gina that when the federal and state

investigators got involved she would probably be exposed. What Miranda didn't expect was her omission would be used against her. The politicians' flaks called it a cover-up. Garrett Giles's office insinuated that Miranda and Gina had set Giles up. His loyal wife stood up for him, saying her darling would never violate their marriage unless shamelessly lured.

Meanwhile, Ravalo had a small interest in KATX-TV that few knew about. Its board of directors chose now to throw its weight around and demanded that the station manager fired Miranda. A dozen calls from the politicians' friends in Austin echoed that and the station manager buckled under the considerable pressure. Miranda became a sacrificial lamb.

Not slowing down long enough to let the turn of events demoralize or depress her, Miranda fought to save her reputation, and her job. She boldly admitted to her mistakes and tried to refocus attention back on what was most important – the criminal and unethical behavior she had exposed. Unfortunately, much of it was lost in a cloud of controversy and conflicting information.

While many appreciated the validity of her expose, the public in general was mired in an overload of fact and fiction being spewed by the public relations gurus. It worked. By the time the stories about Ravalo and the capitol versus Miranda Randolph began to peter out, San Antonio was so desensitized to it that it had become apathetic. Giles and his state house cronies would most likely survive another election and the two fired Ravalo vice presidents were quietly re-hired as consultants.

Daniel remembered the day Miranda came to clear out her desk. She had the unquestioned support of the newsroom. The news director had to be given an ultimatum before he would carry out the station manager's reluctant command to fire her.

Even so, it would have been easier if she had waited until after hours to claim what was left of four years of work. Instead she arrived at ten in the morning, when everyone from sales to production was sure to see her and be reminded of the injustice. Daniel had been proud of her. It took courage. But even while she was saying goodbye with calm dignity he could see the fight had left her.

He hoped then that she would recover, and that was why he hadn't contacted her until he knew she was ready to be reminded of the pain of the whole ordeal. For while he might have been the one who helped her the most during the troubles, he was still a reminder of them.

Looking at her now, Daniel had to admit Miranda would never be the same optimistic dragonslayer she was just this time last year. She was different. Forever. Not to say that was for better or worse. The scars would have to heal before he could make that judgement. Saddened, he realized he didn't know this Miranda, but hoped he got the chance to.

A roommate of his in college told him once women and men could never be friends. It was men's fault, the friend admitted, because if they were attracted enough to a women to be her friend they wanted to be her lover, which precluded friendship.

While he prescribed to the philosophy as a young man, he rejected it now. Maybe middle-aged men can be friends with women, he pondered a way around the wisdom he embraced so long. Or maybe you have to be in love before you can be friends with other women. For, in retrospect, it was after he fell in love with Cindy that he found himself able to make friends with other women. Or maybe it was just his luck to be married to such a special woman who supported and did not feel threatened by such friendships.

Whatever the reason, Daniel counted Miranda as one of his greatest friends. He did not think of her as a daughter, nor did he feel sexually attracted to her. While their relationship had begun as more mentor and student it had grown to one of mutual trust, need and support. Miranda would not admit it, he knew, but Daniel relied on her just as often as she did him. Specifically, he remembered when their younger daughter Angie had been in a serious car accident. Daniel had read the story on the news along with the heartstopping video of the mutilated cars, before he'd been told his daughter was 'the victim in critical condition.' The call came in the middle of the newscast. While shock paralyzed Daniel, Miranda took over, getting him off the set, finding a replacement in the ninety-second span of the commercial break, getting him and Cindy to the hospital, and mercilessly badgering the doctors until they would tell all. Seeing her caught up in conversation with Cindy now, Daniel could feel she was guarded. He hoped she would be able to care again.

Miranda, her attention suddenly caught by a slightly overweight man dressed in a tuxedo two sizes too small, was bidding them a distracted goodbye. Cindy pledged to call Miranda soon for a lunch date. Dan gave a 'see ya later in the evening' and was going to say more but Miranda touched his arm affectionately and headed toward the man who was now gesturing.

'Must be her client,' Cindy guessed as she leaned lovingly into her husband's shoulder. Her upturned face searched Daniel's eyes. 'I know. She doesn't seem herself.'

'It takes time,' he answered on a sigh.

Miranda beat a path to Wayne before he made a spectacle of himself.

'What are you doing?' she whispered. Seeing Cindy and Daniel had left her feeling unraveled – happy at being with good friends again, guilty for not seeing them for so long, and melancholy for what used to be.

'You are supposed to be Cole's date. Where is he? I don't want Vicki smelling what's up, with you lurking around alone. She might figure out you're working for me.' A sheen of nervous sweat covered Wayne's face.

'Oh, and you think motioning me over here like a crazed orangutan is not suspicious?' Miranda barely kept her voice under control. 'Lurking? I wasn't lurking. I was talking with some dear friends of mine. It might seem

116

more strange if I stayed attached to Cole like some kind of leech, ignoring the people I know.'

'I'm not saying ignore them, just hang around Cole more. There he is, over there.' Wayne was whining now, and that Miranda could not stand.

'Alright,' Miranda snapped then turned to look where Wayne had indicated. Cole was talking animatedly to a young beauty with hair that hung in a rippling golden sheet. Her strapless form-fitting sequined dress in the same gold as her hair showed plenty of her still-deep summer tan. Yet the effect wasn't sleazy. She wore it with panache and Miranda felt as if a rock dropped in her stomach. It felt strangely like jealousy, though Miranda told herself she had no right to be jealous. That could be his girlfriend for all she knew. Or one of his girlfriends.

So I'm supposed to walk up there in my plain dress, messy hair and half made-up face and try to regain his attention? Right. Wayne gave her a hard nudge with a hand as clammy as his face. Yuck. Wiping at the sweat stains he left on her black silk, Miranda decided standing next to that goddess was better than putting up with Wayne.

Cole had been aware of Miranda since they separated at the door and he saw her coming toward him, but kept his attention on Kitty. For months, Victoria Lambert had been tactfully trying to set them up. Kitty worked on the board of the Children's Safehouse with Victoria. Kitty Alexander was a professional volunteer from an old San Antonio family. Cole wasn't sure what her father did. Probably manage his own money. She was beautiful, bright and a witty conversationalist. It was what she'd been raised to be and she often reminded Cole of a well-bred, well-groomed Maltese.

With Kitty what you saw was what you got. Miranda was something else, a package of contradiction and mystery. She walked to them with the grace of a ballerina. The blaze in her eyes could take on a prizefighter. Her pinned up hair, falling softly around her face looked like it might

117

the morning after a long night of lovemaking, the way her curves moved under the black silk made him want to find out. Her voice, changeable as a chameleon, made him want to think twice. Remembering it so intimate on the phone in the bedroom, Cole heard it now with a hard edge. The words were a surprise.

'I'd wondered where you'd run off to. Sorry I left you with Lena. I'm a coward.' She smiled at Cole. Fake. Purely for Kitty's benefit. It irritated Cole, but he played along, making introductions.

Cole had not given Miranda's reason for standing at his arm, so Kitty looked her over with a question in her eyes. They managed some small talk. Kitty, proving more insightful than Miranda would've given her credit for, did not mention missing her on the news and, instead, opened a discussion of the free trade agreement, asking Miranda's opinions. The woman obviously internalized the newspaper every day to have such current knowledge.

Miranda was impressed. This amused Cole who knew why Kitty was such a news dilletante. Better to catch a husband with, my dear. Beauty and brains, in that order, attracted who Kitty was looking for – pre-politicians, future CEOs, surgeons-in-residency. Ambitious in her own way, Kitty didn't want someone who'd made it. She wanted to help them make it.

That was what was so ironic about Victoria's match-making. She saw Cole as a good-looking second son of a well-respected and well-heeled old Hill Country family, which he was. But Victoria, and maybe Kitty too, believed he would 'outgrow' the flaky music business and get back to his father's lucrative ranch and seemingly bottomless family money and take his place in the hierarchy, right behind his famously underachieving brother.

What they didn't understand was that Cole was doing his life's work now. But even at this he was not terribly ambitious by their definition. He played and sang because he loved it, needed it like he needed to breathe. He toiled for days, weeks, to make a song exactly the way it should be – making his audience feel something. If it hit the charts, great. If it didn't, he would not change it just to reach the lowest common denominator. One slimy agent told him he'd starve trying to be 'too much of an artist'. Cole saw it as a compliment, even though it was meant just the opposite.

Kitty was attracted to him, he knew. What he didn't know was whether she saw him as an amusement to keep her warm until she chose Mr Right or whether she hoped to make him into Mr Right. It was undeniably one of the two, and Cole didn't want to be either. He had great fun flirting with her, though.

Cole turned the charm on Kitty now, although he realized he was doing it not to tease Kitty but to irritate Miranda; something he, in a perverse way, also seemed to enjoy. His eyes rolled up and down her perfectly petite, sequined frame. Breasts not too big, not too small, waist a precise ten inches smaller than her hips. Those hips, Cole was sure, would measure exactly the same as her chest. Barbie.

Kitty, aware of his attention, winked and her nipples hardened at just the right time. Maybe she practiced. Cole wondered fleetingly what her parents would have done if they had spawned some genetic throwback who had frizzy hair and a skin problem, was flat and hippy and had to wear bifocals. Probably pay to get it all fixed, or trade her for the kind of girl standing in front of him now. Cole laughed at himself.

His laugh, being out of context of the serious conversation they were having, caught both women off-guard. They looked at him strangely.

'So, Kit, are you wearing any underwear? Are you trying to get all the old men in here to forget how many zeros they are writing on their donation checks?' Cole gave her a half-lidded look.

Loving it, Kitty giggled. 'You're worse than Howard Stern!'

Cole doubted she'd ever heard Howard Stern. But having read about his reputation as a shock master, gambled that this was the right context in which to use his name to sound worldly and well-read.

Cole was pleased to see he'd accomplished what he'd set out to do with the comment – antagonize Miranda. For some inexplicable reason he couldn't resist. Her exquisite ivory skin blushed as only redheads will. She was embarrassed and angry at his tasteless remark.

Already put-off by the attention Cole was paying to this socialite, with his eyes and conversation, Miranda now looked around for someone to escape to. She wasn't quick enough.

'Oh, there's Reynold McKinney,' Kitty bubbled, her eyes already on the thirty-ish, bachelor state Senate candidate as she waved to catch his attention. 'I just must talk something over with him. Nice to meet you.' Her cheek brushed Miranda's as lips kissed air. 'And, you scamp, you watch yourself,' Kitty's lips actually made contact on Cole's cheek.

They both watched Kitty as she moved with purpose toward McKinney. Cole smiled, his earlier question answered. He was definitely 'fling' on Kitty's agenda. Kitty McKinney. Sounded good. He wondered when the wedding would be. Before the election surely. Probably the day absentee polls opened.

Miranda surreptitiously searched his face. She saw affection and bristled. She couldn't blame him, Kitty was everything a man must want in a woman. I even like her, despite myself. Miranda's hackles came down in resignation. How could I possibly compete?

Miranda caught herself. Compete? For what? An arrogant, chauvanistic, conceited, irritating, energetic, mysterious, sexy . . . Whoa. Okay, so I'm attracted to him sexually. I can rationalize this. The physical draw I can resist. Keep thinking: Suspect. Suspect. Suspect.

Cole was watching her. He'd seen the most vulnerable look cross her face, then it closed again. Cole wondered what made her control her emotions so tightly. Who and what had she been thinking about?

CHAPTER 6

A tuxedoed waiter approached with a tray of champagne, various wines and what appeared to be sparkling water. He broke what had stretched on long enough to become an uncomfortable silence. Cole scanned the tray.

'You have a Merlot?' he asked the waiter in a most dinner-party tone of voice.

'Yes sir,' the waiter nodded his head toward the crimson-purple liquid at the center of the tray. Miranda tried to look detached while battling feelings of irritation – that Cole had not even bothered to ask what she wanted to drink; and elation – that he had remembered what she'd been drinking the first night at Electric Blues. The former emotion won the battle and with an icy stare she reached past the proffered Merlot to grab the champagne from the confused waiter. With a questioning look at Cole which was met with an amused grin, the poor man moved gratefully off to the next couple.

Cole kept the Merlot for himself, sipping it with over-emphasized relish. Miranda was left to wonder whether he really did choose the Merlot for her or whether she'd done the presuming.

'Are you a schizophrenic drinker or are we supposed to be celebrating something?'

Unable to explain herself, Miranda gulped ungracefully at her champagne while again searching the crowd for someone to save her from Cole's presence. He unsettled her. Her body was on high alert, her mind paralyzed. It

121

was how she imagined being on drugs might feel. Out of control. That's why she'd never tried drugs, and that's why she didn't want to be around Cole Taylor.

While waiting for her reply, Cole's eyes danced across her face. He felt the attraction. It was undeniable. But it had to be denied. Circumstances dictated life, Cole thought wryly. And the dynamics here were too combustible. She's a private investigator. I'm her chief suspect. I'm implicated in rapes and God only knows how close she is to that. She's too damned beautiful. And too damned difficult.

Finding no one available to rescue her, Miranda turned back to Cole. He stood in cocky relaxation, looking as if the world could go straight to hell and he wouldn't care. His coat hung open recklessly, that lock of hair shaking loose to hang over his forehead rakishly. A smile playing on his lips. The look of the boy-next-door with mischief on his mind. The kind of boy who hits baseballs through windows and runs, charming his way out of it later. The kind mothers didn't want their sons to hang around with or their daughters to even look at.

But suddenly, as she watched, his face changed. The gray eyes hardened to steel. The muscles along his jaw and neck corded. His lips thinned. The tension moved down his body like a wave. Cole turned in an uncharacteristic jerk and grabbed Miranda's arm with a single, almost furtive, glance back.

'Let's go see if there's something we can't live without at the silent auction.' Casual words through clenched teeth.

Curious and confused, Miranda let him propel her toward the tables of goodies set up against the wall while she tried to find what disturbed him. The only likely candidates were an attractive middle-aged couple who were just walking into the room. The tuxedoed man, who Miranda guessed was around sixty, was overly tanned and handsome in a rugged, Clint Eastwood way. He greeted a friend who approached.

Miranda was about to turn away when she noticed the

woman's eyes. They were trained on Cole, staring almost desperately at his back. They overflowed with such emotion, Miranda, feeling as if she'd violated some privacy, had to look away. There was something strangely familiar about the pair, although Miranda could not discern what it was.

Miranda glanced back once more before they reached the auction table. The woman, now drawn into conversation with her husband's companion, looked at least fifteen years younger than her husband though Miranda guessed she could easily be fifty and had aged well. An elegant willowy blonde, she wore her straight hair shoulder length and was dressed in a forest green, gold-trimmed wool suit. Tailored but feminine. A simple but extremely expensive gold necklace and earring set was her only adornment. Miranda approved of her style.

But something about her, or her husband, or both of them, threatened Cole. The transformation in his demeanor shocked Miranda. Tense and distracted, he made a show of looking through the items up for bid – landscape paintings, boutique and restaurant gift certificates, jewelry, furs. His eyes, turned inward, didn't see what they were looking at. His hand still held her, but Miranda could tell it didn't feel.

Love or money? She wondered which it was. In her experience, Miranda had found one or both of them were behind every conflict. If she had to guess, Miranda would say love. Some tortured form of it was on that woman's face as she stared at Cole. She felt a choking feeling rise in her throat. Jealousy. She didn't like it and had no right to feel it.

Digging deeper, Miranda admitted she knew so little about Cole that she shouldn't even venture to guess about what was going on. Wasn't she supposed to be doing a job here? She needed to find Victoria Lambert and get on with it. Away from this man and his troubles.

But the harder she fought to put distance between them the tighter the pull. Like a magnet to her soul. She felt his internal struggle and, inexplicably, needed to ease it.

'Are you alright?' It came out of her mouth before she could stop it. And she did want to stop it.

Cole looked surprised, as if he thought he'd been alone and suddenly realized he wasn't.

'Fine.' His voice was tight and left no room for challenge.

Put off, Miranda reached down to finger an intricately detailed concho belt on the auction table. The silver alone weighed at least five pounds. The etching probably took months. She found the opening bid: four-hundred dollars. Miranda let go as if it had burned her hand. The sudden laugh behind her made her jump.

'You don't have to pay to touch it.' Cole seemed determined to cover up his distress with good humor. It wasn't working on Miranda, but she let it go.

For the next ten minutes they eased their way down the auction line, joking at ridiculous bids on items both seemed to agree unworthy. Their similar tastes surprised and pleased both of them. Several times Miranda fleetingly thought of a way she could wangle an introduction to Victoria Lambert. Then something else captured her attention.

'Oh.' She let out a gasp of admiration.

It was a simple teardrop pendant of at least four carats of blue topaz. It hung from a gold chain nearly invisible and so delicate it did not look strong enough to hold a gem of such size.

'It's the color of your eyes,' Cole observed, looking at the stone, not her eyes.

Usually a washed-out azure, this topaz displayed a rich, deep tone that glowed almost turquoise. It had a dazzling clarity.

'Topaz is my birthstone,' Miranda said half to herself.

Not one for costume jewelry, Miranda had a few classic pieces of real jewelry; gold, pearls, the diamond earrings she wore now. Rick had told her once she was made to wear only the real thing; that the pure alabaster of her skin revealed the lie of fake baubles. Miranda loved hearing it

124

then, but only thought of it bitterly now, and discarded it as the words of a charlatan.

While she might not agree that she was made for jewels, Miranda knew she liked this jewel. Very much. Mrs Lunz of the terribly affluent '09' zip code had listed the last bid of nine-hundred and twenty five dollars. It will go well with the thousand other pieces of jewelry that woman surely owns, Miranda thought, and moved on without looking back.

'Cole Taylor, why haven't you introduced me to your lovely date?'

Miranda turned to find the source of the voice that chided in a warm, affectionate way. She found Cole already kissing an older, very classy woman on the cheek. She caught Miranda's eye and smiled. Open and friendly. Miranda didn't know who she was but liked her immediately.

She exuded richness the way only old money can. The way many heirs to San Antonio first families did.

Looking past that, she might be considered average. Five-foot-six, a nice but not exceptional figure, hair naturally grayed, well-styled in a permed shag common of women her age, which Miranda guessed was around seventy. The way seventy should look without plastic surgery and stringent dieting. Her patrician face was strong more than attractive and her clear brown eyes made no excuse, for herself or for others. Her gold lame dress showed some risk, but the gold, diamond and rubies at her ears and throat made it acceptable.

'Victoria, this is Miranda Randolph.' Cole was smiling with pleasure, obviously fond of the woman. 'Miranda, Victoria Lambert, one of the greatest women I've the pleasure to know.'

Miranda hoped her mouth hadn't dropped open in her shock. This confident, classy woman was the last thing she expected to find as Wayne's wife.

Victoria was laughing, a tinkling, happy sound. Incongruous. Surprised again, Miranda realized she'd expected a low chuckle or a dry ha-ha.

'I'm so honored to be at or near the top of what is certainly a legion of ladies.'

'Oh, very few are ladies,' Cole interjected, looking pointedly at Miranda.

Miranda's fist clenched as she felt the color rising up her throat. 'So nice to meet you Mrs Lambert.' She offered a stiff hand to shake the older woman's. She could barely contain her anger at Cole.

'Ah, you must know my husband.'

Once again, Miranda was sent reeling. How did Victoria know? Had she seen her with Wayne?

Then her mind started working again. No. Cole had only introduced her by her first name. Miranda had added the 'Mrs'. Big slip, dummy. Watch it. This woman is quick. And Cole is trying to distract me. On purpose?

'Miranda's been to the club.' Unexpectedly, Cole chimed in to cover for her.

Miranda squirmed under Victoria's questioning gaze, which Cole's explanation hadn't quelled.

Finally, after a few seconds of silence, Victoria spoke. 'Randolph? You are that talented reporter on the news. You really did quite wonderful work.' The older woman smiled reassuringly. 'You looked so familiar. I'd been trying to place you.'

Miranda relaxed some then, smiling in return. Victoria was still looking from Cole to Miranda as if wondering how long this relationship had been going on without her knowledge. Miranda made note of Victoria's attitude. It was as if she knew most of what went on at Electric Blues, whether she was present or not.

Cole, his eyes twinkling, knew what she was after, but was quiet, waiting to see how long it would take curiosity to overcome breeding.

It never did, and Victoria deftly changed the subject.

'You are still going to sing for me, aren't you, dear?'

Miranda decided it would be appropriate to look politely curious. Victoria picked up on it immediately.

'He didn't tell you? Well, it's no secret, Cole,' she

126

chided him then explained to Miranda. 'He's promised to do one of his songs after dinner.' She lowered her voice conspiratorily. 'Really it's to warm up the crowd for the silent auction. I hope he gets them so romantic the husbands can't help but spend tens of thousands of dollars on their darling wives on cruises, rubies and priceless artwork.'

'What about wives buying for their husbands?' Miranda could have squelched her feminism, but she wanted to see Victoria's answer to her question. She was a woman who could buy her husband a thousand times over. Was this a sore spot in the marriage?

'Of course, dear.' With a wave of her hand, Victoria casually acknowledged and dismissed the notion at the same time. Then she turned back to Cole.

'You know your parents are supposed to be here this evening. Have you seen them?'

'No.' Staccato. Uneasy and trying too late to hide it. 'But I did see Kitty, looking more gorgeous than ever.'

Victoria shot a warning look at Cole that said talking about the glowing physical attributes of attractive ladies of your date's age in front of your date is bad form.

To Miranda she said: I've known Kitty her whole life. A darling girl. She's done some good work this year on the board of the Safehouse. Though I doubt she'll have as much time for it next year. I hear she and Reynold are close to making an announcement.'

This last comment was punctuated with another look at Cole that said: *you dropped the ball on that one, buddy*.

Cole flashed an impish smile and shrugged.

'Don't say that too loud, Victoria. Lena's in the build-ing.'

Victoria didn't respond, but her eyebrows raised slightly.

'Oh, I get it,' Cole laughed. 'Now Kitty's got you doing her publicity, too. What? Is Reynold dragging his feet all the way to the jewelry store?'

Now Victoria started laughing too. 'You are an irrepressible cynic. Good luck with him, my dear, you'll need it. And you,' she hugged Cole. 'I will see you on stage after dinner.'

Miranda had been watching their conversation with the absorption of a voyeurist. So much affection there. They could be mother and son. She wondered how long they'd known each other. Victoria had said his parents would be at the dinner. Miranda was instantly intrigued. She knew so little about Cole. Was he a member of San Antonio's upper crust, too?

Something nagged at her sub-conscious. His reaction to Victoria's mention of his parents had been so strange. Cold? No, there was more emotion involved than that. Defensive. That was it.

A model pranced by, showing off a floor-length gray fox coat that would be up for live auction later. Miranda watched distractedly as the blonde stopped to talk to Cole. Rolling her eyes, Miranda wondered if he knew every female in the building.

Suddenly Miranda noticed the strap of her beaded black evening bag digging into her left shoulder. Switching the purse to the right side, she wished she hadn't brought her .38. It was too heavy. It was illegal to have it in a place that served alcohol. And futhermore, what would she need it for tonight anyway? Certainly not to fend off Cole, she thought, as he opened up the fox coat to see what the model had on underneath.

Needing something to do, Miranda signaled a waiter and got herself another glass of champagne. As she sipped it something in the corner of the room caught her eye. He looked like Secret Service. Standing alone, navy blue suit, all antennae up. That obvious intimidation factor. Miranda guessed he was a plainclothes cop, new on the job. She was shocked that he had followed Cole into a charity dinner. How did he get in? Was he going to stand up against the wall while everyone had dinner? Miranda smiled at the ludicrous notion. Then it occurred to her that the cop had probably been following Cole all day. To her house. What would Rick think? She felt panic rise. Why should she care what he thought?

The fact that she'd been watched for hours made her skin crawl. The man moved his face toward her and suddenly Miranda recognized him as one of the goons that had been with Rick yesterday at the police station. Infuriated, without thinking of the consequences, she walked over to Victoria, who was caught up in conversation with a man in a western-cut tuxedo, silver bolo tie and big black Stetson. The auctioneer, no doubt, at least Miranda hoped that was his excuse for dressing like that.

Excusing herself for interrupting, Miranda pulled Victoria off to the side.

'I'm sorry to bother you, but I thought you ought to know. I think you have a party crasher. Don't look but he's standing against the far wall. In the suit.'

Victoria, without moving her head, glanced at the cop and nodded.

'Thank you for being so observant, dear. I think you're right. Can't imagine what he's up to, but you can't be too careful these days. I'll have it taken care of.'

Miranda smiled at Victoria's back as she glided unhurriedly out the door. She knew he wouldn't flash his credentials because that would cause an uproar among the city's most influential dinner guests and it would draw Rick's ire at his not so invisible surveillance.

Stopping to say hello to a few acquaintances along the way, Miranda finally made her way back to Cole who was now standing alone near the auction table.

'Where have you been?' Cole put his arm around her waist and pulled her away from the table, walking with her to the other corner of the room. They had to weave their way through the room, which now had become rather crowded with hundreds of guests. Pressed along the side of his body, Miranda could feel the powerful line of his thigh. His warm, strong fingers squeezed into her waist. She felt so supple and feminine next to him.

They weren't making much headway, so he grabbed her

hand and led her through the throng of sequins, silk and taffeta. She looked down once at his hand. It was not a pretty hand. It was square and strong and purely masculine. Fingernails that looked worn down from the guitar strings rather than often trimmed. Remembering those hands on her bare breasts. Wanting that again . . .

Finally finding a few feet of breathing room, Cole stopped, turned around and with no excuse to keep holding it, released Miranda's hand.

Just then, Miranda noticed a man who looked like he might be a manager of the hotel escort the now-surly looking cop out of the room. She laughed out loud.

'What did I miss?' Cole regarded her with curiosity.

It really wasn't funny when Miranda thought about why the cop was there in the first place. That sobered her up immediately. 'Nothing.'

The brush-off bothered Cole. She could see his face close. Another uncomfortable silence stretched between them. Miranda opened her mouth to try to smooth it over, but the call to dinner stopped her. Separately, they both nearly ran to the table. She hoped they didn't have to sit next to each other. Her eyes scanned the placecards. Miranda was between Wayne and Cole. Hell and high water.

CHAPTER 7

Actually the dinner passed pleasantly enough, with Victoria guiding the conversations between the five couples at the table. The bartender at Electric Blues, Trey, had brought his girlfriend, a big-boned brunette from Kansas.

They bubbled with excitement because Trey had bid on an autographed Dallas Cowboys' football in the silent auction and they'd enough money saved up to bid on a Carribbean vacation in the live auction. Miranda didn't have the heart to tell the poor saps they didn't stand much chance against the hundred millionaires in the room with them. Maybe the vacation could be theirs, since most of these folks had homes of their own on the ocean somewhere. But the football was definitely out of the question. The town was Cowboys crazy and the craziest guy with the fattest wallet was going to get that football.

Trent was there with his wife, a pretty, petite Japanese-American girl named Tomori. She seemed like she'd be fun in about six months, once she got used to sleep deprivation and the need to talk constantly about her three-month-old son.

The other couple was the man and woman Miranda had seen talking with Wayne at the club the night before. They were old friends of Victoria's who seemed to love her enough to tolerate Wayne. They said they remembered seeing Miranda at the club. She was glad Wayne played smart then, ignoring her, because now they assumed she'd been there to see Cole.

While making small talk, Miranda watched the inter-action between Wayne and Victoria. She touched him often, on the hand, on the shoulder, on the cheek. Once she smoothed back a stray bit of hair on his head. Wayne caught her hand and kissed it. Though she searched for signs of affectation, Miranda could find none. Their demonstrative behavior was completely genuine. Miranda had expected to find latent hostility. Instead she found love.

With Victoria, Wayne became almost likeable. In his presence, she radiated happiness. Victoria was no fool. She must know about his affairs, or at least the rumors of them. What possessed her to overlook them? Miranda knew she had to find out. If not for the case, then for herself.

Finally, Victoria crooked a finger at Cole, stood up and took the stage. She thanked the crowd for their support of the Children's Safehouse and explained to what projects their donations would go. She was an engaging public speaker, evoking both laughter and tears as she told little vignettes to illustrate what the organization did and introduced a few of the children who benefited from it.

Cole stood up slowly and ran his hand lightly across Miranda's back as he made his way to the steps leading to the stage. His touch sent tremors cascading down her shoulders, over her breasts. Her nipples tightened. She shivered.

During dinner, Cole had been quiet and withdrawn. Unlike himself. Trent coaxed him into conversation a few times, but he hadn't seemed to want to talk. Miranda wondered if Cole was nervous. He obviously knew quite a few of the people in the audience. Maybe it was harder to perform in front of friends than strangers.

'Now, one of our talented and famous guests has generously agreed to perform a song for us before we begin the auction,' Victoria smiled and welcomed Cole up on the stage. 'Ladies and gentlemen, Cole Taylor.'

The applause was louder and more enthusiastic than she expected from this crowd. Trent Simon, who'd left the table fifteen minutes before, already had his guitar set up at the rear of the stage. Cole strode confidently across the stage and took the microphone. It surprised Miranda that he wouldn't be playing. Trent would play the lead guitar. Cole would only sing.

The melody was soft, a little melancholy, a lot introspective. When he began to sing, Cole's voice was rich and romantic. His body language was sensitive and sensual. It amazed Miranda that he could be such a musical chameleon. Rocking and rolling with raunchy tunes and hip-grinding moves last night and tonight he was crooning with his heart in his hand. Or was it her heart in his hand? As she listened to his words, she felt herself relinquishing it.

His song was about a man who had good looks and talent. Made money doing what he enjoyed. Great friends and plenty of lovers. He had a life many would envy. But still, he felt something missing, though he didn't know what it was. Until he saw the woman of dreams he'd never remembered before. And then he knew what was missing. Love.

As she had the night before, she felt as if Cole was singing to her. Their eyes met. The electricity made her heart race, her breath short. Again she brushed it off. He'd barely spoken to her for hours, only doing his minimum duty as her date. But she was so touched by the song, that when he was finished she looked around the room to see if others had been similarly affected. She saw a few damp eyes, nostalgic looks between husbands and wives and several women looking enviously at her.

I'm just here for show, she wanted to tell them. Although Miranda felt her swelling heart and wished she was, in fact, his inspiration.

Tomori had scooted across Cole's empty chair and was now trying to say something into her ear. Miranda smiled apologetically and shook her head. The applause drowned out her soft voice. Tomori repeated herself.

'Great song, huh?'

'Wonderful. I wonder where he found it.'

'In his heart,' Tomori answered in a quiet, wise way. Miranda wondered how many generations she was removed from Japan. She must have seen doubt in Miranda's eyes because she explained further. 'It's his song. He wrote it.'

Miranda nodded politely, speculating over who could have inspired the song. Seeing Miranda still didn't understand, Tomori continued. 'He wrote it two days ago. You are very lucky.'

Miranda opened her mouth to dispute Tomori's assumption. Was everyone around here a romantic or what? 'I . . . ah . . . no . . . I think you have the wrong woman.'

Tomori's almond eyes regarded her seriously. 'No, I think you do. Have the wrong woman, that is. He sings for you.'

Miranda flashed a smile she hoped was polite but disbelieving. Instead it felt timorous.

Just then Cole and Trent returned to the table and Victoria got the live auction into full swing. The best auctioneer in South Texas was at the microphone, which meant little could be understood until the gavel came down and the guy with the itchy nose found out he'd paid four thousand dollars for a two-inch metal sculpture of a bear.

Auctions always excited Miranda, even when she wasn't in the market to buy anything. The knowledge that, with one movement of her hand, she could buy something completely outrageous was a bit heady. That was the reason for her pounding heart, wasn't it?

Because Tomori had moved over next to Miranda, Trent and Cole sat down together on the other side of Trent's wife. He caught Miranda's eye and gave her a searching look. How should she respond? If she gave him any encouragement she felt she might be swept away. Lost. It was too dangerous. She reached toward her champagne glass and took a sip that turned out to be more like a swig.

Tomori launched into another baby Luke story and Miranda let her mind wander. It was unlike her, for she was famous among her friends and co-workers for being a good listener. She added the right sympathetic noises at the right times to keep Tomori going as she reviewed Cole's song in her head. It had been a song about love at first sight. A life with a piece missing. Was she the missing piece that made that life complete? The answer was yes if she was to believe Tomori, and she wasn't sure she did. The woman was obviously operating under diminished capacity, Miranda thought, as Tomori recounted her dismay over Luke's constipation.

'Prune juice,' Miranda said as she continued to juggle her split concentration.

Tomori thought it a fine idea and struck off on some new baby problem. Miranda admitted to herself that what she was feeling could be construed as love at first sight. Then again, she could be desperate. There really hadn't been anyone since Rick. A waiter came by offering a tray of wine and champagne during the intermission of the auction. Miranda had already had two glasses of champagne and wine with dinner. But without stopping to consider, she took another glass of champagne anyway. Tomori shook her head at the waiter.

'Breastfeeding,' she explained self-righteously to Miranda.

Miranda smiled back with enough approval that Tomori then took the virtues of nursing on as the topic of conversation. Drawn in by the new mother's enthusiasm, Miranda began to think about having a child of her own. She really hadn't thought much about it. Even when she and Rick were serious and she thought about marriage, children weren't included. Not that she didn't want children, it was just she and Rick were so ambitious and so involved in their careers that a family was not part of any five-year plan.

Miranda was not so emotionally blind that she didn't realize some of her hesitancy to think about kids had to do with her childhood. Honestly it had never been bad, just parts were lonely and painful. From what she could remember, life before her mother's accident had been nearly idyllic. Loving, attentive parents and a close sister and brother.

In a way that had been worse than if her younger years had been filled with parents who weren't as nurturing, because when they were no longer there for her, it was devastating. With no coping mechanism in place, she foundered in an abyss with no one but an overburdened Melanie to hang on to. She eschewed any attempts by friends or more distant family to get close because she was so afraid she would be drawn into another cocoon, only to be thrown out into the dark again.

So when thoughts of children – her children – crept into her head she shoved them out. Afraid that she could die and leave them to the same darkness she'd lived through. More terrified that they would abandon her. Reject her. Not love her.

'Do you want children?' Tomori's question shocked her mind into a blank. She stared dumbly into sensitive eyes. Patient eyes. Eyes that truly wanted to know. Had she sensed what Miranda was thinking? Or was the question merely a coincidence? Suddenly her thoughts came flooding back and tumbled out of her mouth. Too much champagne her conscience told her disgustedly. But still she couldn't stop.

Tomori accepted the flood of words and emotion as if that was exactly what she expected in response to her simple question. Before Miranda became overwhelmed the younger woman led her unobtrusively outside and onto a bench in the tropical courtyard.

Then the tears came. And more words. Under the cover of palms and crawling vine. The clamminess of the concrete crept through the thin silk of Miranda's dress. The ice-laced breeze buffetted her bare arms. Tomori said little, except one-word comments that seemed to elicit another torrent of feelings. A human catalyst.

Miranda didn't know how long they sat there, but gently Tomori stood, gathered Miranda's hands in hers and held them to her heart. Then she left Miranda alone.

Still sobbing slightly and still facing the interior of the lush courtyard, Miranda straightened her weakened legs. She was surprised to find that instead of feeling embarrassed at her outburst, she felt physically lighter. Cleaner almost. She turned around. And almost fell into him.

Cole stood just behind and to the side of the concrete bench. He blocked the path between the bench and an overhanging palm frond. Speechless, Miranda stared at him with rising outrage. How long had he been standing there? Had Tomori left to clear the way for Cole? How much had he heard? Had it all been a set-up?

Letting her anger take control, she took a long stride and put her hand on his chest to push him out of her way. Suddenly his arms enveloped her, crushing her arms to his chest. She fell into him, giving in to his embrace. Strong, still and comforting. It made her want to weep more, but she fought the tears back.

Pulling back a few inches, she searched his face. She saw compassion, understanding. And knew how much he'd heard. She looked for pity, knowing she'd see it as she had when she told Rick just a trickle of the flood Tomori had unleashed tonight. But Cole's face held no pity. She let herself relax.

Neither one spoke. Neither one moved. Locked in a safe embrace. Until Miranda eased away. Chilly air invaded the small space between them and the spell was broken.

'How long have you been standing there?' Her voice sounded raw and was slightly accusing. She was beginning to realize her vulnerability.

'Long enough.' His eyes, the color of an overcast sky, held hers as if waiting for her to speak.

Miranda, not knowing what to say, returned his stare. A few more locks of his slicked back hair were asserting their independence over his forehead. His tie, loosened and slightly askew, made it look as if his body was trying to reject the formal clothes he wore. Not that he didn't look great in his suit, but Cole Taylor was made for blue jeans and T-shirts. Miranda felt the corners of her lips curl up.

Cole saw her smile as an opening. He motioned to the bench. 'Do you want to sit back down?'

Turquoise eyes flashed. 'Why? So you can bleed me dry? Psychoanalyze my troubled adolescence? Find out how screwed up I am so you can use it against me when I've got dirt on you?'

Cole was shocked. What had he said? 'Maybe I'm just trying to be nice, maybe I care, maybe . . .' Nothing he said came out right. Usually so sharp with his tongue, Cole was becoming frustrated with his sudden inability to think.

'Nice? I don't need nice.' Miranda's voice transformed from husky to brittle. 'Go back to your flashy girlfriends and adoring old mentors. They need you. I don't.'

Spinning away from him, Miranda marched across the courtyard, dodging leaves and branches. She intended to go in the opposite doors and walk back around to the gala. Suddenly it occurred to her what she must look like after crying for what seemed like hours: racoon with a bad allergy. The restroom first, then a cab home. No, that wouldn't work. She'd left her purse at the table. She'd have to slip back in for it. Damn.

She reached for the knob of the glass door. A hand circled her wrist and yanked her roughly around. He'd followed her so silently she hadn't heard anything. His face was set, his eyes now dark as an approaching tornado. Miranda tried to wrench her arm away. He held it tighter, and grabbed the other wrist, his fingers indenting her soft pale skin. Her breath was coming quick and hard. Exhilerated and terrified.

'You don't understand, do you?' His words choked out of a tight throat.

'I understand that you feel threatened and you are trying to make me feel that way too. I understand that you insult me one minute, compliment me the next, sing to me, then ignore me. All so you can throw me off-balance, find my weak spot and zero in for the kill –'

Miranda felt her back and buttocks molding to the cold glass as Cole pressed her suddenly, urgently into the one of the windows that encased the courtyard. His breath cascaded across her cheekbones as his lips rested on hers. 'You got it right. And here's the kill . . .'

Through wool pants and silk dress, his hard, hot ridge dug into her belly. Urgent. Impatient. She stiffened and tried to fight. But his powerful chest closed in on her breasts, their nipples hard from the breeze and him. Then, hands still gripping her wrists, his mouth claimed hers, not demanding as she expected, but soft and sweet.

His tongue explored the wet, tender inside of her mouth. His hips pinned her to the glass, but his chest rode her nipples lightly, teasing. She heard a moan, and several seconds later realized it was hers. Her eyes flew open and were lost in his, burning.

Miranda tried again to pull her hands free, maybe to run, maybe to feel more of him. She wasn't sure. But he decided for her, placing her hands on his rump. Unable to resist, her fingers traced the contours. The groan that came from his mouth was a sound of pleasure and pain.

Half-drunk with desire, Miranda felt herself going so far she couldn't stop. Her hands slid slowly up to his chest, to feel the wiry hair and hard muscle that lay beneath the proper shirt. Something hard and heavy in his inside jacket pocket knocked against her hand. She unbuttoned two of his shirt buttons before she realized what the familiar weight must be.

Her hand flew back. A gun. Desire became fear. His words rushed back to her. 'The kill'. She shoved his chest and bit his tongue. Cole yelped. Miranda fumbled for the doorknob, wrested the old door open and flew through it. She ran through the hall, grazing the shoulders of two curious and confused hotel guests as she searched for a way out of the hotel. Her heels clicked on the marble corridor. Seeing a side door, she pushed her way through.

139

Across the flagstone lined street stood the wall to the Alamo.

Miranda darted across the deserted street without looking, without knowing where she would go. She glanced back several times to see if Cole was following her, but could not see anyone except the couple she passed in the hotel. They had stopped to watch her through the glass wall. She slowed her pace, but hurriedly followed the solid stone wall around to the left. Finally coming to the end of the wall, she cut right toward the front of the historic fort and then found the path leading to the gardens inside the fortress wall. Except for the glow of the street lights beyond the wall, it was dark. Taking a deep breath, to quell her racing heart, Miranda stopped and considered what to do now. She eased up to a short rock border of a pansy-filled flowerbed and sat down.

Cole carried a handgun. On a date. To a *Who's Who* filled gala. While he sang on stage, for God's sake. Miranda didn't know why she should be shocked. He was a suspect in two crimes. Miranda tried to tell herself that she had been staying true to the constitution, that this man was innocent until proven guilty. But she knew that was a rationalization. A weak one at that. She was just a fool to have let her desire overtake her suspicions of him.

As her adrenaline wore off, Miranda began to feel the cold. Tiny goosebumps rose on her bare arms. Wishing she had her overcoat, she considered going back to the hotel. Cole was probably long gone, escaping before Miranda could confront him about the gun.

Miranda decided to wait another ten minutes, then head back to the hotel, collect her purse and coat and hail a cab home. Even if he was there, surely he wouldn't try anything in front of hundreds of people.

Clouds slid over the moon, shrouding the Alamo grounds in a deeper darkness. Suddenly Miranda was aware of her surroundings, the sounds and movements in the bushes. A cat? A rat? A bird?

An eerie half-light played off the fortress wall. Her head

140

spun around when she thought she heard a footstep to her left. She felt a presence and remembered the stories she'd heard of guests of the Menger Hotel seeing, from their second floor windows, ghosts of the defenders of the Alamo floating through the grounds. Miranda shivered and tried to shake off her imagination.

While neither actually rejecting nor accepting the notion of ghosts, Miranda imagined if they did exist they would be more benign than evil. Still, the idea of sharing the garden with spirits who'd died prematurely in battle was unsetting.

'A little spooky here, isn't it?' The voice out of the darkness so shocked her that she felt her organs rearrange in her body. She leapt to her feet to back away from the figure in the shadows. Her back hit the Alamo. She was cornered.

The breeze blew the clouds off the moon and its glow lit his face. Rick. He held his nine millimeter, loosely, pointed at the ground. She relaxed at the familiar face. He almost looked like he was enjoying being a spook. Miranda thought, knowing him, he probably is.

'What are you doing lurking in the shadows of the Alamo, Lieutenant? Chasing a warrant on Daniel Boone?'

'I saw you run across the street. I was worried about you.' Rick moved closer, clicked the safety on the gun and dropped it in his holster, hiding it once again under his houndstooth blazer. 'Are you alright?'

'Sure,' she lied. 'I was at that stuffy gala and just needed some fresh air.'

Rick looked skeptical. 'Without your coat?'

Miranda rubbed her arms briskly in answer to his question. 'You're right, I should have brought it. I didn't realize it had gotten this cold.'

With characteristic chivalry, Rick shrugged out of his blazer and swung it over her shoulders. His cologne filled her nostrils. His mounded biceps strained the broadcloth of his tailored shirt. His hand brushed her breast. Miranda was sure his movements were planned for effect, but

141

knowing that didn't change her response to him. After everything, she still found him incredibly arousing.

A master of timing, Rick felt Miranda's vulnerability and gently drew her to him. His head bent over hers as his hand lifted her chin. Mobile lips closed over hers. His kiss was probing and anti-climactic. Unable to stop herself, Miranda felt herself comparing this kiss to the ones she and Cole had shared earlier. That was the difference. Sharing. When she and Cole kissed she felt as if they were one, their passions igniting a single fire. Now she felt like Rick was using a good technique as a means to an end – to get her to bed – instead of enjoying the kiss for its own sake. Rick was more than good; he was excellent. He still could turn her on, physically, if not emotionally. And right now, he was familiar and that was comforting.

Miranda moved her arms, bulky with his jacket, up around his neck. His hands moved down to her taut breasts, index fingers tracing her hardened nipples with circles growing faster. His hands migrated down her soft stomach coming to rest just where her legs met, probing through black silk.

Rick gave a short laugh. 'I knew you'd feel this way again, all in heat. Nobody gets as hot as you do.'

She heard his words and hated them, hated herself. But she felt herself giving in to technique as he reached around to push her hips into his hardness barely contained in tight dress pants.

During their affair, Rick had always avoided exotic locales for his lovemaking, preferring the security of his bed, where he could be the undisputed boss. Several times, Miranda had suggested elevators, the kitchen table, a romantic lookout trying to fulfil her own secret fantasies. He'd always flatly refused. Miranda figured out, long after her side of his bed was filled with another, that it wasn't convention that stopped him, but fear that he wouldn't be able to control the situation completely.

So here they were in the middle of the night at the

Alamo, with dozens of ghosts looking down on them and Rick spoke again.

'Let's go home, I can barely wait.'

'Then don't. How about right here?' Miranda challenged, wondering how much he'd changed over the years.

Rick just laughed at her and wrapped his arm around her waist as he headed to his car. Disappointed with him, Miranda squirmed out of his grip and followed quietly. It wasn't that she would have ever gone through with it. She and Rick were history. But something in her wanted him to jump at her offer, to be less like Rick and more like . . . Cole.

As they turned toward the street and Rick's car, Miranda thought she saw, out of the corner of her eye, a figure move just beyond where they had been standing. She stopped and concentrated into the darkness.

'What is it?' Rick asked, suddenly alert.

'My imagination,' she dismissed.

But the flash of movement haunted her as they walked on. Was she becoming paranoid?

Almost reluctantly, Miranda shook off the feeling and climbed into Rick's Lexus. It was then that she remembered the purse and coat she'd left at the hotel.

'Stop outside and I'll just be a minute.'

'No, I'll go get them.'

'Rick, that would be too suspicious. I'll be right back.'

People were filtering out of the party and only a few stragglers remained inside. No sign of Cole. Tomori and Trent were just getting up from the table. Tomori, her delicate brows drawn together with concern, asked how she was doing. Miranda was cool, still not sure of Tomori's role in trapping her with Cole.

'Have you seen my purse?'

Tomori looked thoughtful, then said: 'Not since I came back in from the courtyard.'

Miranda thanked her and hurried off to the front desk, giving Victoria a wide berth so she wouldn't be roped into her conversation with Wayne and an elderly couple. She reported her lost purse to the night manager, but did not mention the gun. She didn't want Victoria to find out from the staff that she was a PI.

Collecting her coat, Miranda rushed out into the night air. Rick was waiting just outside the front door. She jumped in, slammed the car door and he sped off.

'Nice car for a cop,' Miranda observed, more sarcastic than impressed.

'I have a generous ex-wife.' Rick's smile of pleasure was for the car not Sheila, Miranda was sure. But she did notice he said 'have' and not 'had' which made her wonder again about their current relationship. Then again, she was probably reading too much into it. Once Rick had something it was always his, in his mind anyway.

She knew without asking how he felt about her. To Rick, their affair had simply been on sabbatical during his marriage. He made it clear when she came to the police station that she would come back to him. His arrogance was infuriating, but at the same time Miranda tried to be honest with herself. If she hadn't had the case as an excuse to see him, would she have eventually found another excuse?

His marriage still hurt her, and she wasn't sure whether the pain was a bruised ego or a broken heart. As he manuevered through the quiet streets of downtown, being with him felt like falling into a old habit. A bad habit.

'It's so nice of you to give me a ride home,' Miranda said with her most innocent smile.

Rick turned to look at her so suddenly he nearly ran a red light. He slammed on the brakes and skidded halfway into the intersection. The cross traffic tentatively went around him and a bicycle patrolman stopped next to driver's window. Rick flashed his badge and the patrolman waved him on.

'Yeah, I'm giving you a ride,' he paused. 'To my house.'

'No, Rick, I want to go home. I need to go home. This case is important to me. I need to work on it.'

Rick whipped the car around the corner and into the

King William Historical District. Halfway down the block, he pulled the car over onto the side of the road.

'What happened there at the Alamo, Miranda?' His eyes burned into hers. 'I thought you wanted to finish it as badly as I still do.' His hand moved from her knee up her thigh, pushing her dress up with it. His fingertips grazed the black lace of her panties. He laughed, soft and low.

Miranda grabbed his hand off her leg, holding it between her hands. 'Rick, it's just too complicated right now. I'm involved in my case, you're involved in your case, and coincidentally or otherwise, the cases seem to be overlapping.' She took a deep breath. 'This is just not a good idea.'

Rick's dark eyes glittered. Miranda braced for a smooth talking argument, but got none.

'Alright. But you are going to be back in my bed again, now or later.'

Miranda fidgeted, uncomfortable with the conversation. She let go of his hands.

Rick continued. 'You brought it up, so let's talk about the cases. Maybe it is more than coincidence. Maybe we can help each other.'

Miranda looked indecisive, not trusting Rick or herself. 'Okay, we can talk here for a minute.'

'No, let's go in. You haven't seen my house. You'll love it.' Rick jumped out of the car and went around to Miranda's side to open her door. Miranda was confused. She'd assumed Rick had moved out of his apartment when he married, but she never imagined he kept the house, especially not one in the oldest, most prestigious neighborhoods in San Antonio.

The King William District was in the south end of downtown, where history meets slum. Most of the homes were mansions, but the neighborhood was not homey. Businesses had moved into some of the homes, others had fallen victim to the high cost of their upkeep, while others had been expensively restored to their original splendor.

Rick's home was one of the latter. Miranda slid off the

leather seat and straightened slowly, looking up at the magnificent two-storey mansion.

'This is where you live?'

The house was built in 1882, Rick explained. It was about four-thousand square feet of mahogany and marble. They walked up the steps of what could only be described as a veranda, past carved columns. Miranda imagined sitting in a corset and hoop skirt in the wicker chairs, sipping a mint julep. She was enchanted.

'I knew you'd love it,' Rick pronounced, studying her twinkling eyes.

Rick unlocked the glass inlaid door. It was so heavy it swung open on its own, to reveal a chandelier-lit entry hall, leading to a cathedral-ceiling dining room on the left and a narrow staircase on the right.

Miranda followed Rick down a dark hallway that opened into the kitchen. She was surprised to find the kitchen so small. A tiny island in the center was the extent of the counterspace. A bar built into one wall looked as if it may have sacrificed most of the space. It probably fit Rick perfectly. He never cooked for himself and she doubted his spoiled wife did much in the kitchen either. Priorities, Miranda thought. I bet the bedroom is a thousand square feet all by itself.

As he reviewed his bar stock, Rick called out: 'Can I get you a brandy? Cognac? More champagne?'

As she peered out over the lush grounds, Miranda heard the twinge of sarcasm in his voice in his last suggestion. She looked over her shoulder but his back was to her. How did he know she'd been drinking champagne?

'You never answered when I asked what you were doing in the Alamo in the dark with gun drawn?' Her breath blew mist on the window.

'You didn't tell me why you were running around in the dark at the Alamo with no coat and no companion and no gun.'

'Why do you have to assume I need a companion and you don't?'

146

'Because it's women being raped downtown, not men.' Rick stopped reading the label of the Bailey's Irish Creme bottle in his hand, and turned his dark eyes on her. 'Of course, it wouldn't help much if you picked the wrong companion, now would it?'

Miranda didn't respond and turned back to the window. She tried to control her rising anger at his presumption by studying the view. In the dim glow cast by the moon, she could see the landscaping was simple: autumn-bare pecan trees mixed with live oaks, rye grass that would be bright green in the sun and three large beds of pansies. The lawn rolled down to the river, just the far bank of which was visible from the window. A tall wall hid whatever was on the other side of the water.

Rick's estate was beautiful and romantic in the moonlight. But, Miranda reminded herself, it was a oasis bordered by the city on one side and the welfare housing projects on the other. Miranda could not help but notice the irony. Was this a metaphor for her relationship with Cole? And when would the dangers that surrounded them finally overtake them, just as the city and slums of San Antonio would eventually meet to squeeze out this historic neighborhood?

147

CHAPTER 8

Since Miranda had not chosen her drink, Rick chose for her and walked over with her snifter of the creamed whiskey. She took it without a word and without looking at him.

'Pretty nice house for a cop,' Miranda said, breaking the silence.

'Like I said, courtesy of Sheila.'

'So, she still pays the mortgage?' Miranda always knew Rick could be bought, but she never considered him the type to be a 'kept' man.

'There never was a mortgage,' Rick paused and she could hear the satisfied smile in his voice when he continued. 'She gave it to me as a going-away present. Said I was worth every penny.'

Miranda never stopped looking out the window, but now she wasn't seeing the view. She should have appreciated the humor in the statement, made even funnier by the fact that Rick missed the double meaning completely. Instead, her thoughts turned back to the humiliation and hurt the name Sheila still wrought . . .

Miranda had floated into work that morning high on life. She'd never imagined things could be so perfect at just twenty-five years old. Working in a top-forty television news market for a network affiliate, she was the station's number-one investigative reporter. She was mentioned in the gossip column nearly every week, if not for her work then for her affair with one of the city's top cops. She was in love with him. And Rick had told her he was in love with her.

He came to see her the night before. He'd been working on a case, he'd said, but couldn't keep her off his mind. He could only stay a few minutes.

'To touch you, to feel you, to love you,' he'd said.

Miranda didn't need any convincing. They made love with wild, sudden passion and Rick left while she was still breathing hard. It seemed so illicit and so delicious.

Miranda lay there and thought about her great life. It all seemed too good to be true.

And it was, she found out the next day.

As she walked into the newsroom, Tanya leaped from her desk to run over and sit on top of Miranda's.

'What's up? Big assignment?' Miranda asked, still humming a love song she'd heard on the car radio.

'Nooo . . . not exactly.'

'Oh, juicy gossip?' Miranda reached for the paper and tried to pull it out from under Tanya's ample rear. 'Excuse me, paperweight.'

Tanya didn't budge. 'Miranda, there's something I have to tell you. I know it can't be true, but you ought to know what garbage Lena's written today.'

Miranda felt her heart speed up and stomach tighten.

'Tanya, for God's sake, spit it out.'

'She says that Rick got married,' Tanya looked sorry enough to have written it herself.

Miranda laughed. 'She certainly doesn't have very good sources, does she? Unless I got married in my sleep.'

'Miranda, Lena didn't say you got married. She said Rick got married.'

'What? Where? To whom?' Miranda grabbed desperately at the paper, ripping the edges before Tanya could leap off of it. Oblivious to the stares of her co-workers, Miranda flung sections of paper on the floor looking for Lena Howland-Hansen's column.

Finally she found it with a headline 'SURPRISE WEDDING'. It read:

149

'*San Antonio's sexiest police officer, Rick Milano, tied the knot last night with one of the city's richest, most beautiful women, Sheila O'Connor. Sources tell this column that the car heiress was wed in a small affair with only about fifty family and friends, including Senator Rich Garcia, in attendance on the grounds of the O'Connor family home in Alamo Heights. Reverend Dick Walling officiated. The marriage will certainly break hearts across the city, that of one famous TV reporter in particular. Miranda Randolph and the studly cop dated for over a year and were last seen in an intimate dinner at a posh Broadway restaurant just last week. This columnist wonders if she was invited? The Milanos are expected to leave for their honeymoon in the Cayman Islands this afternoon.*'

Miranda felt her world caving in on her. Out of the corner of her eye she could see Tanya waving her arms to get the rest of the newsroom back to work. She must have been swaying because Tanya pushed her down into her chair.

'You okay?'

'I know it has to be a joke,' Miranda reasoned. 'One of the guys Rick works with is probably playing some kind of joke on him and planted this with Lena.'

'Maybe you should talk to Rick,' Tanya suggested weakly.

'I just saw him last night. He came over . . .' Miranda stopped, feeling lost. 'He didn't say anything about this.'

Picking up the phone, Miranda touched the number one on her speed dial. One ring and an unfamiliar voice answered. 'Homicide.'

'Rick Milano, please.' Miranda's voice sounded deceptively in control.

'I'm sorry, ma'am. Detective Milano is on his honeymoon. Can I connect you with Detective Villareal, who's handling his cases?'

Miranda hung up without answering and stared blankly at the wall.

Phil Hart, the assignment editor, yelled from across the room. 'Line five for you Miranda.'

'Take a message,' Tanya barked. 'You idiot.'

Phil spoke into the phone for a minute. 'It's Lena. She wants a comment on –'

Tanya cut him off. 'We know what she wants, Phil.' She picked up line five. 'Lena, it's Tanya.' Pause. 'What a scoop you got! You really are better than Liz Smith. If we're not careful, New York will snap you up. But then what would we do for fun?' Tanya looked as if she might throw up. 'You really do have spies all over town.' Pause. 'Oh, she did. Well, aren't you lucky it just fell in your lap.' Pause. 'No, Lena I haven't seen her yet this morning. I think she's out on a story, but I sure will have her get back to you. Bye.'

Tanya hung up and turned to Miranda. 'Sheila's publicity-shy mother called Lena with the scoop last night. Never guess who put her up to it. I'm sorry, Miranda.'

'Thanks. You're a good friend.' Miranda managed a smile. She felt weak all over.

'I think you need to take a sick day.'

'No!' Miranda shouted and caused a few heads to turn back to the center attraction.

Somewhere deep inside she found a reserve of strength and tapped into it. 'Everyone in San Antonio will turn on the news tonight to see if they can detect red-rimmed eyes on the jilted lover. If I'm not there it will be a hundred times worse tomorrow, with people speculating over me having a breakdown or something. I'm going on tonight and the interest will die down a lot sooner when there's no weeping, knashing of teeth, or public mudslinging.'

'I'd like to sling some mud right into Sheila O'Connor's expensively made-up face.' Tanya looked like there was someone else she'd like to sling mud at, but she held her tongue for Miranda's sake.

Miranda had picked up the phone and was rifling through her Rolodex. She found what she was looking for and dialed.

151

'Lena Howland-Hansen.'

'Lena, this is Miranda Randolph. Listen, I just got your message and don't have much time so here's my comment: I wish Rick and Sheila the best in their marriage.'

'I never expected you to call. Aren't you devastated?'

'Lena, I gave you my comment.' Her voice gave nothing away.

'Nothing off-the-record?'

'What would I have to say off-the-record?'

'Okay, okay. One last question. Are you surprised?'

'No. I don't think surprised is what I am.' She replaced the phone in the cradle and let out a long breath. Tanya looked at her and shook her head.

'How did you manage to sound happy for the jerks without lying. You are amazing.'

Miranda was already walking over to the assignment desk.

'What you got for me today, Phil?'

When Daniel Cox stepped in and tried to talk her into taking some time off, Miranda forced a cynical smile. 'C'mon think of the ratings. They'll go through the roof. And, that's what it's all about, isn't it?'

Miranda didn't stop all the rest of that day, or the next or the next. She insisted on doing two stories each day, one for the early and one for the late newscast. The ratings did indeed skyrocket, although Miranda wished that was because of her backbreaking work instead of the viewer's gossipy interest in her mental state. There she disappointed them, because she never broke down. The only time she ever even cried was privately when Daniel kidnapped her coming out the door one night and took her home for dinner with him and Cindy. Their caring touched the hurt. But after that painful night, Miranda shoved the feelings back down deep and resolved to keep them there.

When she had thought about what had happened, which wasn't often, she never blamed Sheila. Miranda had met her a few times, at charity dinners and Junior League luncheons that Cindy sometimes dragged her to. Of Scandinavian-Irish descent, Sheila was tall, lithe, fair – a spoiled rich girl who Miranda neither liked nor disliked. She'd always struck Miranda as not having much character, someone who, when the going got tough, would get gone. She wasn't far wrong. Although Miranda didn't know what happened to end the marriage, she did know Sheila didn't work too hard to fix it.

Instead of blaming Sheila, Miranda blamed herself – for not seeing Rick more clearly. She shouldn't have been so trusting. She should have noticed the warning signs that he was cheating on her, for she learned later that he and Sheila had been having rendez vous for three months. She should have realized he was using her for sexual satisfaction while playing the field for a partner with better finances and better political connections . . .

So, as Miranda turned to look at him now, as he eased into the leather loveseat in the den just off the kitchen, she wondered what he was after.

Had he learned his lesson and realized that he really loved her? Miranda doubted it but some part of her wished it was true. What would she do then? Fall back into his arms, or throw it back in his face and walk out of his life vindicated? The scary thing was, Miranda didn't know which urge would win out.

'You know we aren't going to get very far by answering each other's questions with more questions,' Rick's voice drifted to her from the other room. She wandered over to the doorway, still hugging his blazer around her as if it were a shield.

'I'm not the one who started it.'

'You're right. I confess. Let's both ask one question and the other will answer, then we'll see how it goes. I'll even let you go first.' He motioned for her to sit down next to him. She did, but in the chair not the loveseat. She kicked off her shoes and pulled her feet under her.

'What were you doing before you found me at the Alamo?'

'Surveillance on a suspect.'

'Cole Taylor?'

'Ah, that's two questions. It's my turn. What were you doing at the Menger?'

'Two things really. Doing a favor for my client and studying some of the subjects involved in my case.'

'Why did you arrive with my suspect?'

Miranda held up her hand. 'It's my turn.'

'Go.'

'What kind of surveillance is Cole Taylor under?'

'Twenty-four hour. He's going to slip up and we're going to catch him. Now, why did he pick you up and take you to the party?'

'You were at my house?' Miranda was disgusted.

'Quincy followed Taylor there. Now answer.'

'I made a deal with my client and part of that deal was to be Cole's date tonight. It served my purposes as well.'

'Oh, and what are those purposes? To climb into bed with him?' His voice was so polite, his words so ugly, that it took a moment for their meaning to sink in.

'Go to hell, Rick.' Eyes afire, she stood up threw her drink at him, picked up her shoes and took off down the hall. Wiping the creamy alcohol off his face with the back of a mongrammed handkerchief, he raced her for the door and blocked her before she could open it.

'I'm sorry, baby. I just get so jealous when I see you with another man.'

Miranda laughed humorlessly. 'That's rich, isn't it? The man who left me for another woman gets jealous when I'm with another man. You have no more right to be jealous than a stranger I've never met. Let me out of here.'

'Let's try this one more time.' Rick took a deep breath. 'I promise, no more personal comments. We'll keep it strictly professional. For the next few minutes, let's forget we share a past. I can do it. Can you?'

Miranda debated. She wanted nothing more than to slam the door in his face right now, but she had enough presence of mind to realize that tomorrow she'd wish she'd swallowed her pride and pumped him for more information on the rape investigation.

'Okay, Rick. Let's try it again.'

They returned to the sitting room. Rick retrieved the unbroken glass from the Oriental rug, looked with distaste at the liquor slashed on the leather couch and wiped at it with a tiny cocktail napkin. He always hated disorder and messes, Miranda recalled. Visual ones, anyway.

'I'm working on getting a search warrant for Taylor's apartment. The judge is dragging her feet. Taylor's dad is a big shot around here and apparently is very free with his political contributions. Hence, the delay.'

'How is his dad a big shot?'

'You don't know?' He searched her face. 'Usually you do better homework than that, Miranda. His name is Caldwell Traynor, sixth-generation Texan, or something like that. He owns a pretty big ranch north of town, between Boerne and Bandera. They run cattle, breed horses. The ranch is only passably successful, so I assume their considerable money comes from his wife. Her family's estate, trust funds.'

To Miranda, this news was both shocking and plausible. It explained why he seemed to know so many of the elite at tonight's gala. It didn't explain why he appeared the starving artist. Again she wondered why Cole's parents, if they had indeed been at the party, had not at least come up to congratulate him after his song. The answers seemed to breed more questions.

'Traynor? Is Taylor a stage name?'

'His given name was Colton Traynor. When he was eighteen he had it legally changed.'

Miranda digested that information without comment. Rick was watching her intently. 'There's something else we've come up with. Off-the-record.'

Miranda nodded.

'When Taylor was seventeen, he was accused of molesting a girl he'd dated. No charges were filed because Old

155

Man Traynor paid the girl off. She wouldn't testify.' Rick spit the words out as if they tasted bitter.

'How do you know there was a payoff? Maybe he didn't do it and that's why she wouldn't testify.'

Rick's eyes narrowed. 'Whose side are you on?'

'No side. This isn't a football game. I was just throwing out a suggestion that you obviously didn't consider.'

Agitated, Rick prowled around the small den for a few moments while Miranda sat, willing herself to be patient. She needed to think about this new information, but not now, not when Rick could read her thoughts in her eyes.

'And, of course, there is the matter of the missing band member,' Rick said casually, though he watched her closely.

'Which is the title of a Hardy Boys mystery, right? I didn't realize you refer to those in solving SAPD cases,' Miranda shot back sarcastically. She was tired of his baiting game.

Rick glared, but didn't tackle her sarcasm. 'We've found out that a couple of years ago, when Taylor had his band in Austin, his first bass guitarist vanished. Taylor reported him missing, but wasn't real cooperative with investigators. This guy, Greg Pittman, has never shown up.'

'Did they ever really look for him?' Miranda studied her steepled fingers and forced calm into her voice, even though her heart was pounding.

'What do you mean?' Rick asked sharply.

'You know what I mean. Some musician takes off. Cops think all those creative types are flaky anyway. They assume the band probably had a fight over what song to play. They take the report, but don't really look. He didn't have family did he?'

Rick swallowed hard, and answered stonily, 'No.'

'See? No body turns up. The cops figure the guy is off with a new made-up name playing in some dive in some other city. So who cares?'

'I'd watch out who you're criticizing. Or you won't get

much cooperation with solving your case. The information exchange might just dry up.'

'This – tonight – was your idea, not mine,' Miranda reminded him.

Rick's fingers drummed on the bar. His jaw clenched. 'You came to me first.'

'Yes, when I thought you might have adopted some humility after the failure of your marriage.'

Miranda realized too late that she had said too much. In his eyes, being called a failure was worse than being called a wop. Her words hung heavy in the air between them. Rick stood deathly still. Miranda stared out the window. Finally she heard him expel a breath.

'Okay. Score one for you. I guess I deserve that.'

Miranda narrowed her eyes at her ex-lover. Rick never admitted defeat. He was manuevering. But to what end?

'What's new with your investigation?' Rick was trying to swallow his irritation with her, but Miranda could see it was still caught in his throat.

'Not much.'

'Come on, Miranda. You've only gotten the one contact?'

'We got a second, with terms.'

'Which are?'

'None of your business.'

Rick ignored her snub and walked around behind her chair. His supple fingers started to massage her shoulders.

'I've got a way we can help each other solve our cases, baby.' Rick's voice was as smooth as the flat side of a butcher knife.

'I bet you do.'

Here it comes, Miranda thought as his fingers probed.

'You seem to have gotten,' Rick paused, searching for the right word, 'familiar with Taylor. Maybe you could get him in another situation where you'd be alone with him. Maybe he'd force himself on you. We'd have him covered so we could nab him.' Rick leaned down to whisper in her ear. 'I don't want you hurt, baby.'

Miranda became so still she was hardly breathing. So, that's what Rick had been after this evening. He wanted to use her as bait. She was appalled and disappointed and furious, but she sat quietly and waited for him to finish digging himself into a hole.

'Once we got him in custody, I'd break him for you, make him confess to the blackmail. We'd have it wrapped up all neat and tidy.' Rick stopped and waited for her response.

'Why me, Rick?' Miranda asked in a saccharin-laced voice. 'Why not one of your smart policewomen who are trained to be minnows?'

After a split-second pause, she continued, her voice now flinty. 'Maybe because your boss vetoed your plan. Maybe because it's too dangerous or too dumb to sacrifice a policewoman on. Maybe because when Cole's attorney accused you of entrapment you could call me a liar, deny any attempts to set this up and say I'm just a horny bitch in heat who got herself in a bad situation. If I wouldn't testify, you could use whatever I told you in a disheveled state of being nearly raped to compare with the reports from the other victims and whatever you find from your search warrant and nail Cole on circumstantial evidence.

'What do you have to lose? Cole would be in jail. A gullible jury and a dumb lawyer would ensure he'd stay there. Now I might be mad at you, but that's happened before. Right? It wouldn't be long before I'd get over it. Look at me now. Just sitting here asking to be made a fool of again.'

Rick was looking at her, speechless. Finally he whispered: 'You've lost it, Miranda.'

'No. I think I've found it. I just have one more question, Rick. Why do you hate Cole Taylor so much?'

CHAPTER 9

'Excuse me.'

The night manager of the Menger Hotel looked up. At the desk stood a man in a rumpled suit, a shirt with the top button undone and a tie hanging half-tied around his neck. He looked like he'd been drinking the night away. Or wanted to. The manager braced himself. 'Yes sir?'

'The Children's Safehouse Gala is over, right?'

'It has been for quite some time.'

'Did you see a striking redhead . . . well, her hair's more auburn. Anyway, she's beautiful. Had a black dress on. Did you see her at all after the gala?'

'No. But I came on duty at midnight.' The manager was about to let it go there, but something in the man's face (desperation?) made him offer some extra help.

'Listen, I'll look and see if the evening clerk left any messages. Don't get your hopes up though.'

The manager walked back into the small office behind the front desk and sifted through some papers. He found something written on a notepad and returned to the disheveled man.

'It says here someone named M Randolph reported a lost purse at 11.15. Is that your girl?'

'It doesn't say there if she left with someone, or whether she had to call a cab?'

'Nope.'

'Thanks for your help.'

The night manager watched the man's shoulders slump

as he walked away and felt sorry for the guy. A lost girlfriend. Or did the urgency he saw in the guy's face mean something more?

'Hope you find her,' the manager called out as the man pushed through the front door.

Miranda stepped out of the shower and reached for her towel through clouds of steam. Still chilled despite the twenty minutes of nearly blistering hot water pouring over her body, she hugged the terrycloth tightly around her. The taxicab she'd ridden home in had no heat and the near freezing temperatures that had blown in with a cold front had seeped straight to her bones.

Toweldrying her hair, she weighed her options. It was three in the morning. She should go to bed, but she knew she wouldn't sleep. She looked at Sheba stretched lazily out on the goose down comforter and felt a twinge of guilt at neglecting her for the past few days. Not that the cat was any worse for wear. Or even looked like she cared.

Oh, to be a cat, mused Miranda with a little envy.

Sighing, she decided to make some coffee and scribble notes on the case. That always helped get things in perspective.

Quickly she threw on her most worn, most comfortable pair of jeans, a turquoise turtleneck and seafoam sweater, and a pair of low-heeled boots. She finished drying her hair, covered up the dark rings under her eyes and swished some blush across her cheekbones.

Feeling refreshed, she sat down at the kitchen table and took a new spiral notebook out of her case. Miranda wrote for about a half-hour straight about the facts of the blackmail case. Then she began to fill the book with random impressions: Wayne and Cole disagree over the management of the club. Cole wants a bigger share, but says he can't afford to buy Wayne out. His parents are rich. Cole isn't. Cole isn't close to his parents. Victoria is fond of Cole and vice versa. Victoria loves Wayne. Sable is hiding something. Sable is involved in the blackmail.

Miranda sat thinking for a while, chewing on her pen's end. Then she flipped the page and filled the next one with questions. Why did Cole change his name? Did he have a trust fund? If so, what would be his motive for blackmailing Wayne? Why couldn't he 'afford' to buy Wayne out if he wanted to? Did he have a history of molestation? Who was the woman who stared so desperately at him at the gala? Were Cole and Sable conspiring? How do the rapes fit in?

Miranda stared at what she'd written for another half-hour then decided she had to answer the questions in her mind about Cole before she could go any further with the case. They nagged at her. And her intuition was telling her that answering the questions about Cole would lead her to all the answers in the blackmail case.

Twenty minutes later, after signing in with the night guard, she was in her office. She scanned the messages on her desk and saw Tony's team had finished identifying the type and photo sources. She would have to wait until the office opened for the day to pick up the results. Tony didn't release anything from his division to anyone but the investigator who turned it in. Nothing was ever dropped on a desk, for security reasons. It was easer to slip past Marjorie than it was to slip past Tony.

Miranda entered the computer right away and began searching the database for anything on Cole Taylor. She found a few newspaper mentions of him: when he performed in Austin, when he bought into Electric Blues, when he opened at the club.

Reviewers loved him. The only mention of his roots were vague: 'son of a Hill Country rancher' or 'Boerne High School graduate'.

That was a lead. Miranda walked down the hall to the lounge to pour herself another cup of coffee. The digital clock on the table showed 5.45. If she left now she could make it to Boerne by 6.30 or so, maybe she could find a teacher who remembered Colton Traynor.

* * *

Downtown was stirring by the time she got out on the road. The traffic headed north on Interstate 10 was light and she got into Boerne five minutes earlier than she expected. She stopped at a convenience store to ask for directions to the high school.

'You look kinda old to be a student. You a new teacher or somethin'?' Her question reminded Miranda that Boerne was a close-knit small town. She wondered how much information residents would give an outsider.

'Oh, I'm just here checking up on an old friend.'

'Maybe I know 'um,' the clerk suggested brightly. 'What's your friend's name?'

Miranda considered giving her a fake name, but figured this woman probably knew every family in Boerne and would be onto her right away.

'Colton Traynor.'

'Oo hoo hoo,' the clerk hooted as she gave Miranda an exaggerated once-over. 'Yep, Cole sure always did have an eye for the ladies. My sister was in his class. He was one of the rich boys, but didn't hang around with the rich bunch much. He and his friends were kinda artsy fartsy, y'know. You a college girlfriend or somethin'?'

'Yeah,' Miranda answered vaguely.

'Well, he don't live up here no more. His folks do. Got a spread halfway to Bandera. You probably know that though. Probably been there, huh?'

'No. We never got there.'

The clerk looked at her sadly. 'Oh, that's right. I forgot.'

'Forgot what?'

'Y'know, about his folks and all.'

Miranda made a sympathetic noise to try to draw more out of her without admitting her own ignorance.

'Yeah, I think it's been real hard on his mom. She comes in here sometimes, y'know to get gas and stuff. She seems so sad. Must be hard not to see your son anymore.

'Hard on both of them.'

The clerk nodded understandingly. 'Musta been one helluva fight.'

Another customer had come in and was standing impatiently behind Miranda.

'Thanks so much for the directions. What's your name? I'll tell Cole I saw you.'

'I'm Deanna,' she laughed. 'But he won't remember me. We ain't from the same side of the tracks.'

By the time Miranda got her car parked at the high school it was seven o'clock. She found the principal's office. A woman who looked like a geometry teacher was bent over an open drawer of the filing cabinet but didn't look up when Miranda walked in. Miranda stood there for several minutes before finally clearing her throat loudly.

The woman turned around, irritated at being interrupted. She looked to be anywhere from thirty-five to fifty-five years old. She wore her lifeless mud-brown hair cropped short in a no-care style. Small tortoise-shell glasses framed eyes that were a nondescript color. Her skirt and blouse were thrift-shop chic, at least ten years behind the style.

'Yes?' When she spoke, Miranda was startled, because her voice sounded as if it had come from someone else. It was lovely, musical, beautiful.

'I'm sorry to bother you. I'm here looking for some information on a former student.'

'I don't have the authority to release any information. The secretary isn't in yet. Usually gets in about 7.15.' The woman looked at Miranda more closely. 'Are you a relative?'

'No,' Miranda answered hesitantly, not sure how to explain herself.

'Who's the student?'

'Colton Traynor. I think he graduated sometime between . . .' Miranda let her sentence drift off at the look on the woman's face. It was nostalgia and something else. Anxiety?

'1984'. The teacher looked as if her mind had traveled back to that year as she continued. 'Cole was my best student ever. And I've taught for nineteen years.'

She must have seen the question in Miranda's eyes, because she brought herself back to the present.

'I'm sorry.' She extended her hand. Miranda took it. 'I'm Elaine Farber. I teach music here at Boerne High. Choir, music theory, music history.'

'Miranda Randolph. It's nice to meet you.'

'Aren't you a TV reporter?' Elaine looked at the door as if she expected the cameras to come in at any minute.

'Used to be. Now I'm a private investigator.'

A veil of wariness dropped over Elaine's face. 'Is Cole in trouble?'

'He is. I'm trying to help him.' It surprised Miranda when she realized what she'd said was true. 'I came here to find someone who knew him well in school. I need some information.'

Elaine regarded her for several minutes.

'Maybe you could give me the name of someone else I could look up who was teaching at that time,' Miranda finally suggested.

A man approaching middle age who Miranda assumed was the principal walked in, glanced at both women and sat down at the secretary's desk. Elaine must have figured out what Miranda was thinking because she chuckled.

'Come on, I'll help you.' She led the way out the door and down the hall. Teenagers were filtering onto the campus. Groups of boys were roughhousing and joking loudly. Girls stood by lockers whispering and giggling. Miranda had been one of those insecure, self-conscious teens nine years ago, but it seemed more like nine lifetimes. She got a few catcalls, which flattered and amused her.

Miranda tried to imagine a young Cole walking the halls, elbowing his pals as they passed a girl he had a crush on. She had a feeling he broke more hearts than the other way around. She thought about what Deanna had said. Hanging around with the creative crowd, he probably wasn't the typical rich rancher's son.

They had reached the end of the hall, and Elaine seemed

to stop and consider. 'I think we'll talk in your car, if that's okay. There's not much privacy on campus right now.'

'Fine,' Miranda said, taking over the lead. A few students stopped to ask the music teacher a few questions about class. She seemed to be well-liked.

They got in the car wordlessly, but once inside, Elaine got down to business. 'What can I tell you about Cole?'

'What kind of young man he was.'

Elaine's features softened. 'He really was a sensitive kid, more in touch with his feelings than most boys are in their teens. More emotionally mature. I don't want you to think he was nerdy, though. He was sensual, animalistically so. The boys wanted to be like him. The girls wanted to be with him. He wasn't popular in the traditional sense of the word, because he wasn't a follower or a leader. Nor was he a loner. He was an individualist, his own person. If you were around, that was okay with him but he wouldn't change himself for you. If you bailed out, it didn't phase him much either.'

Elaine's voice was so lyrical, so full of her emotion that Miranda found herself almost transported back in time. She closed her eyes as the teacher continued.

'Cole wasn't an honor roll student. Not because he didn't study, but because he didn't play the game the way school demands it be played, with memorization, good behavior, politics. I would bet my last dollar that Cole learned more than half the straight-A students who come out of here.

'Sometimes I think that frustrated him. But he, more than many of the teachers here, understood the big picture. What was really important. He threatened the more short-sighted administration.' She stopped, a look of infinite sadness crossed her face for a moment. 'And they eventually made him pay.'

Miranda sat quietly, hoping Elaine would continue. But the older woman just looked out the window and remained silent.

'I've been told something about an alleged molestation Cole was accused of . . .' Miranda began gently.

165

Elaine sighed heavily. 'Yes. It was a wonderful opportunity for them to make him knuckle under, fit the mold.' Her voice took on a bitter edge.

'She was a stunning girl from a big family, lower middle class. Not particularly bright, but charming and very popular. She really had an eye for Cole, probably because he didn't want anything to do with her.

'I think he became a challenge for her. She signed up for choir just to get his attention, I'm convinced. Turns out she had a lovely singing voice and was cast opposite him in that year's musical, *Phantom of the Opera*. Not that she was talented, mind you. Because talent goes beyond ability. Music must come from your soul, an expression of emotion. It's something that can be nurtured, but not acquired. You either have it or you don't. This girl didn't. Cole did, more than any other student I've seen.'

Elaine glanced at her watch, a bulky, black 100-meter waterproof scubadiver's model. It looked like it weighed down her thin arm.

'I have to make this long story short. The play was a success, and the crew and cast had a big party. This girl's crush on Cole had only gotten worse over the weeks of rehearsals. Certainly Cole saw it and in front of everyone he asked her out on a date the next night. I really think he was trying to save her from embarrassing herself, which she was. You know, figuring they could have a date, claim it didn't work out and they could both move on without her being ridiculed. Believe me, that was how sensitive Cole was.

'Anyway, everyone at the party heard they would meet in the parking lot on campus here. Her father was terribly strict and didn't let her date. And, well, there aren't any witnesses to this . . .' Elaine looked uncomfortable talking about this, but forced herself to continue. 'She claims Cole drove up, dressed up like the Phantom of the Opera, her friend dropped her off and left. Once she was in his car, he didn't talk, but just started raping her. She fought him off and got free before the sex act, and ran to the nearest

166

telephone where she called her brother to pick her up.'

Miranda felt nausea building in her tightening throat. A hard edge began to overrun the lyricism in Elaine's voice.

'She had some nasty bruises on her arms and face, a black eye she admits came from hitting her head on the car door as she ran away. There's no doubt someone attacked her, but I am convinced it was not Colton Traynor.'

Miranda had been totally absorbed in the narrative and was startled when Elaine stopped talking.

'Why? What makes you so sure it wasn't him?'

'The most compelling reason is that such an attack would be totally out of character for Cole. Then there are other parts of the story that raise doubt. It was Cole's car, but she never saw Cole's face. Her attacker had on a dark face mask. He never spoke, so she couldn't identify his voice.'

'What did Cole say about it?'

'When they found him, he was in the barn, walking one of his father's best broodmares. She'd come down with colic. He claimed he never made it to the date because he found the horse writhing on the ground before he was due to pick her up. He didn't call because he didn't want to risk her family finding out she had a date. The veterinarian did report Cole called in at 6.30. Their date was set for 7.00.'

'A sad coincidence,' Miranda observed. 'that the horse would get sick.'

'It was no coincidence. The horse had been overfed its grain. In effect, poisoned.'

Miranda shook her head to clear the shock. 'Cole wouldn't have –'

'Of course not,' Elaine cut in. 'Anyone who knew anything about horses could have done it.'

It seemed like such an elaborate plot. All just so some crazy could attack a girl? Miranda was having trouble swallowing it.

'Did the girl press charges?'

'No. Actually the girl's father found out and brought her to the Traynor ranch that night supposedly to let

Cole's father see what his son had done. Cole told me later he was shocked and professed his innocence. His dad didn't believe him and the principal didn't help by discrediting Cole, calling him a troublemaker.

'Caldwell Traynor offered to pay off the girl and her father in exchange for them not filing charges. I don't know how much it cost him but they accepted the deal. Her father was convinced her reputation would be ruined and suggested she leave town. There were only a few weeks left of school and the principal agreed to work out a deal for her to get her degree by mail. I heard she moved to Hollywood to become an actress. But who knows?' Elaine shrugged.

Miranda weighed the teacher's words carefully. She was painfully aware how much she wanted to believe what the teacher was saying.

'Cole argued against the payoff. He wanted her to file charges so there would be an investigation and he could be cleared. But he never was, from then on he was presumed guilty. A lot of the kids rallied around him, but as their parents started to cut off privileges as they were seen fraternizing with him, their numbers dwindled. The teachers were very hard on him for the most part, most hearing just part of the story and believing it. Where grades were subjective, he was penalized. He lost a lot of his heart those last few weeks of school.'

Elaine paused and glanced at her watch. She started up again, the pace of her monologue quickened. 'But the worst was yet to come. Cole had long wanted to make music his career, but he hadn't told his dad. He had worked on the ranch since he was a little boy. He enjoyed it, but saw horses and cattle as a hobby. Music was his passion. When he told his father he was going to the University of Texas where he could get his degree and have a band on Sixth Street, his father was furious. His dad was an Aggie and expected Cole to go to Texas A&M too. His sons were expected to take over running the ranch.'

Miranda closed her eyes. She realized she felt a twinge of envy and knew it was misplaced. What would it have been like to have a father care what she did with her life? Her father sure as hell hadn't. She could have flown to the moon for college and he wouldn't have noticed. But she realized now she wouldn't have wanted a controlling father either.

'Obviously desperate, Caldwell brought up the payoff of the girl and told Cole he owed it to him to do what was expected and go to college. When Cole told him he didn't owe him anything since he didn't believe his own son's integrity, Caldwell threatened to find the girl and insist she file charges. He said he would even testify against Cole, his own son, in court. Cole walked out and never came back.'

Stunned, Miranda sat in silence for a few moments. The story explained a lot. If she could believe it. Elaine was obviously biased. 'Caldwell never pursued the case.'

'Of course not. I'm sure he never intended to. It was just a cruel threat.'

'Cole's never been back since?'

'Actually he owns a piece of land near his parents' spread. A hundred and fifty acres or so. His mother's family owned the land before her marriage to Traynor. She signed it over to Cole a couple of years ago. He has horses there, and his dog. A friend of his lives there and keeps an eye on things for him.'

'Does he ever talk to his mother?'

'I don't think so. From what I hear, Caldwell Traynor made it a "him or me" kind of deal.'

Elaine, who'd been lost in nostalgia, now looked sharply at Miranda. 'Now, are you going to tell me what kind of trouble Cole's in now?'

'Have you heard of the Riverwalk Rapes?'

Elaine nodded, eyes widening.

'Cole is one of the suspects.'

'Oh dear, God help him. Do they know about the high school attack? Is that how you heard about it?'

'One of the police detectives knows. I don't know how, since there wouldn't be a record.' Miranda tried to sound reassuring. 'Don't worry, they can't use it against him in court.'

'In court! Oh, poor Cole. Can I do anything to help?' Elaine looked at her watch again, though Miranda realized it was more from anxiety than fear of being late.

'Just one more thing. Do you remember the name of the girl?'

'Let me think,' she paused, closing her eyes. 'Erika. But the last name escapes me. I'll look it up and let you know.'

Miranda handed her a card as Elaine stepped out of the car.

'That has my home number as well as my office, beeper and mobile phone. Call me anytime.'

Elaine nodded and turned to go. Miranda called after her.

'Have you seen Cole since he graduated?'

'He sent me an invitation to the opening of his club. He was fantastic. He has a bright future.' She paused, her smile fading slightly. 'In music.'

As she pulled out of the parking lot, Miranda remembered something that caught her attention during Elaine's story. She hadn't wanted to interrupt her at the time and then forgot to pursue it. She'd said Caldwell Traynor wanted his sons to follow him in the family business. Did Cole have brothers?

She looked back, but Elaine had already disappeared into the building. Miranda decided she could ask when she called her about the girl's last name. But as she passed the convenience store and she decided Deanna might be able to help.

'Hi. Did ya find the school?' Deanna was sitting behind the counter chomping gum and reading a tabloid. A black and white TV behind the counter was tuned to an old rerun of *The Price is Right*. A pre-gray Bob Barker was holding off a three-hundred pound woman who was trying to jump up and down and cover him in kisses at the same

170

time. Deanna leaned forward and turned down the sound.

'Yes. Thanks. Listen, I thought of something else you might be able to help me with. If you don't mind?'

'Sure. Shoot.'

'You know with the rift in the family I haven't had the chance to meet Cole's brothers or sisters.' Miranda affected her best pout. 'Really he won't tell me if he even has any.'

Deanna snorted. 'Well, I don't blame him there.'

'Why is that?'

''Cuz his brother is about as weird as a two-dollar bill.'

'Oh?'

'Yeah, Crayne is good looking and all, looks a lot like Cole as a matter o' fact, but he's a lot older than Cole. And creepy.' Deanna shivered dramatically to punctuate her point.

'Creepy, how?'

'His eyes, they make your skin crawl. They're not really mean so much as sad and mad at the same time.'

'Does he live around here?'

'Oh yeah. He sorta helps run his Daddy's ranch. Lives in a bunkhouse there.'

'He's not married?'

'Not now, but he was once. She run off though in the middle of the night a coupla years ago. Nobody never saw her again.'

'Was she from around here?'

'Nope. I don't think anybody around here's crazy enough to marry him.'

'Even for money? Aren't the Traynors supposed to be rich?'

'They ain't gonna be rich for long the way Crayne's runnin' things into the ground.'

Miranda was halfway back to San Antonio and deep in thought when she realized the phone beside her was ringing. It was the vibration against her thigh more than the sound that got her attention.

171

'Miranda Randolph.'

'Finally, I find you. I've called damn near everywhere looking for you.'

'Wayne, what is it?'

'I've got another note.'

'Okay. I have to stop by the office, then I'll come to the club.'

'You can't come now? You gotta be here,' Wayne whined.

'Wayne, I'll be there as soon as I can.' Miranda hung up on more pleading.

An hour later, Miranda walked into the office. Traffic had been heavy, which she wasn't used to. Making her own hours had its privileges. Poured into a fuchsia coat-dress a size too small and three inches too low cut, Marjorie was on the phone and waved wildly at Miranda.

'I haven't heard from her yet, sir.' Her eyes asked Miranda a question.

Miranda shook her head and walked down the hall to her office. She could hear Marjorie promise to give her a message. Then she hung up and yelled: 'He sounds really pissed, gal. Said you knew who it was. Call him back quick so he'll get off my caboose.'

Miranda laughed. 'It's better than him being on mine.'

She threw her bag on her desk and headed for Tony's division. From down the hall she could hear angry voices coming from Tony's office. Then Peter stormed out and knocked her against the wall as he went by. His face, usually so handsome it was almost pretty, was so red he looked like he was having a heart attack. He muttered obscenities just barely above his breath.

When he was safely out of sight, Miranda peeled herself off the wall and tentatively made her way back to Tony's office.

Tony was standing in the doorway, his usual urbanity completely intact.

'Ah, *mi bonita*. You are alright? Yes, you are tough, I know. But such rudeness is unforgivable.' Tony looked down the hall, past Miranda, his eyes turning dangerous. 'I'd like to put his *cojones* in a sling. *Gringo pendejo*.'

Miranda smiled. Such a fate might be good for pretty boy Pete.

'Now it is I that must ask for forgiveness, to speak so crudely in front of a lady.'

'Don't worry about it, Tony. I'm sure whatever he did deserved more than that.'

This time Tony smiled, but it didn't travel up to his eyes. 'Accurate as always, Miranda Randolph. Now, I have those reports for you.'

He unlocked a drawer in his desk and extracted two papers, handing them to Miranda. She scanned the results.

'Tony, you're amazing. Thanks.'

'My analysts are amazing, for them, I thank you.' Tony paused and looked hard at Miranda. 'This is just between you and me, but when you need help with this case, you call me. That goes for anything, even beyond analysis. You understand?'

Miranda was alarmed. 'No, I don't Tony. What aren't you telling me?'

His private phone line started ringing. He pushed a card into her hand and went to answer.

Miranda didn't need to be told to leave and shut the door behind her. Outside his door, she looked down at the card. It was professionally printed and all it said was 'Tony' and two numbers, his private office line and his cellular telephone. Miranda was honored and alarmed. She was sure no one but Doug in the office had these numbers. Tony only gave them to his outside 'specialists'. Something must have happened to make Tony concerned about her case. But what?

Wandering back down to her desk, Miranda sat down and looked again at the analysis. It showed the make and model of the printer used, the brand of paper, the make and model of the photographs, the developing paper and, finally, the make and model of the videocamera. All routine. Nothing there indicated the reason for Tony's distress.

Then Miranda remembered Peter's explosion. Was that a coincidence, or was there a connection? Stuffing the analysis in her case, she picked up a stray piece of paper and headed ostensibly for the copy room. Passing Peter's office she slowed down and casually looked in on him. He was talking on the phone but hung up on whomever it was when he saw Miranda.

'Hey, sorry about that in the hall. I blow out sometimes. Major, y'know.'

Too cool for school, dude. Miranda bit her tongue before the sarcasm spilled out of her mouth. Peter flashed an ultra-bright smile, but his hands nervously jangled a plastic cube of paper clips. Something about that niggled at the back of Miranda's mind, but she wrote it off to the aftermath of Peter's run-in with Tony. She admitted she'd be edgy too if Tony turned his ire on her.

'Tony's pretty ticked at you,' Miranda couldn't resist rubbing it in. Peter was so insufferably conceited.

He snapped to attention as if she'd slapped him. 'He told you that?'

'No,' Miranda answered slowly, a little perplexed at his reaction. 'One look at his eyes and anyone could tell.'

Peter visibly relaxed. He flipped his hand at her. 'Oh, he's all bark and no bite.'

'I tend to think it's the other way around.' Miranda shot over her shoulder as she finished her fabricated trip to the copy machine.

She fiddled with the copier and waited a few minutes before heading back down the hall. As she passed Peter's office, he called out, 'Working early this morning, huh?'

Miranda stopped in her tracks. 'How do you know that?'

Peter looked trapped for a moment, then said. 'Oh, I saw your coffee cup in the lounge.'

Miranda walked on without comment. Something about their conversation disturbed her and she was beginning to think she was paranoid.

174

Miranda slung her case over her shoulder and headed out the front door. A young bachelor Doug had just hired was making Marjorie's day by taking a peek down her cleavage while trying to con her into typing a report for him.

In between giggles, the receptionist told Miranda that Doug had wanted to see her but Marjorie had told him she had an appointment.

'You're a peach, Marj.' Miranda whisked out the door.

'Peaches and cream, babe. Peaches and cream,' slipped out the door as it eased shut.

Miranda turned around to see the guy nuzzling Marjorie's hair. She could have sworn she saw his tongue in her ear. But, then again, maybe not.

What she didn't see was someone watching from the hall as she headed for the elevators.

CHAPTER 10

Miranda decided to walk to Electric Blues. It bought her some time to think. She was anxious about seeing Cole after what happened between them the night before. After talking with Rick, Elaine Farber and the store clerk, she'd convicted and acquitted him in her own mind at least twelve times in the last twelve hours. But the more she learned the more latent trust was building under her suspicion. And the more uncomfortable she became, the further her feelings for him moved from black and white and deeper into gray.

The sun was breaking through the morning clouds, setting the stage for what promised to be a mild autumn day. As she strolled along the flagstone walk, Miranda passed a hotel restaurant kitchen and smelled breakfast. Her cramping stomach reminding her that she hadn't eaten, Miranda stopped inside and ordered toast and coffee. She knew she was dragging her feet, but indulged the urge.

The phone in her bag rang. The other diners, a pair of middle-aged tourists and a businessman, looked around for the source of the interruption. Miranda pulled the phone out and they went back to their meals. She hoped it was Elaine Farber.

'Miranda! Where are you?'

'Wayne, calm down. I'm about a block away.'

'Thank God. Hurry.'

With a heavy sigh, Miranda estimated her bill, threw

down a five and was at the door to Electric Blues in a minute. She'd barely knocked when the door flew open.

'Get in here.' Wayne yanked her in and locked the door behind them. Miranda stumbled into a barstool. It rocked back and forth, then clattered to the floor.

'Why don't you turn on a light or raise the blinds? It's dark as the inside of a pocket in here.'

'I don't want anyone to know I'm here.'

Miranda rolled her eyes. 'How am I supposed to see the note? Or is it in Braille?'

'We'll go in the office.'

He pushed her inside and fumbled for the lightswitch. The sweat from his hand bled through her shirt. Her nose wrinkled at his strong body odor that smelled like soured scotch. Light filled the room and Wayne squinted as if he'd been in the dark a long time.

Wordlessly, Wayne handed her a manila envelope that looked exactly like the previous two. Inside was another typewritten note and more photographs.

'When were these taken?' Miranda asked, not even trying to hide her disgust.

'Day before yesterday, I guess.'

'You guess?'

'I know.' Wayne even had the rare grace to look embarrassed. Miranda guessed it was because she had seen him in a loving display with his wife the night before.

Miranda studied the pictures. Most were extreme close-ups, unlike ones taken before. Chains were visible, but Miranda did not want to figure out where or how they were used. What caught her attention was the location. It was obviously not the stage of the club.

'Where is this?'

'In the dressing room.' Miranda recognized it now, the couch where Cole had laid her, both of them caught up in passion. Miranda felt sick.

'Excuse me.' She stumbled into the bathroom, regained her composure and began checking stalls. In the handi-capped one she saw a small crocheted wall hanging.

177

Looking closer, Miranda saw it hung from a nail that was driven into a tiny plug cut out of the wall. She pulled on the nail and the plug came out to reveal a hole cut through the sheetrock to the dressing room. Miranda was looking at the back of a picture. She went around to the dressing room, removed the picture and saw the hole had a direct view of the couch. She replaced everything and returned to the office, where Wayne was wringing his hands.

'You okay?'

'Fine.' She noticed Wayne was holding a small paper sack. 'What's that?'

'Oh, I just found this on the desk. Has your name on it.'

Miranda took the sack from him and opened it. Inside was the evening bag she had lost at the Menger. Opening the clasp, she saw her .38, lipstick and credit cards still inside.

'Lose that last night?' Wayne leered at her.

'Yes,' Miranda stared into the open purse, as if the answer were inside. 'I wonder who found it.'

'Who else? Your date.' Wayne tipped himself back in the chair, obviously enjoying himself now, the anxiety over his own predicament temporarily forgotten. 'Y'know Miranda you don't have to be coy. If you got some last night, I'd be the last to judge.'

'Wayne, how do you know Cole found this?'

'I recognize his handwriting on the bag.'

Suddenly everything came into focus for Miranda as she flashed back to the embrace in the courtyard. Cole coming out to find her. Finding her upset, encouraging her to talk. Her rejection. Their desire. Feeling the heavy metal object in his pocket. Realizing it was a gun. Had it been her gun in her purse that he had found at their table? Had he been trying to give it to her?

It could've happened like that. But if it had, why didn't he leave a note that explained what happened? Maybe because he didn't want to beg for her trust.

Or, she admitted, it could have been his gun. He could have gone back to the party after she ran off and found her purse, brought it here to make it look like he'd been carrying her gun. But that would be a lucky coincidence. And Miranda was not a great believer in coincidence.

There was something else, too. Tomori had said she hadn't seen her purse after coming back from the court-yard. But could she trust Tomori?

'Aren't you even gonna read the note?' Wayne de-manded shrilly.

'What?' Miranda asked, still caught up in supposition. Wayne waved the note at her in answer.

For a moment, Miranda thought Cole had left a message for her. Then it dawned on her that Wayne was talking about the blackmail note. Shelving her problems, she took the paper from his outstretched, clammy hand, she noticed it was a lot longer than the others.

Time is up. I hope you've made your decision. I can prove when all these hot shots were taken, too, so don't get any ideas about lying to your dear sweet wife about them.

I want the contracts to sign over your shares in Electric Blues to me. You will leave all references to the recipient blank. My attornies will take care of that. You will give the paperwork to a taxidriver who will meet you at Market and San Saba at eight Saturday morning. You must say 'Blues' and the driver must answer 'Phantom' or you have the wrong cab. I must have the papers in hand by nine Saturday morning or a package containing the juicy pictures and video you received plus others will be hand-delivered to your wife.

You will get some instructions soon on how I want the club run. Nice doing business with you sucker.

Miranda leaned back in her chair. 'So, we have three days.'

'Two and a half,' Wayne corrected.

'You are still insistent on not telling Victoria? You know Wayne, she just might forgive you. She does seem to love you.' The last comment left a bad taste in Miranda's mouth. Like biting into a green banana. But it did seem to be true.

179

'That's why I can't tell her. Because she loves me, because she is understanding, because no one like me deserves great gal like her, because I ain't gonna cause her anymore pain. And because I'm a chicken. I could never tell her.' Wayne's voice choked up. He started to sob.

Miranda was surprised to find herself unmoved by his hystrionics. 'Wayne, why don't you pull yourself together? We need to work out a plan.'

Wayne nodded and walked out of the office. As soon as he was out of sight, Miranda scooted to the computer. She checked the model and make of the printer with Tony's report.

'Bingo,' she whispered to herself.

Then, hearing the toilet flush in the men's bathroom, she accessed the computer and began searching for any record of the notes. After five minutes of wading through accounting records, marketing ideas, payrolls and schedules, she decided her search was in vain. She heard the faucet at the sink turn on. Returning to the employee information, she quickly copied down Cole's address. She switched off the monitor just as Wayne returned, his face red, swollen and slightly wet.

'What are you doing?'

'I had to make some phone calls.'

'Don't you have a mobile phone?' Wayne glanced nervously at his desk.

'Yes,' Miranda thought quickly. 'But the battery is low and I wanted to save it. You don't mind do you?'

'Guess not,' Wayne slumped back into his own self-pity, forgetting his skepticism 'What're we gonna to do?'

'Well, Wayne,' Miranda tried to sound as matter-of-fact and efficient as possible. 'I'm going to continue to try to find out who is blackmailing you and you have to decide what you're going to do if I don't find them in time.'

'Okay,' Wayne accepted the order better than Miranda had expected. 'Are you close at all?'

'I have a couple of great leads, but I really don't want to

tell you yet, because in dealing with those who might be involved, you might tip your hand. It could become dangerous or could send the perpetrator into hibernation,' Miranda explained quickly.

'Hibernation? We're not talking about a Goddamn bear here.'

'It might scare the blackmailer into laying low for a time, and either giving up altogether or lulling you into a false sense of security and hitting you with this or something else down the line.'

Wayne sat in thought for a moment. He grabbed a pencil and cleaned his ear with its eraser. Miranda tried not to gag.

'No,' he finally said. 'I ain't gonna live knowing somebody out there is eyeballing me. You do it your way.'

Miranda sighed. 'If you really mean that, I want you to do something for me. Stop sleeping with Sable. It's complicating things.'

'Yeah. Okay.' Wayne sounded uncertain. 'I can wait till Saturday.'

Shaking her head in disgust, Miranda stood. 'I'll talk to you later.'

'Will you come to the show tonight?'

'I don't know yet.'

Once outside, Miranda paused at the top of the stairs to take several deep breaths, clearing her nose of the lingering odor of stale scotch-sweat. When the toast in her stomach seemed somewhat stable again, she trotted down the steps and headed for the nearest street access. Feeling the weight of the .38 in her bag, she knew where she had to go.

Cole lived in a small high-rise adjacent to the historic Majestic Theater, a few blocks off the Paseo Del Rio. There weren't very many apartment buildings in downtown San Antonio, so, a few years before, when an architect renovated the old building to accommodate residential units, it made the evening news. Miranda didn't cover the story herself, but vaguely remembered seeing the video of a half-finished apartment. She'd been impressed with its vogueness and the view.

Halfway up the stairs, Miranda slowed her ascent and questioned her reason for being there. It was the blackmail case. She could use his return of her purse as an excuse to gain access to his apartment. She told herself she hoped to surprise him, catch him with a video camera, tripod and zoom-lens in his closet or under his bed. Why was she thinking about his bed? She shouldn't even see his bed. She wanted to be in his bed.

Miranda grabbed at the handrail to catch her breath. Her heart beat almost painfully and her lungs didn't seem to take in enough air. Getting her vital signs under control, Miranda tackled the rest of the stairs and walked into the apartment hallway. There she paused again. How should she appear when he came to the door? Apologetic? Grateful? Wary? Wanting? Wanton?

'Stop,' Miranda shouted at herself, hoping no one else was in the stairwell. She looked down at the rise and fall of her breasts and felt his hands there, his chest pressing. Her desire was overtaking her intellect again. She wondered if the two had fully developed into separate entities. The devil and the angel on her shoulders. Only which was which?

Here she was, obsessed with their physical attraction. Maybe that was exactly the way Cole wanted it. Their chemistry was an accident of nature; maybe he'd decided to use it to his advantage. To distract her. To confuse her. If so, it was working.

With a deep sigh, she drew the blackmail case back to the top of her mind. She had to concentrate on that now. Greeting Cole in a businesslike manner was the route she had to take right now. But it occurred to Miranda as she raised her fist to rap on the door that cool may not get her into his inner sanctum. And she had to check out his most obvious hiding place, his home.

She decided to sprinkle a little friendliness into her approach. Just a little. Like warm acquaintances. No, wrong word, not warm. Maybe amiable. Yes, she would be amiable. She let her tightly closed lips upturn a centimeter or two but carefully stopped the smile before it reached her eyes. Adjusting her case, she held it with straight arms in front of her thighs.

But a moment later Cole when opened the unlocked door in answer to her quick and efficient knock, she lost her well-planned control for an unnerving instant. Seeing him, with hair tousled from sleep and morning disregard, eyes underlined by tired gray smudges a shade darker than his irises, rough and somehow inviting stubble that led to the mass of curly brown hair on his bare chest, sparked an uncontrollable fire of emotion that she couldn't douse for what seemed like forever but was really only seconds. Even after she reined in the urge to drop her bag, reach out and touch his haggard face, she couldn't keep her eyes from continuing their journey south, down to where the hair tapered to a point and disappeared in some hastily pulled on gray sweat pants from which hung untied drawstrings, down the length of his finely muscled legs that the fleece couldn't hide, down to bare ankles and feet so long and inexplicably sexy.

Miranda's head snapped up at the sound of his voice, raspy and ragged. 'Go away.'

Cole started to close the door in her face. In the minute since he'd opened the door he'd seen so many conflicting emotions flash in her eyes that he thought he was starting to hallucinate. Desire. Hope. Longing. Distrust. Anticipation. Apprehension. Or was it still fear? He'd felt both her desire and her fear last night and spent all morning trying to figure out what game she was playing with him. Deciding he couldn't afford to play.

Taking one hand off her case and letting it drop to her side, Miranda put her right hand on the door and took a step inside. 'Cole, I need to talk to you.'

Maybe it was the timbre of her voice, so sincere yet unsteady. Or maybe it was that she'd said 'need' and not 'want' or 'have to'. Maybe it was because it looked like she'd had less sleep than he had. Maybe it was because her rich, untameable hair was coming loose from its clasp at her neck in wavy tendrils around her face. Maybe because he couldn't resist her. For none or some or all of those reasons and despite his best intentions after a nightlong debate, he felt himself yield to her pressure. She wedged her way inside as Cole pushed the door closed.

He pivoted around, his back pressed against the door, less than a foot from where she stood. Their eyes locked. He could smell her, not a fragrance – for she wasn't wearing any – but the clean scent of her hair, her skin. They were having an unspoken conversation that he understood on some level but not a conscious one. As he felt passion begin to overtake his uncertainty, Cole realized his loose sweatpants would make what he was feeling obvious in a matter of seconds. Suddenly, he tore his eyes away and walked to the coffee pot.

Dazed and overwhelmed by the power of their gaze, Miranda stood immobile for a moment trying to collect her paralyzed wits. She heard him speak from across the room, but didn't listen. The sudden impatience in his voice as he repeated his question finally caused her to return to reality.

'Do you want some coffee?' Spinning around to face him, she looked in his eyes and saw that they were different. Guarded. She let hers ice over immediately, closing the channel of emotions that had run between them.

'Yes, thank you.'

'Milk, sugar?' Cole relied on the mundane conversation to put more distance between them.

'A little cream.'

Cole brought the steaming mugs to the coffee table and motioned for her to sit down on the emerald suede couch. When she ignored his gesture, he perched on the edge, elbows on his knees, warming his hands on his coffee mug.

'Are you going to sit or conduct this inquisition standing?'

In response to his antagonistic tone, Miranda became defensive, her words clipped. 'This is not an inquisition. I came to find out if you are the one who found my purse.'

To show him she was not uncomfortable, Miranda sat. On the matching armchair, not the couch where he was perched.

Cole's brows lifted. 'You've been to the club this morning?'

'Wayne called.' She paused, unsure of how much to tell him. 'About some business.'

He was regaining his composure, his arrogance. He put his cup on the sofa table and leaned lazily back, regarding her with sarcastic eyes. 'Ah, feeding his paranoia like an old lady with a pet poodle.'

'He is my client,' Miranda snapped, angry at herself for jumping to his bait. She regarded him warily now, wondering how he could seem so vulnerable one moment and so cruel the next.

'He is a fool,' Cole mocked her, dismissing further discussion of Wayne with the hard evenness of his tone. It made Miranda shiver and fleetingly think he could be capable of blackmailing his partner.

'Look, I didn't come here to talk to you about Wayne . . .' she began, uncertain of where to go next.

Cole cut in before she could decide which way to tack. Curious and wary. 'Why did you come here?'

'I already told you. I came to ask if you left my purse at the club.'

'Do you have your precious purse back?'

'Yes.'

'Then what difference does it make?'

Cole stood jerkily and Miranda tried not to notice that his sweatpants pulled farther down as he stood, exposing a tan line and pale skin beneath. Her eyes lingered over the band of muscle above his hipbones and the indentation of his navel that made her think of a nail driven into a hard, corrugated board. She felt a tingling run between her own hipbones and settle between her thighs.

'I want to know if you had the purse with you when you found me in the courtyard last night.'

His face betraying no emotion, Cole walked over to his sophisticated stereo system, set into a large oak and glass entertainment center that rose nearly to the ceiling. He flipped a switch on the control panel and the voice of Nat King Cole filled the apartment. Then, with the grace and agitation of a caged lion, he walked over to the wall behind the couch. The tension that had built all night returned, knotting the muscles that flanked his spine. Turning away from her to look out the window, he didn't answer.

Determined to wait for his answer, Miranda began to look around the apartment for the first time. Amazingly, in the ten minutes she'd been there she hadn't noticed anything but Cole. Now she took in the beauty of the room. Structurally it was quite simple, a large room separated into three by virtue of furniture placement: a kitchen alcove and dining area and living area. Two entire walls were nothing but stucco and glass, a series of windows that began at hip level and rose to the ceiling.

Lightly stained oak hardwood covered the floor. But it was how it was decorated that so fascinated Miranda. He had merged the light simplicity of Scandinavian pieces in wood with upholstery in rich, heavy jewel tones – burgundy, emerald, lapis. A plain rectangular pine coffee table sat on an antique Turkish rug. A combination of obvious and mysterious. Simple and complicated. Miranda thought the home reflected the personality of its owner well. It also solved the mystery of who decorated Electric Blues.

Suddenly, Cole broke the silence, his voice soft. 'Yes. I was ready to leave and couldn't find you. Trent told me you and Tomori had gone off somewhere. I picked up your purse, hoped to find you and hoped you'd want to leave too. Slipping away seemed easier than having to say goodbye to everyone we knew at that damn party.'

He was watching her now from the window, the expression on his face unreadable.

186

She had her answer, but what did it mean? He could have fabricated that tale to convince her he didn't carry a gun. He certainly took long enough to answer her question with the truth. Mulling this over, she was startled when he spoke again, his voice even lower than before, his face turned back to the view of the city.

'Why did you carry a gun to the party?'

In that moment, her doubt was erased. The tables turned in an instant and she found herself scrambling to defend herself to him.

'I'm a private investigator. I'm on a case. I'm licensed to carry a gun. I'm –'

His quiet voice, volumes lower than hers, stopped her in midsentence. 'Scared. You don't trust me.'

Stunned, she didn't know how to answer. Disembodied words came out of her mouth without passing through her mind first.

'I want to.'

Slowly he turned back, their eyes connecting along with some inner, unreachable part of themselves. All the emotion they evoked in each other, that had run in an undercurrent between them since they'd met, that made them raw and unsteady, now pulled them together physically.

Meeting in the middle of the floor, their bodies joined quietly and calmly seeking something indescribable. Hands gentle and questing. Mouths sensitive and yearning. Somehow this was more powerful than the near violence of their last two kisses.

After what could have been minutes or hours, their lips drew apart – by just inches – while their bodies remained locked together. Miranda explored the muscles along his back. His skin felt like suede on stone. Her hands drifted down the small of his back, around to his waist, stopping at the waistband of his pants as if reaching an invisible barrier then traveling up, her fingers getting tangled in the curly mass of hair that covered his chest, over his nipples that hardened under her touch. A tortured groan

187

escaped his lips, vibrating the hair along the back of her neck.

Then his hands – that had stilled at her waist during the journey of hers – came alive. Finding their way under her turtleneck and sweater, his palms slid up along her ribs, his fingers probed the tight muscle on her back. His fingertips brushed the sensitive skin beneath her armpit and made her shiver. Her shivering grew stronger as he reached her breasts heavy and taut. With a featherlight touch he traced their curves and tested their weight. His thumbs barely brushed her nipples that were so tight they hurt. Then his hands drifted down to the dewy softness of her abdomen. The tingling within her pelvis became a burn. At her navel, his hands tiptoed around and down. They caressed the curve of her rump and gently pressed. Her hips responded in arching to his and the heat and hardness of his desire pushed through the thin fleece of his pants. Urgency was building in both of them. Slowly, his breath uneven, Cole pushed himself away from Miranda, and returned to the window.

Confused and feeling she'd lost part of herself, she asked in a desperate voice: 'Cole?'

His buttocks tightened in trying to keep his desire under control and his fingers, white-knuckled, gripped the windowsill.

Harshly, he whispered: 'Just leave. Go.'

His words had a physical effect on Miranda. She felt dizzy as if something had sucked all the oxygen from the room. He didn't want her, it was the second time he'd told her to leave since he'd opened the door. Shaking her head to try to find where her reason had gone, she wondered how she could have felt such strong emotions all by herself. Imagining he felt what she did.

Slowly and wordlessly, she turned around, fumbled for her case and shuffled to the door. His whole body throbbing with passion, Cole watched her reflection in the glass. He'd never wanted someone so much. He didn't just want to take her to bed, he wanted to share himself with her. His feelings stunned and scared him. He was vulnerable. For while he accused her of not trusting him, the fact was he didn't trust her either. That had never stopped him from sleeping with dozens of girls in college and while touring with the band, but it stopped him now.

As Cole heard the strains of *Unforgettable* drift from the stereo, he turned and studied her.

Miranda looked like a fire that had just been put out, ashen but, from somewhere underneath, still reluctantly glowing. It tugged at his heart. He'd expected her feisty spirit to ignite at his rejection, accusing him of being a tease and leaving in a fit. It would have been easier to see her go fighting. This was unbearable.

He caught her at the door, his hand reaching the brass knob just before hers.

Although he was not touching her anywhere, Miranda could feel the heat of his body through the back of her sweater and jeans. Afraid of what her own body would do if she moved, she stood still and waited for him to open the door.

He didn't. Seconds ticked by in slow motion. Finally, Miranda tried to gently brush his hand off the knob so she could turn it. But her touch was like a magnet and, from behind, she felt his body press up the length of her. Instinctively, Miranda pressed into him and felt a burning hardness dig into the small of her back. His lips drew to her ear.

'Christ, Miranda I just want you too much. But there's so much distrust surrounding us. I know it would be damned beautiful right now, but in a couple of hours, tonight or tomorrow, it would be ugly again. I couldn't stand that.'

'You're right.' Miranda knew it was true, but hated herself for saying it.

Cole closed his eyes and took in the scent of her. He had an idea, but before he could weigh the pros and cons, he'd blurted it out.

'I tell you what. I have to go out to the country to check on my dog and horses. You could come along and finish

189

those questions you started the other night. I know I wasn't very cooperative.' He paused and she was silent. 'If you don't feel comfortable with that, we could meet before the show tonight . . .'

'Okay.' Miranda's voice sounded weak to her ears. Cole took her shoulders and turned her around to face him. Inches away from his face was too much for Miranda. She stepped away, knocking into the metal coat rack causing it to wobble slightly.

'Okay. Which?'

'I'll go with you to the country. We'll take my car.' Miranda tried to tell herself she'd keep control that way and could leave if things got out of hand. Further rationalizing, she thought she could look for the camera and video equipment at his ranch.

Looking vaguely surprised by her decision, Cole disappeared into the bedroom, shutting the door behind him. While he was gone, Miranda did her duty by searching all evident drawers and kitchen cabinets for the blackmailer's equipment. Nothing. Relieved, she opened the last cabinet door and noticed some Waterford crystal wine glasses hidden behind a collection of aluminum pans, metal bowls and a cookie sheet.

It seemed monumentally incongruous, for the rest of his cabinets had been a shambles; odd numbers of cheap, mismatched dishes and glasses and only a single pot and frypan that Miranda guessed had seen more dust than burners in their lifetime. But the crystal was precisely arranged and a complete set of twelve. It must have cost at least eight hundred dollars and Miranda wondered what possessed him to buy it. Perhaps it was a gift. But for whom and for what?

Her head was still stuck in the cabinet, her backside in the air when she heard a sound behind her and started, bumping her head on the underside of the counter.

'That is way too tempting,' Cole laughed lasciviously. 'You'd better stand up quick before I have to go take another cold shower.'

Embarrassed by his words and uneasy at being caught, Miranda extracted her head from the cabinet, pulling her hair loose in the process. She felt completely ungraceful and felt her face growing flush.

Cole sucked in his breath and seriously considered jumping back under the icy stream of water that had restored his sanity and good humor. Standing there, sheepish and blushing with her hair a tangle around her face, Miranda was breathtaking. He knew she had no idea how irresistible she was. He felt himself growing hard again and thanked God his jeans were relatively tight.

'So, what are you doing spying in my cupboard?'

It took Miranda a half-beat to realize he was teasing her. She opened her mouth for a retort but had trouble forcing the words out. All she could think was she wished she'd been in the shower with him. His hair wet and slicked back, his face still dewy with moisture. He'd put on a red T-shirt under a thick plaid flannel overshirt, faded jeans and some old black roper boots with a serious history. He hadn't shaved.

Finally, Miranda found her voice, improvising. 'Haven't you ever heard the saying: "Know the kitchen, know the man"?'

'Can't say that I have,' Cole was clearly amused. 'So what do you know now that you've explored my deepest, darkest culinary secrets?'

'That you appear to be the stereotypical bachelor, undersupplied in cookery and what is there is obviously underused,' With mock seriousness, she surveyed him from head to toe and back again. 'Seemingly well fed, but apparently not from your own hand.'

'Hey,' Cole held up his hand in protest.

'But,' Miranda continued with dramatic flourish. 'A single mystery in these cabinets threatens to unravel the stereotype.'

Suddenly Cole became guarded, unsure now of where she was headed with this, even though her tone was still

191

teasing. She noticed the change and moved quickly to explain. She pointed at the open cabinet. 'The Waterford. It doesn't quite fit.'

His smile disappeared and he slammed the cabinet shut. Put off by his reaction, Miranda stepped back out of his way as he charged to the kitchen table and began throwing bills and newspaper around in a search for something. Finally finding his keys, he stuffed them in his pocket. He looked up to see her viewing him with confusion and regret. And immediately he was sorry. How did he expect her to trust him when he shut her out like that? He had to give trust to get it. Intellectually, he accepted that. Emotionally, he challenged it. He wasn't ready to share the hurt with anyone. But maybe he never would be ready, maybe he just had to do it.

'I bought it as a wedding present a long time ago.' Cole held her eyes. 'For my brother.'

Miranda felt like he was telling her more than he wanted to, but she took a gamble and asked for more. 'Why didn't you give it to him?'

'Good question. I'm not sure even I know the answer. I didn't go to the wedding. I was on the road. Well, hell, I wasn't really even invited.'

Miranda wanted to ask why but let him continue on his own. He bent down and began to collect the papers he had strewn about the floor in his search for the keys.

'My brother tracked me down, called me, and told me he got married. You know, if he told me her name I don't remember it or really anything about her.' That realization seemed to surprise him. 'Anyway, I bought the glasses and spent the next few years debating over whether to send them or not. Then I heard they split up, which made the question moot.'

Miranda thought about what the store clerk had told her about Crayne Traynor. Creepy. She'd said his wife had run off. Why? Miranda wondered. From this morning she knew what caused the rift between father and son, but now was curious about the relationship between the brothers.

They weren't close but did communicate, at least they did five years ago.

'Is he an older brother?'

'He's eight years older than I am.' Cole saw what was in her eyes and answered the unspoken question. 'I'll be twenty-nine in two weeks.'

Miranda smiled but tried to hide her disappointment as he stood up, indicating the conversation was over. She wanted to know more, but she resolved to be patient. Pushing him would be counter-productive.

'Let's go,' Cole invited as he opened the door. She followed him out and he locked it behind her. Then she remembered her car was in her office parking garage. Not wanting to waste anymore of the morning going to fetch it and trusting Cole more than she had an hour ago, she agreed to go with him in his car.

Miranda prayed her intution was not failing her this time.

CHAPTER 11

Soon they were headed back the way Miranda had come a few hours before. They sat in comfortable silence, both lost in their own thoughts. As they moved away from the city, flatland gave way to rolling hills that grew rockier and steeper the farther north they moved. The sun had warmed the clear day from cool to merely crisp and Miranda rolled her window down halfway to smell the cedar-lined air. The wind whipped her hair – now russet and gold in the sun – around her face. Cole smiled to himself at how free she looked. He'd dated women who had avoided wind because it mussed their hair or dried out their skin. Miranda seemed unconcerned about the damage the wind might do to her appearance. Maybe, Cole thought, being part of nature was more important. That evoked another inner smile.

At the exit to Boerne that Miranda had taken earlier that morning, Cole turned left instead of right and they traveled on in silence. Civilization was apparent along the road only in the occasional gravel driveway marked with a cattleguard and wrought iron arch proclaiming it to be 'Cedar Valley Ranch' or 'Home of the Smiths'. Miranda noticed a few large ranch houses perched on the top of hills, but they were set far-off the road.

Cole finally broke the silence.

'I thought you were going to finish your interview.'

'Oh, if you don't mind I think I'll enjoy the day a little longer.' Her smile lit up her face. 'I can't resist.'

'Neither can I,' Cole answered, although he was talking about something other than the weather. And, in the moment, he wished they could stay out in the country forever. Where everything seemed easier between them. Where he could have an uncomplicated courtship with a woman he was attracted to. Where cops weren't breathing down his neck. Where his partner wasn't being black-mailed. Where Cole could shake the feeling he was being hunted.

'You know, you can listen to music if you like,' Miranda offered generously.

Cole shook his head. 'Sometimes it's nice just to listen to the quiet.'

Miranda was pleasantly surprised. Somehow she ima-gined that a singer would want to be surrounded by music constantly. That he could appreciate silence lent him a new dimension. But, Miranda supposed, it wasn't really silent. The wind rushing through the car was actually loud and the stray sounds of birds and cows from outdoors made their own music.

Cole clicked on his blinker, although they had not passed one car on the road, and turned onto a gravel driveway that was marked only by a rusty cattleguard. They followed the path down through a canopy thick with cedars and live oaks. Under the trees there wasn't much but limestone rocks of varying sizes, which was why the Texas Hill Country was known more for cattle than crops. Feed was easier to produce than soil.

As they descended deeper into the valley, Miranda wondered if the driveway would lead to one of the homes she saw on the top of a hill. The view from there would be incredible. But a few moments later, Miranda saw a small log cabin ahead, partially hidden among the trees.

Cole was telling her some of what she already knew. 'I have a hundred-fifty acres, although I can ride about seven hundred. The owner of the adjoining property to the west lives in Houston and doesn't get here very often. He likes to think Bubba and I keep an eye on things for him.'

195

'Bubba?'

'A Texas cliche,' Cole admitted ruefully, 'but it fits. He's a good ole boy. His real name's Ray Schond. We've known each other since kindergarten, ran around together in high school. He's perennially down on his luck. Right now as a mechanic. He stays here as sort of a caretaker for me.'

'It's gorgeous here. And not really that far from town. Why don't you live out here full-time?'

Cole finally pulled the car to a stop next to a red Ford Explorer. He turned to look at her.

'Well, when I first moved back I had planned to, but Bubba had just been fired from his last job and I knew there was no way I could live with him. I also didn't have the heart to throw him out, so I heard about the apartment and thought it a good investment while Bubba got his life back together.'

Miranda got out of the car before Cole could come around to open the door. He seemed amused by that although he didn't say anything.

'Am I going to meet Bubba?' Miranda asked looking questioningly toward the house. She tried to ignore the disappointment that had lumped in her stomach.

'Oh, no. He's at work.' He nodded toward the Explorer. 'That's my car.'

Miranda followed Cole up to the house, still a little let down that it wasn't on the top of a hill. And all of a sudden she saw why. A stream that had been hidden among the cottonwoods and cedars came into view. It ran along and behind the cabin. The crystal clear water in it gurgled and bubbled with an unseen energy, leaving the limestone rocks on the bottom polished and shining in the streams of sunlight that penetrated the forest.

Cole came back down the steps to stand with Miranda. 'It's so charming,' she whispered as to not disturb the peaceful melody of the flowing water.

'When I was deciding where to build, I thought of the hill first. The view is spectacular. But this stream really

196

drew me. I felt . . .' Cole paused, searching for the right word to explain to this special woman who seemed to share many of his feelings. 'A kinship. It's like a friend.'

Miranda smiled in understanding. She too had always felt a strong attraction to water, whether it be ocean, rivers or even an indoor fountain. She remembered that he'd said his birthday was was in two weeks. A Scorpio. Water sign, like her. Never putting much stock in astrology before, Miranda found herself considering that perhaps there was something to it.

'When I want to see the view,' Cole continued, looking up toward the hilltop. 'I ride up there and it's almost more powerful that way. Being on horseback . . . having it suddenly unfold before me . . .' He paused, almost embarrassed at revealing a part of himself he had never shared with anyone before.

Out of nowhere came a crash in the woods and the sound of a small stampede. Miranda whirled around to her left and saw three magnificent horses galloping down the embankment with a golden retriever at their heels. All but one of the horses jumped the stream. The dog barked impatiently at the straggler and the horse finally picked her way across slowly.

Splashing happily alongside the horse, the dog waited until his equine charge was all the way across before he ran at full speed for the house. The horses were stopped short by a wooden fence, which the dog easily squeezed under, leaving the horses pawing and whinnying. Cole crouched down and the dog jumped into his arms, licking his face, his tail wagging so fast it looked like a blur.

Startled at first by the thundering hooves, Miranda started laughing now. The dog and horses seemed so happy to see Cole it was like he'd been gone for years.

Cole pulled his face from the licking dog long enough to make introductions. 'Miranda, this is Reggie. Reggie, Miranda.'

Reggie pointed his lolling tongue at Miranda and regarded her for a split second with warm brown eyes.

Cole held his breath, remembering the first time he met Sable, growling and trying to nose Cole away. While Reggie had never hurt her, he'd never liked her either. It was mutual, for Sable hated Reggie's sloppy tongue and protectiveness of Cole. She hadn't cared for the ranch either, so he'd only brought her out there twice and she had been nervous and tense. She refused to come after that.

But now, Reggie restarted his wagging tail and pranced over to Miranda to give her a kiss. She was given the canine stamp of approval and accepted his wet nose gracefully. She stroked his gleaming golden coat.

'He's great. Does he always round up the horses for you or was that a coincidence?'

'Actually he trained himself to do that. He hears my car and knows I'll go riding. He loves following along, so I think, to facilitate things, he gathers the group for me,' Cole smiled with pride.

'Smart boy.' Miranda gave him one last pat before following Cole into the house.

They passed an old-fashioned front porch with a swing and a set of mahogany-stained wicker chairs. Cole tested the brass knob of the heavy wood door. Finding it unlocked, he held it open for Miranda to go in first.

'Bubba never locks anything. He thinks the rest of the world is as honest as he is.'

Suddenly somber, Miranda answered: 'I wish it were.'

Stepping inside, Miranda looked around, and was instantly enchanted. The inside of the cabin continued the theme of the outdoors: rustic, roughhewn and masculine. It was, however, a masculinity that invited rather than repelled femininity. Miranda remembered the first time she stepped into Rick's apartment and felt unwelcome. Everything inside was so complete in its maleness. But Cole's home had a certain empty place on a wall, a space on the mantel, a chair that needed re-covering that seemed to be waiting for a soft touch. There was room here for a woman.

The walls were rough-wood panel. The floor in the main room, which opened up lodge-style, housed the living area, dining area, and kitchen and was wall-to-wall saltillo tile. The same red-gold tile covered the countertop and kitchen island. What appeared to be a single bedroom was set off to the right and carpeted. Another doorway on the opposite side led to another carpeted room. A cathedral ceiling gave the illusion of space. A limestone brick fireplace rose to the roof. Miranda could look straight ahead through a unique western version of French doors and see the back porch and into the stream below.

Although it was surrounded in dark wood, the room seemed to glow with light from windows that let in the outside. A thick, woven Indian rug was the centerpiece of the room, on which sat a haphazard collection of furniture. On the walls were Western and American Indian art pieces in a variety of mediums: beaten metal, sand, even oil paint on bark. One traditional canvas painting hung over the fireplace. If it wasn't a Georgia O'Keefe, it could have passed for one, Miranda thought.

A small round oak dining table was set off the kitchen and was cluttered in breakfast dishes and coffee cups. The sink was piled with empty containers and dishes too.

'Bubba's no housekeeper,' Miranda observed.

Cole shrugged and moved to the table and began clearing it off. Miranda pitched in to help. Cole dove his hands into the sink next. 'Why don't you ask your questions about the case now and we'll get it over with and have a nice afternoon.'

Miranda didn't answer right away, as she debated whether delving into the case now would ruin the day for good. She felt safe and content and was reluctant to arouse her own suspicions from the wraps she'd put them in during their drive.

'You do ride, don't you?'

Cole asked the question in such a way that Miranda felt like a 'no' answer might be a hanging offense. Laughing, she admitted to knowing how. 'But I haven't been on a horse since college.'

'Oh, it'll come back right away. Your hands, your legs, your seat, they all have incredible memories.'

They sure do, Miranda thought as she looked down at her palms and recalled what they'd felt when she and Cole had kissed that morning. The corded muscle. The suedey skin. She looked up at Cole, intent on his dishwashing, that errant lock of hair dancing over his forehead.

Oh, she did want to trust him . . .

Deciding that Cole was right, that they should get on with the questioning, Miranda tried to adjust her mindset. She dragged her attention away from the sexy way he cocked his head when he scrubbed a plate, to trying to figure out who was plotting to destroy Wayne Lambert's life.

'Who has access to the office at the club?'

She felt Cole's body tense slightly when their conversation turned from pleasure to business, but he answered without missing a beat. 'Supposedly, only Wayne, Trey and I do. We have keys, but it's never locked so you or anyone who's in the club, theoretically, could have access.'

'Great. That narrows it down. Who has a key to the front and back doors?'

'The three of us, plus Sable and Trent.' Cole was looking at her with questions swirling around in his head. With Herculean restraint, he kept them to himself.

'Tell me how long you've known Trent and Sable and how they got in with the band.'

'Well, Trent.' Cole began with the better of the two subjects. 'I met him my freshman year at the University of Texas. We sort of "found" each other at registration. Both of us were looking for a roommate, so we rented an apartment. It took us a whole week before we realized our mutual interest in music. Six months later, we had our first gig. He's from Sugarland. Has great parents. We stayed with them when we did a gig in Houston a couple of years ago.'

'So, you, Trent and Sable started the band?'

'No, actually Trent and I and another guy we hooked up with down on Sixth Street. One of the most talented bass guitarists I've ever run across . . .' Cole trailed off, lost in thought for a moment.

'He joined another band?'

'I don't know. One day Greg just disappeared. Greg Pittman was his name.' Cole paused again, clearly disturbed by the memory. 'Although we'd played together for a while I really didn't know much about him. He wasn't in school. He worked as a lunchtime waiter when we didn't have gigs. I talked to the restaurant after he didn't show and they hadn't heard from him. He was just gone without a word.

'The funny thing was, while he was a close-mouthed and private guy, he'd always been really dependable. And he was excited about the plans for going on the road.' Cole shook his head. 'Wonder where he is now.'

'How did you come across Sable?'

Cole knew he had to be careful what he said now. He planned to tell Miranda about his affair with Sable but somehow didn't feel this was the right time. Their truce was too tenuous.

'Sable was new to the bass guitar, and had nowhere near Greg's skill, but she was adequate and in the right place at the right time when we needed someone fast. She's really improved a great deal since, by sheer will more than talent,' Cole added as an afterthought.

'I really don't know anything about her family. In fact, she's probably more of an enigma than her predecessor. Maybe it's a trait of bass guitarists.' At least that much was true, Cole told himself, still a little guilty at not telling Miranda everything.

Miranda ignored his philosophical commentary, instead latching on to something he'd said earlier. 'So, you'd say Sable was lucky. I mean, if this guy had given you some notice and you'd auditioned guitarists she probably wouldn't have made it.'

'That's exactly right. As it was, Trent kept after me to do just that, but by that time Sable had learned how to play up to the audience. The guys lusted after her. The women hated her. All were fascinated. Some came to see the performance more than to hear the music. Trent and I learned how to compensate for her musical weaknesses and made it work for us. Our following grew and bookings for our tour – if we can use that lofty term for what we did on the road – went up when bars heard we had a girl in the group. Especially such a naughty girl.'

Miranda could see the logic in what Cole was saying. Sable was riveting, reminding Miranda of a shiny blue snake behind glass at the zoo. The only problem was she wasn't locked up. Miranda was beginning to think she should be.

Cole noticed a familiar look pass across Miranda's eyes. Suspicion. For a moment he felt a wave of panic, but it faded as he realized it was Sable and not him who was the object of that doubt. She's jealous, he decided. I was right not to tell her about Sable and me now.

Miranda was thinking the disappearance of the guitarist and Sable's sudden appearance in his place seemed more than coincidence. Intuitively, she sensed Cole was keeping something from her but chose not to push him at the moment.

The dishes had been dried and put away for a while although Miranda still gripped the damp dishtowel and Cole was absently wiping the tile countertop. Miranda hung the towel on the oven handle.

'Okay, you're off the hook for now. Let's go have a ride.' She showed more bravado than she felt.

Throwing the sponge toward the sink with exaggerated abandon, Cole grabbed her hand and led her out the back door. The cozy, unexpected gesture both took Miranda aback, while at the same time pleasing her. She felt like she was back in high school on a date with the hunky varsity quarterback.

They wove their way through roughhewn pine outdoor

furniture that looked homemade and down the steps. As they strolled along the creek, Miranda stifled the urge to skip and instead reached down and felt the clear water. It slid through her fingers like melted ice. Cole crept up behind her and pushed, grabbing her back to safety just before she pitched forward. Reggie barked happily at their silly human antics.

They finally made their way to the small barn. It was camouflaged so well by the thick cedars and live oaks that Miranda hadn't even seen it until they were virtually right on top of it. Three stalls were open to the fenced land too rocky and hilly to be called a pasture. A tackroom, long and skinny, ran the length of the stalls and was separated from them by a wide aisle. Bales of alfalfa hay were stacked at the far end of the aisle.

The horses, sensing a ride, were standing at the fence, pawing and whinnying. Halter in hand, Cole strode up to the largest horse, a sleek jet black Irish warmblood gelding that Miranda guessed stood near seventeen hands. His withers grazed Cole's shoulder.

'Hey, O'Malley.'

Miranda laughed. 'That's his name? That's the name of a jolly Irish bartender with a red face and a big belly, not the name of a glorious beast like that.'

'That was his name when I bought him. I just couldn't see making him get used to another one.'

The horse shoved his nose into the halter. Cole buckled it and led him over to the hitching post where he saddled him up. O'Malley was dancing impatiently. Scratching him on the withers, Cole talked to him in low tones to soothe him then turned to Miranda.

'Now, be honest. How much riding have you done?' Cole turned his gaze to the two remaining horses, both mares, as if considering which would suit her. He shaded his eyes from the sun. Something innately masculine in that movement sent a shiver of sexual awareness through Miranda. He turned his attention back to her.

'Well?'

She flushed slightly as if he could read her mind.

'Oh, ah, I showed up to second level dressage in college,' she admitted somewhat reluctantly.

'Ex-cuse me. Maybe you ought to be the one to ride O'Malley, then.'

Miranda glanced at the gelding, now jogging in place and shook her head emphatically, though smiling at his put-off tone.

'Alright, Rocky it is then.' He reached up and grabbed the dapple gray mare's mane and she followed him docilely out the gate and to the hitching post. There she stood while he fetched the bridle. Miranda enjoyed watching him work with the horses so easily, as if it were as natural to him as breathing. Then she remembered he'd grown up with it, probably sat a horse before he could walk.

Cole poked his head out of the tackroom. 'Miss Second Level Dressage, all I have are western saddles. Can you lower yourself this once?'

Miranda played along, answering with a haughty air. 'I suppose so.'

But when he came out, carrying the saddle, Miranda took it from him. 'Let me finish. I haven't helped at all.'

Cole protested but gave in, letting go of the heavy load. He was surprised Miranda handled it with such ease. She'd tightened up the cinch and hopped on before he could reach O'Malley.

Miranda heard a phone ringing and realized she'd left hers in the car when they'd gone into the house. Her beeper was at home. If it's Doug, he's going to be ticked, Miranda thought. But at the moment she didn't care.

'How did you get home last night, anyway? I was worried about you,' Cole called out to her back. He saw it stiffen slightly.

Miranda was glad he couldn't see her face. 'Oh, I ran into a friend who gave me a ride.' To his house, she kept to herself. She didn't want to get into Rick right now.

'Why is her name Rocky?' Miranda asked in a casual

attempt to change the subject. She stroked the dappled coat along the horse's shoulders.

'From the time she was born she could pick her way across the rocks better than a mountain goat. O'Malley here could win any race on the flat, but Rocky loses us in her dust going up or down a hill.'

At that, Miranda pressed the heel of her boot into Rocky's side and the quarter horse took off at a lope up the hill. Cole took off on the chase and Miranda urged Rocky into a gallop. Miranda used all her concentration to guide the horse around low-lying trees, dodging and ducking. Finally, the trees thinned and then cleared and they reached the top of the hill.

Her neck and flanks bathed in sweat, Rocky pulled up without a cue, apparently used to stopping at the peak. Exhilerated by the cool air and hard ride, Miranda absorbed the breathtaking view before her. Hill Country autumn. An undulating pallete of colors stretched out on all sides: the deep emerald of the evergreens, the maroon of the red oak, the lime of the mesquite, bone-like hunks of sun-bleached limestone. She could see the small town of Boerne in the distance, but it seemed as far away as another country.

Belatedly, she registered the labored breathing of O'Malley as Cole reined in beside her. No words were necessary and would have been superfluous. This scene spoke for itself. They stood there until the horses' breathing had returned to normal and the equine sweat had dried into salty waves on their necks.

Eventually, Cole clucked to O'Malley and led the way down the opposite side of the hill. This time Miranda followed without a race. They rode for another hour, then turned back toward the cabin. After pausing at the top of the hill for another look at the view, Rocky responded to an imperceptible cue from Miranda and took off headlong down the steep incline.

With a shake of his head, Cole laughed and urged O'Malley to follow. The gelding wanted to keep up but wanted to avoid stepping on any rocks more and that slowed his pace. Within a hundred yards, Cole could no longer see or hear Miranda or Rocky.

Miranda was determined to have Rocky unsaddled and rubbed down by the time Cole made it home. She was so preoccupied by that goal that she didn't notice a dark figure running through the woods to her left. But Rocky did and, now at a quick jog, the horse suddenly shied away. Miranda looked for the source of her fear just as the dark, hooded figure jumped into the path. Rocky whinnied and reared. Miranda lost her stirrups but gripped hard with her thighs. Hands reached out from the cloak and grabbed for the reins. Miranda wrenched them away and kicked Rocky, who leaped past the figure and headed for the stream at a gallop. Miranda felt her heart beating in her throat.

At the stream, Rocky stopped short and too late Miranda remembered that she was the horse which Reggie had to coax across the stream earlier. Miranda flew over her neck.

'Cole!' She screamed automatically in her terror. A jolt to her knee, her hip, her thigh. Her head hit something hard. Her world went dark.

Halfway up the hill, Cole heard the whinny. Pricking his ears nervously, O'Malley whinnied back. It made Cole's blood run cold. It wasn't her sound of greeting or play. It was her snake scream. Reggie, who'd taken off at the first whinny, was already out of sight. Not wanting him to get hurt, Cole tried in vain to call him back. Then the scream. His name carried through the thick brush. A branch raked his face. Cole didn't feel it. What he felt was the danger. It was palpable.

CHAPTER 12

The first thing she felt was the cold. Liquid cold. On her
skin, in her boots, weighing down her hair. She opened
her eyes and brushed away the wetness. Tried to focus.
Shapes and colors swam together like an impressionist
painting come alive. She felt a presence. Her horse?
Instead, a dark human form loomed above her. Mena-
cing. Miranda fought to regain her senses. Was it a dream?
She tried to sit up, to move away. She seemed frozen in
place.

Scream! Her mind commanded. Her mouth wouldn't
move. A hand gripped her shoulder roughly. Tried to pull
her up. She was limp. What was that? A noise getting
closer. The figure let go of her shoulder. Kicked at
something. Barking, growling. A coyote? A dog? Reggie! She heard something rip. The figure swore. Water
splashed into her face. The scene before her eyes blurred
again just as it had begun to clear. A strangled voice spoke
in her ear. What did it say? Everything went dark again . . .

Rocky had run to the barn. Cole could see her from his
vantage point, but he still couldn't see Miranda. Was she
safe in the barn? He didn't think she'd leave Rocky loose
and still tacked up. An experienced horsewoman wouldn't
do that. Rocky was trembling. Reggie was barking, not far
ahead. Cole urged O'Malley on. He turned when he
thought he saw something out of the corner of his eye.
Whipping his head around, he saw nothing but trees.
Then he saw her.

She was laying on her back in the ice-water of the stream. Her eyes closed, her body motionless.

'Oh God, let her be okay.'

He jumped off the black gelding and ran, tripping over rocks and roots, calling her name. Reggie stood next to her barking insistently. Cole jumped into the stream, wading through the thigh-deep water. Thank God her head had landed so near the bank, he thought. She could have drowned. Maybe she had anyway. Grabbing her under the arms he tried to haul her to dry ground. But her sweater, completely saturated, pulled her back down. Yanking harder, he dragged her onto the bank and began doing CPR before he realized she was already breathing. He cradled her in his arms.

'Randi, Randi. Wake up.' Desperately, he raised his voice. Reggie quieted and began licking Miranda's wet hand. 'Come back to me.'

Her fingers began to move under Reggie's warm tongue. She sighed deeply and her eyes fluttered open. Unseeing for a second, she struggled to focus. She heard a man's voice call her name and, instinctively, began to struggle.

'Miranda, stop fighting. It's alright. It's Cole. Relax.'

From somewhere deep in her subconscious, his soothing words and worried tone began to register. Her muscles slackened. She leaned against his chest and began to shiver.

'We have to get you inside. Can you walk?'

Miranda wanted to talk but couldn't find the breath to get the words out. '. . . have to catch him . . .'

'Miranda,' Cole interrupted, thinking she was hallucinating after her fall. 'We have to get you inside. Get you dry and warm. Then you can tell me.' Quickly, he heaved the sopping sweater off and left it on the bank. Her turtleneck had come with it and Cole tried to concentrate on the task at hand instead of the creamy skin and full breasts encased in a lacy peach bra. Gathering her in his arms, he hurried to the cabin. Reggie followed and settled patiently by the back door.

Inside, Cole set her on the couch and heard her wince. He wondered how badly she was hurt. Grabbing a well-worn Indian blanket, he laid it over her.

'Miranda, we need to get these clothes off you.' He began fumbling under the blanket for the button of her soggy jeans. His fingers began way off the mark, at the inseam of her right thigh. They slid up until the seams met. They found the base of her zipper and inched their way up. His thumb and forefinger released the button and eased the zipper open. His pinkie trailed along the satin panties, scorching the skin underneath,

A low moan escaped Miranda's lips.

'Oh,' Cole apologized, withdrawing his hands. 'I've hurt you.'

'It's alright, but I can do it,' Miranda wasn't about to admit her moan was not the result of pain but of pleasure.

Cole turned his attention to building a fire. Her hands took over where his left off, peeling away the wet jeans, panties and then her bra, leaving them in a pile by her feet.

By the time he turned around only her damp head peeked out the top of the blanket. He scooted her closer to the fire.

'Are you any warmer?'

Miranda nodded blankly. Studying her eyes, Cole could see her pupils weren't dilated. A good sign. Shock hadn't set in yet. Cole moved to the stove to heat water for tea. He busied himself with finding a tea bag and mug until the kettle began to whistle. He dipped the tea bag in and handed the mug to her.

'I'm going out to untack the horses. I won't be five minutes.' He threw off his wet flannel overshirt, but decided to wait to change his soaked jeans.

After Cole left, Miranda tried to regain her senses. Shivering under the blanket, she opened it up to let the fire's glow penetrate her skin. Hazy images swirled in her mind as she went back over what had happened. Rocky spooking. The black cloaked figure. Falling into the stream. The figure hostile and rough. Angry with Reggie. She could hear the barks she knew they'd been real, but the rest . . . Was it just her imagination? She hadn't had any sleep in thirty-six hours and she'd knocked her head pretty hard on the ground. He (it had been a man, hadn't it?) said something to her. What was it? And how long had she been unconscious before Cole appeared to rescue her.

Wrapping the scratchy blanket tightly around her, Miranda struggled up and shuffled over to the back door. There, she searched the woods for any sign of the figure she thought she had seen. It was quiet and still with sunlight streaking through the trees and bits of azure peeking through branches.

A scene in repose.

The creak of the front door made her jump and spin around.

'It's just me. Who were you expecting? The boogyman?' Cole's joking smirk faded at the starkly anxious look that passed across Miranda's face. He moved forward tentatively, still worried about the possibility of shock.

'What's wrong? Do you want to tell me what happened?'

'I . . . I'm not entirely sure what happened,' Miranda admitted.

Cole waited patiently while she made her way slowly back to the fire.

'We'd almost reached the creek when Rocky spooked.'

'At a snake?' Cole asked

'No . . .' Miranda considered whether to tell Cole of the images in her mind and risk him thinking her crazy or to lie and tell him she blacked out and didn't see anything. But the concern in his eyes urged her into honesty before she could debate the issue with herself any further.

'Things are a little hazy and confused, but this is what I remember: a figure in a dark hooded cloak ran up – from behind a tree – and tried to grab the reins at Rocky's neck. Rocky reared and bolted for the stream. She balked and I flew over her neck. I blacked out for . . . I don't know how long. When I woke up, the person was standing over me, trying to get me up. I remember being scared . . .'

210

'Did this person touch you?' Cole's tone was neutral. His eyes were not.

'Umm . . . on my shoulders. Then Reggie came up and started fighting with him. He was mad. The guy, that is. All of a sudden, he pushed me back into the water . . . my face got wet . . . he kicked water in my face, that's it!' Miranda brightened as the images grew clearer. Her brow furrowed again. 'He leaned down close to my face . . . no . . . more at my ear . . . and said something.'

Cole watched as her face drained of color.

'What?' he demanded with urgency.

'I can't remember,' Miranda whispered. 'I just know it terrified me. Then I blacked out again. The next thing I remember, you were there. Holding me.' She stopped as she felt a flush rising. She recalled the way Cole held her. The caressing way his voice called her name.

'You said "he". You're sure it was a man?'

'I can't be sure. The hood was pulled up over his head. I don't remember a face. The figure seemed big and the hands are a blur, so I couldn't say. The voice . . .' Miranda struggled with her psyche, 'was gravelly. Like it was being disguised. And something about it was familiar.' The last thought surprised her.

'Someone you knew?' Cole was growing more tense and agitated with every answer.

'No . . . I don't know. It's just too vague . . .' Miranda was becoming frustrated with her own confusion.

'Just one more question right now,' Cole promised. 'You said it was a cloak. Like a black cape?'

Miranda nodded vigorously. 'A cape! That's it exactly!'

With her answer Cole's face became hard, making Miranda cringe inwardly.

At first, Cole believed Miranda's story to be a hallucination. But the more she said the more plausible it became. Then it became all too familiar.

Cole hadn't noticed that he'd frightened Miranda. So when he touched her arm and she jumped again, he attributed it to leftover nerves. 'Why don't you rest?

211

Come on,' he took her arm and propelled her to his bedroom. As she sat on the bed, he pulled out a T-shirt and sweat pants from his dresser, laid them next to her and ordered her to sleep. Distracted, he closed the curtains and shut the door behind him without another word.

Miranda had no intention of sleeping. Cole's reaction to what happened in the woods was troubling. The familiarity of her attacker's voice was unsettling. And there was something nagging at her. A connection begging to be made.

She let the blanket drop to the carpet and, for the first time since her spill, she checked the damage. Her right hip and thigh were bruising already, but that was about it. She found a brush and ran it through her nearly dry hair. The back of her head was tender, but no knot. She went to the bathroom and ran a warm bath and decided she'd gotten off lightly, remembering her junior year in high school when her horse had refused a fence and she'd flown headlong into the oxer. She'd broken a rib and the accompanying concussion had caused temporary amnesia.

Toweling off quickly after her bath she put the borrowed clothes on. They smelled like Cole. She found herself becoming aroused at the musky masculine essence. A heady combination of fresh split oak and the air washed clean by rain. Her bare nipples rubbed against the soft cotton. The fleece ruffled her pubic hair. She threw herself on the bed and lay still, trying to stay her sudden and poorly timed craving.

Trying to distract herself, she looked around the room. Here too, the combination of the windows and decor brought the outside in; plush evergreen carpet, a walnut stained ceiling fan, a rust and evergreen canvas plaid chair and an ivory-and-evergreen down comforter covered the high four-poster bed that looked so old and banged up Miranda wondered sarcastically how much action it had seen. The dresser, equally as worn, needed refinishing but showed promise in an exquisite beveled mirror and fine grained wood. The art on the walls was an eclectic blend of professional and amateur: a fine charcoal sketch of a cattle round-up, an ordinary framed photograph of O'Malley and a wood-on-wood wall sculpture of a horse's profile that looked like Cole's junior high woodshop project.

Miranda closed her burning eyes for a moment. Before she could fight it, she slipped into sleep.

A few minutes later Cole knocked on the bedroom door and getting no answer, peeked in. Her face was angelic, so relaxed, so at peace.

Closing the door, he went out on the back porch. At the creek, he searched for proof that the story Miranda told was true. He knew it wasn't coincidence. Someone was setting him up, either Miranda or the ghost from his past. But what would Miranda have to gain from playing mind games by renewing an old nightmare? Nothing. It didn't have anything to do with her blackmail case. But it might have everything to do with the rapes. So she had nothing to gain, unless she was working with the police. But why would she do that and how would they have found out about that night almost ten years ago?

Cole had ignored Reggie, who'd followed him, whining slightly, from the porch down to the bank. The dog now began to whine loudly and poked at Cole's hand with his nose. Finally looking down, Cole patted his golden head.

'What's wrong, boy?'

Then he saw what Reggie had carried in his mouth, a piece of black material. Reggie dropped it into Cole's hand and then turned and began to bark at the woods. Cole fingered the wool/polyester that had apparently been ripped from the corner of something. A cape?

The years fell away and Cole remembered the heady feeling he got when he wore the heavy black cape. Suddenly, he was embarrassed at his wild suspicion of Miranda. What she'd described was true. But what did it mean?

He called Reggie back and hurried to the cabin. He didn't want to leave Miranda alone. Just then a piercing

213

scream came from his bedroom and shot through the woods. Running into the house, he burst through the bedroom door and saw her sitting bolt upright in the bed, her eyes wide with terror, her body shaking. Seeing she wasn't quite awake, he clasped her tightly in his arms and made a visual check of the room to be sure no one was there. It looked just as he had left it.

'It's okay. You're alright,' Cole crooned softly. He could feel Miranda's heart pounding against her ribs.

Still drugged with sleep, she was struggling to make sense of the images that had haunted her in her slumber. The caped figure with a dark chasm instead of a face, behind trees watching her on their horseback ride, in the car behind her on the freeway, outside her window at her townhouse. Her subconscious had clearly exaggerated, but who was to say that she wasn't being watched and followed?

'He said something to me.' Miranda hadn't realized she'd spoken and was startled when Cole asked: 'Who?'

'The man who spooked Rocky. He kept whispering . . . in a melancholy way. "I'm watching you." Then his voice changed . . . turned mean, threatening. He said: "I will take you away".'

Sudden realization dawned on Miranda and she spoke with fervor. 'That is exactly what he said when he leaned over me in the creek: 'I will take you away'. But from what? What does that mean?'

Miranda felt an involuntary shiver rack her body. The sense she'd had earlier – that the voice had a familiar ring to it – was getting stronger. Cole continued to stroke her hair.

She pushed back and looked him in the eye. 'Do you think I'm crazy?'

Cole answered solemnly, drawing her into endlessly deep gray eyes. 'No, I don't think you're crazy.'

They sat there studying each other for several minutes. Her nightmare had left Miranda's cheeks flushed. Her hair was in a tumble about her face and shoulders. Her eyes, now more green than blue, reflected the colors in the room. His old T-shirt molded tightly to her gloriously rounded breasts and fell away to hide her small waist.

Cole's face looked tanner after their morning ride, his razor stubble darker, thicker. Worry lines ran down his forehead to just between his expressive eyebrows. He kept running his long fingers through his hair. The front of his T-shirt and his jeans were still damp from carrying her from the creek, the brown hair on his chest made more visible underneath.

His proximity ignited the desire she thought she'd quelled. Miranda took a deep breath to try to calm her beating heart. She motioned to his wet shirt. 'You should change out of those clothes before you get a chill.'

Cole's eyes held hers.

She stood up. 'I'll go.'

'No,' Cole answered quickly as he grabbed her hands in a light grasp. 'You're the one who might be getting a chill.' His voice was teasing and he couldn't resist letting his eyes linger on her now taut nipples.

Miranda glared at him in affected reproach. She tried to yank her hands away. He held tighter.

His voice was raw and full of sex. 'You don't want to go, do you?'

Angry with herself for letting him see how much she wanted him, Miranda squeezed her eyes shut. Maybe he'd disappear and she wouldn't have to find the strength to lie. But when she opened her eyes again, he was still sitting there, still holding her hands in his sensitive yet powerful ones. She could see his desire matched her own and she forgot she ever wanted to lie.

'No, I don't want to go.'

Her answer ignited the smoldering in his eyes, and slowly he rose. Gently he cupped her face in his hands and his mouth tasted hers. His more mobile lips molded to her softer ones, his rough stubble teasing and tickling. She felt herself pressing her breasts into his chest, her hips arching invitingly into his. His hands slid into her hair as his lips nibbled a path down the side of her neck, across her collarbone and back the other side to her bare earlobe. Her body stayed still, letting his ministrations send tiny jabs of pleasure and pain through her.

Her arms finally awoke from their sweet paralysis and tentatively slid along the side of his hips. His lips parted in a moan and again found her mouth, this time his tongue explored the contours and flavor of her lips until she could stand it no longer. Her mouth opened to invite his tongue in with her own and together they moved in a dance that somehow was both natural and erotic.

Miranda's nerve endings were tingling and her mind was losing focus. Her hands began to move without being told, under his shirt, exploring the muscles of his back, his abdomen, his chest. Bravely they reached just beneath the top of his jeans and traced the mark of the waistband, part of her wanting to whip him into the frenzy he had her in. His breath was coming in short pants now, his erection straining his zipper so hard that Miranda was both fascinated and frightened by the power that was barely contained there.

With a tenderness that belied the urgency his body was feeling, Cole lifted her shirt. His knuckles just grazed the silken skin along her ribcage. She sighed softly as he pulled the shirt over her head, her hair falling on her bare shoulders in an auburn cascade.

She stood, surprised to feel pride under his gaze instead of uncomfortable embarrassment. His mouth quirked into a half smile that was both naughty and nice. Just the tips of his fingers lightly ran from the hollow at her throat, through her cleavage, around the swell of her full breasts. Like lascivious spiders his fingertips tickled their way to the sensitive center, meeting at the nipples that Miranda thought couldn't get any tighter. A small shiver of desire racked her body.

Then it was Miranda's turn. With a sense of disembodied amazement she felt herself pull his shirt off, then boldly reach for the top button of his jeans. His hand caught hers and held it still.

'Not yet,' he begged thickly.

Instead, his head bent to taste her nipples, teeth and tongue teasing as her breasts rose and fell with quickening breaths. Then down it moved along the center line of the tender skin of her abdomen. The heat of her desire hurried in front of his mouth, ducking beneath the mound of red brown hair and into where she wanted him to be. Now.

Feeling what she craved, but determined not to rush, Cole deliberately eased to his knees and gently tugged her sweatpants to her ankles. She kicked them off impatiently and he chuckled, deep and low, his breath on her tightly curled hair. Finding her already extremely hot and wet, he teased there only for a moment then nibbled the delicate skin of her inner thigh, in the hollow of her knee, at her sweet tender toes.

Heavy lidded eyes looked up at her with a grin so mischievious, Miranda laughed. He rose from his suppli-cant position and hugged her to him, crushing her breasts to his hard, hairy chest as she raked her fingernails across his back.

'Okay,' he whispered hoarsely. 'Before you do permanent damage.'

Cole held his hand up in surrender and Miranda quickly released his button and zipper, but instead of wriggling out of the jeans as she'd expected, he waited, one eyebrow arched in a playful challenge. She took it and eased to her knees, teasing his hardness with a fingernail, kissing lightly, then as he had done, moving down his muscled legs to ankles and those sexy feet.

Cole pushed her onto the bed and time lost all meaning. They explored each other with hands and mouths, fin-gertips and tongues until their passion had built into a crescendo. Cole slipped into inviting legs that wrapped around his hips, pushing him toward the source of her desire. But even after he had discreetly slipped on his condom he teased around her white-hot center. The already throbbing point of her sex swelled even more at the touch of his sheathed point.

Miranda arched her neck, throwing her head deep into the softness of the down pillow. Her breasts jutted upward and into his eager mouth.

'Cole, you can't torture me anymore,' Miranda panted. He opened his mouth, his tongue flicking her nipple as he let it go. Miranda gasped.

'You know what they say, "No pain, no gain",' he murmured as his chest slid over her bare stomach and breasts until his lips reached hers. His tongue teased hers, feinting and jabbing playfully as his slick hardness pushed right at the entrance to her core. With an urgent moan, Miranda dug her heels into the backs of his rock-hard thighs. Her hands slid down his back to urgently knead his buttocks. But he resisted with muscles stretched so tight they seemed to be at breaking point.

Their standoff didn't last long until both knew it was time. With a rumble of intense pleasure escaping his lips, Cole slipped inside her molten den of desire. He plunged again and again to meet the undulating arch of her hips. Miranda felt herself rushing deep into an abyss where it seemed the skin of their bodies melted into a single soul. Together the waves of release shook them.

But they both knew it wasn't over. For them, this had just begun.

'Randi . . .' he said in his husky whisper.

She started to cry. 'No one has ever called me that but my sister. And my mother . . .'

'If you don't want me to . . .' he began tentatively, kissing a tear.

'No, those are the only people who've truly loved me. The only people I've ever really trusted. I want you to call me that.' Just then Cole felt he'd been given a greater gift than the one she'd given him with her body. They held each other until they both drifted off to sleep.

An hour later, Cole roused himself and slipped carefully from under the covers. Seeing Miranda virtually glowing in her sleep, her skin the color of blushing ivory, made him

218

smile and feel a strange sense of contentment. He glanced at the clock and saw it was already four o'clock. They'd have time for an early supper before they had to head back to town for his show. He pulled on some old boxer shorts, went to the kitchen and opened the refrigerator. The one thing Bubba was good at was eating and he always had the cabin well-stocked. Cole found two ribeye steaks, threw them on the indoor grill and put a decent salad together.

The smell of grilled beef drifted into the bedroom and the growling of Miranda's stomach woke her. She opened her eyes feeling sinfully sated. She threw the covers back and, naked, walked to the closet, hesitantly peeking in. Finding a terrycloth robe, she put it on and tied the sash around her waist and followed the smell of cooking beef out of the bedroom.

She watched Cole chopping tomatoes for the salad, savoring the way his muscles bunched as he wielded the knife and jealous of the way his fingers held the tender fruit. Miranda laughed inwardly at herself, unable to believe anyone could make her feel jealous of a tomato. Feeling eyes on him, he turned, saw her and smiled.

'Hungry?'

'I didn't think I was until I saw you,' Miranda admitted slyly.

'Well, if we eat quick, we might have time for dessert. That is, if you're still hungry for it.'

'Oh, I'm sure I will be.' Miranda's eyes twinkled.

Cole had the newly cleaned kitchen table set, so he plunked a steak on each plate along with the big bowl of salad and they sat down to a feast. He poured them each a glass of Merlot.

Miranda picked hers up and ran the tip of her tongue around the lip of the glass. Cole blew out a breath as he felt the immediate tightening in his groin. His fingertip grazed her jawline as he returned the wine bottle to the kitchen counter.

'So,' Cole asked, forcing a conversational tone. 'Was the pain worth the gain?'

'You don't know how much,' Miranda breathed, as she watched him extract the cork from the corkscrew.

'Oh, I bet I do,' he said as he slipped the cork back into the wine bottle.

Fighting back the blush that threatened to creep up her neck, Miranda sat down at the table.

Cole studiously avoided touching her again, knowing if he did they would never get to their meal. As it was, he could hardly concentrate on his food. Even in his bulky robe, Miranda was incredibly sexy. The effortless grace of her movements, from the tilt of her jaw when she sipped her wine to the way she stopped eating to tie her hair in a chignon on top of her head all combined to give him both a sense of joy at being in her presence and a sense of restlessness at wanting to be part of her again.

When they finished eating and Miranda had started washing dishes, Cole moved up behind her, his hands on her buttocks, his breath on her neck.

'Leave those. Bubba owes us one.'

His hands reached around to untie her sash as he rubbed his pulsing hardness against her back. She arched her head back against his shoulder, exposing her neck for him. He ravaged it with passionate kisses, his hips pressing her urgently against the counter. He grabbed for her bare breasts and kneaded them. For a split second, as she clung, white-knuckled, to the tile, she thought he would take her right there. And she knew she wouldn't have stopped him. Wouldn't have wanted to stop him.

Corralling his reluctant body instead, Cole turned her around and kissed her long, slowly and passionately.

Unwilling to give up their embrace, but both needing to become part of each other more quickly than the last time, they sidled to the carpet by the fire. There, Cole lay down, pulling Miranda on top of him. Watching her face in the firelight he saw it become incandescent the moment they both flew free.

Later, during the foreplay they had saved for afterwards, Miranda spoke with disbelief.

'The first time I thought . . . just it had been so long for me since I . . . maybe I thought I was imagining how special it felt between us.' She stopped, embarrassed, but the strength of his steady gray gaze forced her to continue.

'Special?' Cole urged gently as he kissed the tip of her nose.

'You know. It felt so magical.' The flames behind her hair turned it into a mass of burning liquid gold. Cole struggled to concentrate on what she was saying. 'It felt like something once-in-a-lifetime. Something I would be incredibly lucky to experience twice.'

'And now? What do you think?' His eyes danced although he felt a lump forming in his throat. 'That it's old hat?'

'No, I think I might even be lucky enough to feel that special three times,' Miranda teased back, as her hand moved down his contoured chest.

Cole's muscles tightened under her touch. 'Three times in one day? My, you are a lucky woman.'

Knowing it was time to go, but unable to resist, Cole pulled Miranda's face to his. One more time.

CHAPTER 13

Cole pulled his sportscar out onto the road just as the sun was setting. A few clouds had moved in during the afternoon to make the sunset just that much more vibrant. The sun's rays penetrated the darkening sky to outline the puffy cumulous clouds in red, orange and gold.

With the sun went any vestiges of warmth and the air was left sharp with chill. Miranda's sweater had not dried by the time they had to leave the cabin so she had borrowed a well-worn beige fisherman's sweater of Cole's, which she wore now, over her turtleneck. 'I think I'm going to like this – you wearing my clothes,' he'd said as he nuzzled her neck. Suddenly he felt very possessive.

'Why? Because it leaves so much to the imagination?' Miranda teased as she flopped the loose knit around her waist.

His hands had slid down to trace the outline of her breasts. 'Not everything is left to the imagination. Plus, I have a pretty good one.'

She had sniffed at the sleeve. 'It smells like you. I probably won't be able to have a rational thought until I take it off.'

'Promise?' Cole had grinned.

Cole had put on his black alligator boots, size 12, Miranda had noticed, a black sweatshirt and a pair of faded jeans tighter than any she'd seen him wear. 'If I'm going to have to watch you all night, I'd better wear these.'

Now, as the high beam headlights cut a swath through

the deepening darkness, Miranda wanted to know everything about Cole. Not only the mysteries, but the ordinary things. She started with those and began 'twenty questions'. He agreed to comply, but only if she answered the same question for him.

'Favorite color and why?'

'I have two: black and white. Black because it is sensual and mysterious and deep. White because it is clean, light and direct. They are opposites yet are alike in a way no other colors are.' He clarified at her questioning look. 'They are both true. There can be no shades of either. No light black or dark black. No pale white or deep white. It's just white and black.'

Miranda mulled this over until he demanded: 'And yours?'

'Red. It's passionate. It's happy, angry, impatient, sexy, but most of all it's alive. Red makes you feel. You can't look at it and be impartial. You hate it or love it. It demands attention, demands a response.'

Cole cocked his eyebrow, but said nothing.

They talked about their first loves. Cole's was Marsha Reininger in the eighth grade. He'd thought himself in love with her since the sixth grade. She was his first kiss and she had braces which made for an unromantic, rather painful, sloppy event. Cole thought that was how kissing was and resolved not to do it again ever until two weeks later when Treena Wadkins cornered him at the lockers and showed him how it was really done. That was so wonderful it scared him to death. He was so confused that he didn't ask a girl on a date until a year and a half later.

Miranda was laughing as she started her story. She was in the ninth grade, by her account a gangly girl with red hair who was slower than her classmates to mature physically. For some reason that Miranda still couldn't fathom, the drop-dead gorgeous quarterback on the junior varsity team was after her. He hinted around but never asked her for a date. But a sensitive, not-bad-looking honor-roll student in her journalism class invited her to the movies.

223

Impressed by his bravery she said yes. The quarterback found out and picked a fight with the aspiring journalist. The nice guy lost but they still went on their date, his black eye and all. The sparks didn't fly, but they stayed best friends through high school.

'He's an anchor in Salt Lake City now. We still keep in touch through rather sporadic letters.'

Cole tried to stifle the small twinge of jealousy he felt knowing Miranda might be close to another man, even platonically. 'So, you never dated the quarterback?'

'No, thank goodness. He plays with the Washington Redskins now. Can you imagine if we'd gotten married? As a Cowboys fan, I would've had to divorce him for "irreconcilable differences".'

Cole chuckled in understanding. 'You certainly have famous classmates.'

Miranda looked at him, thought of the girl he was accused of attacking and her exit for Hollywood, and asked: 'How about you? Any of the kids you went to school with hit fame and fortune? Besides you, of course.'

Cole's face became brooding in the dark car. He wondered fleetingly whether her question was as guileless as it seemed. 'Not that I know of.'

Miranda jumped in surprise when Cole honked his horn at a beat-up blue pick-up truck coming toward them on the road. An arm sticking out of the window waved.

'That was Bubba,' Cole explained.

Miranda glanced briefly in the rearview miror at the truck's red tail lights and noticed another car's headlights about a quarter mile behind them, then continued her questioning.

'Did you go to public school?'

'Yes. Boerne. My folks had enough money for private school, but my father thought the only way to grow up to be a normal healthy Texas boy was to go public, with football and all that.'

Miranda could hear the hostility in his voice. 'Did you ever play football?'

'No. I was a forward on the basketball team, hurdler on the track team, third baseman on the baseball team but no football. Spring practice coincided with rehearsals for the annual school musical and I made my choice. My father never accepted that. Period.'

'He didn't like you singing or acting?'

'No, it's more like he hated the idea of me singing and acting. It was sissy, no future in it. Furthermore, I was born and bred to run a ranch, I couldn't do all that traveling around like some glorified barfly. My father considered music a waste of time, both making it and listening to it.' His voice adopted an exaggerated drawl. '"Music is a product of oversexed, untalented junkies with overactive imaginations who pander to the lowest common denominator in society. No boy of mine is gettin' mixed up with that horseshit."'

Cole had nearly spat out his last words. It was clear his father's attitude still hurt him.

'He told you that?'

'Not quite so eloquently. He's a redneck. Being rich doesn't make him any less ignorant. Anyway, that was the gist of his attitude when I was growing up.'

'That was a long time ago, maybe he's changed his mind.'

'I doubt it. But I haven't talked to him in almost ten years, so who knows?' A mask descended over his face. It grew cold and unforgiving. 'I was given an ultimatum. Basically it was: your music or your family. You see which I chose.'

Miranda remembered what Elaine and Deanna told her this morning and filled in some of the blanks Cole left. She felt like he couldn't be pushed far back onto this memory lane. But she knew she had to try. Carefully.

'Your mother . . . she must have been heartbroken.'

Cole sighed and as he did, his face softened. 'She is. Most of all I hate what he's done to her. I haven't talked to her in all that time, either, although she's tried. I just won't put her in the position of choosing him or me. He'd do that to her if he ever found out she'd contacted me. This way she won't have to choose, I've done it for her.

'She changed the ownership of that land where my cabin is from her name to mine while I was a sophomore in college. She knew that was all she had to give me. It was the first piece of land my great-grandfather owned when he moved to Texas. Later he amassed a small fortune through land speculation around the Hill Country. What my father and mother have now is what's left of that fortune. What my father hasn't squandered away, my brother will. He's running the ranch, supposedly, and from what I hear the bills are mounting.'

Cole seemed lost in thought for a few moments and Miranda left him in his reverie.

Soon, he began talking again, but almost to himself. 'You know, she has always been a sweet, generous, caring person and she used to fight for the people she loved. I remember, when I was little, she would stand up for my brother when my father picked on him. For some reason, Crayne was always the whipping boy. My father beat him with a belt, but more often with his words. He never hit me. Now that I think about it, Crayne should have resented me but I think he tried hard not to. Anyway by the time I was four, my father had sucked all the strength from my mother and she stopped challenging him.

'What really amazes me is Crayne still lives on the ranch with them. If I were him, I'd put as much space as I could between me and that power-hungry bastard.'

'What is your brother like?' Miranda asked quietly, disturbed by the look of raw emotion in Cole's eyes.

'Crayne was a great big brother when I was little. He was my idol. I walked the way he walked, talked the way he talked and rode the way he rode. He wasn't given the time for sports in school because Dad made him come home and work on the ranch so he was around a lot. He used to encourage me with my music. Crayne even gave me my first guitar. I still have it.

226

'He never went to college and I don't really know why. I was around eleven then and I didn't notice that he stayed home when his friends, what few he had, left for various universities. By the time I was going into high school he'd turned sullen, secretive and generally unhappy. Always a loner, he'd become a virtual hermit. All this I saw in retrospect, because at the time I was so busy with sports, music, school and girls that I didn't have time for my brother.'

'Does he look like you?'

'People used to say so. We both take after my mother, she has the Irish and Scandinavian blood. My father is dark, some kind of English-German, mutt combination. Crayne's no more than an inch shorter than I am and used to be a little stockier, not much though. He has brown eyes. But, man, we really sound alike. I used to practice his voice for hours when I was a kid. I thought it was so cool – raspy and old-movie-cowboy tough. We used to tease Mom, calling her and making her guess who was who. Even she couldn't tell.'

'So you haven't talked to him since he got married?'

'Yeah. He sounded really happy then. I should have sent that gift. Oh well . . .'

They were quiet for a moment while he manuevered from the on ramp to Interstate 10. Then Cole moved to divert the conversation away from his life and to hers. 'From what I heard last night your dad isn't a model parent either.'

'From what you overheard, you mean,' Miranda stalled.

'Again, I apologize for my lamentable moral error. I realize now I should have cleared my throat or somehow announced my presence. Instead, I allowed my desire to hear the secrets of my fascinating date to overcome my good judgement. Please forgive me, dear lady.'

Cole reached over for long graceful fingers and brought them to his mouth in a chaste kiss of forgiveness. But instead of letting her fingers go, he grabbed them in his mouth, sucking and tickling with his tongue.

'Rhett Butler meets Lady Chatterly's lover,' Miranda laughed, pulling her hand away as the feel of the inside of his mouth began to rekindle her passion.

'If you are going to deny me that, then you must distract me with conversation,' Cole continued in character.

Miranda humored him with the condensed version of her life story. 'We were the perfect little family, a mommy, a daddy, two girls and a boy, a dog and a cat. We lived in Rosenberg, south of Houston. My parents had a fairytale love for each other, which filled everything in our lives with a kind of radiance. Even then I think we knew Mom came first with Dad. If the ship was sinking, she would be the first he'd save. With Mom you never got that impression, it was more like she had enough love to go around. Twice. Dad was there for school plays and ballet recitals and softball games. We took trips together.

'Then, when I was ten, my mother died in a car accident. Dad went into a sort of emotional paralysis. He walked around as if he were sleepwalking. My sister Melanie took over the family. Because of us, she chose to stay near home and went to college in Houston even though she had good enough grades to get in at most any college in the country.

'Dad never allowed himself to love or care again, as if Mom took all the love he had with him to her grave. I realize now he's afraid of being hurt again, but that didn't make it any easier for me as a child. Sometimes I think it would have been better if he had abandoned us. Because he was there, physically, we – at least my little brother and I – were always hoping he would someday just wrap us up in his arms and tell us he loved us. It never happened. The most we got was an absent pat on the head. Eventually, he started staying away for long periods on business and I guess he finally did abandon us. But it was long and painful . . .'

'What about your sister and brother? You see them often?'

'Not as often as I'd like. My sister is business manager at

a newspaper in Boston. She's great, except for being a workaholic. Who can blame her? It's how she coped all those years. And my brother, Mark . . . well, he suffered the most from the loss of our parents. He was so young then.

'He's a professional thrillseeker. Takes people on thrill tours, anything life-threatening qualifies. He avoids attachments, personal, professional, physical, emotional. But I know he loves me, wherever he is.'

'Where is your father now?'

Miranda shrugged. 'He doesn't keep in touch.'

Cole opened his mouth to ask another question, but she held up her hands. 'No more. I've given you enough revelations for one day.'

'Okay,' he conceded. 'But, I'm warning you, I'm going to start up again tomorrow.'

She answered with a grin and was struck with a giddy feeling of happiness that there would be a tomorrow they would share.

Cole stole a sideways glance at Miranda. *God, she was beautiful.* It wasn't her high cheekbones or flawless skin that made him think that, but the sweep of her lashes, the slight upturn the edges of her mouth took when her face was in repose.

They'd just crossed the city limits and the neon signs of city businesses and restaurants were becoming more frequent. Miranda looked idly in the rearview mirror and noticed the same set of headlights she'd seen just after they left the cabin. It certainly wouldn't be much of a coincidence that the driver would also be headed for San Antonio, but it would be unusual that they also would be going eighty miles an hour the whole way. It was undoubtedly the police tail. Miranda had forgotten about it, and now she wondered how closely they'd been tailed. Surely not onto the ranch property. He must have stayed out on the road. Right?

Miranda began to tense in her seat, although Cole seemed not to notice. Was that incident in the woods one of Rick's mindgames? Suddenly Miranda remembered what Elaine had told her about the high school attack. The attacker had dressed in his costume for *Phantom of the Opera*. That would be a hooded cape! But what did that mean? The one who attacked the girl then had returned to haunt her now? Seemed a stretch. With her blackouts, she had no idea how long the whole incident had taken. Could Cole have planned it, let her get ahead and then ambushed her? No! She told herself I trust him. Don't I?

Oblivious to her new uncertainty, Cole popped the Lyle Lovett tape out and tuned into a newsradio station. The weatherman was predicting the first freeze of the season for the coming weekend. The Spurs were undefeated two weeks into the regular season.

'And now updating our top story this hour: another young woman has fallen victim to the Riverwalk Rapist.' Miranda saw Cole grip the steering wheel tighter. 'Sources tell WOAI that she is a young socialite and daughter of a well-known Alamo Heights citizen who was attending a charity function last night. She got separated from her escort and was attacked near the Riverwalk.' Cole turned to Miranda. She met his gaze that was almost desperate.

The radio continued. 'Her escort, whose name is also being withheld by police, rescued the victim as she was being taken into an alley. The suspect, fitting the description of the man police are looking for for two previous rapes, fled on foot. Details on the story at the top of the hour.'

Cole murmured. 'It's Kitty.'

'What?' Miranda asked, dumbfounded.

'I just have this . . . awful . . . premonition,' Cole said, half to himself.

'But there were at least a hundred women at that party that could be called "socialites" and daughters of well known Alamo Heights citizens,' Miranda reasoned weakly.

Cole didn't respond but suddenly made a decision and

230

cut across three lanes of traffic to take the next exit. Within ten minutes of running yellow lights and whipping in and out of traffic they made their way to Broadway and then onto a side street. A moment later they pulled up in front of a mansion. Miranda assumed this was Kitty Alexander's home and chose not to wonder how Cole would know how to find it. Tall columns painted a blinding white held up two stories of wide southern porches. The grounds were so green and well manicured that the foliage and flowers looked fake. Despite the obvious charm of the architecture, the whole effect was sterile and hygenic. It was too clean, too perfect. It looked unlived in and unwelcoming.

Miranda laid her hand on Cole's arm as he moved to open his door. 'I'll wait here for you.'

He merely nodded with distraction and worry and hurried up the steps with poorly disguised impatience. He rang the bell and Miranda could hear the royal gong from out on the street. The porch light went on and a maid dressed in a traditional black and white uniform opened the door.

She appeared to recognize Cole, but was obviously not very happy to see him. After they had argued for a minute or so, Miranda saw a middle aged man appear behind the maid and the door was shut in Cole's face. He stood there for another minute, his shoulders hunching slightly, his eyes cast down, before he turned around and walked slowly back to the car.

His face dark and brooding, he got into the driver's seat and started the car. As Cole popped off the clutch and jumped into first gear, Miranda looked back at the house and thought she saw a silhouette of a young woman on the second storey, looking out the window. But before she could be sure they turned the corner and the window was out of view.

'They think I did it,' the tortured voice beside her said. 'They think I'm the rapist.' He hit the dashboard with his open palm in fury and frustration.

'But, how could Kitty say that? Didn't you, ah,' Miranda paused, unsure of how to speculate on their relationship. 'Date? I mean, wouldn't she know it wasn't you who tried to attack her?'

A dry laugh escaped Cole's lips. 'No. We never dated. Kitty and I are friends. Victoria Lambert tried to set us up many times but our concepts of what a relationship should be never did . . . mesh. Still . . . I can't imagine Kitty accusing me of . . . unless she is suffering some kind of emotional shock.'

'Was that her father, at the door?'

'Yeah. Old Man Alexander. He's probably thrilled, ready to ship me down the river. He's always been afraid Kitty would run away with my sorry ass and ruin her future.'

Cole turned to look at Miranda with distant bitterness. 'He told me that once, warned me too, with bodily injury and career ruination and all that. I liked to irritate the old bastard and Kitty and I would play up a fictional passion in front of him. She liked provoking him as much as I did. Well, I guess he sees his chance to destroy me now. Gee, and I didn't even get the girl.'

It hurt Miranda to hear the caustic irony in his voice. A trace of helplessness had crept in too. Why? Because he knew it was inevitable that he be caught? Miranda wouldn't allow herself to believe that he was guilty. But maybe he was beginning to feel as if he were being set up. But why would someone want to set him up?

'Look, Cole, if they had any evidence against you they would have already arrested you by now. Or at least put a warrant out for you, and when they do you'd better believe the news organizations will be some of the first to know. This is such a high-profile case. The police want to make it look like they are doing their jobs.

'As for an alibi, what did you do last night, after . . . I ran off?'

'I ran after you, but apparently not fast enough. I asked a couple in the hall if they'd seen you they said no.'

Miranda remembered the couple at the window, she must have looked so desperate they thought she was running from Cole. Well, she was. Then.

Cole was still talking. 'So, I searched over half of downtown, finally ending up back at the hotel. Everyone was gone, including you. I asked the night manager if he'd seen you, he hadn't.

'So, my alibi is that I was walking all over downtown in the middle of the night by myself. Sort of like . . . the rapist.' They both realized that was more than coincidence.

By the time they reached the Riverwalk, Miranda had debated over what she should tell Cole as his lover, and what she shouldn't tell him as a private investigator. Indecision prevailed which meant work won over emotion by default.

Her cellular phone rang and they both jumped. It was Doug, sounding first worried then irritated at her disappearing act. His humor didn't improve as Miranda was evasive considering Cole's presence and the fact that she hadn't done much in the way of investigating that day. He finally hung up in frustration.

'My boss,' Miranda explained. Cole nodded, tight-lipped.

As they headed for Electric Blues, Cole slipped his arm around her waist and, instinctively, she leaned into his warm, hard body. Her eyes followed the reflections of lights as they danced across the rippling water and she realized with more irony that they were now one of those romantic couples she'd envied just a few nights before. But appearances are never what they seem, and Miranda had to admit their lives were a lot more complicated now than if they'd never met. Right now those questions, doubts and fears were weighing so heavily on their new relationship that Miranda had to accept that there might not be a sequel to the bliss of today.

A horse drawing a buggy clip-clopped on the bridge

overhead and suddenly Cole stopped and pressed Miranda against the cold stone of the wall next to a man-made waterfall. She caught her breath and his lips sealed it in. After a long, deep, sensual kiss, Cole rested his forehead against hers and broke the contact of their mouths.

'I just want you to know . . .' his sentence was broken by a series of quick kisses before he pulled back again. 'That even though I'm worried like hell about what's going on, all I can think about is you. The way your skin feels when I close my eyes, the way your hair smells, the way your face looks when I'm inside you, the way you call my name when you want me.' His speech again came to a halt, this time because Miranda put her hands to his face and brought his lips back to hers.

Oblivious to the stares of passersby – the disapproving middle-age tourists, the nosy waitresses headed for work, the envious bachelors, the understanding newlyweds – Miranda and Cole remained locked in their embrace for several more minutes.

Reluctantly they parted and strolled hand-in-hand, slowly, toward the steps leading to the club.

CHAPTER 14

Standing at the window of Electric Blues, he could see them as they stopped under the bridge. In almost morbid fascination, he watched their kiss. He'd been informed as to where they'd been all day and he could guess what they'd done. Now he knew. They both had that worn-out look, but something else was there too and that, more than knowing they'd gone to bed, made him hate Cole Taylor more than he'd thought possible.

Even now, when Taylor must be feeling the walls closing in on him, he was so damn cocky. Maybe the asshole thought he could buy his way out of trouble like the way his old man did for him ten years ago.

'Not this time,' he whispered. 'This time I'm going to get you.'

He kicked at the chair next to him. It clattered to the floor. Conversation at the other end of the room stopped. Feeling eyes on him, he forced the bile down his throat and turned back to the window.

He saw Taylor say something to Miranda as they wound their way through the people waiting in line to get in and her laughter, husky and sexy, drifted through the glass. He felt himself growing hard and all of a sudden he wanted to hurt her too. For hurting him. For not wanting him like she wanted that damned Cole Taylor.

'Aren't we going to go in the back door?' Miranda asked.

'No, I want to show you off,' Cole answered, his finger tracing the skin along her jaw.

235

'It might be easier –' Miranda began, but saw the people in line begin to recognize Cole and knew it was too late.

They cut their way through to the front door. Men gave him some high-fives. Women and girls reached out to grab his biceps, brush his buttocks, whisper something teasing in his ear. Cole flirted back, but kept Miranda's hand firmly in his. As she felt prickles of jealousy, Miranda admitted she didn't know if she could handle this constant open adoration of her lover. Good thing I won't have to, she told herself, dooming their relationship to failure in her head if not her heart.

Feeling she was being watched, Miranda looked up at the smoked glass window that overlooked the river. She thought she'd seen a flash of movement there out of the corner of her eye, but she must have been wrong. Except for a few tables and chairs, it was empty.

They finally fought their way to the door where Statue the Doorman let them in with a flourish and a buck-toothed smile. Miranda almost fainted.

'Thanks Emilio,' Cole said.

'I thought I'd never see him smile,' Miranda said reproachfully.

Cole chuckled. 'Only for me, doll. He's gay.' Miranda had to stifle a laugh.

They waved at Wayne who was behind the bar looking sweaty and nervous. 'Cole, what the hell do you think you're doin'? I thought you were gonna stand us up. I was getting ready to put Sable and Trent on by themselves and charge half price. Do you know what that would've cost us?'

'Half profits?' Cole answered sarcastically.

Wayne stuck his lip out in a sulk. 'You coulda called and told us you were gonna be late.'

His worry over profits allayed, he now was openly curious as to why Miranda and Cole were arriving together. Trey and the waitresses were trying to prepare the club and eavesdrop at the same time.

'So, how come you're with him?' Wayne asked Miranda. 'You two spend the night together or what?'

'No, actually I took Miranda home last night.'

Shocked, they all turned toward the voice coming from the half-lit jumble of tables and chairs that sat empty. Against the wall, bathed in neon light from the sign, stood Rick.

Wayne was confused. Unfortunately, Cole was not. He was putting it all together a little too quickly. That gossip columnist's words of the night before came back: 'I thought you were getting back together with Rick?'

His hand went cold and dropped Miranda's hand. He turned to her with accusing eyes.

'This is your *friend*?'

Her eyes met his, pleading. Her mouth opened to explain but her mind couldn't figure out how.

Rick stalked closer. 'Yes, it seems you scared her. And you, probably more than anyone, realize it's not good for a beautiful woman to be running around alone right now.'

His voice was thick with vicious sarcasm. Miranda bit the inside of her cheek.

'So, we ran into each other,' Rick continued. 'And I took her home. To my house. It just seemed the familiar thing to do. You see, Mr Taylor, Miranda and I were lovers.'

Miranda could feel Cole tensing during Rick's painful monologue. His hands balled into fists and she wondered who he wanted to hit. Her or Rick?

'That was a very long time ago!' Miranda turned to Cole. 'Nothing happened last night. He wouldn't take me back to my house. I had to catch a cab –'

Cole's eyes hardened into cold, wet granite. 'You, at one time, shared a bed with the cop who's trying to nail me as a rapist. That's an interesting coincidence, don't you think? Why didn't you tell me Miranda? Didn't you think it would be pertinent? Or were you trying to get some evidence for your old boyfriend? Maybe you can compare notes with the girls who got raped. How nice for you.'

He looked for a moment like he might floor Rick, but instead turned and strode into the dressing room, slamming the door behind him.

Miranda glared at Rick, who looked terribly satisfied, then hurried down the hall. The bartender and waitresses had abandoned their charade of working and were now openly watching the drama unfold.

'Cole,' she called softly. 'You don't understand.'

It was quiet for about thirty seconds before he spoke from behind the door. 'You're right. I don't. And I don't want to. Go. It's my fault I didn't follow my instincts and let you leave my apartment this morning. Go back to your cop boyfriend and you two can wrap up this case together. What a headline that will be. Good luck and get lost.'

'No!' Miranda was trying to choke off the desperation in her voice. 'I don't want anything to do with him. It's not what he's made it out to be.'

Cole opened the door partially, blocking her from entering but she could see a trace of hope creep into his eyes. 'You can't deny that you were lovers?'

'That was over two years ago.'

'Can you deny you went to his house last night?'

'He found me by accident. I didn't know he was taking me to his house. I thought he was going to give me a ride to my home.'

'And you're telling me that's the only time you've talked to him in two years?'

Miranda paused, dreading what was to come, knowing she had to be honest. 'No.'

'You've talked to him before, about the case, haven't you?'

'Yes.'

Silence. His eyes narrowed as he watched her face, reading things he didn't want to see in it.

'Miranda, I don't ever want to see you again. If I do have the misfortune of running into you, I'm going to pretend you don't exist. Most of all I want to forget this day ever happened.' The door shut in her face.

Turning around, Miranda came face to face with Sable. A wicked smile pulled her olive skin over her sharp-boned face as she pushed Miranda out of the way with long

238

taloned fingers and let herself into the dressing room. Miranda caught a glimpse of bare muscled back as Cole changed out of his sweatshirt. Her heart ached as, unseeing and unhearing, she rushed out of the club.

Taking deep breaths and biting her lip now to fight off tears, Miranda tried to to run past the restaurants and clubs. She passed the waterfall where not fifteen minutes before they had been so close. But . . . even then, Miranda told herself, she'd known they were living on borrowed time. She'd expected it, now she should accept it. But she couldn't.

'Miranda.'

Automatically, she turned toward the voice calling from the left even as she recognized it as one she'd rather avoid. Rick was sitting in an open air restaurant at a table for two just inside a waist-high stone wall.

'Come here. I want to talk to you.'

Miranda folded her arms across her chest, her bag slung over her shoulder, and moved closer to the wall so she wouldn't block traffic along the walkway. 'I don't want to hear anything else you have to say.'

'Maybe not. But you should.' Rick studied Miranda's hostile expression. 'Look, I'm sorry I broke up your little love affair, but you have to understand that I'm concerned about you. That's a suspected serial rapist with a past history. He takes you off in the woods . . .'

'First of all,' Miranda cut in in a cold voice, 'Cole is not a that. I know he's just a case to you, but you might want to remind yourself he is a person too. Secondly, he did not take me anywhere, I went with him. Willingly.'

'You are wrong about one thing. He is not just a case to me.' Something in his face made Miranda remember the night before, his palpable hate for Cole as he proposed the risky set-up. That was before she'd gotten involved with Cole. So it couldn't be mere jealousy that was driving him to be so cruel. What was going on?

She fixed Rick with a piercing look. 'Why are you so hot for this case?'

'Why?' Rick looked as if he might explode and Miranda drew back. His obvious emotion was uncharacteristic. He was an extremely controlled person, forcing cool on what Miranda always suspected was a hot temper.

'Miranda, come sit down,' he ordered through clenched teeth. She followed his order because she thought she might actually get an honest answer to her question. But by the time she'd come around past the maitre d's stand to the table he had recovered his cool exterior.

'I am 'hot' for this case, as you call it, because I have half of San Antonio crawling all over my back. The mayor calls the chief every hour and the chief pays me a visit. The Chamber of Commerce president keeps reminding me how much money this is costing the city. I have messages from just about every city council member waiting for me every time I get back to the office. After last night, I have not only the victim's rich daddy telling me how to do my job, but the boyfriend too, who inconveniently happens to be a state Senate candidate with great connections, making all sorts of threats if I don't make an arrest. That is why I'm so "hot".'

Miranda knew there was more to it than that, but she played along, challenging him.

'Sounds like enough pressure to make you want to make any arrest, even the wrong man.'

'Just because he didn't rape you, doesn't mean he didn't rape those other women. Don't let your first orgasm in two years blind you to the facts.'

Embarrassed that he guessed one truth and infuriated by his presumption, Miranda felt color rush to her face. She forced herself under control. She didn't want Rick to see how right he might be. 'Look, *Lieutenant* Milano, if you had enough evidence you would have thrown Cole in jail by now. But you don't, do you?' Miranda studied his face and saw she was right. 'If you'd get off this inquisition and look at the facts yourself you'd see it looks more like a psycho trying to set Cole up.'

Miranda stood up.

Rick's hand clamped down on her wrist. 'I'm not finished.'

'Well I am.'

'Your lover is also sleeping with that whore in his band.' Rick's tense face watched her closely, looking for the prime time to twist the knife. 'He didn't tell you that did he? Or was he so good you were willing to share?'

Miranda felt her heart go into a tailspin, taking her stomach with it. Her mind went blank, then was filled with ugly images from the blackmail videotape. 'Sable?' she asked weakly as she sank back into her chair.

'Ah, yes, the charming and lovely Sable Diamonte. It seems they've had a good thing going for years now. Maybe when he couldn't find a woman to rape, she'd fill in nicely. Probably like taking a viper to bed. Interesting.' Rick looked as if he were ruminating over the possibility.

Miranda, just seconds before tingling with anger, now felt the blood drain from her body. Her fingers and toes felt numb.

'You're lying,' Miranda said, her eyes turned inward. Her mind's eye showed clear images of Cole replacing Wayne in the encounters on the videotapes. She could see Cole and Sable in the bed at the ranch. Her stomach wrenched painfully as she remembered Sable go in with Cole as he changed for the show a few minutes before. How stupid they must think she is!

'I got it out of that nice guy, Trent Simon. Poor guy. I think he was sorry he told me, but it seems he hates that cold bitch. Didn't like the fact that she was screwing his best buddy. He doesn't trust her. Go ask him if you don't believe me.'

Suddenly Miranda felt as if she were suffocating. She gulped for breath and gathered her bag to her chest. 'I have to go.'

'Let me drive you home. You don't have your car here,' Rick reminded her with righteous certainty.

Suddenly something Rick had said earlier came back to

her. 'How did you know I was out in the country with Cole, anyway?'

Rick met her flat stare with one of his own.

'Oh, I get it,' Miranda answered herself. 'You're following him. Or me.' She thought of her attacker in the woods. Her eyes blazed. 'Just quit playing the mindgames, Rick. They aren't going to work on me. Remember you're dealing with a veteran, one with plenty of Milano battle scars.'

'Yeah, you're tough. You're smart,' Rick agreed smoothly. 'You think you'd have figured out Cole was double-timing you, too.'

The hurt flashed across her eyes for a second and Rick carefully used his opportunity.

'Look, I know you're having a hard time dealing with this, but you need to accept that he's been lying to you. Come on. Help me. Help those girls.' He paused to let his plea sink in. 'Did he use a condom? What kind was it?'

Miranda snapped to attention. 'You manipulative bastard.' She ran out of the restaurant, as patrons stared after her, then reprimandingly at Rick when he didn't follow her. He smiled at their outraged stares, pleased with the results of his machinations. It would all pay off. He knew it would.

Inside the dressing room at Electric Blues, Cole had a fresh white T-shirt on. He grabbed his sweatshirt off the floor and without thinking held it up to his nose. It smelled like her.

He sank into the couch, ignoring Sable as she stripped in front of him, zipping herself leisurely into her blue leather skin. Maybe Miranda was telling the truth. Nothing happened last night between her and that self-righteous cop. But why hadn't she told him about their affair? For the same reason he hadn't told Miranda about Sable? Cole felt his resolve against her soften. He knew it was more than coincidence that Miranda and her former lover would be involved in these two closely knit cases. Cole

wanted to believe that Rick Milano was doing the manip-
ulation and not Miranda. It was obvious the cop was after
him, and for more than these rapes. Cole doubted he got
this vengeful about all his cases. Why now?

A short stack of eight-by-ten glossies fell into his lap.
Cole looked up.

'I thought you might want some proof that your
girlfriend is lying,' Sable explained, the edges of her
thin-lipped mouth curling up.

With dread, Cole looked through the photos. They were
grainy and dark. He recognized the Alamo grounds. He
peered closer and could make out the figures of a man a
woman. Miranda in her black cocktail dress. A dark haired
man. His back was to the camera, but Cole knew it was the
cop by his arrogant stance. The next shot showed them
kissing, her arms around his neck. In the next shot, his
hands went to her breasts. Miranda didn't look as if she
were fighting. Cole threw the photos across the room.
They hit the wall and slid in a jumble to the floor.

'Where did you get those?' Cole took a deep breath to
clear the buzz in his head.

'I had a friend at the right place at the right time,' Sable
answered. Something about the satisfaction in her voice
reminded Cole of the arrogant cop.

Cole was beginning to lose faith in himself. Why had he
trusted Miranda? He'd almost given her a second chance
to put his hands in the cuffs.

My God, he'd thought he'd loved her. He had almost
told her so a dozen times today. At least he hadn't done
that. But, sitting there, betrayed, he knew he still did. His
heart had chosen a woman who'd lied to him from the
start. In all the years with Sable she'd never deceived him
and his heart remained untouchable. Why was he losing it
now?

Maybe his new song was all wrong. Love wasn't what
his life needed. To forget all about love was more like it.

CHAPTER 15

Miranda ran up the first street access she could find. Rick's words ricocheted in her mind. Somehow her intellect took her body over, guiding her back to the office and her car.

A driver honked as she jaywalked in front of him and Miranda took hold of herself until she got to her building. The security guard in the parking garage insisted on walking to her car with her.

'Are you alright, miss?'

'Yes, thank you.' Lie. No, really I'm dying inside, but don't bother yourself about it.

Fingers searching her bag for her keys, she heard the security guard's keys jangling against his pocket as he walked back to the elevator. It opened and shut behind her while she tried to fit the keys in the lock. Then a hand grabbed hers and she let out an abbreviated scream.

'It's okay, Miranda. Let me do this. It looks like you're having a hard time.'

Miranda swiveled to stare into a familiar face. Peter from the office. Relieved yet still unsettled, Miranda relinquished control of her keys to him. He turned them in the lock and opened her car door with a flourish.

'What are you doing working so late?' Miranda asked, trying to make sense of his sudden appearance.

'I could ask you the same thing,' he threw back, putting on his ultra-bright smile.

As Miranda slid into the seat and tried to fit the keys in

the ignition, they dropped to the floorboard. She ducked her head under the dash and finally, with unsteady hands, located them under the seat. As she started the car, she put the window down to thank Peter. He leaned in.

'Drive safely.'

She put the car in reverse but as she was about to ease her foot off the brake she remembered her case. 'Peter, could you hand me my bag, please?'

'Oh, uh, sure. Where is it?' He made a show of looking around, but Miranda saw it sat right next to him.

'There it is,' she pointed impatiently.

He handed it through. 'Where you off to?'

She looked at him curiously. 'I don't think that's any of your business.'

Pressing on the accelerator, she squealed toward the exit ramp. In her rearview mirror she thought she saw Peter put something in his pocket of his jacket.

The whole incident left her feeling uneasy. Why did Peter keep popping up? First in that clash with Tony that left her with a feeling it involved her. Then here he was in the parking lot after dark almost as if he were waiting for her. She'd heard the elevator close after the security guard left. It hadn't opened again. Neither had that squeaky door to the stairs.

He must have already been on the floor. Coincidence? I am getting paranoid, Miranda told herself.

Her cellular phone rang, She jumped and stared at it as if it were a tarantula. Who was it? Cole, calling to make up? Rick, wanting to continue his interrogation? Doug, firing her?

That would be the best, she decided. It would put me out of my misery. But she knew that would be the easy way out. She'd never taken that and wouldn't now. She'd finish the job then lick her wounds.

'Miss Randolph?' A woman's voice. Cultured.

'Yes.'

'This is Victoria Lambert. We met at the gala last night.'

'Yes, Mrs Lambert. Please call me Miranda. What can I do for you?'

'I need to talk to you. It's very important. If you have the time right now, would you mind coming to my home? I assume you know where it is.' Her tone was friendly and calm.

Miranda's antennae went up. 'Uh, why don't you give me directions?'

Victoria complied succinctly. Extreme curiosity superseded Miranda's tattered emotions. 'I'm on I-10 right now, I'll be right there.'

She took the next turnaround on the freeway and was at the Lambert home in just a few minutes. She parked on the street in front of the stately home. Victoria, who must have been watching for her, opened the front door before she'd made it all the way up the walkway.

'Thank you so much for coming. I never dreamed you'd make it here so soon.'

Miranda followed the gracious older woman into the white marble foyer. The ceiling was open to two storeys. What was surely a Waterford chandelier hung over their heads.

'I have to admit Mrs Lambert, I'm curious about your call.'

'I would be honored if you would call me Victoria. I won't seem quite so much your senior.'

Her classic face lit with a smile, which in and of itself dropped a decade from her age. She led Miranda into a small sitting room off to the side of the hand-carved oak banistered staircase. They sat in Chippendale chairs that flanked a Tiffany lamp. Miranda knew she ought to feel like she was sitting in an antique store, but she didn't.

While all the furnishings were of the highest quality and expensive, Victoria had added homey touches that made the room seem welcoming: a needlepointed pillow with enough mistakes to look homemade, a rather ugly crocheted afghan, what looked like a child's ceramic sculpture of a dog, several framed snapshots of Victoria, Wayne and family and friends.

Victoria saw Miranda looking at the dog sculpture and explained: 'My godson made that for me thirty years ago. I was so proud of it I wanted to put it in an art show that my husband was sponsoring. He talked me out of it, bless him, and suggested it would be a perfect complement to my favorite room. He was right, of course.'

A warmth spread through Miranda's chest as she listened to Victoria speak with such love of her first husband.

'Ah, well, you didn't come here to hear an old woman's ramblings of the past. Let me get straight to the point. Forgive me if I'm blunt. I've been told by some it's my best quality and by others that it's my worst. I suppose it depends on your perspective.' She chuckled to herself.

Miranda waited patiently, finding herself liking this woman even more than she had the night before.

'I know that you are a private investigator.' Victoria paused at the shock in Miranda's eyes and then explained. 'Doug is an old friend, although I doubt he admitted it to you for obvious reasons. I called him last night and he didn't deny that you were working on a case for my husband.'

Miranda was seething. Why hadn't Doug told her he'd talked to Wayne's wife?

Victoria held up her hand when Miranda opened her mouth. 'No, let me finish. We'll have plenty of time to discuss this. I should get it all out before I forget. I have tended to do that lately.'

She took a deep breath, smoothed the skirt of her midnight blue linen dress and continued. 'After Harry died I was depressed and felt very alone. We never had children, but always had each other and never noticed a void.

'When he was gone, I felt the loss of both him and the lost opportunity of children. If we had had them, I may never have married again. I did not want to be alone, yet there was no one I wanted to be with until I met Wayne. He made me feel alive again. He made me laugh for the first time since I'd been widowed. He made me feel like a woman again.

'Believe me, I knew what he was. I realized his faults, being a womanizer among them. And I knew I would never change him. I married him anyway. Not because he was the only one who asked, not because he was youthful, not because he swept me off my feet, but because I wanted to share the rest of my life with him.

'I love him. Not the all consuming way I loved Harry, but in a way I can only describe as fun. We are happy. We have a good time when we are together. I know he would never leave me. In his own way, he loves me.'

'Now, he thinks I don't know about his indiscretions. I want it that way. He has always thought I am a better person than he is and that is not true. If he thought I knew about his womanizing and accepted it, it would confirm his assessment of me and of himself and it would destroy him, which ultimately would destroy the happiness we share. Above anything in my life, I don't want that to happen.

'Now, while I don't know exactly what you are working on for my husband I have figured out – through things he's let drop and my own observations – that he is being blackmailed and proof of his womanizing is being used against Wayne. Beyond that I don't know and don't want to know.'

'What can I –' Miranda began.

'I'm getting to that, dear. Why I called you here is to tell you this: no matter what, I do not want this proof to end up in my hands. Wayne can never know that I have found out about about his infidelity. So, whatever the black-mailer is after I will help you find a way to get it taken care of. Perhaps I can give Wayne an expensive gift of jewelry or a painting he can then hock and claim was stolen. I will pretend to go after the insurance settlement. He would never know because he does not ever see our finances . . .'

'Victoria, I'm sorry to interrupt . . .'

'No, my dear, please go ahead. I've talked too long

anyway. Tea?' Miranda nodded and Victoria served them from a silver tea service. Any servants she may have seemed to have been dismissed for the night. They were alone in the house.

'First of all, Wayne is my client. He is the one I serve. It's his wishes I must follow,' Miranda tried to sound hard. She wanted to make a point. Like Victoria or not, she had to make sure this woman would not manipulate her.

Victoria smiled slightly. 'But I imagine that what Wayne wants and what I want are the same. Are they not? He has told you to keep the evidence out of my hands at all costs?'

Miranda couldn't argue there. She tried a new tack. 'But, what the blackmailer is asking for is probably the one thing on earth you can't help with.'

The smile slipped away as a look of profound concern muddled Victoria's features. 'What do you mean?'

Miranda weighed her options. She knew she should protect her client's confidentiality, yet by admitting she worked for him probably already breached that. She was presented with a rare opportunity to corner one of her suspects.

She gambled. 'The blackmailer is demanding that Wayne sign over his shares in Electric Blues. Then, from now on, the blackmailer will give Wayne instructions on how to run the club, presumably sending his share of the profits back to the new 'owner'. So Wayne would keep the outward appearance of owning the club while giving and carrying out someone else's orders.'

'Oh dear Lord,' Victoria's hands flew to her face. Her voice cracked. 'That club is the only business he's been able to be successful with in fifteen years. It's given him such a sense of pride and confidence. How cruel.'

Suddenly, she looked up, her warm eyes meeting Miranda's. 'And how cunning. This is not your average blackmailer, is it? Instead of going for the money he knew he could get out of Wayne, he's instead set out to emotionally torture him.'

249

Miranda had been watching Victoria for signs that she was putting her on. For though she wanted to accept this grand dame's sincerity, she still needed proof that her theory was unfounded. That Victoria had not set out to teach Wayne a lesson. She had convinced Miranda of her love for Wayne, yet that could be a motive for the blackmail ruse. There was such a fine line between love and hate.

'Please, you can't let him do this to Wayne,' Victoria begged, taking Miranda's hands into her own.

In that moment, Miranda saw the love and fear shimmering in the older woman's eyes. Fear, not of being found out, but of how her husband may be hurt.

'Maybe you can help after all.'

'How?'

'Just answer a few questions. Tell me about the people Wayne works with.'

'Well, you know Cole.'

'I don't know him all that well,' Miranda interjected suddenly. Victoria gave her a curious look and Miranda explained. 'I just met him a few days ago. I don't know him like you do.'

Then Victoria smiled gently, as if she understood something Miranda didn't but would.

'Cole is one of the finest young men I have ever had the pleasure of knowing. And one of the most talented. In some ways he reminds me of my Harry when he was young. All fire and brimstone. Carrying around those rough, raw and deep emotions he tries to cover up by being sarcastic and cool. That's cool with a big "c". I'm probably generations behind in my lingo. What do you kids call it now? Hip. Yes, he tries to be hip. But you know deep down he's just old-fashioned. He has all those ingrained principles and morals his conscience makes him adhere to.'

Guiltily, Miranda wondered if this gentile old lady would think Cole old-fashioned if she knew what they had done all afternoon.

Victoria continued. 'He has character, that kid. Always has. I've known his family since he was born. You know he's estranged from his parents. Mostly the doing of his unyielding hard-hearted father. His mother is lovely.' Victoria looked nostalgic and a little sad. 'Here I go rambling again. That's probably more than you wanted to know.'

Yes, it was, Miranda wanted to scream. She couldn't hear anymore about how wonderful Cole Taylor was, it hurt too much. How great would this nice old lady think he was if she knew what a lying philanderer he was? Old-fashioned indeed! Like Lothario.

'Are you the one who got Cole involved with Electric Blues?'

'Oh no, in fact, I had lost touch with Cole while he took his band on tour. I didn't even know he was back in town until Wayne mentioned his name during the auditions. I put in a good word for him but by then Wayne had already decided to take him on as partner.'

Suddenly, Victoria sat up straighter. 'Surely you don't consider Cole a suspect?'

'Well, he does own a share in the club and has admitted he wants a bigger share. He and Wayne are at odds over how to run the place.'

'Perhaps over little things, not the overall picture. I think the main reason Cole gives Wayne a hard time is because he knows Wayne has these affairs and he resents that. Cole is very fond of me and also it offends his principles. To his credit, Cole has never mentioned it to me. He values our right to a private life.'

Miranda dropped the subject of Cole and covered the other members of the staff. Carefully, she asked about Sable. Victoria hadn't ever really talked to her, didn't like her much and trusted her less. Trent was a 'charming boy, but not very ambitious.' Trey was going to college part-time in the hopes of becoming an English professor. The waitresses were mostly a transitory lot, except for one who supported three young kids and a disabled husband by

251

working every night they were open. Button-nose. Miranda reminded herself humbly that appearances were deceiving.

Putting down her teacup, Miranda readied herself to go. 'Thank you for being honest with me. I'm going to do my best to catch whoever is blackmailing your husband before he has to decide whether to meet the demands or not.'

'How long do you have?'

'Until Saturday.'

Victoria gave her a look of confidence, wrapping her well-manicured, liver-spotted hands in Miranda's young, alabaster ones. Somehow, Victoria's hands looked so much wiser and Miranda felt an incongruous pang of envy.

'I know you can do it, dear. You are bright; you are intuitive; and you care. That will make the difference.'

Climbing into her sedan, Miranda fought the urge to go home and crawl into bed. The work ahead of her seemed an insurmountable, unsolvable muddle. Yet something about what had happened over the last twenty-four hours was nagging her more urgently. She referred back to her list of suspects.

Confidently now able to eliminate Victoria, she had Cole, Sable, Wayne and a yet unknown person. Of course that Cole and Sable were sleeping together, if Rick was to be believed, made a stronger case for their collusion. Miranda had suspected Sable was involved in some sort of set-up. What if Cole had used her to get control of the club? He'd be calling the shots. It was logical. But if they called his bluff, could he really hurt Victoria by showing her those pictures? They were so fond of each other he might let the game go. Or would he?

He could have seduced me to try to delay my investigation into the blackmail threats, Miranda thought. The knot in her stomach tightened. It all fit so well.

Not quite. What about the attack in the woods? How was that related? The caped man was either the rapist or pretending to be him. To confuse me? To scare me into backing off or backing into Cole? Had the 'Phantom of the Opera' returned to haunt Cole, wrongly accused in high school, or had Cole resurrected him for some kind of sick game?

'Phantom. That's it,' Miranda said out loud as she frantically began searching her bag for the blackmail note Wayne received that morning. Soon her car was strewn with papers, photographs and notes. And there it was. The last blackmail note. She read it again and found what she was looking for: 'Use the password "phantom". This was what her mind had failed to grasp all day. This was no coincidence. Here was proof the rapist and the blackmailer were one and the same.

Cole was either guilty of both crimes or innocent of both. He was either the hunter or the hunted and in a split second she made her decision. She would try to prove Cole innocent. He may have used her and lied to her but she loved him. If she didn't try to find the truth she would never know. Rick would have enough evidence soon to arrest and charge Cole. Miranda knew the justice system was far from fair and he could be convicted by a gullible jury. Especially with Rick on this mysterious inquisition.

With a few wrong turns, Miranda made it to the Alexander home in twenty minutes. At the door, she paused slightly when she remembered the unpleasant maid and the stern face of Warren Alexander. The imposing door bell gonged. She prayed the old guy was out. The maid opened the door.

'Hello, my name is Miranda Randolph. I met Kitty Alexander at a dinner last night and she suggested I come by sometime. I wonder if she'd see me now?'

The maid moved to close the door. 'Not tonight. Some other time.'

Miranda stretched to be her most patient and charming. She must not appear too anxious. 'Oh, I am disappointed. I'm going to be leaving for England tomorrow and Kitty and I had talked about me picking some things up at Waterford for her. We never did get the list finished.'

The maid looked at her with indecision and slight recognition. 'Weren't you that reporter on TV?'

'Well, yes, I used to work for KATX. I'm no longer on the air, but how nice of you to remember me.' A dazzling smile.

'Well, if you have a card I will take it up to Miss Kitty. But,' she added in slightly accented English, 'she may not be up to seeing you.'

'I understand,' Miranda handed her a card. The door closed and Miranda let out her held breath. She'd gambled that Kitty would see her despite the lie she told. Five minutes later her bet paid off.

'Miss Kitty will see you in her sitting room,' the maid announced. 'But please don't stay long. She's not feeling well.' Her bony figure led the way through the palatial mansion that was as sterile inside as it was outside. Miranda would have, without qualm, eaten off the pink marble floor.

On the second floor, the maid pointed to a closed door at the end of the hall. Miranda nodded and let herself in with a light knock.

Kitty, clad in a feather-lined satin robe, sat in a pastel suite filled with flowers, not only in the wallpaper, couch and curtains, but in live bouquets. At least ten dozen roses, carnations and irises were scattered in crystal vases throughout the room. Kitty followed Miranda's eyes. 'Daddy thought these would make it all better.'

Miranda looked sharply back at Kitty who went on to explain. 'I know they aren't using my name in the news stories, but I saw you in Cole's car earlier. So I knew you knew what happened. Have the police questioned him yet?'

'Did Cole attack you?' Miranda ignored the question and asked her own, fearfully.

'No. I know it wasn't Cole. He would never do anything like this. And, you know when you can feel a person's presence, even when you can't see them?' Miranda nodded encouragement.

'Well it wasn't Cole's presence. I couldn't see his face. He had that awful hood on. But he sounded so much like Cole, like he was copying Cole's voice. His build was close to Cole's. He was about the same height. But the thing I keep going over and over in my mind is . . . him grabbing me, on my shoulders, my arm.'

She shivered and touched her left breast. 'Here. And his hands were rough. Really rough. I don't mean the way he used them, but the skin. It was calloused and cracked. It was so rough it scratched me. Look.' Kitty dropped her robe down and Miranda could see the reddened skin on her tan shoulder. 'Cole's hands are not rough,' Kitty pointed out with certainty.

Fleetingly, Miranda wondered how Kitty would be so certain Cole's hand would feel on her skin. He said they hadn't dated. Impatiently, she pushed that thought out of her mind. Only to have it replaced with her own memories – the feel of his fingers trailing across her stomach, teasing her breasts, between her legs.

No, she agreed silently, they were not rough.

'Did you tell the police?'

'Well, first Daddy wouldn't let me say anything without a battery of lawyers present. Then, when I could start talking I could only answer direct questions. Not, how tall was he? But, was he six-foot-one? Not, was his voice familiar? Instead the detective asked: how was his voice familiar? It was like the detective was trying to fit the description to match Cole, instead of the other way around.

'I couldn't add anything of my own initiative. When he finally asked me if I thought it was Cole who attacked me and I said no, he turned off the tape recorder and my dad started saying something about me being in shock and not knowing for sure. I was hustled out of there and Daddy and this cop huddled up, whispering, for a minute.

'On the way home, Daddy started working on me to try to turn Cole in. I refused, but still feel like I didn't do enough to dissuade them.' Kitty's eyes teared up. Curled up on the couch she looked like a child. 'Now I'm locked in here like a prisoner. I feel so helpless.'

Miranda fought the urge to tell Kitty she was an adult and could actually walk out of the house without her Daddy stopping her. She had enough to worry about without helping Kitty grow up. 'What was the cop's name?'

'Lieutenant . . . something Italian.'

'Milano?'

'That's it.'

'I'll be back in touch.' Miranda rose and patted the younger woman's shoulder.

Kitty grabbed her arm. 'Is someone trying to frame Cole?'

'I hope so,' Miranda reached for the door knob.

'What?' Kitty looked at her incredulously.

'Consider the alternative.'

CHAPTER 16

It was almost ten o'clock by the time Miranda reached the police station. She'd bluffed her way into the Alexander home, but this would be more difficult. She had to see Rick's files on the victim's statements. If they mentioned the rough hands she had something. Not much, but something.

Walking up the front steps, Miranda heard her name and froze. A young investigator who worked for Rick rushed up beside her.

'Miss Randolph! It's great to see you again.'

Usually good with names, Miranda couldn't remember his. She did remember he was sweet, polite and seemed to have a crush on her. Two years ago, anyway.

'I heard you were back together with Lieutenant Milano. I think that's great. We sure missed seeing you around here. His wife was a real . . . uh . . . kinda . . .' He began to stutter, afraid he may have embarrassed Miranda with mention of Sheila.

She touched his arm and smiled. 'It's okay. That's what I heard too.'

He relaxed. 'You meeting Lieutenant Milano?'

'Uh, yes. I'm supposed to meet him at his office.'

'Let me walk with you.'

'Thanks, I appreciate it.' Miranda smiled again, pleased that for once she could use the hyperactive rumor mill to her own advantage. Nodding at cops she recognized along the way, they made small talk until they reached Rick's office. Miranda hadn't decided what she was going to do if Rick was there. The light was on but the office was empty.

Her noble, if ignorant, escort asked a grizzled old cop on the phone if Rick was in the building.

'Yea, he's here somewheres,' was the answer barked as he covered the receiver.

Miranda realized she didn't have much time. She treated the young man with an inviting smile. 'Do you mind if I wait inside?'

He hesitated only half a second, then opened the door for her. 'Sure, I'll let folks around here know you're waiting for him.'

'Don't go to any extra trouble.' *Please*.

'Oh, it's no trouble, Miss Randolph.'

Damn, she thought as she flashed him what she hoped looked like a grateful smile.

Miranda sat down and watched him get out of sight. The grouchy guy on the phone was rifling messily through some papers on his desk and wasn't paying attention to her. Miranda scooted her chair carefully to Rick's desk, put her bag on top and looked for the files. It was too easy. They were stacked on his desk calendar. One was open to Kitty's statement.

She reached underneath and pulled the two files out. With one eye on the bullpen, she flipped through the first one. Scanning the account her skin began to crawl. She felt the girl's fear. Finally she found what she was looking for. She read '. . . grabbing at my leotard from behind, down by the crotch. I could tell he was mad he couldn't get it off. He tried to rip it. His hands felt so scratchy on my skin. Rough . . .'

Quickly, Miranda closed that file and opened the next. It took her longer to find any mention of the rapist's hands. The cop in the bullpen slammed down the phone and Miranda jumped, letting the files slide to the ground. He looked over at her, as if checking on her. She had put her chin in her hand, elbow on the desk, striking a bored pose. He looked a little suspicious, but apparently had to do something more pressing than babysitting her, so he stormed off. When he was gone she reached down for the files, stuffing papers back inside.

The second victim's statement had slipped under the desk. Recovering it, she found where she'd left off. While the first victim had seemed relatively composed by the time her statement was taken, this victim was a basketcase. Her words were frequently broken by bouts of crying. Miranda became engrossed in her description. '. . . I feel all rubbed raw, like his hands were brillo pads or something . . . (more crying). My back, down here is so sore, scratched up . . .'

The office door opened. Miranda's head shot up, her heart in the throat.

Rick looked supremely confident; like a lion who'd found the lamb in his den. 'Decided your boyfriend's not Prince Charming after all?'

Miranda bit the inside of her lip. She had to maintain her composure long enough to get out of there. Rick glanced at the files in her lap. Miranda's pulse pounded in her throat.

'Find anything in his MO that matches up?' Rick's eyes glittered. He knew he should take it slower but he couldn't help himself. 'Did he like to turn you around? Did he like to hum while he was in you?'

Miranda leaped up, fighting the urge to throw the files at his smug face. 'I can't do this right now.' She reached for the door.

Rick held her shoulders and whispered in her ear, forcing his voice to be gentle.

'Look, baby, I'm sorry. I promise I'll be nicer. This guy just has me crazy.'

Miranda turned around, her face inches from Rick's. 'You got that right, but why?'

A curtain dropped down over Rick's inky eyes. 'I hate him because he's used you. He's hurt you.' If that was true, Miranda realized it wasn't the whole truth. She turned back to the door and opened it.

'Miranda, this is serious. He might be after you now, remember he thinks you and I set him up. If you help me, we can arrest him tonight.'

She walked out without looking back. Rick realized he'd played her the wrong way. She'd come around, but it would take awhile. She needed a little push, some pressure. Maybe that would get more of a helpful statement from the Alexander girl too. Rick reached for his Rolodex and the phone. He'd waited long enough for his revenge.

Miranda sat in her car a few minutes, shaking with release of pent-up anxiety. She successfully and, most likely temporarily, misled Rick into believing she was turning against Cole. She'd found the rapist had rough hands which might prove to her Cole's innocence, but would mean little in front of a jury.

Miranda knew who she had to talk to now. She dialed Electric Blues. The bartender answered and she asked for Wayne. She could hear the music in the background and her heart ached. Wayne, with a stomach full of scotch, wasn't making much sense, but she did manage to get him into the office where he gave her Sable's address off the computer. She hoped he had it right. She hung up on his questions about the blackmail case.

After consulting her map, Miranda drove to Sable's address. She lived in a trendy apartment complex. Though it was late, Miranda took a chance that the neighbor in the next unit would be awake. A man in his forties came to the door looking irritated, but brightened at the sight of Miranda.

'I'm sorry to disturb you sir.' She flashed her private-eye identification quickly hoping he'd get the impression she was police. 'I'm investigating a crime that may involve your neighbor in 24-E.'

The man looked eager and justified. 'I told my wife there was somethin' kooky about her. What d'ya wanna know?'

'Anything you can tell me about her.'

'Well, probably not much. She never introduced herself or nothin'. We'd say "hi", she never said "boo" back. That one guy comes to see her and that's it. No family, no friends.'

'One guy?' Miranda wondered if it was Cole. Wayne said he'd never been to her house. Of course he could be lying.

'Yeah. He's creepy too. Look all skittish and nervous. Shifty eyes and all. He don't talk either.'

'What does he look like?' Miranda breathed.

'Little younger than me, I guess. Around six feet. Dark blond hair. Tan, like he worked outside some. I dunno . . . my wife says he's good lookin', but there's something about him that gives her the willies. Y'know.'

The physical description, vague as it was, could fit Cole, Miranda admitted. 'Did you ever see them act affectionate toward each other?'

'Y'mean like kissin' and huggin' and stuff? Nah. That bitch is a cold fish. But, now that y'mention it, he did look kinda goofy at her a coupla times. Lovey-dovey, maybe. Never did figure out that deal.' He stood there shaking his head.

Miranda thanked him and walked back to her car to wait for Sable. She closed her eyes while she pondered the possibilities and not a minute later, fell asleep.

Miranda woke up, disoriented. Her eyes fought to focus on the neon light in front of her. A clock. Where? In her car. What did it say? 2.30 am.

Someone moved across the parking lot and Miranda recognized Sable climbing the steps to her second-floor apartment, unlocking the door and letting herself in. Miranda desperately needed a cup of coffee. She grabbed the brush out of the glove compartment and ran it through her hair, hoping to massage some sense back into her brain. Finished, she twisted it into a messy chignon. Her hand on the door, she stopped. A figure was bounding up the stairs to Sable's door. Miranda peered through

261

the dark. A man. Too tall. Too thin. The door opened. He went inside quickly.

This mystery man did not fit the description the neighbor gave of Sable's only visitor. Miranda stuffed her .38 into the pocket of her jeans, beneath the oversized sweater, got out of the car and hid beneath the stairs. This way she could see what he looked like, if and when he left. She'd just settled on the concrete slab under the stairs when she heard a door open.

'Don't come here again.' Sable's voice was hard in warning.

'Okay, I got it.' A familiar voice. The door slammed shut and feet thumped down the stairs. Miranda could see his face now. Peter!

Keeping her surprise and temper in check, Miranda followed stealthily behind Peter as he wound his way through several neighboring buildings. When she saw the parking lot he was headed for she went around to waylay him. As he turned the corner he nearly ran into her. The color in his face drained away so that his complexion almost matched his sun-bleached hair.

'We keep meeting each other in parking lots tonight. What a coincidence.' Her eyes showed she thought it was anything but a coincidence.

'Uh, ah, Miranda . . . I'm in a real big hurry . . .' He tried to get around her.

She grabbed his arm. 'What are you doing here?'

His blustery bravado was recovering from the shock of seeing her. He shook his arm loose. 'That's really none of your business.'

'Oh, I think it is precisely my business.' Her words cut through the heavy night air. 'What are you doing with Sable Diamonte?'

He was uneasy but stubborn. 'She's my client. And that's all I'm telling you.' He turned to leave.

Pulling her gun from her pocket, she crossed her arms and leveled the gun from the crook of her arm at Peter, concealing it from all but her target and the empty parking lot.

Ten feet in front of Miranda, Peter jumped as the safety clicked off her gun. 'I think you ought to think twice about that.'

Peter turned slowly and saw what he expected. 'You wouldn't shoot me,' he said with surfer-boy nonchalance.

'No? Let's see . . . I have my career riding on this case. This case that you are helping to complicate. You are working for one my prime suspects. A woman who I just found out has been sleeping with the man I've fallen in love with. What is that about a woman scorned?' The dangerous sarcasm in her voice apparently convinced Peter she was either serious or crazy, or both. His eyes shifted around the parking lot for help. It was deserted.

'Okay, put your piece down and I'll talk.'

'No. I think you'll just talk. What were you doing here tonight? Bringing her something you stole from my case when you so conveniently appeared to help me at my car?'

Looking nervously from her .38 to her face, Peter nodded. 'I got some notes. She wanted notes in your handwriting.'

'Why did she hire you?'

'I'm supposed to keep tabs on how you're doing on the case. She calls me for updates. When I got the notes I decided to deliver them right away. She didn't like that. She's a little paranoid about stuff.'

'Is she the blackmailer?'

'I don't know,' Peter said desperately and, despite herself, Miranda believed him. 'She just told me she's being used as blackmail bait and wants to keep tabs so the photos and video don't go public.'

'Why would you do this? Doug obviously didn't accept the case. You know he doesn't allow freelancing.'

'She's paying me triple. I, uh, need the money.' He suddenly looked like he wanted her to understand. 'I've had a run of pissy luck lately and my new bookie's not too patient.'

He'd gone from puffed-up to pitiful. Miranda waved him quiet. 'What did the notes you took her say?'

'There was enough there that Sable knows you're onto her,' Peter admitted.

'Onto her doing what?'

'I'm just telling you what she said. I dunno what she's into and I don't wanna know, if you know what I mean.'

'Get out of here,' Miranda dismissed him.

Peter walked slowly to his car, as if reconsidering something. As he turned his car alarm off, he turned back to Miranda. 'There's one more thing. Sable asked me to follow you and Cole Taylor to and from that party. She wanted photos of whatever I saw.'

Miranda closed her eyes, anticipating what he'd say next. 'I saw you run to the Alamo. I took pictures of you with that guy you met there. You guys got pretty hot. Sable seemed excited when I gave her the shots this morning. Even gave me a bonus.'

Miranda knew who saw them next. Cole. She tried to shove aside her realization that those pictures would make her look like a liar in Cole's eyes. Suddenly she thought of something and ran in front of Peter's car before he drove away.

'What?' He yelled out the window. 'I told you all I know.'

'Did Sable give you the camera to use?' He nodded and she continued. 'Do you still have it?'

'Yeah, she told me to keep it and shoot you anytime you met that guy again.'

'Let me see it,' Miranda demanded urgently. Peter dug in his car console and then pulled the case out. Miranda looked at the brand, style and model number. It matched the camera that took the photos of Wayne and Sable. She slung it over her shoulder.

'Hey, I need that back.' Peter protested.

'No you don't.' Miranda said confidently.

Inside her apartment, Sable watched the clear liquid slide across the chunks of ice in her glass. Setting the bottle down, she brought the glass to her lips. She didn't feel the vodka as it burned a path down her throat. She studied the maze of veins distended on her bony left hand. Her hand might look old, but her body didn't.

She brought the icy glass to one nipple holding it there until it was hard and aching. She slid it to the other one. Then to the mound of hair between her legs until the hair dripped with sweat from the glass. She looked in the mirror. She was taut and tight. Why didn't he want her anymore?

Sable let the glass drop to the tile floor. It shattered, the vodka splashed up on her bare legs. Without avoiding the shards of glass, she stalked to the sofa. She felt a sharp pain in her left foot and relished it.

She slid onto the cold leather, staring unseeing at the notes written in flowing script on the coffee table. The red-headed bitch had fingered her, but didn't look like she had any evidence, except the holes cut out in the bathroom. Anyone could have done that. She hadn't figured out the connection. She hadn't even begun to guess the whole of it. And there was no way in hell she ever would. They were safe. Or were they? She probably put together more than she put down on paper.

'No sense taking any chances.'

Sable reached for the cordless phone on the glasstop table and pressed number one on her speed dial. He answered.

'Don't just scare her this time. Do her. Do her all the way.' She hung up and smiled at her image in the mirror across the room.

CHAPTER 17

Feeling justified in her suspicion of Sable and excited by the break in the case, Miranda drove home in an adrenalin rush. She knew she couldn't sleep but she had to at least shower, and feed her cat. Mundane chores that perhaps would give her some perspective. That, she needed. Some part of her conscience recognized that an escalating series of events was threatening to suck her into a blinding vortex.

In her mind, Miranda worked the new facts she had gathered into her theories. Sable was behind the blackmail attempts, and if they were indeed connected to the rapes, then she had to be collaborating with someone or had hired someone to commit the rapes. Together Sable and her partner could be framing Cole.

If Cole and Sable collaborated on the blackmail, then how did the rapes fit in? Coincidence? It was highly unlikely. Perhaps Sable had gotten greedy and framed Cole for the rapes to get him out of the way. Then she could control the club, free and clear.

Miranda pulled into her garage and let herself into her house. Sheba complained loudly at her recent neglect. Distracted by her own thoughts, Miranda fed her and showered before she remembered to check her answering machine. Toweling off, she noticed the red message light.

'Miranda, this is Elaine. I haven't been able to reach you at the other two numbers you gave me, so I took a chance that your answering machine would be a safe place to leave this message. I found the name of the girl. Erika Milano. There wasn't much else I could dig up. Her parents moved into the school district when Erika was a freshman. One of her teachers remembered she had three older siblings. They had already graduated high school by the time the family moved here. Her diploma was sent to an Iris Avenue in Pasadena, California. That's it. I hope it helps.'

Miranda stood at the machine, staring into space, letting the pieces of the puzzle fall into place in her mind. Milano. An uncommon name in South Texas. She had to be related to Rick. His sister? Miranda searched her memory for any references Rick had made to his family during their affair. He had two sisters and a brother. They were scattered all over the country, Rick had said, although he told her they had been extremely close growing up. His parents lived in the country, north of town. She met them once, she and Rick took them to dinner at a downtown restaurant. She recalled his father, a management consultant, as an extremely strong, opinionated man. That would fit Elaine's description of Erika's father.

What had Elaine said? After Erika was attacked, she called her brother to pick her up. Could that have been Rick? Ten years ago Rick would have been in his last year of college. In San Antonio. He could have easily driven the twenty minutes to Boerne to rescue his sister. Miranda tried to imagine Rick arriving to find his baby sister beaten up and abandoned. Could he be seeking revenge after all these years?

Her mind awhirl, Miranda dressed frantically, leaving drawers pulled out, panties and socks strewn across the floor. Somehow, she managed to pull together eggshell chinos, a silk lavender shirt and some low-heeled boots. The weather, not yet ready to give up summer, had turned warm again, but she pulled a brown bomber jacket from the closet just in case a cold front blew in.

French-braiding her damp hair, she tied it up with a silk ribbon and was ready to go. But go where? she asked herself. It was just 4.30 in the morning.

267

All this new information had Miranda restless, ready to act. She had to confront Rick with his blinding revenge. Erika, who could hold a clue to the identity of the Riverwalk rapist, had to be found. Sable was a problem she must deal with carefully, though she was not yet sure how. And she had decided to show Cole the pictures of Sable and Wayne, confident that his face would tell her whether he helped plan their liaisons or was betrayed by them.

Saturday morning the deadline was fast approaching and Miranda felt the pressure. Stretching out her tired legs on the couch, she welcomed Sheba into her lap, began to plan how to trap Sable and her co-conspirator. But, as she had in the car earlier, once she stopped moving, Miranda fell asleep.

The sharp ring of the phone awoke her. Bolting upright, she caught her bearings, then stumbled to the kitchen receiver.

'Hello.'

'Terribly sorry to wake you. I seem to do that a lot.' A thin layer of politeness did not conceal the impatience in Doug's voice.

'What time is it?'

'Eight-thirty. I thought you were coming in for a meeting this morning.'

Eight-thirty? 'Oh, no. I don't have time.' She ignored his incredulous silence and continued. 'Can you put Tony on?'

'In case you've forgotten, I am your boss, a relatively lenient one I might point out. And at this moment I am completely in the dark about your case. Your only case. An important case. The last I heard, you hadn't even interviewed all the players. You can talk to me before you talk to Tony.' Doug's voice brooked no argument.

Miranda's own impatience made her bolder than she normally would be. 'Look Doug, everything is coming down today and I don't have much time to wrap this thing up. I know who's blackmailing Lambert, well half of who, anyway. But it's connected to the Riverwalk rapes too. I need one suspect to lead me to the other –'

Doug interrupted. 'I'm calling Phil in on the case . . .'

'No. Do you realize how much time I would lose just bringing him up to speed? Forget it.'

'I'll jump in then. I know some basics of the case.' Miranda was surprised Doug offered to get out from behind his desk. He rarely did field work anymore. She wasn't sure whether it was a compliment that he wanted to work with her or a lack of confidence in her ability to solve the case.

Doug's expertise would undoubtedly help her in some areas, but his presence would also hinder her in others. She wanted to finish this alone. More than that, she needed to finish this alone to prove to herself that she could. She knew she couldn't refuse his help, but she could distract him.

'I think you're going to have your hands full taking care of another problem.' She explained Peter's interference in her case. The silence on Doug's end of the line grew more and more tense. In her mind's eye, Miranda could see him grinding his teeth the way he did when extremely angry. 'You might want to talk to Tony about it. I think he caught Peter trying to get a hand on some of my evidence while it was in there for analysis.'

'Maybe you're right. I should get on this right away. You check in this afternoon to let me know of your progress. If I don't hear from you by three o'clock, I'll consider you MIA. You understand?'

It was an order. Miranda assured him she understood it. Doug transferred her call to Tony. '*Mi bonita, como esta?*'

'*Asi asi*. I'll be better once I get this case behind me. I have a big favor to ask. There's no one else I know to ask who can get it done and get it done in time.'

'I am honored,' Tony answered smoothly.

Miranda gave him a condensed version of what she'd

learned so far, in both the blackmail and rape cases. She was careful not to be too critical of Rick, not knowing how loyal Tony was to the police brotherhood.

'I need you to find this Erika Milano, last known address Iris Street, Pasadena, California. She may be an actress or otherwise involved in the entertainment industry.'

'And when I find her?'

'I need to know about that attack ten years ago. I found at least one person who doesn't believe Colton Traynor did it. Get what you can out of her about "the phantom". Maybe she can give us a clue to who it is.'

'Maybe I should tell her her brother is trying to railroad an innocent man to avenge the loss of her honor?'

Tony read between the lines pretty well. Miranda smiled to herself. Or maybe her intent was that transparent.

'You make the call,' she responded trustingly. 'I'll keep my mobile phone with me all day.' She started to hang up.

'Wait. You have not seen the newspaper this morning,' Tony observed correctly. 'Look at the front page before you do anything else.' He broke the connection.

He'd pulled into her street just before dawn. He parked the car on a small rise above her house. It was ideal. Perfect vantage point. He could see her, but his car was partially hidden from her. If she looked his way, she wouldn't see him behind the big firebush. His biggest problem would be nosy neighbors. But he hunkered down in the seat and hung a windbreaker up on the hook above the driver's window to fix that. He wanted it to look like the car was empty. Like he was inside visiting inside one of the fancy high-class homes. *Yeah, right.*

He should be able to afford to buy five, six, ten of these houses, damnit. But things weren't the way they were supposed to be. He felt the familiar burn grow in his middle, between his stomach and his heart. He tried taking those deep breaths, the way she told him to do, before the burn became uncontrollable.

In a few minutes, the rage had slipped back into its secret place inside him. He felt better. Everything would be fixed soon. And he wouldn't have to be mad ever again. *Yeah.*

His brow furrowed and he looked at himself in the car's mirror. He was starting to look old. The wrinkles got deeper when he frowned, and didn't go away anymore when he smiled. They were always there. That bothered him.

He got out a comb, dipped it in a pot of gel and slicked the bangs off his forehead. He was pleased with the likeness. Not exactly, but close. *Yeah.*

Something moving down the street caught his eye. It was her. Why can't I get a beauty like her? It was always Cole. Even the one woman I got, Cole took away, without even trying. But I get to touch this one soon. She'll be mine, even if only for a little while. Then it will all be fixed. *Yeah. All better.*

Miranda strode out to the front lawn and rolled the rubber band off the paper. On the front page was a picture of Cole with the headline: RIVERWALK RAPE ARREST EXPECTED. The story quoted 'police sources' as leaking parts of the victims' statements, including that the rapist hummed Cole Taylor's *Loving without Love* while attacking the women. All three victims had attended events in which Cole Taylor performed just before they were raped, in Kitty's case attempted rape. All three women talked to Taylor just hours before they were attacked. The story again pointed out the similarity in the suspect's description and Cole's. It all but said Cole would be the one arrested.

Miranda was furious. 'Damn you, Rick.'

Marching back into the house, Miranda threw the paper into her bag and quickly made half a pot of coffee. Spooning grounds into the filter, she suddenly realized what Rick was trying to do. He didn't have enough evidence to arrest Cole, he expected this story to draw

271

Miranda out, maybe draw Kitty out, get one of them to finger Cole, give him one shred of evidence to put the cuffs on. If he didn't do that today, the heat would be turned full force on Rick. It could cost him his career. It had probably already cost Cole his. Even without an arrest, the bad publicity could do him in. The extent of this hate, that he would gamble with his own life to ruin Cole's, made Miranda wonder how far Rick would go for vengeance. A least she knew why. Or thought she did.

Armed with her 32-ounce mug of coffee with cream, Miranda juggled her bag, jacket and Sable's camera in the other arm, setting her house alarm with her elbow. She was about to pull the door shut when the phone rang. She debated whether to free her laden arms and pick up the phone or wait to hear who it was on the answering machine before she went to that effort.

What if it was Cole? What if he hung up when the machine picked up? Her heart thumped in her chest. She dropped her things and reached for the phone just as her taped message began to play.

Beep. 'Miranda, dear, this is Lena. Just wanted to get your reaction to that terrible story in the paper this morning about that gorgeous man of yours. As you well know, reporters will be crawling all over you by noon. Thought you might want to talk to a friend about it instead of those bloodthirsty fiends. Do call, dear. I'll help you out.'

Miranda punched the erase button. 'Oh sure. You'll be a big help.'

She repeated the exit routine, but this time the door closed behind her before the phone rang again. She stood with her ear to the door as the caller left a message. One of the 'fiends' Lena warned about wanted a quote on Cole's impending arrest. Miranda reminded herself she used to be one of those fiends, and most were just doing their jobs. It was the few insensitive and overzealous ones who gave the bad name to the rest.

With Cole the most sought-after news item of the day,

Miranda doubted she could walk up to his door and expect him to open it and let her in. Neither did she expect him to be answering his phone. By Miranda's best guess, he was a prisoner in his apartment. Unless he was tipped off to the story last night by the newspaper reporter calling for a comment, then he would have never gone home. Where would he go? The ranch. He felt betrayed by her, Miranda doubted he would want to go back to where the bed was barely cold from their lovemaking. Or would he? The smart thing to do would've been to go home with Trent, then he and his family would be Cole's alibis should the rapist strike again. But Miranda knew Cole would never subject his best friend to the inevitable sensationalism. Suddenly, she knew where he'd spent the night. On the small couch in the dressing room. Her heart ached for him.

So absorbed had she been in her own mind, Miranda was almost all the way downtown before she noticed the tail. Rick's doing, she thought angrily, probably hoping I'll lead them to some secret lair where Cole keeps his phantom costume. Well, where I'm going is no secret. Miranda didn't bother to shake the car following her, ignoring it instead in her search for a parking place.

As luck would have it, she eased into a rare parallel spot along a side street. She laughed as the gold Jeep with the tinted windows zipped past her. Thinking it was a strange car for a police tail, she shrugged and got out.

As she hurried the few blocks to Electric Blues, Miranda steeled herself for Cole's reaction to her. Sable's pictures and Rick's words undoubtedly had convinced him she had been lying. Miranda found it hard to believe just fourteen hours ago she was lost in his arms, in his voice, in his soul. She still felt him against her, in her. She prayed he did too.

For some inexplicable reason she looked behind her and thought she saw Cole's face in the crowd waiting for the walk sign across the street. When she did a double take she couldn't find him anywhere, and smiled to herself. She was getting herself in such a frenzy that soon she would be seeing his face in the clouds, dancing on the surface of the river. She already saw it in her dreams.

At first she considered going to the front door of the club, but decided against it. There was an off-chance that a reporter may be hanging around outside, hoping to catch Cole. She backtracked toward the alley that led to the back door. Still feeling she was being followed, she cast a look over her shoulder. No one she could pick out of the crowd. Miranda brushed off her paranoia impatiently.

She had almost reached the door, raising her hand to knock when she heard a sound behind her and froze for a split second. The police tail wouldn't follow her this closely, would he? A ticklish sort of fear began to knaw at her. The alley was completely hidden by concrete and asphalt, a cinderblock wall, the brick building. Then she heard his voice and relaxed, her hand falling down to her side.

'Miranda . . .' A warm whisper, teasing and inviting.

A smile spread across her face. She was relieved that love was stronger than his suspicions. Miranda tried to turn around. A steely grip suddenly clamped onto her shoulders. She gasped in surprise and pain. He was angry, after all, but she never suspected he'd be violent. Fear escalated with the beating of her heart. A trickle of sweat ran between her breasts.

Powerful hands shoved her against the side of the building, her cheek jammed against the unyielding brick. His hood had fallen off his head and she saw a flash of his face, Cole's profile, his slicked back hair. Instinct took over and she began to struggle.

He swore under his breath as he fought to control her, his voice becoming mean, evil and ugly. Miranda could feel his hands snagging on the delicate fabric of her blouse. She kicked out, trying to catch his shins. Her fear transformed into terror with the sound of her blouse ripping. His strength was overwhelming her. He was trying with one hand to free her belt. His hands racked across her bare stomach, rough and scratchy. He began to hum. A high

274

pitched, demented sound that was the tune of *Loving without Love*.

It all came together for Miranda in a second . . . the voice familiar enough at first for her to be fooled. Who else had been fooled by that voice? Cole had said his mother had. He and his brother used to trick her. Crayne! How had she not seen it before, when all the clues had been there? She felt like a fool. A fool who was going to pay for her mistake.

Her belt was gone, the buckle broken, and the humming grew louder and higher. Suddenly Miranda realized she'd been fighting so hard she'd forgotten to scream. But now her lungs seemed deflated, unable to take in enough air to make any noise. She concentrated hard as she felt her zipper torn apart. Then it came, drowning out his awful squeaking. It shocked both of them and for a moment, he stopped. She used all her strength to push against the wall and got free, still screaming. She ran. Three steps then he grabbed her braid, yanking her head back, cutting off her scream.

'I'm sorry, I don't want to hurt you.' Cole's voice in a madman's body.

Miranda felt her body weaken as she began to drift into another reality. Her eyes began to lose focus. Then she thought she heard the voice on the right and the left, surrounding her. The voice talking to itself. The cape flew past her face and she grabbed it, holding on for dear life, before she drifted away forever . . .

Cole stood at the sink, dipping his hands in the cold water, splashing it on his face. It was so cold it hurt and that was good. His life had been hell since Miranda Randolph walked into it and yet she was all he could think about. He wanted to freeze her out of his mind's eye. He cocked his head. Did he hear something in the alley? Probably reporters digging through the garbage, or waiting for him to slip out the back door. Well, they could wait out there all day.

He'd spent the sleepless night studying those pictures of Miranda and Rick until he thought he'd go blind, searching for some sign of struggle, of rejection. Some sign that she was telling the truth and she hadn't gone to bed with the man trying to lock him up for good. Some sign she hadn't made love to him just to get evidence. Some sign that he hadn't fallen in love with a lie.

Finally he thought he saw it in the turn of her head, the placement of her hand. But by that time he was also seeing himself in her arms instead of Rick. That's when he tore the photos to shreds. He knew he should be thinking of how keep himself out of jail, calling a lawyer, setting up alibis, but all he could do was . . .

The scream pierced through the wall and went straight to his heart. He moved before he consciously realized he recognized it. He'd heard that same scream yesterday. In the woods. Miranda!

Flying through the back door, he saw them against the dumpster. Miranda, her clothes ripped, struggling, against a figure in a black cape, who was humming, mumbling, clawing at her.

Before he could think, Cole acted. Running toward them, he yelled. 'Let her go.'

The figure spun around, still holding Miranda. Cole saw his face and stopped in shock.

'Leave us alone. She doesn't want you. She wants me now! Like all the rest! All the rest!'

His brother? Cole's emotions were confusing his mind. 'Crayne . . . What are you doing? You're hurting her. Let her go. Come on.'

They heard the footsteps running toward them from part of the alley hidden from view. Crayne looked indecisive for a moment, unwilling to let Miranda go, but knowing he had to if he wanted to escape. Releasing her, he lunged toward the only escape route left, the door Cole had come through. Miranda still gripped the cape and he ran out of it. Black wool billowed down as Miranda fell against the dumpster and slid to the ground. In milliseconds Cole's mind ricocheted between his options. Should he chase after the man who had betrayed him or comfort the woman who had?

He heard the door click shut behind him as he leaned over and gently cradled Miranda in his arms.

'Randi, Randi. It's Cole.'

Her mind still confused by the two similar voices and not registering what he was saying, she began to fight his caress. 'No, no . . .'

The footsteps came to a halt, but Cole was still too worried about Miranda, afraid she was going into shock. He draped her tattered clothing with the cape and stood with her in his arms. The nose of a pistol dug into his kidney.

'Put her down slowly and put your hands up,' came the familiar voice that belonged to the footsteps. 'You're under arrest.'

Cole didn't move, knowing that if he gave the cop any excuse at all, he'd have to undergo dialysis the rest of his life, or worse.

'I need to get her to a doctor. I think she's in shock.'

Rick mocked him with a mirthless laugh. 'It's a little too late to seem so concerned. What do you do? Attack them then take them to the hospital? It's not at all original, so drop the act.'

Miranda, who had gone limp, now started to stir. She closed her vacant eyes and used the dark to pull her mind together. She could smell Cole and began to feel his arms around her. On an unconscious level she understood what had happened and, feeling safe now, she snuggled against his shoulder.

The trusting, intimate gesture sickened Rick, he rammed his Glock deeper into Cole's side. His words cut like a knife. 'Put her down so I can get the cuffs on you before I kill you.'

Cole's eyes hardened at Rick's power play. 'You idiot. You've been chasing the wrong guy, and now you caught him. I didn't attack Miranda. Ask her. The creep ran

277

through the club. If that joker who was sleeping in front wakes up, he might catch him running out the front d . . .' Cole's sentence trailed off as he saw the cop that had been stationed on the riverfront door come jogging down the alley. Cole shrugged with exaggerated nonchalance. 'Oh well, you lose.'

'No, it's you who loses,' Rick pointed out coldly, then yelled over his shoulder at his partner. 'Cuff him and read him his rights.'

'No,' Miranda croaked through a throat raw from screaming.

Cole and Rick both turned their attention from each other to her. She opened her mouth to continue, but nothing came out.

'Stay quiet and still,' Rick ordered a little more sharply than he needed to.

Miranda shook her head, still trying to get the words out. 'It wasn't Cole –'

'You don't need to protect him now, Miranda. We'll get him in custody. Then he can't hurt you if you tell the truth.' Rick motioned at the other cop to hurry with the handcuffs. His gun was still dug into Cole and he tried to grab Miranda from him with his free arm. Cole wasn't letting go, and neither was Miranda.

Miranda shook her head more vigorously now, as if trying to get her wits about her. She sounded stronger when she spoke again. 'Rick, let go of this revenge thing. I know all about it. You've lost your perspective –'

'Shut up,' Rick barked, then harshly wrenched Miranda from Cole's arms.

The other police officer twisted Cole's hands behind his back and snapped on the handcuffs. 'You've done a good job, we'll go over this later,' Rick commended Miranda in an artificially loud voice.

Rick cocked his head at the uniform, silently urging him to get Cole out of there.

'Job?' Miranda murmured, asking the question in Cole's mind.

As sick as he was about that attack on Miranda, Cole had to consider what she was doing to him. Was the whole thing another set-up? Had Milano used Miranda as bait to catch Cole? Where did Crayne fit in? What did Miranda mean about Milano's revenge? Was it all just part of an act? Cole fought the waves of confusion that threatened to drown him. All he knew for sure was he was going to jail and he didn't know why.

His eyes desperately searched out Miranda's and held them, asking for answers. Sadness and helplessness shimmered on their turquoise surface, but underlying those was what? Trust? Hope? Love?

The uniformed cop dragged him down the alley, then propelled him forward, leaving Miranda behind. He looked back once, and saw her shaking loose of Rick's arms to stand alone.

The few reporters that had camped out in front of Electric Blues must have heard the commotion behind, because they finally found their way to the alley and surrounded Cole with shouted questions.

'How does it feel to be under arrest?'

'Do you have anything to say to your victims?'

Cole stopped listening as he fixed a stony stare straight ahead. Behind him, Rick and Miranda heard the reporters descend. Suddenly aware of her disheveled appearance – the torn clothes, her hair half pulled out of her braid – she shrank toward the back door of the club.

Rick, tempted to bask in the glory of his arrest and yet also aware of his duty to get Miranda in for questioning, could not resist pursuing the fame. A quick comment he told himself, then he'd hustle Miranda to the hospital and on to the station.

'Go inside, and I'll come get you in a few minutes,' Rick ordered her, pointing at the back door.

Miranda looked at him like he was crazy. 'That's where he went . . .'

'He, who?' Rick asked impatiently as the voices of the reporters moved farther away.

'The man who tried to rape me. Cole's brother, Crayne.'

Rick dismissed her answer with a wave of his hand, jogging off to catch the horde following Cole, confident she would go inside.

For several moments, Miranda stood rooted, staring back and forth from the door to the alley. Realizing that she still had the cape wrapped around her she discarded it as if it were poisonous. Then she looked down at her blouse. The delicate material was virtually in shreds. One strap of her bra hung, torn, from her shoulder.

Irrationally, she was embarrassed and ashamed, blaming herself for not being aware, for not anticipating the attack. But those feelings would have to wait. Right now she knew she had to get away before Rick came back. She refused to endure the degrading examination by doctors, then the more degrading interrogation that would undoubtedly be conducted by Rick.

'Good job?' Miranda repeated sarcastically to herself. She realized what Rick had been trying to do and was incensed. Talking sense into him was obviously hopeless. She had to show him the truth some other way. Getting out of there would be the first step.

CHAPTER 18

'Cut. Cut. Cut,' the director blurted out in a patronizing way that so irritated the actors and crew who worked for him.

'The problem is,' he announced to the assembled group both in front of and behind the cameras. 'We have no passion here.' He strolled up to the lighting director and, after a dramatic sigh, began explaining what was wrong with their placement.

'The problem is,' Erika mocked to her co-star. '*He* has no passion. And it permeates everything around him.'

She preferred volatile directors to this bloodless cretin. Even that director who'd determined the validity of a scene by the strength of his own hard-on was better than this guy.

'What's "permeate"?' asked the blond god who was still standing pressed against her wearing nothing but a vacant look.

Erika rolled her eyes and wedged herself out of the dummy of an airline lavatory that was missing one wall so the cameras could shoot the scene. A wardrobe assistant handed her a robe and a cigarette. Gratefully, she took the proffered light and took a long draw.

She loved what she did: the acting, the semi-stardom, the money, living in southern California. That half the people she dealt with on the job were morons was a small drawback, she told herself, as she watched her pretty co-star call over his make-up artist for a touch-up. At least this moron was pretty harmless.

The director was another story. This was the biggest budget picture she'd been in yet and could be a break, if the director stuck to the plot. So many of her directors had abandoned the plot in favor of what they thought sold the movie. Sex. As explicit as possible. But plot was what would make this one successful and could take her to another level on the Hollywood pyramid.

Erika pulled her long, thick, dark hair, artfully disheveled for the scene, back into a ponytail. They would have to re-do her hair for the next take, but she didn't care. She'd had it hanging in her face for two hours now and couldn't stand it a minute longer.

Her attention was suddenly drawn to a man who'd just come in the stage door. The scene was such a crowded, chaotic one that Erika might not have noticed him except he was large. Burly and tall with a thick neck and rump roast shoulders, he looked like he was a football player. Or used to be. He had to lean over to talk to the director's assistant who looked rather intimidated and pointed in Erika's direction without a word. He lumbered over to her on barrel thighs.

Before he could reach her, the director stopped him to question why he was there. It was a closed set and even husbands, wives, boyfriends and girlfriends had a hard time getting in. But after a few minutes of discussion, the director nodded and dismissed the cast for the day. The crew, he said, would stay to do preliminary work for next day's shoot.

Forgetting the interloper in her joy at having an early evening, Erika turned toward her ratty dressing room. She debated over whether to go home and review a few proposals she'd been sent, including one to appear half-clad in a European music video, or to head to Rodeo Drive to browse. She walked in and flipped on the lightswitch. Nothing.

'Damn,' she said out loud. 'When am I ever going to get a decent dressing room?'

'I guess when you get in a decent movie,' came the response from the darkness. The voice belonged to the pilot in the movie, the good guy who's supposed to save her from the international terrorist she was with in the airplane lavatory. It was a stretch for Evan Creamer, who Erika knew in real life to be arrogant, crude and often cruel. Fortunately they didn't have many scenes together.

'Get out Evan. I'm going home.'

'Isn't that funny? That's exactly what I had in mind. Let's go home and rehearse the final scene.'

Erika could see his capped teeth leer in the darkness. She felt nauseous. There was no way she was doing that last scene without a director and at least two dozen people looking on.

'Forget it,' Erika answered, dropping her cigarette and squashing it with her gilded pump.

He made a grab at her breast in the dark and got her lower ribcage instead. 'I have some things I want to ad lib in that scene like . . .'

'The lady told you to get lost, so do it.' His voice was as big as his body and that took up the whole doorway. He grabbed Evan's shoulder and shoved him out the door. Evan never looked back as he tripped over his own feet getting out of there.

After a few moments of confusion, Erika finally realized her rescuer was the stranger she'd noticed talking to the assistant director. She laughed a little stiffly. 'I'm grateful. Whoever you are.'

She fiddled with the lightswitch and the bulb on the ceiling reluctantly flickered on.

While his body was imposing, his face was kind. And older than he looked from a distance. He was maybe in his mid-forties. Erika relaxed before she realized she'd been a little nervous.

'Have we met?' Erika asked when the silence stretched on.

'A friend of mine asked me to come to tell you something about your brother.'

'My brother?' Erika was instantly concerned. 'Rick or Vince? Is he hurt?'

'The cop. Rick. He's not hurt. It's just he's screwing up someone else and he's using your past to do it.'

'My past?' Fear crept into her eyes.

'Yeah. The guy you fingered for trying to rape you back in high school is in jail. Your big bro arrested him today.'

'How do you know about what happened to me ten years ago?' Erika was indignant, confused and frightened. She glanced at the door and back at the stranger. She didn't want anyone else to hear this, but should she risk being alone with him? Pausing for a moment, she pushed the door closed with her foot.

'Charges were never filed . . . What's going on? What are you doing here, anyway?'

'Hold on. Lemme get what I have to say out, first. Then you can ask your questions.'

Erika nodded uncertainly.

'Your cop brother got this guy Cole Taylor . . . or I guess his name used to be Colton Traynor . . . for a bunch of rapes on the river in San Antonio. He told the reporter-types today that the big break was, they found out about some girl who'd been attacked at Traynor's high school ten years ago. He's talking about you. Only thing is, seems he's been after this guy since day one. Like he's got a grudge or something.'

'What evidence does he have against him? Against Cole?' Erika's voice was weak to her own ears.

'These girls were all raped after talking to this Cole that same night. I guess the biggest thing is, he carves the letter "C" into their shoulders afterward.'

Erika felt the color drain from her face in a spilt second. Decade-old images haunted her mind.

'What did you say?'

'What? He cuts 'em up? Yeah, writes his initial in their arm with a knife. Now, whether it's this sicko's own initial or he's setting Cole up, I dunno. I've been told Cole didn't do it.'

Erika's eyes turned inward. Her mind zoomed into reverse. She saw a tree. A hunting knife. The sharp point at her shoulder. That familiar voice no longer sounding familiar. Threatening. Evil.

'Cole didn't attack me in high school.'

'Well, it's not me you gotta tell, lady. I'm just a messenger. Or I guess an escort would be more like what I am,' he mused, his thick brows drawing together.

'What do you mean?'

One beefy hand extracted an envelope out of his slightly frayed blazer that had to be a size fifty-two long. 'I got plane tickets to San Antonio. You leave in two hours. I take you to the airport.'

'You're kidnapping me?' Her eyes widened with incredulity.

'Oh no, ma'am,' he looked offended. 'I'm just here to give you the information and to facilitate anything you might decide to do because of it.' The words sounded awkward, as if it were something he'd been coached to say.

'Who asked you to do this?' Erika demanded.

'Well, the guy who called me is my friend Tony.'

'What's Tony got to do with any of this?'

'I don't really know. We go way back. He's an ex-cop, works for some gumshoe outfit in San Anton.'

'Gumshoe?'

'Y'know private investigator.'

'So, somebody hired Tony to look into this case?' Erika struggled to make sense of what was going on.

'Oh no. This is personal. This ain't his case. He's just doing a favor for someone else. I dunno who.'

'Great, so the trail ends there,' Erika sighed. She didn't know what she was walking into but her conscience wouldn't let her not go. She'd kept the lie buried so long that once unearthed it was going to fill her mind like a rancid odor until she could give it a proper burial.

The seconds ticked by as she considered. Her 'escort' waited patiently.

'I'll change. Can you wait outside?'

A few minutes later, they were in his sedan headed to LAX. She wondered if he was a private investigator, but she doubted it and something about him told her not to ask.

'How did you get Marco to give us the rest of the day off?' Erika realized now he was responsible for her sudden free time.

For the first time since she'd seen him, he smiled a big, happy grin. He had a wide space between his front teeth. 'I'm a persuasive guy.'

He didn't just drop her off. He parked and walked her all the way to the stewardess who took her boarding pass. It was only after she was seated on the jet that she realized she didn't know his name.

When they landed in Dallas, a bland middle-aged man in sunglasses met her at the gate. 'Miss Milano, I'll help you with your bag.' Normally, Erika would have thought it was a fan of her movies, but since she used a stage name this had to be another link in a strange chain of 'escorts' who intended to get her to San Antonio. Apprehensive, she followed and he took her to the connecting flight without another word. As he walked her onto the boarding ramp he tipped his hat and was gone.

CHAPTER 19

Steeling herself with a deep breath, Miranda recovered her bag from where she'd dropped it next to the club door. She planned to be ready, if he was still inside. She pulled her gun from a zippered compartment and held it down next to her thigh. She opened the door cautiously, but quickly, aware she didn't have much time before Rick finished basking in the limelight and came looking for her.

The club was dusky, lit only by the sunlight filtering in through the mini-blinds at the front windows, the two skylights and a light turned on from somewhere down the hall, perhaps the dressing room. The places to hide were innumerable and Miranda forced herself not to think about it as she jogged soundlessly to the dressing room, closing the door behind her.

Her slacks were not torn but were smudged with grime from the dumpster and alley floor. They might have to do, but she had to find a new shirt. Opening the closet she surveyed the options; several of Cole's white T-shirts, Trent's blue leather coat. The only women's clothes she could see were the baby blue leather jumpsuit Sable wore on stage and a pair of black jeans.

Miranda refused to even consider the leather outfit. It fit Sable's boyish body like a second skin but Miranda was more generous in the hips and smaller in the waist. Not to mention that the odd style and color would draw attention to her on the street. So would her stained slacks, now that she thought about it.

With an anxious eye on the door, she slipped out of her clothes, including her broken bra, which wasn't doing any good, and put on the jeans. They were tight but laying down on the couch, Miranda managed to get them zipped. She prayed the denim would loosen with wear or she would be virtually disabled. She pitched her torn shirt in the garbage and it landed on the black sweatshirt Cole had worn yesterday. It would have to do. Retrieving the sweatshirt, she pulled it over her head. Her .38 in her hand, she listened at the door before opening it.

Silence.

Running on tiptoes, she made it to the front door, it was unlocked. Surely Cole had it locked while he was hiding out, so she guessed Crayne had already left this way. The hairs on her arms pricked with an instant of fear.

Keeping herself alert to moving shadows, she ran down the stairs and onto the Riverwalk. Her heart gave a jump as she remembered the gun in her hand. Nervously slipping it into her bag, she looked around to be sure it hadn't been seen. But the only strollers in her line of sight had their backs to her. Miranda let out a breath.

She had forgotten to check her hair and her hand flew up now to pull the braid all the way loose. Slowing to a walk, she headed the way she guessed she would be least likely to run into Rick or reporters.

Miranda passed several accesses before she finally climbed the steps to the street level. By going a block or two out of her way, she hoped she'd miss the horde following Cole but be quick enough to get to her car before Rick started searching the streets for her.

She knew now that the Jeep following her had not been a police tail, but Crayne. So the police didn't know where she was parked. Yet.

Before she rounded the last corner, she peeked around. Just tourists and businessmen passing her car, so she hurried toward it. As she jumped in a news van swooped across three lanes of traffic to get in behind her car. At first, Miranda panicked, thinking they were going to jump her for an interview, but then she saw all they wanted was her parking space.

Turning on the ignition with trembling fingers, she waited for a break in the traffic. A young man had got out and was waiting on the sidewalk for his cameraman to park the van. Miranda recognized him as the police reporter who worked at the CBS affiliate. She turned her head so he wouldn't recognize her. Too late. His face lit up and he began gesturing wildly, but Miranda pretended not to see him. She pulled out in front of a tour bus, risking a collision. In her rear-view mirror she could see him standing in the street, slightly bewildered.

'It'll all make sense to you soon, Carlos,' she said out loud, though she hoped it wasn't too soon. She needed time before reporters would be after her like a pack of dogs, because she knew they'd find her before the cops would.

Now that Miranda was safe in her car, she relaxed and trembling in her fingers took over her whole body. Gripping the steering wheel, she fought for control. The emotional stress she'd undergone in the past twenty-four hours – finding love and losing it, Rick's revenge, Peter's deception, Sable's blackmail, Crayne's evil – was looking for an outlet. There wasn't room in her soul for it all. But she'd have to make room, because there wasn't time to deal with it now.

With some inner reserve of strength, she wrestled her body back under control and pointed the car toward Boerne.

If she had guessed right, and the 'phantom' of the blackmail note was the phantom who was raping women, then Crayne and Sable were partners in crime. But their motives and their connection remained a mystery. How would Sable and Crayne have met, if Cole hadn't seen his brother since he left home at eighteen and hadn't even talked to him for five years? Why were they setting Cole up? By this time Miranda had decided Wayne had been nothing more than an ignorant pawn in the scheme.

289

Miranda knew the Traynor Ranch was where she could find all the answers. She'd get them out of Crayne at gunpoint if she had to. Her hand slipped into her bag to double check her mini-recorder. It was there, loaded and ready.

As she drove, as fast as she could without attracting the attention of police, who surely by now had an APB out on her, Miranda tried to ponder the strange twists of the case. But her mind kept returning, instead, to Cole. She didn't think Rick would hurt him, he usually prided himself on being fair and professional. But in this case he'd lost both his professionalism and his perspective.

Rick was out to avenge his sister and, somehow, the attack on her ten years ago didn't quite explain it. True, it was a nightmare for a teenage girl, for which she had been, in effect, exiled. Yet, something else had happened, Miranda was sure, that Rick blamed Cole for. Something so terrible that Rick wanted to make Cole pay. He already had in one way. His reputation and career could be ruined irreparably. Miranda might not be able to win those back for him, but she was going to get him his freedom.

Miranda knew the Traynor land adjoined Cole's, but wasn't sure how to get there. On impulse she took the turn-off to the town of Boerne and pulled into the same convenience store where she'd stopped before. Deanna was behind the counter and recognized her when Miranda pushed open the glass door.

'Hey. You're back.'

Miranda nodded with smile. 'You give such great directions I came back to get some more. I need to find the Traynor Ranch.'

Deanna's eyebrows pulled together as she studied Miranda's face. 'Geez, what happened to you?'

'Why?' Miranda began to get edgy. Was Cole's arrest already all over the air? On the opposite counter a television was showing an *I Love Lucy* rerun. Miranda knew the independent station that ran that sitcom didn't have a news department, so she relaxed. Sort of.

'Oh, your cheek is scratched up . . .' Deanna rubbed her own cheekbone empathetically. Miranda's hand automatically went to her face. It did feel sore. She hadn't noticed before and chastized herself for not looking in the mirror before she got out of the car.

Deanna reached under the counter for a packaged wet washcloth and handed it to Miranda.

'I ran into a brick wall,' Miranda looked sheepish as she explained, dabbing her cheekbone 'I didn't think I'd really hurt myself.'

'It's not so bad. You're so pretty nobody's gonna notice,' Deanna encouraged before turning her attention to Miranda's question. Curiosity and a trace of small-town suspicion crossed her face. 'How come you wanna know where the Traynors live?'

Miranda willed herself to be convincing. She adopted her 'ah shucks' lingo to make Deanna feel more comfortable. 'Well, you know the stuff I found at the high school got Cole sort of nostalgic. We started talking about his parents and all that and I thought while his heart was softened up I would try to get them all back together. I wasn't sure his mom would talk to me if I just called.'

Deanna didn't look completely convinced, but apparently wanted to believe the story. 'Miz Traynor is so nice. You'll really like her. It's not right, a mama and her boy to be separated like that . . .'

Miranda could tell by the look on her face that Deanna was about to impart on a mother and son reunion story and she stopped her in mid-sentence. 'I'm in kind of a hurry. Gotta get back to work on time or my boss'll kill me.' Miranda prayed she wouldn't ask what kind of work she did.

The clerk brushed the frizzled orange-blonde hair off her forehead and smiled with understanding. 'I know whatcha mean. My boss is a real hard ass . . .'

Miranda implored her with a look and Deanna put on the brakes. 'Let me letcha go. This is how ya get to Traynors . . .'

She began to give her the directions and Miranda pulled a notebook out of her bag. With it came the manila envelope that fell on the counter, spilling the photos of Wayne and Sable all over the counter. Miranda scrambled to pick them up, but not before Deanna saw them. She looked closely at one that showed a good view of Sable's face and Wayne's bare rear. Miranda blushed in spite of herself as she jammed the rest of the photographs deep into the bag.

'Hey, what are you doing with these?' Suspicion was overtaking Deanna's friendliness.

'Uh . . . someone gave them to me . . .' Miranda could not think quickly enough.

'This looks like . . .' Deanna trailed off.

Miranda was suddenly alert. 'Looks like whom?' she demanded.

But Deanna's face had closed off now, she wasn't going to tell Miranda anymore.

'Nah, just thought I knew her . . . can't be.'

'Who did you think it was?' Miranda wasn't going to let go.

With all her defenses up now, Deanna shook her head. 'Hey what are you doing here, anyway? Who are you – some kinda reporter or police or somethin'? What's going on?'

Miranda considered flashing her credentials and claiming to be an investigator but she didn't think that would get anymore out of Deanna. Snagging the photo out of clerk's hands, Miranda headed toward the door. She turned around when she got there and answered, love and truth shimmering in her eyes.

'I'm just what you guessed the last time. Cole's lover.' She just hoped that would still be true tomorrow.

Deanna had outlined the directions before the sudden appearance of the photos stopped her, so Miranda had a general idea of where to go. She didn't have any trouble finding it. The Traynors' driveway was off a sideroad and maybe a mile from Cole's cabin, less as the bird flies. She parked on the side of the road, a hundred yards in front of the gate. She wanted to see them before they saw her.

Miranda put on her bomber jacket, not because it was cool – actually it was a mild overcast day – but because her borrowed jeans were too tight to put anything in the pockets. They had managed to stretch out enough, however, so that she could wedge her .38 between her abdomen and the waistband. Slipping the recorder in one pocket of the jacket, she locked up her car and crawled through the barbed wire fence next to the road.

She was thankful for the dark clothes she'd found to wear; they'd help camouflage her in the brush. She wanted to find the main house and the bunkhouse where Crayne lived, see who was there and get her bearings before she decided what to do next.

The hike to the house proved longer than she expected. Miranda tried to keep the driveway in her sight but, because it was white gravel, it blended in with the white limestone that covered the ground and she frequently lost the road altogether. The thick low-growing cedar often obscured any view.

Miranda was getting tired and frustrated. She felt directionless. Something grabbed her jacket. Her breath caught in her throat and she wheeled around, knocking it with her elbow in a karate-like move. Something snapped and fell to the ground. A tree branch.

Relief flooded through her and the vision of how ridiculous she must have looked popped into her mind. She started to laugh and became hysterical, she couldn't stop herself and in a sort of out-of-body way recognized she must be in shock. After what seemed like fifteen minutes, her laughter subsided and something moaned behind her. Spinning around she drew her gun. On a cow. More startled than she was, the heavily pregnant black angus bolted into the brush. This time she stifled the laughter before it started.

'Well, now that I have the trees and cows intimidated, I

can move on to the humans,' Miranda said into the woods. 'That is, if I can ever find any.'

As if in answer, a bell clanged over the small rise on the right. The call for lunch, Miranda assumed. She headed cautiously over the hill and stopped at the top. Below her was a shallow valley, completely cleared of brush. A convoy of pick-up trucks was parked haphazardly around several barns, pens, cow chutes and a bunkhouse. Miranda assumed this was where Crayne lived. There was no sign of the gold Jeep. Just beyond the clearing, a gravel road led up a taller hill and at the top was the main house.

Back in the valley, a man who looked like the cook was still clanging the cow bell outside one of the barns and about a dozen men and teenage boys were gathering at the picnic tables. The cook finally put down the bell and lumbered in the barn, emerging with steaming pots of food. The hungry men dug into lunch without much talk. The way they were eating, Miranda decided she didn't have much time before they got back to work, so she made her way around the clearing, keeping well into the trees.

She scared one of the cattle into the clearing, causing the men to jump. Miranda froze. The ranch hands all looked at one another, laughed raucously and went back to their barbeque.

A few minutes later, Miranda reached the house, a Spanish-style hacienda with pale stucco walls and a red tile roof. A generous porch decorated with black wrought iron furniture greeted visitors at the front door and a large multi-level courtyard with several fountains offered various views. From what Miranda could see through the oaks, this panorama was even more exquisite than the one she and Cole shared during their ride yesterday.

Had it only been yesterday? It seemed lifetimes ago.

Seeing no activity outside the house, Miranda began to get bolder and peered in a few windows. The interior seemed to be wall-to-wall saltillo tile, broken up only by various rope-weave area rugs. The Traynors seemed fascinated with hunter-gatherer art with rooms done in

American Indian, African, Arabic, much of it seemed authentic and, Miranda suspected, expensive.

So absorbed she was in the art, that Miranda didn't hear the footsteps until a lovely middle-aged woman appeared in the living room. She seemed agitated to the point of being distraught. As she turned around, Miranda forgot to shrink back from the window, for the woman she was looking at was the same woman she'd seen at the gala. The woman who had looked so desperately at Cole. The woman Miranda had assumed was one of Cole's lovers.

Looking at her now, Miranda realized why she looked so familiar. Her face was a feminine version of Cole's face. Especially the eyes. The same deep gray that seemed to radiate from her soul. Miranda chided herself for not seeing the resemblance before. His mother. Her insecurity had made her jump to a ridiculous conclusion.

'Don't you run away from me when I am talking to you.' The voice from down the hall commanded with such brutal authority that Miranda jumped. She noticed Cole's mother had not been nearly as surprised but her body grew suddenly tense and very still. Footsteps rang heavy with purpose, then a man appeared in the doorway.

He was physically imposing, maybe only an inch or two over six feet, but very wide across the chest, solid through the hips. Still well toned for a man who looked to be in his sixties. It was a beefy version of Cole's body, but that's where genetics left off. Miranda couldn't see any other resemblance. His face was blatantly ruthless. It was tanned from a life in the sun and a naturally dark complexion. Its lines reflected a character that was controlling, stern and disciplined. His ice-blue eyes offered a stark contrast to his dark skin and clearly left room for no arguments and no opinions other than his own. The world according to Caldwell Traynor. Miranda wondered if that glitter in his eyes ever warmed to a twinkle. She doubted it.

'Vanessa, you're not going to go to the police station. He can rot in there for all I care. This is proof that that damned boy lied to us ten years ago.'

'He did not lie, and this is some mistake. Cole could not rape anyone. He couldn't hurt anyone. It wasn't him ten years ago and it isn't him now.' Vanessa challenged her husband, her eyes shimmering with motherly love and complete confidence.

'Bullshit,' Caldwell stormed. 'He's no longer my son. I won't acknowledge him.' He said it with such finality, Miranda believed him. His wife apparently didn't.

'That is exactly what you said when you threw him out. Yet you kept him in your will as executor of your estate and inheriting everything, aside from the insurance policies you arranged for me.'

What about Crayne? Miranda asked herself.

'Oh? And what other option did I have? Leave it to your bastard son who's not worth the powder it'd take to blow him up? Crayne's worthless,' Caldwell dismissed callously. Vanessa's head bowed and Miranda thought she could see tears glimmering in her eyes.

The strength seemed to have ebbed from her. She stood there as if awaiting punishment. Caldwell pressed his advantage, bearing down on her shrinking figure. 'He's running the ranch into bankruptcy court. Just when I get to the time in my life when I think I can concentrate on the horses, I have to go back to the cattle management because he's too dumb and too lazy to handle it.'

'Like father, like son,' Vanessa almost whispered.

Maybe she did have some fight in her yet, Miranda silently cheered.

'He's not my son,' Caldwell boomed, slamming his fist against the couch table. A picture of Cole and Crayne as teenagers fell onto the tile and shattered. Their mother looked at it with foreboding.

'Yes he is. He was born a Traynor. You raised him . . .'

'He was born a Traynor because I married you. I never promised to love him, make him a son. But here I gave him a good home, a good job and what does he do? Screw up *my* son. I know he did something to turn Colton against me, to give up our dreams and chase after music.' Caldwell

296

looked as if that was akin to Cole running off to join some satanic cult.

Vanessa's chin lifted and her eyes met his again, with quiet resolve. 'You are the one who turned Cole against you. Imposing your will on him, treating his hopes and dreams as nothing better than garbage. Undermining his integrity, refusing to believe in him, and trying to force him into your plan by buying him out of trouble. How did I ever let you get away with it?' She looked more disgusted with herself than her husband.

'You don't *let* me do anything,' Caldwell reminded her harshly. 'I do what I want to do.'

Miranda didn't doubt that. She had moved closer to the open window, transfixed by the drama unfolding before her. She knew she was in danger of being seen, but she couldn't pull herself away. Belatedly, she reached for her recorder, turning it on and placing it on the windowsill.

She remembered that Cole said Caldwell used to beat Crayne. She was beginning to understand why Crayne may harbor resentment toward his brother. The seeds were planted at birth by their father with his emotional and physical abuse of one, the glorifying and pressure to succeed on the other. She wondered if Crayne knew he was fathered by another man. Cole apparently didn't.

His anger somewhat diffused, Caldwell stomped over to a mahogany secretary against the opposite wall. He sifted through a few papers, then began speaking with more bitterness than vehemence now. 'Well, I'm changing my will this time. A lazy son-of-a-bitch is better than a rapist. What a choice I have, huh? If that she-devil were still here I'd give the whole thing to charity. Getting rid of her is the only good thing Crayne's done in his life. He becomes the heir by default.'

His words stung Vanessa like the lash of a whip. In her shrinking posture and sagging face, she had aged ten years during their argument. She took a deep breath and it caught several times before she finally filled her lungs.

She let the air out with a gush, looking for all the world like she hoped her anguish would go with it.

'I'll admit Blase was a strange woman. She seemed to bring out the worst in Crayne.'

'That's an understatement if I ever heard one. I told you this before. She had him under a sexual spell. He'd do anything for her and did. He probably had reason to be thankful. He's such a hermit it's probably the only time he got himself any,' Caldwell scoffed cruelly.

Vanessa winced again, but didn't say anything.

'Remember the time we caught Crayne going through the safe? She put him up to it. Out for your good jewelry, I bet anything.'

'I always thought Crayne wanted to see the will. I hope he didn't. It would have hurt him terribly.' Wistful, she tucked some loose strands of hair back in her neat bun. Miranda thought of Cole always messing with his hair. 'Still, you shouldn't have hit him, Caldwell. He's a grown man –'

'He deserved it. He always deserved it,' Unrepentant, Caldwell cut her off with the power of a shotgun. 'I'm just sorry I never showed Blase the back of my hand.'

Vanessa started to weep, evidently overwhelmed by the memory of her eldest son being beaten up by the man she'd chosen to be his father.

Miranda used the break in the conversation to mull over what had been said, and if any of it might help her help Cole. She assumed Blase was Crayne's wife, who Deanna said had run off a few years ago. Something about the name nagged at Miranda. Had she heard the name mentioned somewhere in the past few days?

'Crayne really loved her,' Vanessa finally said softly, as tears still wet her eyes. Caldwell had turned back to his papers when she began crying. Vanessa stood alone in the middle of the room and Miranda felt like crawling through the window to comfort her.

'Love? Love is for fools, of whom Crayne is obviously one. What does love do but impair your ability to think, distort your perspective on reality, waste your time and energy, make you miserable more than anything else and mix up your life with someone you have no business even talking to much less spending your whole damned life with.' Once again, the world according to Caldwell Traynor.

Vanessa looked dismayed and now Miranda wanted to slap her. She couldn't have lived for over thirty years with the man and not know his philosophy on romance.

'Aren't you talking about us now?'

'I'm talking in general, but we happen to fit in with the rules of common sense, so yeah, I guess you could say I'm talking about us,' Caldwell answered matter-of-factly.

'Why get married then, besides the obvious need to procreate the species in a civilized manner?' Her voice now held that same sarcastic challenge Miranda heard so often from Cole.

'You hit on the number one reason. After that, you should get married for convenient companionship, to share the burden of life or to elevate your position in life. It can be one or, if you're lucky, all three of those.' Caldwell was pontificating self righteously almost like a college professor discussing his thesis.

'Which of the three was it for you, dear?' He was missing her sarcasm completely. Or ignoring it.

'I'm a lucky guy. It was all three, of course. You provide damn great companionship. You keep a great house and kept the kids out of my hair mostly. Now you do so much charity work it almost canonizes the Traynor name. And your beauty and money could not but have helped my postion in life.' Caldwell looked as if he deserved a standing ovation. Miranda thought she was going to be sick. What a sad and cold view of life. She supposed it was one her own father probably subscribed to now. But at least he had an excuse in her mother's death. Miranda wondered what Caldwell's excuse was.

Vanessa wasn't giving up. 'So you shouldn't love a member of the opposite sex. What about your children? Should you love them?'

'You do, and look what it's gotten you: heartbreak and all that wasted time and energy. I don't mean the feeding and clothing and teaching them how to tie their shoelaces. Those are necessities. But the rocking to sleep, all that messy fingerpainting, talking to them for hours about girls they liked at school or the part in some sissy school play they didn't get. So damned unnecessary and probably detrimental. That's probably what ruined them.'

Gray eyes widening in disbelief, Vanessa nonetheless continued to press. 'Why have children if you aren't going to love them?'

'To continue the family line, carry on the name. To have someone to leave your life's work to,' Caldwell answered impatiently as if it was a well known fact.

Miranda felt something wet drip onto her hand and realized it was her own tears. The thought of Cole living with such a heartless man overwhelmed her. While Vanessa Traynor seemed to have given her sons a lot of love, Caldwell's callous philosophy must have affected him too. She had seen in Cole his mother's gentleness and consideration, but she'd seen his father's temper as well. Miranda realized she was crying not only for Vanessa and Cole but for herself too. Cole may not be capable of ever saying 'I love you' and Miranda knew she couldn't live with that or any version of the man who stood before her now.

Vanessa straightened her shoulders and walked over to face her husband. 'I feel sorry for you, but even sorrier for myself. You refuse love and I've given my love to a man who won't return it. You never told me you loved me, but somewhere deep inside I convinced myself you did. How pitiful.

'I should have married Gunther. It would have meant living behind the Iron Curtain, but we would have survived it. We were in love and that would have made the darkest times brighter. I made the wrong choice, for Crayne and for me. Growing up a communist in East Germany would have been a better fate for the poor boy than growing up under a worse tyranny here.'

'Stop your mooning,' Caldwell spat back. 'Gunther died ten years ago.'

'What? How do you know?' Her face drained of color.

'I have military friends in Berlin who kept track of him for me. He wasn't an exchange student like the story he spoon-fed you. He was a double agent and they finally caught up with him and executed him. Shot in the head, begging for his life.' The final brutal fact was obviously meant to torture her.

Vanessa stared at him uncomprehending. 'He was a spy? Even when –'

'Yeah, even when he was sleeping with you, getting you pregnant, never planning on hanging around or hanging on to you.'

'You spied on him? But, why?'

'I had to protect what was mine,' Caldwell stated flatly.

The jangling of the phone interrupted the revelation. Vanessa and Caldwell stood in suspended animation until a woman who appeared to be the housekeeper came into the room.

'Senora Traynor, *telefono* for you.'

'Who is it, Juanita?'

Juanita looked uncomfortable. 'They are from the television. They say they want to know something about Senor Cole.'

'Tell them we support our son and the police have made a mistake,' she said firmly.

'No. Tell them we have no son by that name,' Caldwell bellowed.

Vanessa looked at her husband and saw there was only one compromise he would accept. 'Tell them we have no comment at this time,' she offered with a catch in her throat.

Caldwell let that go and Juanita went back to the phone. Vanessa looked at her husband, decided there was nothing left to say and left the room. After a few moments, he followed.

Miranda remained crouched there, next to the window for a few minutes, going over in her mind what bothered her about the name of Crayne's wife. They had pronounced it 'blaze' like the synonym for fire. How else could that be spelled? Blaise. Blase. B...l...a...s...e. That could be rearranged to spell: S...a...b...l...e. Sable! She was Crayne's wife? Was it the product of coincidence and an overactive imagination or had Miranda uncovered the mysterious connection between the two who'd blackmailed Wayne and planned a series of rapes?

Miranda remembered Deanna's reaction to the picture of Wayne and Sable. Had she recognized Crayne's wife in the picture? It all began to fit together. She straightened up as she planned her next step. But before she could, she was knocked to the ground from behind. A piece of duct tape was clamped down on her mouth before she could catch her breath. Roughened hands raked across her cheek and she knew without doubt it was Crayne. Anger rose from the center of her being. Anger at Caldwell Traynor for creating such a monster, anger at Sable for feeding that monster and anger at Crayne for letting himself become one. It was all so senseless.

He was talking now, more to himself than to her, in that voice that sounded like Cole's but wasn't. Miranda was beginning to hear the differences. Crayne's had a thinner, reedy, whiny quality.

'What are you doin' here? What am I gonna do? She didn't tell me what to do if you came here? How come? She always knows everything. Didn't she know you were gonna come here?'

Miranda lay there motionless, listening to his pitiful mumblings that became more and more unintelligible. She felt the hard metallic outline of her .38 displacing her intestines, cold against the bare skin under her sweatshirt. Her trump card, she told herself. If she could just keep it a secret from him until she had time to get her plan back on track. She felt relatively safe for now. It was becoming obvious that Sable was the puppeteer, Crayne her puppet. Miranda just prayed she was not waiting for them somewhere on the property.

CHAPTER 20

Like boomerangs, the reporters' questions would fade away then return in Cole's mind:

'Are you the Riverwalk Rapist?'

'How does it feel to be as helpless as your victims?'

He had wanted to scream out: I am the victim.

Of what? They would ask.

Good question. He would have to answer, because the truth was, he didn't know. He didn't know why his brother had become a monster or why a cop he'd never seen before was on a mission to wreck his life or why a woman he had fallen in love with was trying to frame him.

So, instead, he kept his mouth shut, stoically staring ahead like a guilty man headed for the gallows. The uniformed officer who'd been given charge of Cole while Rick answered questions was taking great pleasure in pushing him around. By the time they'd gotten to the squad car, he'd shoved Cole into a concrete wall and several buildings, even though he'd been walking cooperatively enough. Cole decided the cop had a small man's complex. The policeman couldn't have been more than five-foot-seven, dwarfed by his prisoner's taller, more muscular frame.

Tourists walking along the sidewalk were both fascinated and frightened to see a man being led in handcuffs. They moved to the other side of the street, as if Cole were about to break loose from his handler's grip and attack them. They pointed and speculated openly about his crime. 'Shoplifter,' guessed a balding man. 'No. He looks like some kinda gang member,' said the woman as she grabbed his arm more tightly. 'Don't be ridiculous, Helen. Gang guys have long hair and tattoos. He don't have none of that. He's just some smalltime hood.' Cole looked away, frustrated, angry and helpless.

Shorty opened the back door of the blue and white car and shoved Cole in with his foot. He fell in sideways, and with his hands behind his back, had to struggle to sit up. Trying to maintain some semblance of dignity, he righted himself and then changed his mind as another group of nosy pedestrians stared into the car window. He didn't want everyone along the short route back to the police station to look in, wondering what car he'd stolen or convenience store he'd robbed. Then they'd see the evening news and know it wasn't either of those. It was a hundred times worse. He slumped far enough down in the seat so only the top of his head showed.

Cole had the sensation of his life slipping through his fingers. But instead of trying to close his fist around what was left, he was watching the rest disappear with paralyzed fascination. Somewhere along the way he must have asked for this. But where? Cole had always been spiritual, believing in God and, if not mortal justice, then a divine one. Now he searched for that, wondering if he had been too greedy with his life, sought more than he deserved. He had a comfortable career, good health, a few good friends. Then it had hit him he needed love too. Maybe that was the key that had turned the lock on the wrong door. Maybe he should have been happy with a convenient relationship with a woman he felt nothing for. Instead of looking for love.

The explanation didn't work intellectually, but emotionally Cole needed a reason for the nightmare. Maybe he should accept this as his penance now. Maybe he should, but he couldn't. He was a fighter. He'd had to be to grow up his own person under the thumb of a tyrannical father. Now fate had stepped in to take over where his father had left off. Fate was ready to decide the direction of the rest of his life. But Cole hadn't battled Caldwell Traynor when he was eighteen for nothing. He owed it to himself to fight back now. As he had back then, alone . . .

Back in the alley, Rick Milano held up his hand to stop the onslaught of reporters' questions. The crowd of news-gatherers had grown during his impromptu news conference as word of Cole's arrest was broadcast across police scanners. Rick knew he'd better take advantage of the attention now, because soon the chief and mayor would be vying for the politically enviable position of telling the city it was once again safe to walk the river.

'What would you say was the biggest break in the case?' A newspaper columnist shouted, unwilling to give up Rick's attention.

'We uncovered a woman who'd claimed to have been attacked by Cole Taylor ten years ago when he was a student at Boerne High School. No arrest was made and no charges filed at the time, and of course it can't be used to prosecute him for these crimes, but it did indicate to us that this was no set-up. We began looking at Cole Taylor as the chief suspect from that moment on.'

'Do you have enough evidence for an effective prosecution?' It was the stringer for *Newsweek*. She was extremely bright and Rick hated her. She was always challenging him, looking for places he'd screwed up, and finding them.

'Of course we do,' Rick answered sharply. But he warmed his tone as he realized the photographer she had with her could put his face in the national magazine. 'If you stop by my office later, I'll give you a few of the details.

As the other reporters clamored for similar treatment, Rick looked back at Electric Blues. He'd left Miranda alone too long.

'That's it. The department will hold a complete news conference later.'

The crowd behind him buzzed with the excitement of a

breaking news story. Rick heard a chorus of electronic bleeps as the reporters called their information back to their respective news stations.

Rick grabbed for the back door and pulled. It was locked.

'Damn.'

Miranda must have locked it, afraid the reporters might come after her. Rick was proud of himself, he'd protected her gallantly by keeping a lid on her attack. For now. It would come out later, when Cole was charged and tried. But by then she wouldn't be so vulnerable.

Nodding at the plainclothes officer who was guarding the crime scene, Rick gave him a signal to call the ID team. Then he walked back through the alley and through the dispersing crowd, waving off more questions. As he climbed the steps to the front door, Rick felt the inside pocket of his ultrasuede blazer. It was still there. His insurance. If they couldn't get the rape charges to stick, he'd nail Taylor for blackmail. Rick had proof of the motive. He'd snuck it from Miranda's bag during their little talk at that restaurant last night. She'd been so distraught by the fact that her lover had slept with Sable that she hadn't noticed him reaching into her bag under the table. Rick allowed himself a small self-satisfied smile.

The front door was slightly ajar and Rick pushed it open, locking it behind him in case any enterprising journalists followed him.

He called her name. Silence answered him. Suddenly afraid that she had slipped into shock, as Cole had warned, Rick hurried frantically down the hall, looking in the office, both bathrooms, and finally the dressing room. He saw the leg of her chinos peeking from behind the couch and for an instant thought she'd passed out on the floor. He rushed over and found the slacks lying limply, partially stuffed under the couch. The sleeve of her tattered blouse hung over the edge of the garbage can. He kicked it over and saw her bra spill out onto the floor.

'Damn. Damn. Damn.' He punctuated each word by

hitting the rickety dressing table with his fist. A bottle of cologne rattled off the table and shattered on the floor, sending the pungent odor of its contents wafting through the room. It was Cole's scent and it enraged Rick.

He grabbed a can of shaving cream off the table and flung it into the mirror. With a loud pop, the mirror cracked in a spider web design. Rick stared back at his reflection. His face was caught in a web of his own making.

Shaking off a sense of foreboding, Rick hurried out the back door and nearly ran into the plainsclothes officer, who was calling directions to the ID team. 'I'm headed to interrogate the suspect.' No need for him to know Miranda was missing. The officer, distracted by his phone call, nodded.

At the end of the alley, Rick paused, wondering which way Miranda went. For a moment he considered that Miranda was right, that another guy had attacked her. Maybe he took off with her. Rick dismissed the idea. The perp wouldn't have had the balls to force her to change clothes first, not with the cops standing right outside with a dozen reporters. He would've thrown a jacket over her and taken off. No, he told himself, Miranda either was wandering in a daze from the shock or she'd taken off to save Cole. Either way she was delirious.

'Where are you, Miranda, and what are you doing?' He asked the air as he slid behind the wheel of his unmarked car.

She was probably waiting at the station while Cole was being booked, hoping to get him bailed out as soon as possible. Rick laughed mirthlessly. He wouldn't be getting out any time soon. He'd already talked to the Assistant District Attorney in the sex crimes division and she was prepared to ask the judge to deny bail based on Taylor's continuing threat to society. Not to mention his continuing threat to tourist dollars. Rick's lips curled in a smirk. It was all working out well. Miranda would be the biggest challenge, but she too would come around.

Rick wondered how far she'd gotten to solving her

blackmail case. Did she suspect her lover was guilty there as well? He bet once she got the idea he was involved, she dropped the investigation. He'd be there to pick up the pieces as her career fell apart. Maybe he should call Doug Sandborn right now and get the wheels moving. No. Rick changed his mind. That could wait. It was inevitable, no sense rushing everything.

And when her world was disintegrating all around her, her self-esteem shot, down two careers at the age of twenty-six, her lover proven a rapist and blackmailer, then and only then would Rick propose. She would accept, of course, what option did she have? She might not think she loved him anymore, but he was familiar, handsome, and ambitious with a promising political career. Crime was the number one concern of voters, so what better time than now for a proven crimefighter to run for office. He'd be a sure thing. He'd have a beautiful wife on his arm as he campaigned, a wife so grateful to him that she'd look the other way during his indiscretions.

His game of revenge was turning out to have peripheral benefits he never imagined.

Rick turned down the police radio and switched on the newsradio station. One of the reporters who was at his news conference was doing a live report from somewhere on the river. She ran a soundbite and Rick was pleased with what he said and the timbre of his voice. He sounded authoritative and strong. As he parked the car and walked into the station, Rick mused over whether to run for the open seat on the city council, challenge the mayor for control of the city or go straight to the state capitol in the state Senate race.

'Milano,' a rookie woman cop called to him. 'Chief's looking for you. Your perp's in booking.' She saw which direction Milano headed and offered some advice. 'If I were you, I'd see the chief first.'

'Chief can wait,' Rick answered.

'No. He can't,' the chief of police corrected as he

stepped into Rick's path. Rick pulled up, more impatient than surprised.

'While I am pleased you finally got an arrest in this disaster, it had better be the right one. This Taylor guy seems to be a favorite of "oh-nine" society mavens. You know, the ones who paid to get the mayor elected? Victoria Lambert is leading this as if it were her charity fundraiser. She's got all of her bridge club and anyone else she can enlist calling the city council, me, even the Goddamned mayor. I'm sure you have a list of messages from here to tomorrow. So you'd better have the right perp or you can kiss your fancy political plans goodbye.'

Rick's political ambitions were well known in the department and the police chief treated them with undisguised disdain. He was a career cop, who had risen in the ranks – from the street to the front office – by being completely ethical while walking that fine line between law breakers and law abiders. The temptation to cross over the line was strong. Rick had known some who had and he'd felt a pull sometimes himself. It wasn't the moral obligation to the badge that stopped him as much as not wanting anything he might do to come back and haunt him during his career. When the chief promoted Rick he told him it was because he was good at his job, even though he was good for the wrong reasons.

'Don't worry. I have it under control,' Rick said with more confidence than he felt. 'In fact, the reason we were able to arrest him today is I caught him in the middle of another assault. Attempted, but the girl was pretty beat up. Plus, I got evidence – the cape he used in the other assaults.'

Rick knew he should tell the chief the victim was his ex-girlfriend, but as soon as that came out he would be taken off the case. He didn't want that. Not just yet.

'Where's the victim? At the hospital? Is there a badge with her for the exam?'

Rick wondered how he was going to wriggle out of this one. If he told the chief Miranda had disappeared he would have one of his famous threatened heart attack fits. He was saved from a decision as the assistant DA for sex crimes hustled up to the pair of them.

'I'm so glad I found you, Rick.' The petite brunette with enough energy for three people reached over and shook his hand. Rick always wondered why professional women did that. He supposed it was their way of asserting their power in a world ruled by men. But it always struck him as odd. Stretching their red lacquered soft, sweet smelling hands out for a shake. He always had the urge to kiss their knuckles instead. He mentioned it to Miranda once and got a full-blown Gloria Steinem lecture.

The DA was obviously rattled. 'I don't think we're going to get the "no bail." Our phones have been ringing off the hook with influential supporters of our friendly Riverwalk rapist and the courthouse is feeling the heat. Plus,' she added ruefully, 'Crawley has been assigned the bail hearing.'

Rick groaned. The chief patted him on the shoulder and excused himself as his assistant caught his eye with a stack of phone messages. Judge Philip Crawley was a slave to the conservative members of his district. Normally that would be good news, he had a reputation for putting the criminal's rights just below those of the fire ant under his shoe. The only thing that Crawley let get in the way of his political beliefs were political dollars and apparently these friends of Taylor had thrown a lot of those Crawley's way.

'Maybe pressure from the public to keep him locked up will be stronger than his war chest,' Rick offered with some hope.

'Don't count on it,' the DA disputed. 'I just talked to his clerk and he said Crawley and the mayor are cooking up some crap to spoonfeed the masses.'

'I have to go,' Rick said as he realized he had to find Miranda. 'I'll check back in with you soon,' he threw over his shoulder as he headed for booking.

She touched his arm. 'Let me know when you inter-rogate.' He nodded, thinking he had no intention of doing

310

that. Once the DA had disappeared, Rick began asking around if anyone had seen Miranda. He left orders that if she showed up, to page him immediately. He didn't say what the urgency was but he got a few ribald explanations he brushed off distractedly.

Taylor had already been booked and printed. He was waiting in the interrogation room.

Rick debated whether to find Miranda or to turn his attention to her lover. In a way Miranda represented the future, Taylor the past. He looked at the door to the interrogation room. It drew him like a physical force. He'd waited so long for this confrontation, the revenge he thought would never come. He'd actually resigned himself to it, living with the anger. Then he found Cole Taylor back in his town and that's when he transferred to sex crimes instead of staying in the more high profile homicide division.

It had been luck or divine intervention when old Alvarado had a heart attack and retired. Rick was in the right place at the right time, only two weeks into his new sex crimes beat when he was named to head it up. Then all he had to do was sit back and wait for Taylor to mess up. He hadn't waited long. The bastard had put his own head in the noose. Fate was stepping in and meting out justice. An eye for an eye. One destroyed life for another.

He walked over to the door and instructed the officer posted outside to be sure no one viewed the interrogation behind the two-way glass. If it was requested, Rick was to be notified immediately. He knocked and the officer inside opened the steel door. Rick motioned him to come outside.

'I'll handle this alone,' he commanded, looking past the young man and into the room. He knew it was against the rules, but he didn't care! Now the tables were turned.

The door clicked heavily behind him. Cole swiveled his head slowly and met Rick's gaze unwaveringly. The cop could see he was going to be unrepentant, probably would deny it all, claim he was set up. Perversely, Rick was pleased. It was better this way than if Taylor had already confessed. Rick would get to break him. He'd pull it out of him slowly and painfully. Suddenly Rick had an image of the torture killer they captured a few years before that had dragged tens of feet of intestine out of his victim's mouth while he was dying. Rick smiled grimly at the prospect. Colton Traynor, alias Cole Taylor, deserved nothing less.

Miranda could hear the sparrows' songs and feel the warm sun on her hair. The clouds had burned off and it had become a beautiful afternoon. The balmy, calm weather seemed to mock the danger she was in. Irrationally, she thought no one would worry about her on a day like this. She wished it were overcast, threatening rain.

After fumbling around in the pockets of his work jeans, Crayne had come up with a piece of rough rope that he used to tie Miranda's wrists together behind her back. He continued to hum parts of songs Miranda recognized as Cole's. It sounded like a bizarre advertisement of Cole Taylor's Greatest Hits, an octave too high and a bit manic. Miranda began to believe that it was unconscious, something he didn't realize he was doing.

Crayne sat in the middle of her back, his two-hundred pounds pressing her flat. With the right side of her face to the ground, she could still have seen him had her hair not been loose and covering her face like a curtain. For the first time in her life Miranda cursed the thick russet mane that had always been one of her best assets. Suddenly it had become a liability. Somehow this small, inconsequential moment became analogous of the entire situation. Dreams had become nightmares. Someone she had once trusted had become treacherous. Someone she suspected had become a scapegoat.

As she struggled for breath and against a rising panic, Miranda forced herself to think. It appeared that Crayne needed to check in with Sable for orders on what do about Miranda's unexpected arrival on the Traynor Ranch. As she tried to gauge his mood, she realized he was more irritated than angry, as if he did not deal well without a plan. The kind of man who had to have a list to go to the grocery store.

Miranda was just the opposite, she functioned better flying by the seat of her pants, almost completely spontaneous, which was why she was a good reporter, or once thought she was. And why she'd chosen to be an investigator. Obsessive planners always had made her nervous, even in innocuous circumstances, which this wasn't. In her experience, they became irrational and nonfunctional when they deviated from their outline. In most cases it was completely benign. In this one it was dangerous.

Where would he take her while he contacted Sable? She hoped he was confused enough to take her to his bunkhouse where surely one of the ranch hands would see them. Or maybe he would try to sneak her into his parents' house while he used the phone. It was unlikely. He would probably haul her off into the woods and leave her tied to a tree while he called on his own. That may be the best option, Miranda suddenly realized. If I could get my hands untied I could fire my gun and draw attention . . .

Crayne rose off her back and Miranda took in a big gulp of air. But before she'd filled her lungs a second time, he yanked her up by her hair. Protesting about the pain behind the duct tape, her scream was forced back down into her chest. Crayne checked the windows along the side of the house, apparently to be sure no one could see them, then he pushed Miranda into the trees.

Without the use of her arms, Miranda was forced to walk slowly in order to maintain her balance. Crayne poked at the small of her back impatiently with something hard and pointed and she realized it was his knife. It was sheathed in a hard leather casing now, but she shivered as her insides contracted at the memory of the feel of the cold blade against her skin. Tripping on a branch she fell to her knees. Crayne swore and yanked her back up by her hair, bringing tears to her eyes with pain and fear. The calm she'd imposed on herself was beginning to give way.

Before she began walking again, she saw it. On the tree in front of them maybe two feet above her eye level 'C&M' was carved into the bark. The carving was old and weathered, but had been dug deeply into the tree trunk and looked as if it had once been painted too, with only faded bits remaining. What color was the paint? Pink? She was still ten feet away and couldn't tell for sure. Crayne lost his patience, grabbing her upper arm and dragging her with him. As they passed the tree Miranda's blood ran cold and she nearly tripped again, this time because her legs went weak. The paint was faded red. Her mind sped in reverse, back to the night before, when the photograph fell out of one of the rape victim's files. The 'C' carved into her shoulder, still dripping blood, looked just like the letter carved in the tree. Miranda's own shoulder began to tingle where it had just missed being branded this morning. And might still be . . .

Miranda tried to kick her mind back into drive. If she could puzzle out the reason driving Crayne's violence maybe she could head him off. Save herself. In fact, she was less afraid of him than she was of Sable. Miranda suspected Crayne had a heart, damaged, warped and sick, but it was there or his brother would have never been so fond of him at one time. But Sable, she'd been born without one.

Where is he taking me? Her feverish mind jumped from subject to subject without finishing a thought. They were going deeper into the woods, away from the valley where the calves were being penned and branded. Miranda could hear the bleats and maws of pain as the red-hot brand seared through their hide. Discouraged, she realized that even if she was able to scream or get a shot off, it might not be heard anyway. If the sound of the chaos was this loud hundreds of yards away as Miranda was, it had to be nearly deafening in its midst.

Crayne's feet, having grown up on the land, raced over the rocky terrain without faltering while Miranda stumbled along until he was almost carrying her. The arm he gripped felt bruised, the socket almost out of joint. They did seem to be following a somewhat worn foot path, or maybe cow path. Something caught Miranda's attention out of the corner of her eye. Another tree carved with initials. She strained the focus of her eyes to reach the trunk 'C&P'. Who was 'P'?

Not much farther ahead they passed directly by another tree carved with initials. 'C&S'. With a grim anticipation, Miranda looked for the next tree. She waited nearly ten minutes before she saw it. Again, on a live oak tree off to the right, near the path. 'C&K'. Crayne and Kitty!

Then Miranda knew who 'P' and 'S' were. She felt a chill creep up her spine as she realized Crayne had been keeping score. She felt the goosebumps rise on her arms and looked over at Crayne. He had a proud smile on his face, as if he'd been showing her his trophy room. He knew she knew.

Finally after what seemed like hours and miles, she felt her feet splash into water. The chilly liquid slipped over the tops of her short boots and brought her back from whatever hazy half conscious state she had been in. It was the stream she'd fallen in only yesterday. Yesterday? Her life had been turned inside out in just twenty-four hours? The whinnies of the horses caught her attention and she realized they weren't far from Cole's cabin. A tiny sliver of dread slid into her consciousness. Why had he brought her here? Was Cole involved after all?

Crayne dragged her around to the front. She could see the red Blazer but no sign of Bubba's truck. It had been after dark when they had passed him as he came home last night. Maybe 6.30? Miranda had no concept of what time it was now. The trees blocked the position of the sun, and she'd never been good at that anyway. Maybe mid-afternoon, she guessed.

Miranda thought it was strange that they were walking all the way around to the front when they could have gone up the back steps and in through the back doors. Cole said Bubba never locked the house, and she had a feeling

Crayne knew that. Instead of walking across the yard, he took her all the way to the front walkway that led from the driveway to the house. A huge, hundred-year-old oak tree shaded the front yard and most of the house. Miranda had admired it the day before but now noticed a red ribbon on it that hadn't been there before. How curious.

She peered closer and stopped dead. As if he expected it, Crayne stopped with her. Just under the ribbon, carved into the trunk, at Miranda's eye level was 'C&R'. His next victim. Me?

She could feel him looking at her. She willed herself to walk on, but she couldn't. Why didn't he use an 'M'? Only three people in my life have called me Randi. Mom, Melanie and Cole. Was it a lucky guess? She didn't think so.

CHAPTER 21

The cold dampness of the interrogation room began to work its way into his bones. Cole and Rick had been staring at each other for minutes on end, neither moving, communicating their mutual hatred and distrust with their eyes. The only sound in the room was their breathing, accentuated by the silence. Cole could hear a low mechanical rumbling on the other side of one wall, maybe the air conditioning or the heat. It was one of those mild days that didn't need either, but in a closed-up room in a closed-up building Cole was grateful for any air at all.

Cole realized this wasn't his official interrogation. None of this was going on the record. It was personal and he was about to find out why.

Rick broke their gaze. His message was unmistakable: I am in charge. His attitude had been the same, though more disguised, when he'd come to question Cole after the first rape. The arrogant cop acted like one of the boys on the playground who used to yell, 'I know something you don't know!' And, as he had as a kid, Cole became incensed and defiant.

Circling the table in an affected careless stroll, Rick finally settled at the chair opposite Cole.

'So, you're finally where you should have been put ten years ago.' Rick's voice was thick with pent-up emotion.

Intense suspicion fell over Cole's face like a veil. 'What do you know about ten years ago?'

'More than you want me to know,' Rick said with a cold

smile. He waited a few moments for understanding to dawn on the cocky face in front of him. When nothing but empty belligerence registered, Rick got impatient.

'Does the name Milano mean anything to you?' God, was he so callous he didn't even remember the name of the girl whose life he ruined?, Rick thought.

'Yeah, it's the name of an arrogant asshole I know.' Cole shot back as he racked his memory. He had to be talking about the attack on that girl in the high school. It was the only trouble he'd ever been in. Or, rather, accused of. Her name had been Erika, but what was her last name? He hadn't really paid much attention to her until that party. Then he'd only asked her out because she was making such a fool of herself over him. They were in that play together, he had to have heard her last name, right? Erika Milano? Could it be? Oh God. Why hadn't he seen it before?

Rick clenched his teeth with suppressed rage and stared down at his steel-toed boots. How he would love to slam them right into his ribs. Make him beg the way his little sister must have been begging that night. 'You better watch your smart mouth. You notice we're alone here. Who's to say you don't become violent and have to be subdued?' Rick's eyes glittered like onyx.

'Go ahead,' Cole challenged recklessly. 'You've stolen my freedom, ruined my reputation and used my lover.' He paused and was rewarded with a wince from Rick. 'Why not waste my body too. Make it a clean sweep.'

'What I want from you is an apology and if I have to beat it out of you, I will.'

Cole believed him. But he wasn't going to apologize for something he didn't do. He refused to do that ten years ago and he refused to do it now. He stared defiantly into the raging eyes of the cop in front of him.

'Apology for what?' he finally asked with forced calm.

Rick felt murderous. He clenched and unclenched his fists, unable to breathe. He realized now Cole was trying to bait him, to use Rick's own fury against him. Maybe he planned to sacrifice his body for the sake of public sympathy. It would be a way to make the cops look like the bad guys, and it wouldn't be the first time. Rick made a concerted effort to keep it a psychological battle instead of a physical one. He felt confident he could win that one.

'Listen, Colton,' he leaned back in his chair adopting a pompous air. 'We both know you tried to rape my sister back in high school. I picked her up where you left her . . .' Rick closed his eyes as he began to lose control of his emotions again. He could see her, so small and pure, helpless and beautiful. She was none of those things now.

He exhaled and opened his eyes. 'Nobody went to the cops back then because your old man had a deep wallet. Now, we can't use that in court, but it can be used in other, more indirect, ways to convict you. Like in the media, which I've already done.' Rick paused briefly as Cole's eyes flashed with sudden fury.

'I didn't attack your sister. I never met her for our date. I had a sick horse and couldn't call her because she had said her parents did not let her date. I didn't want to get her in trouble.'

Disbelief written all over his face, Rick cut him off. 'You make me sick with your feeble lies. Your car, your costume, your date with a girl who had a crush on you. You're either saying my sister lied or someone set this whole thing up. Poisoned your horse? Stole your car? Tried to rape your date? Right. I'm not going to waste my time debating this with you. It's so obvious.'

Cole understood now. It was all about revenge. It was driving Rick, blinding him. And, as if the fog suddenly cleared in his mind, Cole realized he could say the same thing about another man. His brother. Crayne was seeking revenge on a life that was unfair and the brother that unwittingly represented that unfairness. Cole was caught in the middle of two men seeking vengeance – one using the law and one breaking it.

Rick mistook Cole's silence for acquiescence. Encouraged, he pushed on. 'Of course, we have a rather damning circumstantial case against you. That, plus the testimony from your old girlfriend – the Alexander girl – and from Miranda, the case will be open and shut. The assistant DA is already salivating.'

Cole was taken aback. He wasn't sure whether to believe Rick about Kitty testifying. She wouldn't talk to him last night. It was possible, he conceded. But what about Miranda? She couldn't have set him up today. Crayne had really hurt her. His heart ached remembering her tattered clothes, the flash of his knife, her wild-eyed look of fear. If it was 'a job', as Rick had said, had it gone farther than they had planned? Or was she coming to see Cole on her own and Rick was using the situation to his own advantage? Cole knew he had to ponder out what happened but all that seemed important now was Miranda.

Rick enjoyed watching Cole squirm in his state of uncertainty. Cole's next question threw him.

'Where is Miranda now?' Cole asked, earnestness replacing his macho posturing.

'You have no right to know the whereabouts of our witnesses,' Rick blurted out. He didn't expect the raw emotion in Cole's face to cut him so deeply. He remembered the kiss on the river. Miranda reaching for Cole as he was led away in the handcuffs.

Cole heard the sharp edge in Rick's voice. He was covering something up. What? Did he know where Miranda was? Cole hadn't seen her when Rick marched up to the horde of reporters. He was surprised that Rick hadn't paraded her out for all the cameras to record the horror of his latest victim. Maybe she was insisting Cole was not the attacker and Rick was trying to change her mind.

'You better not hurt her, or try to play mindgames with her,' Cole warned, suddenly afraid for her. 'She was hurt back there, emotionally and physically. More than you or I could possibly imagine.'

'Oh?' Rick raised his eyebrows. 'Why don't you tell me how you know about that?'

Cole wasn't fooled by the cop's attempt to lead him into a confession. 'All right. I'll tell you exactly what happened.' Cole knew he should demand to have a lawyer present, but what lawyer? He didn't know any and suddenly the truth couldn't wait. 'I was in the club. I slept there last night after a reporter called for a comment on your leak. I knew they'd be swarming my apartment and the outside of the club by morning. I was throwing some water on my face when I heard her scream. I ran out and saw her pushed up against the dumpster with the guy in the cape all over her. He had a knife. I yelled something at them. I don't remember what. He turned around, let her go and ran past me, back into the club. I ran up to Miranda and that's when you saw us.'

Rick could sense Cole was keeping something from him. Or outright lying. The fact that he was making up this fantasy, blaming it on some nameless faceless phantom infuriated Rick. He wanted him confessing, groveling, begging for mercy.

'So you went to Miranda's rescue instead of catching the guy you claim is setting you up. The guy who could keep you out of prison. How noble.'

Cole eyed him coldly, realizing he should have kept his mouth shut. This cop didn't want to hear anything but his own theory confirmed. 'That's right.'

'Well, that's too bad, Colton. Maybe I should give you a chance to rethink what really happened after I tell you what I'm going to have to do. You see, I'm going to have to call in the FBI. The rapes we can handle here in our humble building. But this blackmail, that's a federal matter.'

Cole felt his blood run cold. What hard evidence had Miranda found against him that she would've given Rick? Cole prayed it was another bluff. He was beginning to understand that being innocent wasn't enough.

Letting his words hang heavy in the air a few minutes, Rick slowly pulled a photograph out of his blazer. He threw it across the table at Cole. Like a magnet, it drew his eyes, and his stomach clenched at the sight of the two naked bodies locked intimately together.

'What the hell is this?' Cole choked out as he pushed the picture back at Rick in disgust.

'Well, it's one of your several motives for blackmailing your partner. You found out your long time girlfriend was screwing the guy you can't stand taking orders from . . . on the stage where you work every night.'

Cole pulled the photo closer. He hadn't looked at the faces. It was Sable. And Wayne. Shock spread like frostbite throughout his body.

Rick was watching him closely. 'Kind of a slap in the face. I have to admit I'm not sure I could take something like that without wanting some revenge.'

Cole didn't miss his dig and threw back one of his own. 'I'm not you.'

Rick glared back silently. He resolved not to let Cole get to him.

Cole ran his hand unconsciously through his hair. 'Anyway, I broke it off with Sable and she can do whatever she wants with whomever she wants.'

'Oh ho. Well aren't you a big man. Well these pictures were taken nearly a month ago, when according to even your best buddy Trent, you were still deeply involved with her.' Rick reveled in the expression on Cole's face.

Cole reached for the photo again and saw that the backdrop behind the stage was indeed the one they'd just replaced two weeks ago. He felt betrayed, disgusted and confused. What was Sable up to? As far as he knew she hadn't slept around during their years together. Wayne certainly wouldn't be her first choice of lover.

'Where did you get this picture?' Cole's look was intense. He felt like he was on the edge of a precipice. If he looked a little farther over he'd see what was written all over the side of the cliff. Or he might fall.

'You ask too many questions,' Rick snapped nervously. He'd wanted Taylor to see the picture and lose his temper, not ask about the origin of his stolen evidence. The fact was Rick couldn't call the feds in until he got the cooperation of Miranda and Wayne Lambert, which was not likely. But he gambled some more and left the photo out to keep Taylor distracted.

Cole resisted the impulse to turn the photo down on the table. He didn't want to give the cop the satisfaction of knowing it got to him. But it did. Her naked taut olive skin was twisted in an erotic pose and entwined with Wayne's soft, pasty body. It jumped out from the flat surface of the print. Not that he wanted Sable back or ever loved her even then. He supposed it hurt his pride, but even more than that he sensed a hidden agenda and a pressing need to uncover it.

'Did Miranda give this to you?' Cole pressed him. He was sure Rick had told her about Cole and Sable's affair, no doubt leaving out the fact that they had broken up before he'd got together with Miranda. His heart sunk heavy in his chest. It all made him look guilty as hell. In bed with Sable. Resenting Wayne's management of the club. The blackmail pictures. It certainly would look to Miranda like he and Sable set it up. Now he couldn't blame her underlying suspicion. He wondered what the blackmailer was asking for.

'Miranda is no longer a concern of yours,' Rick pointed out.

Cole gritted his teeth as Rick stood, straightening his designer silk tie. As he did so, his tailored tweed jacket fell open, revealing his Glock in its shoulder holster. Swallowing his annoyance, Cole decided it was an unconscious move Rick made when he felt threatened, flaunting his power through expensive clothes and a deadly weapon. But why would talking about his ex-lover threaten Rick?

Prowling about the confining room, Rick decided to return to the morning attack. 'Okay. Let's say I believe you . . .'

'Why? You don't.'

'Listen, you had better quit that backtalk because I'm

trying to give you a chance before two other cops get in here and aren't so nice.'

'Nice? Is that what you've been? Well, I'm sure I'll appreciate you more when these other guys get in here and start pulling out my fingernails.' Cole was beginning to feel more comfortable. He could feel the momentum shifting. He was gaining more control over the situation and Rick was losing some.

Rick felt it too, but tried to use it to his own advantage. Maybe Taylor would become overconfident and slip right into the snake pit. He leaned his hands on the table and bored a look into the younger man. 'You said the attacker ran right past you. Was he still wearing his black cape?'

Cole's stare shifted to the space beyond Rick's dark head, as he backtracked through the ugly memory. Crayne spinning around. Their eyes meeting. Crayne sheathing the knife. A moment of indecision, then charging by Cole, bumping him in the shoulder. Miranda's half-conscious body slipping to the ground, the cape billowing down with her. 'No, he didn't have it on. Miranda held on to it when he took off.'

'So, you got a good look at the guy's face,' Rick's voice was mocking. 'What did he look like? Who was he?'

It was the question Cole had most dreaded. The one he hadn't wanted to think about himself. He could give the cops a description of Crayne, but of course that could be a description of himself. Would he turn his brother in to save himself? He put his head in his hands.

Rick controlled his elation. He felt the break coming. He leaned forward on his palms in anticipation when the answer to his question came from behind him.

'His brother. Crayne Traynor is the Riverwalk rapist.'

Cole looked up in shock at the sultry voice. Rick's head pivoted more slowly, not wanting his eyes to confirm what his ears told him. He hadn't heard that voice in ten years, but he'd never forget it.

'Erika,' Rick whispered. 'My little Kiki.'

The officer posted at the door was apologizing. 'Lieutenant, she just barged in here, said she was your sister and it was an emergency. I shoulda stopped her, I know, but I didn't uh, wanna hurt her, she was going so fast . . .'

Rick put up his hand. 'Don't worry about it, Trujillo. Close the door.'

A crowd had gathered behind Erika. Rick wasn't sure whether it was what she said or how she looked that drew their attention. He grabbed her arm, slammed the door and pulled her into his arms.

Cole watched them in amazement. This certainly wasn't the Erika he vaguely remembered. At eighteen she'd been pretty, with long silky mahogany hair, big doe eyes, skin the color of burnt cream and a slender body with no curves. At twenty-eight, her face was enhanced by maturity and make-up and her body by plastic surgery. Her D-cups were squeezed into a push-up bra and encased in a white lace bodysuit. A tan suede miniskirt just cleared her perfectly round buttocks and her long legs were bare to tan suede boots that came just below her knee. Cole was damned glad she wasn't his sister.

Rick and Erika pulled loose of their embrace.

'What are you doing here?' Rick looked at his sister with a mix of affection, embarrassment and anger. 'Don't you have a coat or something?' He took off his blazer and put it on her shoulders.

She shrugged it off gracefully. 'I'm not cold.'

'That's not what I meant,' Rick said through clenched teeth, casting a glance at Cole.

'I know what you meant,' Erika said defiantly. Then she turned to Cole, putting her hand on his. 'Are you okay? I'm so sorry about this. It's my fault that you're in here.'

Rick was flabbergasted. 'Is he okay?' He knocked her hand away from Cole's. 'Do you know who this is? This is the animal who tried to rape you. I finally got him. I'm going to put him away for a long time, now, Kiki.'

Turning those deep doe-eyes on her brother she sighed. 'I need to apologize to you too. Look how long you've

325

carried this anger around. It's warped you. I've been so selfish.' She shook her head slowly.

'Stop,' Rick's yell reverberated around the concrete room. 'This jerk ruined your life ten years ago and you're apologizing to everyone? You need to get it through your head. It wasn't your fault! It's his fault! You didn't ask for it, not the way you looked or what you said or didn't say. We'll get you some help.' He wrapped his arms around her. She pushed him away.

'I don't need any help, Rick. Now you listen to me. I never thought it was my fault. I thought it was an opportunity to do what I wanted to do – go to Hollywood and be an actress. When Mr Traynor offered me money I took it and ran. The situation offered the perfect excuse to get out of town. Dad and Mom would have never let me go otherwise.' A cloud passed over her face.

'That night . . . was the most frightening and degrading of my life. I wouldn't have asked for it, but it happened and I tried to make something positive come out of it. It's worked out great for me, but –'

'Great?' Rick sneered. 'You're a porn queen. Don't tell me that was your life's ambition. Don't tell me you just happened to choose that path after this prick stole your self-esteem.'

Erika's expressive eyes threw sparks. 'Look, I'm not going to tell you that because it's not true. But what you are thinking I've become is not true either. I like what I do, and I'm proud of it. I don't do anything that crosses over the line to hard-core and I am actually getting closer to the mainstream with every film. The one I'm filming now actually has a decent plot and might even get an 'R' rating.

'My future's promising. Look, I might not have a future in films if I hadn't chosen this route. Most of it depends on luck, the rest on looks and talent. I have three friends that went with me to the first acting class, one's a call girl and one's a kept mistress for a movie producer and the third is a checker at Kmart. I feel a lot better about what I do than what they do. It may not be something you brag about but I chose my own road and nobody's driving the car but me.' Erika's chin jutted upward with her last statement.

Rick's face mottled in anger. 'Yeah, just a great opportunity. Lucky you.'

'Now, that's not what I said. If you listen you will hear what I am saying. I did not come out of the attack without some scars. I don't trust men. I haven't been on very many dates. But maybe that's good. Maybe I learned a lesson in one quick moment when it takes some women a lifetime of pain and suffering.'

Rick spun on Cole. 'You see what you've done to her? She'll never have a normal relationship with a man. She'll never get married and have kids –'

'A normal relationship?' Erika scoffed. 'What's that? Who has that? Did you have a normal relationship with your wife?' Rick looked away. 'Having a husband and kids never was high on my priority list before so who's to say that changed? I'm not going to say that will never happen, either.'

She stomped the ground in a show of impatience. 'I didn't come here to talk about me anyway. I came here to clear something up. I have exactly two regrets in my life. One is that I'm not closer to my family. I have come to the conclusion that I cannot do anything about that. If you are ashamed of me that is your problem not mine.'

Rick looked ashamed. He'd wanted to call. He'd picked up the phone countless times, his address book open to her phone number only to hang it up again as he sat there reliving the shame and fury he felt when he found out what his sister was doing in California. He was at a party the other police rookies held for him after he got his master's degree. One of his fellow rookies had bought a keg of beer and an armful of the latest porn flicks.

He'd drifted into the living room and absently watched the naked goddess on the screen rolling around a beach with an equally naked pectoral god. His buddies were raucously admiring her physical traits and sexual technique. Rick opened his mouth to agree when the camera caught her face in the middle of a scripted orgasm. He felt he'd been punched in the gut, sickened and hurting. It was his baby sister.

With a string of curses, he ran to the television and turned it off. The cops sitting around the room looked at him in shock, until one blurted out. 'Geez, Milano, just because you haven't gotten any since you started graduate school doesn't mean we have to suffer! That's Kiki Mills, the best in the business.'

Everyone else laughed it off, convinced his bizarre behavior was caused by his self-imposed abstinence during his pursuit of a *magna cum laude* degree in political science. He'd never told anyone. In that moment, an all-consuming hatred had been born for the man responsible for the debasement of the sibling most cherished in his heart.

That she was using Kiki, his childhood name for her, turned hatred into personal vendetta.

Cole had been sitting back, watching the revelations between brother and sister unfold, almost unable to believe that their drama could be so unwittingly woven into his own life. Erika had watched the play of emotions on Rick's face, but when he remained silent she finally continued.

'My second regret has begun to haunt me lately. I didn't know why until today. Maybe I wanted to convince myself that the lie I told ten years ago hadn't hurt anyone.' She glanced at Cole and put her hand on his arm again. Rick fumed as she continued. 'But I know now it has.'

'What lie, damnit?' Rick demanded through his teeth.

Erika paused, searching for the right words, then let them come in a rush. 'That night, when I called you and asked you to pick me up outside the school, I was shaken and confused. You began firing off questions, who had my date been with, what had the guy done, had he hurt me? Well I gave you the impression that it had been Cole who'd attacked me, even though I knew it wasn't.

Then you took me home. Mom whisked me off to clean me up.

'When I got back, you and Dad had already planned it. Not to call the police, to go instead to the Traynor ranch and confront Cole's father, letting him punish his son instead of putting me up for public scandal. I tried to talk to the two of you but you wouldn't listen to me. You kept telling me I was in shock and you would handle it.

'Then Dad drove me to the Traynors'. He went in alone and told me he'd come out for me when he'd told the old man and Cole was ready to give me an apology. I sat there and decided I would tell Mr Traynor the truth. Then the door opened and I expected Dad. It wasn't him. It was . . .' Erika took a deep breath and squeezed her eyes shut against the memory. Rick shot a murderous look at Taylor who looked like he was listening so closely to Erika that he was holding his breath.

'The same hands that hurt me earlier grabbed me out of the car and pushed me into the woods. I was so terrified I couldn't speak. I thought he'd finish what he started earlier. He led me to a tree. My heart was beating so hard I thought I might die and I wanted to. I was so frightened I couldn't scream. I tried to fight, but he was so strong and he pulled out a knife and held it against my arm. He pointed at some initials freshly cut into the trunk. "C&E". He said,' Erika took a shaky breath, 'He said, "So we can remember, forever.' Then he laughed and said. 'Everyone will think the "C" is for Cole. But we'll know won't we?"'

Erika pursed her lips together to stop them from trembling. After a few moments, she continued. 'We heard Dad calling me. Then he squeezed my arm hard and put the knife to my shoulder and told me not to tell anyone that he was the one who attacked me, or he'd carve his initial there, too. He said it was for Cole's own good that he be blamed. That everything would be fair then.

'I ran toward Dad's voice and he got mad at me for wandering off. He told me to look real upset, to cry if I

329

could. To make Cole feel bad, he said. He said Cole was denying everything but that Mr Traynor believed Dad and promised to make it up to us.'

Erika and Cole exchanged a glance that communicated the memory of that awful night. Cole's confusion and frustration. Erika's terror and duplicity. Tears welled in her doe eyes.

Irritated by their sharing glance, Rick drew their attention away. 'So, you are saying that Taylor here was not the one who attacked you?' His voice mocked with disbelief.

'That's right,' Erika answered just above a whisper. She glanced back at Cole and saw he already knew who her attacker had been.

'Well?' Rick demanded 'Should I get down on my knees and beg? Or are you going to tell me who it was?'

'Crayne Traynor, Cole's brother.'

Rick suffered the second biggest shock of his life then. He'd expected Erika to say she didn't know who it was. He'd carried the hate so long that it had become part of his heart. He couldn't accept what she was saying. That his revenge had been focused in the wrong direction.

'You can be sued for libel for that.'

'Not if it's true,' Erika pointed out.

'There's no way you can prove it,' Rick's voice began to rise in desperation. Somewhere deep in the recesses of his gut he felt it all slipping away: the revenge, his career, Miranda.

'And it doesn't matter anyway. He hasn't been arrested for your attempted rape. He's under arrest for a series of rapes near the Riverwalk. That doesn't have anything to do with you.'

'Oh, I think it does,' Erika looked accusingly at her brother. 'You told the media that the connection with the attempted rape of a girl in Boerne a decade ago was the big break in the case. You made the connection.'

Rick's eyes shifted around the room as he began to feel cornered. Cole challenged him with his silence. Desperately, Rick racked his brain for ammunition and he found it. 'Why did you suddenly appear today?'

'Someone thought I should know what was going on here,' Erika answered evasively.

'Someone . . . who?' Rick spat poisonously. 'One of Cole's friends, maybe? Did they pay you to come and lie to get him off the hook. You were bought before to ignore the law, why not again?'

His sharp words cut. His rejection of her because of her movies hurt, but she could almost understand his shame over that. This was different. And the pain would never heal.

'I thought you were seeking to avenge the attack on your sister which, even I can admit, is honorable.' Cole spoke for the first time since Erika came into the room. The brother and sister broke their glare and looked at him. 'But somewhere along the way you stopped doing it for her and began to do it for yourself.'

'That's bullshit.' Rick argued.

'Is it? So what? You hurt her to help her? You sacrifice her to the media in the hopes of nailing me? You accuse her of selling her soul? Who's the one being punished here?'

'Shut up.' Rick jabbed his index finger at Cole. A vein in his neck stood out, throbbing painfully.

'Cole's right,' Erika offered. Her voice wavered slightly with emotion. 'You accuse me of being a whore, in selling my morals for money in more ways than one. You blame Cole for it.

'What do you think is going to happen if you put him in prison forever? That I'll suddenly become a nun and move to San Antonio and live in the family bosom? That I'll always tell the truth and become the woman you thought I should be, as your little sister? You're kidding yourself.

'You are doing this for all the wrong reasons. For revenge. To save me. You should be doing it because someone is breaking the law and making innocent women suffer. And if you do it for that reason you will find you've

331

been chasing the wrong man. And if you put him away more innocent women will suffer, because Cole is the victim, not the victimizer.'

Suddenly, as if her words put out the fire he'd been fighting, Rick sank into the chair and slumped over, his fingers at his temples. A headache throbbed painfully. He had a bitter taste in his mouth. What they said was true, he saw that now. His quest for Cole had become an obsession that robbed him of his perspective. But now that he had it back, he wasn't sure he wanted it. He searched for a politically correct way to extricate himself from the web of lies and deception.

He raised his head. 'So if I am to believe you, and Taylor didn't send for you, who did?'

'I really don't know,' she bored him with an honest gaze. 'Some beefy guy came to tell me about what was going on and had airline tickets for me. I was met at the gate by a guy named Tony who said he was doing a personal favor for someone.'

Cole interrupted. 'Tony who? What did he look like?'

'Hispanic, medium height. Polite, but dangerous looking. I wouldn't want to cross him. Looks like a loyal dog that's made all the friends he needs.'

Erika could see neither Rick nor Cole were familiar with her description. They both looked puzzled.

Suddenly a worried look crossed Rick's face. 'Miranda,' he breathed.

'Miranda?' Cole repeated urgently, his eyes sharp as cut granite. 'What about her?'

Rick's face closed to the question as he went to the wall and dialed the phone. Cole jumped up and twisted Rick around by his shoulder, shoving him against the wall. He got his face inches from Rick's.

'Where is Miranda?'

'I don't know,' Rick reluctantly admitted.

'You don't know. She was almost raped just hours ago. She was bordering on shock. Didn't you take her to the hospital? Or did you just take her statement and say

332

"thanks for giving me enough info to nail your lover" and send her on her way?'

Close to panic with the thought of Miranda wandering around alone, Cole studied Rick's face. It was all there.

'Oh, I get it,' Cole started with deceptive calm. 'You just had to talk to those reporters, couldn't postpone your glory for arresting the Riverwalk rapist. You left her and promised to be right back. When you got back she was gone.' Cole's voice exploded in the tiny room. 'You selfish bastard. She's gone. My brother is gone. She's the only one who can identify him as the Riverwalk rapist. Damn you.'

Confused, Erika asked tentatively. 'Is this the same Miranda that –'

'Yes,' Rick barked.

'Oh my God,' Erika whispered. She didn't need to ask what Miranda was to Cole. It was obvious he was in love with her. 'What a mess.'

Cole strode over to the door.

'Where do you think you're going?' Rick asked with empty superiority.

'I'm going to walk out of here and you're not going to stop me. I'm going to find Miranda before Crayne kills her.'

It was something they'd all thought about in the last few seconds but hearing it spoken crystalized their fears. Erika paled. Rick's jaw clenched.

'First of all, everyone in the station knows what you look like, you would be caught and face another charge. Even if you did get out the door, the reporters out there would be worse.'

'I can handle the reporters. You just get me out of here.'

Rick hesitated. He knew he had to let him go, but he had to think of the way least damaging to himself. He didn't want Miranda hurt, but he didn't want to throw all he'd worked for away without some careful planning either.

Cole wasn't patient. 'I can't appeal to your sense of humanity, because you don't have any. So let me put it this

333

way. If you don't let me go and Miranda turns up floating down the San Antonio River, then you'll have a hell of a lot more explaining to do to the mayor and every other ass you kiss than for a mere false arrest.'

'Rick, for God's sake, listen to him,' Erika pleaded from behind them.

With a glare at Cole and an angry growl at his untenable position, Rick opened the door. The group of cops had remained just outside the door, speculating on what was going on inside. They looked embarrassed at Rick's and Cole's sudden appearance and made a show of discussing work.

Rick pushed past them without a word. He knew they would assume he was taking Taylor to lockup. But their attention was already diverted. Erika had leaned down to straighten one of her suede boots, exposing a foot of cosmetic cleavage. Rick's frown deepened. Cole smiled grimly. She knew exactly what she was doing and he appreciated it.

Once he'd directed Cole out a side exit, Rick gave him a hard look. 'Where are you going to look for her?'

'My brother's house.'

Rick nodded, then looked away. 'I'll call the county cops and see what we can organize between them and SAPD. I have to go take care of your release. Then I'll head out there too. This has to be done.' He added in a weak apology.

Cole shrugged as he started to walk away. 'We all have our priorities.' If he had little respect for Rick before, he had none now. If he was in his position he'd screw the badge and be at the ranch by now. No, he corrected himself, I would have never left her alone in the first place.

The 'good luck' Rick was about to impart remained in his throat. He glared at the broad back and confident stride of the bootclad man he'd taught himself to hate. Then he turned on his heel. He had a lot of lemons sitting in his lap that he now had to turn into lemonade.

CHAPTER 22

Cole had reached the street before he realized his car was ten blocks away, parked near the club. He turned toward the river when someone called his name.

'Mr Taylor, can I offer you a ride?'

A short, swarthy man wearing mirrored sunglasses was leaning indolently against his car, apparently undisturbed that it was parked in a no-parking zone right next to the police station. A reporter would be nervous as a cat. Ex-cop, Cole surmised.

'Do I know you?' he asked warily.

'Not directly,' he answered. Cole had never seen such an expressionless face. 'I work with Miranda Randolph.'

'You're Tony?' Cole took a chance.

The man's lips stretched into a smile that revealed a row of straight white teeth. 'She's spoken of me.'

She hadn't, but Cole let that ride. 'Did Miranda ask you to bring Erika here?'

'She asked me to find the young woman,' he answered vaguely.

'Well, thanks.' It seemed inadequate, but Cole didn't have time to dwell on it. He glanced once in the direction of his car. 'And I will accept your offer of a ride.' If Miranda trusted this guy to find the woman she knew could set Cole free, then he ought to trust him too. He climbed into the black Cadillac.

Cole told him where he was parked. Tony nodded and headed east. The phone in his console rang. He answered and had a short conversation about a 'she' who Cole assumed was Miranda. Suddenly tense and distracted, Tony hung up without a goodbye.

'Miranda is missing.'

'How do you know?' Cole asked.

Tony paused so long before he answered, Cole had to bite his tongue not to prod him. 'She was supposed to check in with the owner of the agency at three this afternoon. He told her if she didn't he would come looking for her. She hasn't checked in yet.' The digital clock on the dashboard read 4.23. 'Perhaps we should notify the police.'

'The cops already know she's missing. At least one of them does.' Cole added with distaste, 'Lieutenant Rick Milano.'

Tony was silent although his shoulders bunched tighter at the mention of Rick's name. Cole took a gamble and gave him a general overview of what happened that morning, about the attack on Miranda, his brother's escape, his own arrest.

When he heard how Rick had handled the day's events, Tony cursed low and hard, a mixture of English and Spanish. Cole had to agree with Erika's assessment of the private detective. He was extremely intimidating. His tirade finally ended and he turned his attention back to Cole.

'Where are you going now?'

'To my brother's bunkhouse.'

Tony nodded once, not registering any surprise. 'I want to go as well.'

Taken aback, Cole hesitated. He'd planned to go alone, but once he located Miranda – if she was indeed on the ranch with Crayne – the escape routes were numerous. Another body in his corner could be an asset. Cole scrutinized the man driving. He had a lot of muscle packed in a short frame and it was incredibly hard for a man in his early fifties. He was wearing a revolver under his jacket and Cole suspected he would have an extra weapon on hand. Another plus.

Tony withstood the once-over, respecting the man at his side for it. He knew Cole was weighing trust, advantages and disadvantages and whether Tony would improve the odds of rescuing Miranda. Neither had any doubt that Crayne would be desperate by now. Desperate enough to go one step farther than he had so far.

'Let's go,' Cole announced.

Cool behind the wheel, Tony whipped the car around the next corner and headed back up the next one-way street. Soon they were on the interstate and speeding toward the Traynor ranch in the thickening traffic.

On the way, Tony asked about the layout of the ranch, insisting on intricate details, exact distances between buildings, the placement of outside lights.

'Tell me about your brother,' he probed with purpose.

Cole told him about growing up with Crayne, how he was a good big brother until Cole got into his teens. He told Tony much of what he told Miranda and more. Confirmation that he was capable of such violence gave him a new perspective on the past. He saw more in his memories than he had just a day before.

'I remember when I was in high school we had a strange rash of deaths around the ranch. Barn cats turned up with their necks wrung. A couple of calves were slit across the throat. A dog was gutted. We thought it was one of the ranch hands. After a few months, my father posted an all night sentry. It stopped and the sentry business faded away. Then the weird killings started again. Dad fired the five new hands and that seemed to stop it. We always thought it was one of them. Now, I wonder.'

Cole sat in thought for a moment. 'Crayne withdrew from me once I got involved in sports and music in high school but every now and then he would quiz me about my girlfriends. Who I was dating, who I wanted to date, who wanted to date me. One of my buddies told me once Crayne cornered him in the feed store and asked him the same things about my dates.' Cole paused as he recalled something else.

337

'That's how he found out about Erika. That I had a date with her. I always thought he was trying to live vicariously through me because he never really had any dates that I can remember. I always thought he didn't have the time or opportunity to meet anyone to ask out because our father made him work so hard on the ranch. Now I don't know. Was he trying to steal something that I had and he didn't; or was he trying to set me up to take a fall? Is he trying to punish me or emulate me?'

Tony treated it as a rhetorical question and sat like a stone. But his hands became white knuckled on the steering wheel, his foot grew heavier on the gas pedal.

Cole continued. 'There was such a huge dichotomy in the way my father treated his sons. I was the golden boy. Crayne was the whipping boy. I still don't understand why. And in a way that explains his violence. Doesn't excuse it, but explains it,' Cole mused morbidly.

Tony leaned down and drew a forty-five caliber revolver out of an ankle holster and handed it to Cole. He took an extra clip out of the car console and gave him that too. 'How good a shot is your brother?'

'He grew up around guns. I've seen him get a deer through the heart at a hundred and fifty yards. He can bag twenty ducks in a half hour on a foggy morning. But he's best with a hunting knife. It's how we used to go rabbit hunting. He could knock the head off one a hundred feet away.'

Cole closed his eyes as he imagined the blade that collected their dinner on round-up nights was probably the same one that was used to mutilate the shoulders of two women. The same one that was held against Miranda's throat this morning.

They sat in silence as Tony wove the Caddy through cars headed home to the suburbs.

'Milano said he'd be sending some of his cops to the ranch,' Cole informed his new partner. He's doing damage control on his own foul-ups before he can come himself.'

'I wouldn't expect anything else,' Tony snapped contemptuously. It was the most feeling Cole had seen him show.

'You don't like the Lieutenant?'

'*La culebra*,' Tony murmured.

'The snake?' Cole tried to draw Tony out.

'That's what he's called at headquarters. Behind his back, of course. One does not intentionally aggravate anything as poisonous as Milano.'

'You used to be a cop?'

'*Si*, I retired years ago, but still have *amigos* there. Rick Milano is not well liked in the department. He is cold, superior, insidious and greedy. You never know when he may strike. And he can operate as low and dirty as *una culebra's* belly on the ground.

'You have to understand I am biased against him. I will never forgive the pain he caused Miranda. It was unnecessary and cruel.'

'What happened?' Cole felt his hands bunching into fists.

'You know they were nearly engaged?' The look on Cole's face confirmed that for Tony. 'As far as Miranda was concerned they were. They were a very high-profile couple in San Antonio, followed by that silly *mujer* who writes the society column. What do you call . . .? Ah, yes, 'media darlings', that's what they were. Milano continued to fool around on the side, flashing his badge to kill gossip. Then he finally attracted a girl from a wealthy family who had a bad reputation. They were seen together and Milano made more threats to keep it out of the paper.

'I assume he wanted to keep the star reporter on his arm to maximize the publicity with her until he finally had a multi-million dollar checkbook in his hand. And he did play it to the very end.'

Cole was finding it hard to breathe. 'What do you mean?'

'Miranda became the . . . what do you say? The cliche. The last to know. She read about it in the morning paper. Her fiance married another woman. And she had to appear on television that night.'

339

Cole felt the rage rising up like a tidal wave from the pit of his stomach. Rick Milano had tried to ruin his life but the anger he felt knowing that was pale compared to this red-hot enmity.

'How could he treat her so callously? Didn't he feel anything for her?'

'Who knows?' Tony shrugged. 'I doubt that he even does. I think whatever he does feel he manipulates in ways that benefit his own ambitions, which are: to be rich, to be famous and to be powerful.

'Is this not what happened with his sister? You and I can understand the fury we would feel if our sister were nearly raped, then becomes a tool of the pornography industry. But instead of merely setting out to vindicate her, he thought only in terms of how the revenge would benefit himself.'

Cole fought the urge to put his fist through the dashboard. He slammed it with his open palm instead. Tony didn't even flinch. 'I wish I'd known this.'

'Why?' Tony's own anger had abated. 'So you could put your fist through him instead of my car? It would never be worth your effort or the consequences. Rick Milano will have to pay for this in ways that hurt him more than physical violence would.'

'I don't believe that. That life is fair. That justice will be served.'

Tony tipped his head once in agreement. 'Oh, I would say life is unfair. But this time Lieutenant Milano has made the wrong people angry. He will find out he's been spending more time making enemies than making the right friends.'

The conversation closed as Cole pointed out the exit to take. Both men grew more tense as they neared their destination. Cole willed Tony to drive faster, even though the older man had already pushed the speedometer up to eighty-five miles an hour.

'Do you know your brother's telephone number?'

Cole shook his head. Tony called information, dialed

the number and got no answer. They both knew that
didn't mean anything. Then Cole thought of Bubba.

'Maybe he could drive over and see if Crayne's car is at
the bunkhouse,' Cole suggested.

Tony looked skeptical. 'Can he be trusted not to do
anymore than that?'

Cole understood what he was saying. 'He'll do what I
ask him to do. I'd trust him with my life.'

Tony nodded and Cole dialed. He looked at the phone
oddly as he switched it off.

'It's busy,' he mumbled with an uneasy sense of foreboding.

341

CHAPTER 23

A numbness seeped into her bones, rooting her to the flagstone walkway. A magnetic force held her eyes on the carved tree. Questions about how Crayne discovered her nickname threatened to undo her manufactured confidence in Cole.

'You like it Randi?' He spoke her nickname with a manic smoothness. The familiar ring in his voice, so like Cole's, taunted her.

When she didn't reply he shook the arm he'd been gripping. 'I carve real good, don't I?'

Miranda bit back the retort she would have loved to give, deciding instead to humor him. She had to keep his guard down, earn his trust.

'It's the best I've ever seen.' She said it flatly, not able to add the touch of warmth she should have.

Still, it seemed the right answer, for Crayne loosened his hold on her arm and nudged her toward the house.

'Yeah. I spent a long time doin' it today, thinking about you and me. I knew you'd come back to see me. We didn't get to finish,' Crayne added petulantly.

A nauseating shiver ran through Miranda at his words, the numbness rushing out of her body only to be replaced with a nerve-tingling dread. Perhaps she had misjudged his capability for self-directed violence.

Dragging Miranda along, he stomped up the porch steps and stretched his hand out to open the door. The bent of his head was so reminiscent of Cole that Miranda felt a tug on her heart. Slipping into a quagmire of emotions, she recognized that she had to stop her descent before she could hope to get out of this.

Help came from a place she should have expected.

They heard the angry barks and simultaneously turned toward its source. A flash of golden fur raced around the corner of the porch, knocking Crayne down onto the wooden floor. Hands still secured behind her back, Miranda leaned with all her strength against the porch post to keep from being propelled with her captor.

Reggie, teeth bared, stood on Crayne's chest, his muzzle in his face. Crayne's eyes widened in fear, but too late Miranda realized it was fear of losing her not fear of the dog attack. For, when she turned to make an unbalanced escape around the cabin, she felt his hand snatch her hair. The brief pain was superseded by the sounds of growling, the scraping of canine nails against the wood floor, the tearing of fabric, and the sickly sweet smell of fresh blood.

'Did the dog scare you?' His voice was disembodied with calm as Miranda saw Reggie literally shredding his legs. Amazed, she studied his face. He was not feeling it at all. 'I'll take care of him for you.'

In slow motion, he unsheathed the knife at his waist. But before Miranda could open her mouth, his wrist flicked like lightning, catching Reggie on the underside of his jaw. Red liquid coursed out of the deep gash. Reggie yelped but did not pause in his attack. Crayne's bloodied hand cocked back for another slash when Miranda finally screamed.

'No!'

His hand froze in mid-air. Ominously, his focus shifted from the dog to her. Her heart stopped beating when she looked into his eyes. Empty gray holes. She had never seen anything more terrifying in her life.

Blood dripped off the knife. Blood soaked his shredded jeans. Man's and dog's mixing.

'Can't we just go inside and get away from him?'

'No,' Crayne frowned. 'He'd just cause problems barking. And he'd bother her when she comes. He hates her.'

So, Sable wasn't here. Miranda had some time. It gave her courage. 'You know, if you kill him and leave him out here, anyone who comes by will see him and it will look suspicious. Why don't you lock him up in the horse barn over there?'

Crayne considered the idea, then narrowed his eyes. 'You're coming with me.'

With his hand on her arm, Miranda followed cooperatively. Crayne dragged his leg, with Reggie still mauling it. Blood dripped a red trail on the sandy path. At the tack room, he detached Reggie by slicing at him. Miranda was afraid Crayne would kill him.

'Hurry. We need to attend to those legs right away,' Miranda urged.

Her concern was real, it just wasn't for him. He pulled the door closed in front of the red-matted dog who somehow still had the energy to throw himself against the door and bark violently.

Crayne wrapped his arm around her waist and led her back to the cabin. Miranda fought off another wave of nausea.

'You had a good time here with Cole yesterday, didn't you?'

Unsure of the answer he wanted, Miranda made a noncommittal sound. She kept her face straight ahead, but watched him through sidelong glances.

'I saw how pretty you was. So happy. I had to tell you, you was wrong. I had to scare you so you would listen. But you didn't listen, did you?' His voice grew louder. 'You went in and let him touch you, didn't you?'

Miranda quaked at the ominous tone. 'I..He..' What had Crayne seen? He'd spied on them. Was that the reason he knew what Cole called her? She felt a flash of anger that such a precious moment had been stolen from her by this sick man.

'The warning idea was dumb. With the other girls I

didn't do no talking. I just showed them I was the one they would never forget. Not him.'

Was it jealousy that drove him? Miranda gathered her wits. 'You know,' she began in a shaky voice. 'I hit my head when I fell. I must have blacked out because I didn't hear you say anything. What –'

'I said,' he interrupted. 'He don't deserve you, just like he don't deserve all the good things that he ever got. I said I was gonna take you away from him.'

She stopped and looked at his eyes. No longer empty, they were now overflowing with hate. Miranda felt a bud of hope. Emotion she could manipulate, the emptiness she could not.

'He'll just hurt you like he's hurt everybody else.' Where had she heard that before?

Crayne had stopped at the porch steps. He began gesturing, his eyes focused on something beyond Miranda. 'I protected him when he was little, I wouldn't let Daddy beat him up like he did me. I taught him stuff. And all of a sudden he gets all high and mighty and don't have no time for me no more. No, just his rich friends and his sluts. He thought he was gonna be a star while I was back here rolling around in cow shit.

'Well he ain't gonna be a star now, huh?' Crayne guffawed as he opened the front door and pushed her inside. ''Cept maybe in Huntsville. He can sing the blues to the cons.'

Staring down at a crack in the wooden stair, Miranda had to admit Cole didn't have much of a chance unless they found Erika before the grand jury met and unless she decided to tell the truth this time. The grand jury would be able to see through Rick's case then. She feared a trial jury would not.

Watching him amble from door to door locking them in, Miranda still couldn't figure out what he planned to do to her, although she was beginning to understand why. Resentment. Perhaps he'd suppressed that resentment in early years for the sake of brotherly love. From what she'd heard from Cole they had been fond of each other then. But eventually that love must have become fuel to the fire of Crayne's resentment when Cole didn't have the time to return that love, or so his older brother thought. He began to manifest resentment and perhaps jealousy at the life Cole had and Crayne wanted a chance to have in the only way he knew how – violence.

Caldwell had taught him well. Miranda suspected Crayne did not know Caldwell was not his natural father. Perhaps if he had none of this would have happened. Crayne would have had a reason if not an excuse to explain why he was the target of Caldwell's rage instead of Cole.

'I know you ain't believin' me,' Miranda jumped at the feel of his breath on her neck. She hadn't realized Crayne had come up right behind her. 'But there's nobody Cole don't hurt. It nearly killed Momma when he ran off and never talked to any of us again. It just made Daddy meaner. And he hurt her, my sweet wife. She just went to him to help me and he treated her like dog shit, too. Poor Blase.' Cole clamped his hand over his mouth as if he'd said something he shouldn't have.

'Oh, oh. She told me not to say her name to nobody.' He was talking to himself now.

Miranda wanted to keep him talking. He could let something slip, information she could use to free herself. Still, she had to be careful. Crayne was so deluded she didn't know what was true and what was not.

'Who's Blase?' Miranda couldn't help baiting him.

Crayne stuck the knife inches from her face. 'You don't say her name.' He stopped just when Miranda expected him to issue a threat. Completely unpredictable. One moment Miranda thought he was a dangerous psychotic. The next he seemed like a confused overgrown boy who was being used.

He mumbled to himself distractedly. 'I gotta call her.'

Seeming familiar with where things were in the house, he went straight to the phone in the kitchen and dialed.

'I got her here.'

Miranda could hear a raised voice on the other end of the line, but not what was being said.

'Cole's cabin.'

He listened to her for a moment then interrupted. 'I know. I know. I didn't do no kidnapping. She came here. I saw her peekin' in Momma and Daddy's house.' Pause. 'I dunno, looking for me I guess. Cole came up on us this morning and I didn't get to . . .'

His face broke into a smile. 'Thanks. Yeah, the cops was right there and got him after I ran off . . . You think I did good, huh?'

Miranda's stomach turned at his childish pleasure at her approval. The corners of his mouth turned down again and he began to hold the phone like it was going to bite him.

'No. I ain't gonna do that. I don't wanna hurt nobody.'

Miranda directed her look of amazement to her feet. What did he think he'd been doing with those women he raped and tattooed with a knife? What was Sable telling him to do?

Crayne was listening intently now to the voice at the other end of the line. 'Okay. That sounds better. Yeah. How long will that take? We can stay here during the day and sleep out at night when Bubba comes home.' Pause. 'Yeah. I know. We won't stay long. Just wanna get somethin' to eat.'

His voice dropped to a low, intimate tone. 'When we gonna be together honey? I miss ya.' He mumbled into the phone, waited for her answer and hung up.

Miranda's heart sank lower with each exchange. He was taking her out into the woods, where it would be near impossible to find her – if and when – Doug figured out where she was in the first place. Why hadn't she taken the time to tell him more? Tony would probably be able to put the pieces of the puzzle together but only with Cole's help. And he wouldn't get that help unless Erika showed up and convinced Rick to let Cole go . . .

What if Cole didn't want to help find her? Miranda felt her heart constrict. She was sure Rick had convinced Cole by now that she had collaborated with the police to set him up. For an instant, she didn't care whether she was found or not.

Sucking in a deep breath, Miranda pulled her psyche out from where it dangled over a pit of self-pity. It would do no good. She realized her second career was headed for an even earlier death than her first, but she had to fight harder than she had last time. She admitted that she'd harbored a sense of self-loathing for not sticking with her reporting job, even if it had meant lawsuits or moving to a smaller market and starting over. She loved journalism and owed herself more than what she had given.

This time it would be different. Even if she failed she would give it her all. And then she could leave, taking her self-respect with her. The first step to doing that was to not let Sable get away with blackmail.

Crayne slid his eyes uneasily over Miranda's bound wrists as he strode into Cole's bedroom. Her gaze followed him then drifted to the rumpled bedcovers. She imagined the sheets still warm. Goosebumps rose on her arms and her nipples grew taut as she instantly recalled the intense and deep lovemaking she and Cole had shared there just twenty-four hours ago. She closed her eyes and felt his hands in her hair, his lips on her flushed skin. Her eyelids flew open. Miranda blushed with embarrassment, the memory was so vivid. She was grateful Crayne ignored her as he rifled through drawers.

'We'll borrow some clothes,' he chuckled. 'Cole sure as hell won't be needing nothing but an orange jail jumpsuit.' Crayne let out a peal of high-pitched laughter. Miranda shivered.

Crayne stopped in the bedroom doorway, and paused. His eyes shifted around the room. He looked lost. Miranda's brows drew together as she tried to find an impetus for his changeable behavior. One moment he was manic,

348

the next he seemed mystified. She realized his capriciousness was the most dangerous thing about Crayne.

Snapping out of his daze, he flung a heavy knit sweater, pillow and blanket at Miranda. In an automatic reflex, her hands jerked up only to be stopped by their binding. Her body absorbed the shock of their impact instead. They bounced off of her and onto the coffee table. The sweater slithered down her lap and onto the floor.

Oblivious, Crayne opened the refrigerator and got out the leftover steak and salad. He stood at the counter and ate out of the containers, using his knife to bring the food to his mouth. The flash of its silver blade was dulled by brown streaks. It looked as if the only cleaning it ever got was being sheathed and unsheathed. Averting her eyes, Miranda thought about what was on the knife: Reggie's blood, the blood of two women and only God knew what else.

Crayne speared another piece of meat. He chomped with an open mouth, a stream of red juice ran out and down his chin. He swiped at it with the back of his hand. Miranda shifted her gaze to the stream outside. She didn't want to ask Crayne for anything, but her mouth felt like sandpaper and she was afraid her stomach would contract in dry heaves any minute if she didn't get a drink.

'May I have some water?' She forced strength into her voice.

Crayne's head snapped up as if he had forgotten she was in the room. He gave a grunt and a nod and grabbed a glass, filling it with tap water. She put her lips to it, trying not to recoil from the greasy imprints of his fingers. She only managed to down a few sips before he lost patience, put down the glass and went back to his meal.

He was nearly finished, and Miranda knew she had to detain him for as long as possible. For once they got out in the woods, her chances of getting free declined considerably. Outside he could outrun her. He knew the country better than she did. Inside there was the phone. And Bubba. He would come home soon.

Crayne had emptied the containers and Miranda watched as he sheathed the greasy knife without cleaning it off. He walked up and kicked her shin. 'Let's go.'

Miranda forced herself to put her plan into action. It was now or never. A gamble that could have dire consequences, but could also make her free.

'Crayne, can't we stay here for a little longer?' She stood shakily and brushed her breasts against his arms. Nausea welled in her throat as she saw his reaction. Masculine desire, but also a sick little boy's confusion.

'Nah . . . we, ah, we gotta get goin'.'

Miranda pressed a nipple, hardened from the chill of fear, into his arm, praying he would not be able to resist asking the next question.

'What d'ya have in mind?' he finally asked. His eyes shifted back and forth.

'That bed in there sure looks inviting. Thought you and I could try it out . . .' She tried her best to look seductive, letting her loose hair drift over her face.

Eyes wide with shock and fear and temptation, Crayne shook his head. 'I'm married. I can't do that.'

Miranda tried to hide her disbelief. Did he not remember what he had done to those other women? Or had he rationalized the brutal attacks? Or had Sable rationalized them for him?

Miranda quickly gathered her wits back and breathed in his ear. 'But I want you, Crayne.'

Her words worked like a magic spell. He looked at her like she was an angel just descended. 'Nobody ever said that to me before. Me? You want me?'

My life, I am fighting for my life.

'Oh yes,' Miranda breathed.

350

CHAPTER 24

Out of nowhere, a silver sportscar appeared behind them, and sped around.

'He must be going a hundred miles an hour.' Cole turned to his companion in amazement.

Tony merely lifted his eyebrows. Cole looked back at the road ahead just as taillights flashed and the car disappeared over the hill. Someone he knew had a car like that. But who? The two men sat in silence for a few minutes.

Suddenly Cole blurted out: 'Wayne.'

'Yes?' Tony questioned.

'Wayne has a car like that one that just passed us.'

Instead of dismissing Cole's observation by pointing out thousands of people in the area had cars like that one, Tony entertained the possibility.

'Why would Wayne Lambert be here?'

Cole shrugged. 'I don't know. Maybe Wayne is headed to see my parents, hoping to find a way to get my shares in the club. I suppose, by now, he's heard I'm locked up.'

'Would he do that?'

'There's no telling with Wayne. The rapes, the police around, had him on edge. Then he was being blackmailed, and I guess I was his number one suspect. With me out of circulation, I suppose he's breathing easier on both counts,' Cole paused. 'Yeah, he might go try to talk to Caldwell and Vanessa . . .'

Tony remained impassive behind the wheel. After a few

minutes, he asked: 'So, would you like to go to your parents' house first, or your home?'

'I care about one thing and that's getting Miranda out safely. Let's go to my parents' house first. That's where you say she was going. Let's pray she's talking to them instead of somewhere with Crayne.'

A few minutes later, they turned into the Traynor Ranch. Speeding down the rocky path, Cole glanced at the bunkhouse. Crayne's car was not there. A few of the ranch hands gave them curious looks, one tried to stop them, but Tony ignored him and slid to a stop on the gravel driveway in front of the hacienda.

'No Wayne,' Cole observed, glancing into the carport. 'And Crayne's car's not here either.'

Tony looked at Cole, his eyes asking Cole's plan.

'You come with me. Maybe you'll see something I'll miss.'

Tony nodded, checked his three remaining guns, a nine-millimeter, a .38 and an old .22. Tony handed the Glock to Cole. He shoved it into the front waistband of his jeans. It was in full view and he wanted it that way.

'Forget the .45. Use this. It's quick and handy, but its bullets are not always deadly, even if put in the right place. Most go in and out. Remember that.' Tony warned.

Cole looked at him but said nothing. He wondered if Tony had given him this particular gun on purpose. A gun that might wound but not kill.

Cole's long strides covered the flagstone walkway in seconds with Tony following, unhurried, a few paces behind. Cole seemed calm, too calm. But when he rang the bell, impatiently, repeatedly, his agitation was obvious.

'Jes, Senor –' the maid who had opened the door stopped with her mouth open. Her polite mask slipped to reveal shock. 'Senor *Cole*?'

He hadn't seen the woman in his life, but didn't have time to wonder how she recognized him. 'I need to see Mrs Traynor,' Cole paused, seeming to steel himself to say the next words. 'My mother.' He brushed past the maid, who had just noticed Tony and looked even more confused. Tony passed her, inclining his head in both greeting and apology.

'Mother,' Cole yelled as he prowled the house, from living room, to kitchen and back.

'Colton?' Vanessa Traynor appeared at the doorway to one of the bedrooms. Clutching a handkerchief she wiped tears from her face as she nearly ran toward her son. Her face asked no questions, just accepted that he was here, with her. And, for the first time in ten years she threw her arms around him.

Cole wrapped his arms around the slender woman, but allowed the embrace to last no more than thirty seconds. Pulling back, he looked into her eyes, now filled with tears of joy.

'Has a woman named Miranda Randolph been here to see you this afternoon?' When Vanessa looked confused, he shook her shoulders with barely contained impatience. 'She's beautiful, auburn hair, turquoise eyes . . .'

Vanessa shook her head. 'What is going on? What is happening to you? Can I help you?'

'The only way you can help me now is to tell me if you've seen this woman. She could be in danger. Think!' Cole was yelling now.

From behind him, Tony murmured under his breath. 'Easy, *amigo* . . .'

Vanessa cradled Cole's jaw in her palms. 'I love you. I have missed you so much.'

'Mother, I just can't . . . We can't go into this right now. I have to find this woman. She is in danger.'

'She'll be in worse danger if you find her,' A voice boomed from down the hall. 'Who is she, your next victim? One that got away?'

Caldwell Traynor loomed in the doorway. The color drained from Cole's face but slowly, painfully, he swiveled to face his father. Behind him, Vanessa, her face stricken, reached for his arm. Cole shook her off.

'So, you've seen her? Is she here?'

'I wouldn't tell you if she was, boy. What do you think I wanna be? An accomplice to a serial rapist? Now, you get the hell off my property,' Caldwell's eyes glittered cruelly at his son. For the first time, Cole noticed Caldwell carried a twenty-gauge rifle at his side. Tony already had his hand inside his jacket.

'I'll get off as soon as you tell me if you've seen Miranda,' Cole challenged.

The two men who shared blood and nothing more locked in a standoff for minutes that to Tony and Vanessa seemed endless. So much that was unsaid hung heavy in the air between them. Finally Caldwell raised the nose of the rifle to point at his son. Vanessa let out a whimper.

'No.'

Cole glanced back at his mother briefly, then trained a hostile gaze back at the tall man in front of him. 'I see you still get off torturing Mama.' Cole was unaware he'd slipped back into the familiar term for his mother. The one he'd used as a boy. But somehow he was struck with a sense of *deja vu*. This was a familiar argument they might have had ten or fifteen years before. Only this time Cole was standing up for not only his mother, as he always had, but also for himself and the woman he loved.

Caldwell glowered. 'I never hurt your mama. I've been good to her since the day we got married, and I will be until the day I die.'

Cole felt his fury seeping away. His father really believed what he had just said, despite all the years of mental torture and verbal abuse. Suddenly he struck Cole as pitiful. An aging man whose mind was so narrow he only had room in it for his perceptions, and a will so strong he tried to impose it on everyone around him. No amount of arguing or threats was ever going to change him.

'Look, you can shoot me or tell me if you've seen Miranda. Those are the only two ways you are going to get rid of me.'

Vanessa was crying hysterically now. 'No, Cole, just go. I can tell you —'

'Vanessa, shut up,' Caldwell warned.

She looked at her husband, then took a shaky breath. 'She hasn't been here. We haven't seen anyone today. Reporters have called . . . but we haven't talked to any of them . . .'

Cole grabbed his mother's hands in his, imploring her with his look. 'How about Crayne? Has he been here?'

Her brow furrowed. 'What does this have to do with your brother?'

'Just answer me. Please.'

'Don't say a word, Vanessa. Get out of here,' Caldwell shoved the nose of the rifle into Cole's shoulder.

Vanessa gave him a look that was both sad and defiant and turned back to Cole. 'I haven't seen him, but one of the ranch hands came looking for him a little while ago. He said Crayne had left at dawn, then came back sometime after noon but no one has seen him since.'

Cole's face softened. He realized how hard defying his father had been for her. His arms wrapped her in a warm hug. 'I love you.'

Knocking the rifle out of his way, Cole strode out of the front door, past where the maid stood shaking, still holding the door. Tony turned on his heel to follow.

Caldwell blocked Tony's way with the gun barrel. 'Who the hell are you?'

'A friend,' Tony smiled coldly. And before Caldwell could realize what he was doing, Tony had jammed a wad of foam rubber into the end of the rifle and he was gone. Juanita slammed the door behind him.

With a string of curses, Caldwell tried to get the rubber out of the gun. When he found he couldn't, he stomped over to where Vanessa stood gazing out the window, her tears still flowing unchecked down her cheekbones.

'What the hell were you thinkin' when you told him all that? You fool.'

Slowly, Vanessa raised her face to his. Her crying

stopped, though tears still glistened in her eyes. 'I was giving my son the help he asked for. And you are the fool.'

Caldwell narrowed his eyes and gripped her arm a little too hard. 'You always did turn real impertinent around him. He brought out the worst in you, always.'

'I disagree. I think he brings me to my senses.' Vanessa turned back to the window, looking at the space where her youngest son had disappeared. Out of her life again.

In a rage, Caldwell's face darkened to crimson. He squeezed her arm once more then released it. It fell limply to her side.

'I'm callin' the sheriff.'

'Look there.' Tony had led Cole around to the side of the house and now pointed at the windowsill. 'That's what I saw from inside.'

Cole reached over and picked up the small tape recorder. His fingers felt the raised lettering of a label. Turning it over, he read, 'Randolph. She *was* here.'

Eyes scanning the area surrounding them, he whispered, 'But where is she now?'

Tony kneeled down, feeling the crushed grass. 'Wherever it is, she didn't go willingly.'

'They can't have gotten far,' Cole said half to himself, half to Tony. 'Let's check the bunkhouse first.'

Jumping into the Cadillac, they drove back down the driveway, parking in front of the barn. The door to the bunkhouse was locked, but Tony picked the lock in seconds and they were inside.

The smell first assaulted them, heavy and thick with mildew, rotting food and sweat. The linoleum floor, brown with dirt in the places that it showed, was strewn with soiled clothes. Dishes that dripped coagulated grease like stalagtites were piled in the small aluminum sink, on the counter and on the kitchen table. The couch, pulled out to a bed, showed sheets yellowed from too much wear without washing.

The bathroom door was closed. Tony drew his gun and

Cole followed his lead. Tony kicked it open. It was empty.

The metallic scent of dried blood wafted out to mix with the other noxious odors in the room. Tony bent down and picked up a T-shirt from behind the toilet. It was splattered with browned bits of blood, along with streaks, as if something bloody had been wiped on it. Cole's stomach heaved. Forcing the bile back down into his throat he reached for the other white shirt in the pile. It, too, was bloody.

Tony straightened and looked at Cole. 'Looks just like the one you have on. What brand do you wear?'

Realization dawned on Cole. 'Hanes.'

Tony checked the tag, confirming what they both guessed. 'Would he know that?'

'I don't know how,' Cole muttered, shaking his head slowly.

Tony looked thoughtful, but said nothing. For a split second, Cole wondered if Tony doubted his innocence. He wouldn't blame him. The frame fit just right.

Suddenly Cole couldn't stand to be in his brother's house any longer. He almost ran outside, gulping in the fresh air. The sudden intake of oxygen heightened his anxiety instead of dispelling it. Desperately, his eyes scanned the barns, the pens. He had to find Miranda. Tony finally emerged. They both noticed a ranch hand approaching from the barns.

'Should we take the shirts? As evidence?' Cole asked.

Tony shook his head. 'No. How can we prove we did not get them from your house, or where you've been hiding them? No. Leave them here. Let the police find them.'

'But what if he gets back here and destroys them?'

'Ah, but you are lucky. I am probably the most credible witness you can hope for. Except for a priest, of course. When I speak, the police believe me.'

Or else. Cole thought. He imagined Tony had a few stories that those in charge at the SAPD didn't want told. 'Okay.'

'Y'all need somethin'?' The ranch hand squinted at the

357

two men as he approached. He shot a stream of tobacco-stained spit at their feet and adjusted the wad in his cheek.

'Just looking for Crayne. You know where we can find him?' Cole asked as he walked toward the cowboy, trying to keep his voice calm and friendly.

'Nah, we was lookin' for him ourselves. He jus' breezed in a coupla hours ago and we ain't seen him since.'

'He take his car?' Cole looked around.

'Nah, it's behind the barn over there.' He gestured with his arm, revealing the line of a farmer's tan at the cuff of his long-sleeved shirt. 'Kinda funny place for him to put it. Usually just sets it right here by his door and all.'

They walked around the building and Cole checked the car, it was clean and empty. Except for a jacket on a hangar lying across the passenger seat. Now that they were in the shade, the cowboy looked hard at Cole.

'Hey, you related to Crayne or somethin'?'

'Why?' Cole asked, on guard.

'You look just like 'im. Or damned close anyways.' The cowboy shook his head. 'Shoot.'

'I'm his brother,' Cole answered cautiously, wondering what poison Crayne might have spread about him around here.

But the cowboy's face only showed surprise. 'Brother, huh? I never knew he had one, is all. You mustn't be from 'round here.'

They were walking on the edge of the clearing, back to where Tony stood waiting, when something caught Cole's eye. On a tree about a hundred yards ahead he saw a glint of red off a tree. He looked again. It was gone. He hurried to where he thought he saw it anyway.

As they neared, Cole could see it was a clump of hair caught in the bark of the oak tree, being buffeted by the breeze. 'What's that?'

The cowboy squinted and spat again, on the ground near Cole's foot. 'Oh, probly jus' some tuft off the en' of a heifer's tail. Switchin' at some fly and she git it caught in that there tree.'

Cole reached out for the hair. It was too fine to be cattle hair. He put it to his nose. Miranda! He looked beyond the oak tree and saw the start of a faint footpath. It wasn't from cattle, the cedars and oaks were too close together to let a cow's belly pass. He beckoned Tony, trying to stay calm and losing the battle.

Tony rushed faster than Cole had seen him move all day. Still it wasn't fast enough for Cole.

'Thanks,' he tried to dismiss the cowboy. But the guy was stubborn and getting suspicious.

'Hey what are you boys gonna do? Why y'all worked up about a lil cattle fur?'

Cole, about to lose his cool, opened his mouth but Tony took in the situation in seconds and jumped in. 'Oh, I agree. Let's leave. We can find Crayne another time.'

Glaring at Tony, Cole turned to the cowboy putting out his hand, barely controlling his impatience. 'Right. Thanks, then.'

The other man shook his hand and wished them luck. 'I'll tell Crayne y'all came by.'

Smoothly, Tony interjected. 'Oh no, let us surprise him when we see him.'

The waving cowboy didn't read the threat in Tony's smile.

359

CHAPTER 25

Crayne shifted his weight from foot to foot as Miranda
rubbed herself against him. What was he supposed to do?
God, he had a hard-on. It hurt. Bad. Real bad. Did she
really want him? He didn't know what that was like, to be
wanted. By a woman. Maybe he could find out. Do it with
Cole's girl. But Blase . . . it would hurt her feelings. She
would be mad. He could do it nice this time and just tell
her it had been like the other girls. But that would be lying,
she made him promise never to lie. Maybe she wouldn't
ask what it exactly was that they did. Yeah, yeah, she
wouldn't ask for details. She hadn't wanted to know too
much about the other girls.

He untied Miranda then let her push him into the
bedroom. Cole's bedroom. Panic struck Crayne. What
if he wasn't as good as Cole? He would be. He knew it.
Better. Because she wanted him.

Her body. It felt so different. Soft and curvy. The other
girls he never really noticed. Blase was hard and straight.

'You are so handsome,' she told him.

But when he reached out to feel her she whispered,
'Wait.' Her hand moved down him. She bent over.

'Let me take off my shoes first. Her hands stroked his
leg. Up high. Crayne closed his eyes and swore. Then
she pushed him onto the bed, then got on top of him.
Her body felt so good. He had to have her now. He
grabbed at her sweatshirt. Pulling. Ripping. She arched
up. She loved it! She loved him! Then he heard the

360

crash, just before his head exploded. A flash of red, and then black . . .

Miranda leaped off Crayne's now-limp form as if he were a leper. She stared from her shaking hands to the oak and glass lamp they still gripped. The left corner dripped blood. Stunned, she raised her eyes to Crayne's head and saw the nasty gash the lamp had made. She had made.

Quickly, Miranda let the lamp drop to the carpet and reached under the bed for her shoes and her gun. The cold steel jarred her back from the shock she was slipping into.

Tucking the gun back into the waistband of her jeans, Miranda raced into the kitchen. She had to find the keys to the Bronco parked in the front. Frantically, but quietly, she searched all the kitchen. Nothing. In Bubba's room, she rifled through his dressers. A lot of boxer shorts, two pairs of white socks and a single pair of jeans. No keys. Should she dare sneak back into Cole's room? How long would Crayne be unconscious or had she killed him? She glanced toward the barn. She could take one of the horses. But the land had fences and she'd be trapped. On foot she wouldn't get far and he could track her. She tiptoed into Cole's room.

Crayne was deathly still. Miranda paused a half-beat to see if he was breathing. Reassured that he was, she decided as she turned back to the top dresser drawer and found what she was looking for. The keys jangled so loudly in the silent cabin that she jumped. Wrapping her fingers around them to silence them, she padded softly to the door.

One foot in the hall and a sweaty hand grabbed her wrist from behind. Miranda screamed and Crayne swore, ramming her body against the wall, knocking the wind out of her.

'You think you're real smart, lying to me. I hate liars. Just like my brother. Liar.' Spinning her around, he spat in her face. Suddenly, his heavy breathing slowed. Miranda forgot her urge to wipe his spit off her face. She forgot everything. His eyes were empty gray holes and they terrified her.

'I'm gonna show you who's boss here.'

He grabbed both her hands in one of his, the cracked, calloused skin rubbing against her smooth skin. With his right hand, he unsheathed the knife at his waist. Miranda had forgotten the knife.

With one sweeping movement, Crayne sliced open the left sleeve of the sweatshirt she wore. Horrified, Miranda looked to see if he'd cut her arm as well. She felt numb. No blood. Yet. Crayne focused on her shoulder. Miranda remembered the photos of the rape victims. The bloody tattoos. They had gone there.

Without thinking, Miranda's hands flew up with all her strength, knocking Crayne's arm out of position. The knife clattered to the tile floor as Miranda accelerated backward. Her hands yanked the .38 out of her pants, clicking off the safety, she pointed it at Crayne. His eyes widened with realization, not fear. Miranda remembered the look he had when Reggie was chewing up his legs. Pain did not intimidate him.

Maybe imminent death would. Crayne crept toward her, his face a hideous mask. Miranda had never fired a gun at anything but a paper target. She hesitated. She couldn't kill him. Maybe a warning would stop him. Praying her aim was as good as it had been at the practice range, she squeezed the trigger.

The gun kicked back in her hand. Crayne flinched. The leather of his left boot splintered and red liquid seeped out. Transfixed, Miranda watched as his eyes slowly dropped down to his mangled foot. He swore. Ugly, low and guttural. His tone, not the words, chilled her.

She turned toward the door and behind her she could hear his footsteps, then a crash as he fell to the floor. His foot apparently refused to support his weight. His fingernails clawed the tile floor, then the wood paneled walls. She had reached the doorknob and turned it, slamming the door behind her.

The fresh cool air was like a tonic for her tortured soul. Her lungs drank it in thirstily. Realizing she couldn't take

362

anymore time, Miranda turned toward the Traynor Ranch. It wouldn't be long before Crayne learned to make his damaged foot work and would come after her. The pain sure as hell wasn't going to stop him. She didn't know the woods like he did, even if she could move faster . . .

The karate chop to her hand sent her .38 flying across the porch. Before her surpise could translate into fear, a knee buried itself in her kidney. Miranda's legs went limp from the pain and she slumped to the floor. Her eyes were on her gun, but her body would not obey her mind.

The door behind her opened.

'She wasn't gonna get away.' It was Crayne, whining. But who was he talking to? 'I was comin' after her. She tricked me is all. She tried to get me in bed, but I told her no –'

'Shut up, you idiot,' Sable ordered harshly. 'Why did you let her keep her piece? You're so Goddamned stupid. She could've killed you, except she's not smart enough. Get in there and leave this shit to me.'

Whimpering, Crayne closed the door softly. Miranda knew his wife's harsh words more than his wound was what hurt him. Miranda finally found the strength to look up at the evil woman above her. She met eyes unlike Crayne's empty ones. Sable's were glowing as they over-flowed with hate, jealousy and pure evil.

'So, you slut, you're not so high and mighty now are you?' Sable's laugh chilled Miranda. 'First you steal away my lover, then you try to do it to my husband too?' Miranda pretended to be surprised, but she kept quiet. She knew her knowledge of the secrets between this entire family might be the key to keeping herself alive.

'You know, you're no different from me. You use people to get what you want. You slept with Cole and your cop boyfriend to solve your case. You should have slept with me, could've had it all wrapped up by now. And had the best lay in your life in the process.' Sable found that amusing, her lips stretching over her teeth in a hideous grin.

Her laughter faded away and she continued. 'Only thing is, you want stupid things. Truth and justice. What does that get you? At least I work for something. Money, power, fame. And I am going to get them.'

Nausea rose up in Miranda's throat. Not now. She tried to control it as she gave another sidelong look at her gun. One of Sable's boots shoved her flat on the ground again. A rope was tied around her wrists again. Her skin had been rubbed raw earlier and with the contact, Miranda winced.

But Miranda knew that it was now or never. Ignoring the pain, she bucked her body violently, away from Sable's grasp and leaped toward the gun. But her hands were so tangled in the rope that Sable reached out first. Sinewy fingers wrapped around the steel and brought the butt down on Miranda's head.

An explosion of stars ricocheted around Miranda's skull, but she refused to allow herself to go unconscious. Being awake was her only chance to stay alive. She had no illusions. She knew now Sable planned to kill her. It was the only way she was going to get what she wanted. Miranda was the last obstacle. The only one of the good guys who knew what Sable had done.

Sable finished tying her captive's hands while Miranda struggled with lucidity. When she saw Miranda's eyes flutter open, she yanked her up by her hair. 'Well, shit. Thought that might have killed you. Would've made my life easier. But I'd miss out on a lot more fun.'

Miranda didn't ask what fun Sable had in mind. She didn't want to know and hoped she never would. Sable put the gun to the small of Miranda's back and forced her forward. They walked toward the stable, with Miranda hanging back as much as she could.

Sable lost her patience and Miranda jumped from the report of the gun behind her before she felt the burning on the side of her calf. She bit her tongue to stop herself crying out. The less satisfaction Sable got the better. Miranda could feel the warm blood welling between her cheek and teeth. She swallowed. Tentatively, she put weight back on the leg and it held. A grazing wound, she guessed, as she felt the cool air whisper through the tear in her jeans.

When they passed the tackroom, Reggie barked weakly. Sable shied away. 'What the hell is that?'

Miranda spoke for the first time. 'Crayne cut Reggie up and locked him in there.'

'Why didn't the fool just kill him? Slit his throat or something? Asshole can't get anything right,' she muttered contemptuously.

Just down the breezeway from the tackroom, Sable pushed Miranda inside the workshop. She rattled around the piled-up items on the workbench, keeping her gun trained on Miranda's head. Finally, she found an eight-inch double-edged knife. She tucked it into her boot, and turned back to Miranda. 'Always pays to have two weapons. You should have remembered that, slut.'

Miranda felt some of her hope dissolving. But she forced herself to engage Sable in conversation. 'So, what do you plan to do with the club once you get Wayne's shares?' They walked back down the breezeway but when they got to the corrals, the horses, which hadn't been there before, were pawing at the gate anxiously. O'Malley whinnyed. Miranda wondered if he remembered her. Why else would he let out his welcome? For that's what it was, her years of growing up around horses told her it was not the sound of fear or nerves. Looking closer at the black gelding she saw his body tensed, his ears pointed to just beyond the cabin. In the woods. What was there? Or who?

CHAPTER 26

Cole and Tony heard the gunshot as they approached Cole's property and both began to run.

'Sounded like a .38,' Tony observed.

'That's what Miranda carries,' Cole breathed. God, how he prayed she was on the right end of the gun.

Leading the way, Cole wove a path through the cedars and oaks. Every now and then he would see a knarled tree trunk or jutting limestone rock that would remind him of taking the trail as a kid. But those memories would lead him to thoughts of his big brother and he didn't want to remember Crayne like that. He had to remind himself his brother was a brutal criminal.

Finally, they reached the cabin and Tony indicated they should crouch down beside it. Cole waved him off and started out onto the driveway. Tony reached out for his shoulder with an iron grip. Cole whipped around angrily.

'Miranda is in danger. There's no time to play war games,' he whispered impatiently.

'Taking time means saving lives. Most especially yours,' Tony reminded him.

'I don't care about my life,' Cole stopped, shocked to hear the words, yet knowing he meant them. 'I care about getting to Miranda before it's too late.'

'We both want that,' Tony said slowly. His cool was unshaken. 'But if you are lying in the dirt bleeding to death, how will that help her?'

Cole glared at Tony for a few seconds, then reluctantly

hunkered down next to him. They peeked around the corner. Everything seemed quiet. Too quiet, Cole thought. Then the horses thundered up. Where's Reggie? Cole wondered. His ears strained to listen for his joyful bark. Tony nudged him, pointing up the drive. About a hundred yards up they could see a flash of gray through the trees. It was a sportscar.

'Could that be the one that passed us on the highway?' Tony asked, his eyes narrowing.

'That would mean Wayne is here,' Cole answered. 'But why? He doesn't even know where this place is.'

'You don't know anyone else with a car like that? Or anyone who might borrow it from Wayne?'

Cole's face changed, becoming dangerous. 'Sable . . .'

Just then, their attention was drawn to the stable, where Sable appeared, shoving Miranda in front of her. Cole's heart jumped into his throat. He saw the ripped jeans, the blood on her calf and knew he might be too late. O'Malley whinnyed. Miranda looked in their direction. He started out after them. Again, Tony restrained him.

'Let me help her.' Cole pushed Tony away.

'Not until we know who else is here.'

'Like who?'

'Where is your brother?' Tony asked. Cole froze. Where was Crayne?

Gravel crunched on the driveway as a car came speeding toward the cabin. Looking at the approaching vehicle, Sable dragged Miranda in front of her, holding the gun to her head.

'You don't move, bitch. Not one hair. I'll kill you.' Sable's breath hissed in Miranda's ear. Miranda flinched. 'What? You don't think I'd do it? Wise up. I've done it before, to people I hated a lot less than I hate you.'

Miranda closed her mind to the hideous words, concentrating instead on keeping her eyes trained on the edge of the cabin where her instincts told her Cole was hiding. As the car drew closer, Miranda went limp in Sable's arms, slipping to the ground. Cole jumped out of the woods, and ran toward Miranda.

'Watch out, Cole,' Miranda screamed just as the front fender of the car threw him into the cedar fence surrounding the cabin. The BMW skidded to a stop and Vanessa Traynor jumped out from the passenger side, her eyes on her son.

'You stay right there mother-in-law dearest, or I will blow this beauty's head away right before your eyes.' Sable's deadly words cut across the driveway, freezing what had been a chaotic scene seconds before. Vanessa looked from Cole, who lay motionless against the fence, to Sable and back, as if making up her mind.

'Mother, do what she says,' came a weak voice from the fence. 'I love Miranda. Please.' Cole straightened up, grimacing at the effort it took. His words shocked Miranda. She longed to reach out and touch him to tell him she loved him too.

'Don't tell her what to do,' Caldwell Traynor stepped out from behind the wheel of the BMW. Miranda could see out of the corner of her eye that he carried a deer rifle with him. He had it pointed at Cole. Cole looked past his father, at Miranda, who Sable had pulled back up. For no more than half a second the rest of the world fell away. He saw love and hope and faith – in him – shimmering in her eyes. He tried to send the same to her and more, much more.

Everyone turned as the door to the cabin opened. Out limped Crayne. Vanessa gasped at the blood that covered his shot foot. Caldwell grunted. 'That she-devil finally shoot you boy? Took longer than I thought. What'd she do? Come back to town to finish you off? Took your balls with her, now come back to get the rest?'

Cole was confused. Were they talking about Miranda? Or Sable?

'No. Cole's redheaded whore shot me,' Crayne threw back. 'He probably sent her to do it too.'

So it was Sable Caldwell was referring to, as if he knew

her. But how? Cole and Crayne locked eyes. He saw the emptiness, the face without a soul, a man he didn't know. Crayne's lips curved to a wicked smile.

'That's right, brother. Daddy knows your Sable. Her name's really Blase and she's my wife. What d'ya think 'bout that? For once I got one first, and *you* got the leftovers. And she only screwed you cuz it was part of the plan. She hated it just like she hated screwing Wayne –'

'Shut up,' Sable hissed, waving the gun at Crayne. 'You're ruining everything I worked so hard for. I ought to put the next bullet through your head.'

Stunned, Cole felt himself being drawn into a vortex of his own emotions. His brother, his ex-lover both capable of such evil. What did it mean about the kind of man he was? He felt eyes seeking his, he looked and caught their message. Miranda was silently pleading with him to come back, to fight, to live. For her. For them.

Vanessa started crying. Cole glanced at his mother, wishing he could take her hurt away and knowing it was too late. He stepped toward Miranda.

'You better stop right there or her brains, what little of them she has, will be spewed all over this prize horse of yours,' Sable threatened.

'Blase, darlin', let me take her over. You don't need to be messing yourself all up and getting into trouble,' Crayne started down the steps, his voice honeyed.

'I said "shut up", you bastard,' Sable seethed.

Miranda took her cue, the opening she had been waiting for. 'He is you know.'

Everyone stared at her, the first words she had spoken since the standoff began. Sable dug the nose of the .38 so far into her temple that her head began to throb. Miranda cleared her throat and her voice was stronger as she continued. She wished for her recorder that was sitting on the Traynors' windowsill. 'Crayne *is* a bastard. Vanessa, you have to tell the truth now. You might not have another chance. Tell them their plan won't work. Their plan to take all of the Traynor estate for themselves. Ask

369

them what they would have done once Cole was disgraced, written out of the will and locked up in prison. Would you and Caldwell be next? It's time. What happens next is up to you.'

'Mama?' Crayne's voice sounded like that of a frightened little boy.

The tears flowing down her cheeks didn't stop, but Vanessa began to talk. 'She's right. I don't know how she knows. No one but your dad – I mean Caldwell – has known all these years. I fell in love with a man from Germany before I married Caldwell. An exchange student. His name was Gunther. He was handsome and charming and promised to marry me. Then he was gone, and I found out I was pregnant. Caldwell asked me to marry him, he promised to be good to the baby, raise you as his own. I agreed.

'I tried to find your real father a few times, but never could. It was as if . . . he disappeared.' She glanced at Caldwell fearfully. His face was beet red, but he remained silent.

'I found out only today that Gunther was a spy, a double agent. That's why he had to leave so suddenly. He was killed. He never knew about you.'

Crayne looked like a volcano about to explode. He turned toward Miranda. His mouth opened, but Sable spoke first. 'So you are nothing but a bastard and a stupid one at that. I just married you for nothing. You're not getting any of the old man's money. You're not his kid. I've been screwing you and kissing you, making me sick for NOTHING.'

In the blink of an eye, Crayne unsheathed his knife and flung it straight at Sable and Miranda. Just as it left Crayne's hand, Cole felt his own nine millimeter go off. He hadn't even realized he'd drawn it. A red stain spread on Crayne's chest. He leaned heavily against the porch post. Sable shoved Miranda in front of her, but Miranda ducked down and Sable put her finger on the trigger as the knife imbedded itself just below her sternum. But before

370

she could get the shot off, Tony's bullet knocked the gun out of her hand. Sable stumbled, grabbing at Miranda to steady herself. Miranda backed away.

'Shit,' Sable spat as she fell to the rocky ground.

The pungent odor of gunfire burned the edges of Miranda's nostrils as she stared at the knife so grotesquely sticking out of Sable's chest. Then Miranda remembered the knife Sable had slid into her boot. But as Sable started to moan and writhe in pain, Miranda decided she wasn't a danger. She wouldn't be able to reach the knife, much less use it.

The urgent sound of sirens approaching filled the oppressive silence that had settled in the wake of the violence. Shivering, Miranda suddenly felt too weak to stand. Then she felt Cole's arms around her. She turned to him and buried her face in his chest.

'I love you, too,' Miranda whispered.

Cole shook his head and her heart skipped a beat. 'I love you more.' His smile began to warm the chill the day's evil had spread through her bones.

A host of police cars sped into the clearing, their flashing lights turning it into a neon twilight. An ambulance manuevered around them, coming to a stop next to where Sable lay. Cole and Miranda could see Caldwell straightening up from behind the car door where he'd hidden when the shots started being fired. Vanessa sat on the steps, Crayne's head in her lap. They could hear her telling him about his biological father, almost desperately, as if she knew his time was short.

Tony shook hands with a sheriff's deputy then walked toward the couple, who still clung to each other amid the activity. He smiled. It went all the way to his eyes.

Miranda smiled back. 'Where did you come from?'

'Ah, *mi bonita*, I just dropped by.'

'Just dropped by to save my life,' Miranda joked, then turned serious. 'Thank you.'

'I did nothing.' Tony shook Cole's hand. 'I just followed his lead. A very honorable man you have.'

Miranda and Cole shared an intimate look. Tony cleared his throat. 'You are alright, no?' He motioned to her leg.

Miranda had forgotten all about her wound. She saw the dried blood, which reminded her of the pain. She felt the throbbing again, but it was dull. Not much at all, in fact. 'I'm okay,' she smiled.

'Your brother will be okay, too,' Tony said to Cole. 'It looks like a clean wound, perhaps the bullet punctured a lung.'

'You knew it might come to this, that I might have to shoot him. That's why you gave me the Glock,' Cole observed.

'It is hard to kill a brother. No matter what he's done. It may be right, but still hard for you to live with.'

'So which is worse: putting him six feet under or seeing him live to take more victims?' Cole looked anguished. Miranda squeezed his hand.

'Neither is easy. Perhaps fate will take that responsibility away from you.' Tony paused, glancing toward the uniformed group who were arguing over where to start. 'Well, then, I must go help these officers do their jobs. You know they hate nothing more than to see an ex-officer at a crime scene. We are worse than reformed smokers.' Tony kissed Miranda's hand and strolled away.

The paramedics were loading Sable onto a stretcher. 'No,' one on the handheld radio reported to the other two. 'The doc doesn't want us to remove the knife. Tricky place. She could bleed to death between here and there. They're going to wait until surgery.'

Another ambulance arrived. Pulling up alongside the first one the paramedics hopped out. Ushering Vanessa out of the way, they checked Crayne's vital signs. He seemed stable, his bleeding had stopped. 'He's gonna make it,' Miranda and Cole heard one of them say.

The paramedics slid Crayne onto the stretcher, the eased him alongside Sable. One of the paramedics walked over to check Miranda's leg.

'We wanna see if we're gonna take you in too,' he explained, bending down to take a look. The other paramedics were readying their vehicles for the journey to the hospital. In that moment, Miranda saw Sable reach down to her leg and pull the knife from her boot. Miranda screamed and pointed, but everyone looked at her. Everyone except Cole. He leaped just as Sable plunged the knife into Crayne's throat. Cole jumped on her, wrenching the deadly instrument out of her hand. But it was too late. With a bloody gurgle, Crayne's life left him. Sable laughed, an eerie sound of triumph before she lost consciousness.

Cole squeezed his eyes shut as the paramedics threw the sheet over his brother after the required attempts to save him. They all knew it was hopeless. Sable's aim had been viciously accurate. The ambulance carrying her left fifteen minutes earlier, followed by a police officer. They weren't giving her anymore chances.

Miranda held Cole closely, searching his eyes in the dark. He looked past her, at the white van that disappeared into the cedars, the lights on its hood off. No hurry to get to the morgue. Miranda felt a wave of relief after the horror he had put her and others through. But at the same time, she yearned to soothe Cole's suffering. Crayne's death would inspire no clear-cut emotions in him. Relief battled with guilt. Loss weighed against a safer society. Questions that could never be answered versus answers Cole probably didn't need to hear.

But Miranda could see more in his eyes. 'We need to talk. Talking will help.'

Cole shook his head. 'He put you through so much hell. *I* put you through hell.'

Miranda rested her fingertip on his lips. 'You have showed me heaven,' she purred. Gently, his hands cradled her jaw and brought her lips to his. The kiss was long, deep, searching and sensitive. She felt his body stir against her. Cole pulled away.

'I love you,' he looked straight into her soul as he said it. Then kissed her once more before walking off beyond the corral.

'Cole, where are you going?' Miranda called, her heart beating faster than it had when her life had been threatened. 'Wait for me.'

He never turned around. Miranda ran her tongue across her lips. They tasted bittersweet.

CHAPTER 27

It was eight a.m. in downtown San Antonio, although to Miranda it could have been midnight in Hades. She had spent all night and all morning being grilled first by Kendall County sheriff's deputies, then by San Antonio police. The crossover of county lines had made the whole mess a complicated jumble with both authorities fighting over control of the investigation. Miranda could have cared less. If someone asked where Cole had disappeared to one more time she was going to scream. Who wanted to know the answer to that more than she did?

'Well, the conquering hero. Or heroine, I should say. Your cowboy lover is the hero.' Rick looked around dramatically. 'Where is he? Putting his white horse away?'

Miranda looked up at him with red-rimmed eyes and ignored his question. 'You don't look any worse for wear after trying to destroy a man's life.'

'Ah, well the top brass don't see me as being that manipulative. In fact, I've been labeled as being "over-worked" and therefore a little careless,' he smiled at her arrogantly.

'Translated, that is: they're covering the police department's ass. They give you a tough punishment and the whole sordid tale goes public and the department looks bad. The public loses confidence. PR disaster.' Miranda delivered the whole analysis in a monotone. It wasn't worth getting upset over. Only one thing left was.

'Oh, don't worry, my sweet. I'm getting my time in purgatory. I'm being transferred to Internal Affairs, just another Joe Investigator.'

'Internal Affairs?' Miranda had to allow a sarcastic smile. 'Where integrity, ethics and morality are the required character traits? Irony reigns. Great place for you. Geniuses must run this place.'

'I'll still join them one day, you know. Before I head to the state capitol on my way to the Congress.'

'You'll certainly fit in all those places. I'm glad to see this incident has humbled you,' Miranda threw over her shoulder as she turned her back on Rick.

He reached over and turned her around. He was close enough that his chest brushed her breasts. They didn't respond. Neither did any other body part. She was finally over Rick. Miranda allowed herself a small sense of satisfaction.

'You know you could be there with me. Wife of the police chief, wife of the state Senator, wife of the US Senator. Just think of the advantages.' His mouth hovered near hers.

'For you, yes, I can think of many. For me, I can't think of one. I'll tell you one thing, though, you do have more balls than a brass monkey.' Miranda put a finger to his forehead and pushed him back.

'Well, there's an advantage right there,' Rick said, rubbing the inside of her wrist.

Miranda had trouble believing he was serious, but looking into his hard, dark eyes she could see he was. Disgusted, she turned away and sat on a bench where she had been told to wait to sign her statement.

'Miss Randolph,' a shiny head peeked around the corner down the hall. It was the kindly cop who she'd spent most of the pre-dawn hours talking to. 'Your statement is ready for you to sign.'

Grateful for the diversion, Miranda took the stack of papers. As she read it over the pain of the incident returned. Her emotions rubbed raw again. Finally, she was finished. It really hadn't taken her that long to read. Why had it seemed to take days to tell?

Before she could sign her name, another police investigator stuck his head around the corner.

'Hey, Will, I just got off the phone with Austin PD. They got a positive ID on that body. It's Greg Pittman, the guy in Taylor's band who disappeared three years ago. Some guys were four-wheeling in a field south of town when one of them got stuck, the wheels churned up the dirt and uncovered a skeleton. They said he had a chain around his neck. Still had prints and bingo, guess whose matched exactomundo?'

Miranda held her breath, and resisted the urge to turn around. The cop next to her answered, 'Blase Traynor, alias Sable Diamonte.'

'Bingo. This bitch is going down.' The cop who spoke blushed as Miranda turned around. ''Scuse me, ma'am. I didn't see you there.'

'Don't worry about it. After what I've been through that is the last thing that would offend me,' Miranda assured him. 'How is Sable doing in the hospital?'

He shrugged. 'She's out of surgery. Knocked out in ICU. Those gut wounds they say are touch and go for at least forty-eight hours.'

'You can go now,' the balding cop said. 'But I need to warn you. Those reporters are crawling the walls of this joint to get at you. And you did decide to wait until later to talk to them. You might want an escort to take you home.'

Sometime during the night she had been *strongly encouraged* not to talk to the press about what happened at the ranch until after three o'clock in the afternoon. Although it was never said, she suspected it gave them enough time to tidy up the mess Rick had made of the investigation. Miranda agreed to the police suggestion. Tit for tat. She'd call in this chit one day.

It irritated Miranda that the cops apparently didn't trust her enough to keep her promise. They wanted to send a chaperone with her through the media horde. Well, screw them. She smiled.

'Thank you, no. I won't be needing any help.'

'Have it your way,' he shrugged, but Miranda could feel him tense at her refusal. 'If you're sure?'

'Yes.'

'If you hear from Taylor, you'll call us, right?'

Miranda nodded and turned to leave. Rick materialized again from behind a cubicle. Miranda had to rock back on her heels to avoid running into his chest. 'So, Colton is missing, huh? Now that does not look good. Maybe there's some secret he's keeping from you. Maybe he's no more lily white than I am.'

'You may be right, Rick. But I love him. And that is the difference.'

Finally rendering Rick speechless, Miranda made her escape. She was halfway down the stairs when she remembered Wayne. It was just about time that the ransom note had ordered for him to be at the Market, she knew he must have been crazy trying to reach her. Unless the whole story was all over the radio and TV by now.

Miranda decided to swing by the Market, only a few blocks away, on a hunch. She snuck out without being seen and crossed over to Market Street. From the veiled disgust in the furtive glances of strangers, she guessed she looked like a bag lady. From an old T-shirt one of the cops had lent her, to her bandaged shoulder and calf, to her ripped jeans and uncombed hair, she didn't doubt she fit the bill.

As she neared the corner, she wondered whether Wayne would be there, waiting to give away his only success in exchange for Victoria's happiness. Because that was what it had boiled down to. Miranda no longer believed and knew Wayne didn't either, that Victoria would cut off his funds if an affair were discovered. But she might cut off her feelings. Victoria had talked a good game to Miranda during their meeting, but she hadn't seen the raunchy pictures. Those would be too much even for Victoria's love.

Miranda was across the street from the designated corner. No Wayne. Miranda felt disappointed. Not only in that alcoholic blowhard but in love itself. She loved Cole and he loved her. She knew that in her heart. But were was he? Maybe the integrity of love was overrated.

But, just as she turned back, she saw Wayne. He stormed away from a pay phone, and back to the curb, looking up and down. He wore a long-sleeved shirt splashed with a loud rainbow of colors. Its silk fabric clung to the loose spare tire around his stomach and his fatty breasts. It was tucked into white jeans so tight they showed the pattern of his boxer shorts. His flushed face shone with sweat, his hair stuck to his neck in wet clumps. Miranda thought she had never seen him look worse. And she was proud of him. In his left hand, he gripped a manila envelope. The contract for the club ownership.

Miranda started to raise her hand, to tell him it was over. That his sacrifice wasn't necessary. But she stopped herself. With a backward glance, she started back downtown. She would leave him to sweat and stew for a while longer. It might do him some good. It might teach him a lesson. Miranda didn't really believe that, but she thought, for Victoria, she would make him suffer. Just a little.

Five minutes later she walked down the hall to Cole's apartment. She didn't know what she expected to find. Him sitting on the couch waiting for her to stumble across him? The yellow police tape warned her not to cross, she reached under it and tried the door. It was unlocked. She opened it and ducked under the tape. It was a mess, the police being indisposed to cleaning up after their search, considering the occupant was a serial rapist who was going to jail. Or so they thought at the time.

Miranda wandered through the small apartment for a while. In his bathroom, she picked the handtowel off the floor and put it to her nose. Closing her eyes, she drank in Cole's scent. Her finger ran across his razor, knocking the razor stubble off. The unmade bed reminded her of his touch. Her heart ached.

She didn't know how long she had been there, mourning him as if he were dead, when a knock sounded. Heart hammering in her chest, Miranda peeked around the corner. A man in a suit, his hair neatly held back in a ponytail, stood in the open doorway.

'You a cop?' Miranda asked, resigned. 'Or a reporter?'

'No. Are you?' he answered, looking around the room with surprise and curiosity.

Miranda had to smile. 'Definitely not.'

'I'm looking for Cole Taylor, but I guess I have the wrong address.' He started to back away down the hall.

'You have the right address. Why are you looking for Cole?'

'I'm his agent,' the man answered, extending his hand. 'Jared Williams.'

Brow furrowed, Miranda shook his hand. 'Cole doesn't have an agent.'

Williams tugged at his ponytail. 'Well, he might have forgotten he had one. I deal only with his manager.'

'Manager?'

'Yeah, Sable Diamonte.'

'Sable,' Miranda breathed, as she sank into the couch. Would they ever uncover all of that woman's machinations? 'She isn't his manager.'

'Well, I don't blame him for firing her. I was getting suspicious that she was out for herself more than for Cole. Especially when this record deal came up and she started trying to convince me that his music was getting lousy, that he was getting unpredictable. She and the other guy in the band were thinking of going out on their own and she wanted the company to still sign them without Cole.'

'Record deal?' Miranda wasn't sure she heard right.

'Yeah, if the execs ever get to meet Cole. It's contingent on that. I've been working on this so long that I finally decided to come drag him to the meeting if I have to.'

'I don't think you'll have to do that,' Miranda said, feeling all the jubilation she would if it were she who was

380

stepping into stardom. 'He'll be thrilled. He doesn't know anything about this.'

Williams looked shocked. 'Are you kidding? What's with this Sable character? Was she trying to ice him out?'

Miranda's eyebrows raised slowly as she nodded. 'Yeah, you could say that.'

He waved his arm around. 'What's with this?'

'Long story. Let's just say Sable's involved and Cole's a hero. Could be great publicity if you play it right.'

Williams looked thoughtful. 'So where's Cole?'

Good question. Miranda thought. 'Tying up some loose ends.'

'Okay, have him get a hold of me as soon as possible.' He handed her his card with the local hotel and room number on the back.

'And you are?' he asked politely, trying not to stare at her ragged appearance.

'I'm the life Cole saved. Miranda Randolph.'

'Wow, this whole thing is blowing me away,' Jared Williams exclaimed as he left, his ponytail bouncing behind him.

'You're not the only one,' Miranda said to the empty room.

CHAPTER 28

There was only one place Cole could be. Once it hit Miranda she couldn't get there fast enough. But as she pulled off the highway and onto the rocky driveway, her stomach lurched. Evil still hung in the air, as strong as the memories. Though it was impossible, she still half expected Crayne to jump out from behind the big oak tree in the front yard. Out from behind where her initial was carved next to his. Forever. She closed the car door.

Miranda stared at the quiet house. He wasn't there she knew. Police tape striped the house and grounds in yellow. Some pieces had broken loose and blew like streamers from tree limbs. It looked like a crime graveyard. Miranda shivered. She knew where she had to go, but her feet stuck to the limestone like it was wet cement.

Would Cole still want her? Every time he looked at her he would remember the hell his life had become since he'd met her. He'd said he had put her through hell, but hadn't she done that to him? If she had believed his innocence from the start, maybe it wouldn't have all ended like this. Maybe their love wasn't strong enough to overcome the mistakes and the memories.

Miranda had to find out. She nearly ran into the tackroom. Dried blood covered the floor and was smeared over some of the saddles. Reggie's blood. A twinge of regret that she hadn't thought about him since the shooting caused her to pause. He was a brave dog. He'd tried to save her. She wondered where he was now. Grabbing a bridle from Rocky's peg, she went to the corral. Rocky stood with the other mare, just beyond the stream. No sign of O'Malley. Miranda went to the dapple mare, pulled the bridle on and jumped on bareback.

Rocky was happy to race through the trees, across the rough terrain. The years since Miranda had ridden regularly seemed to fall away and she felt like a teenager again. A cool front was blowing in and the air was laced with chill. As Miranda rode up the hill, she saw the overcast skies beginning to clear. The sun peeked through the trees, filling the forest with multidimensional patterns of light and shadow.

As they reached the peak, Rocky whinnied. It was answered. Miranda's heart pounded. Rocky slowed to a walk and broke through the trees. Without a cue, the mare stopped.

Miranda saw O'Malley first, tied to a tree. Cole sat with his back to a large rock, facing the valley below. 'Come to join us girls?' Cole asked stonily.

The tone of his voice made Miranda's heart plummet. But after a few moments she realized Cole thought the two mares had climbed the hill on their own. He didn't know she was riding Rocky. Silently, she dismounted and hung her reins in a tree. Miranda's eyes never left Cole as she approached. His profile was hard and brooding, unapproachable. She opened her mouth but his name caught in her throat. She tried again, forcing it out.

'Cole.'

He closed his eyes and took a deep breath. Stopping, Miranda held hers.

'Why did you come?' His voice was raw, as if he been screaming. Or crying.

'Because I love you.'

Cole stood, straightening slowly, as if his muscles were stiff from sitting too long. 'You shouldn't.'

'It's not something controllable. I can't tell my heart not to feel that way. I can't say: "Don't ache when he turns away from you. Don't sing when he looks into your eyes."

Believe me, I've tried. When suspicion was clouding the truth, I tried. I failed. And now I don't want to avoid my feelings anymore. I *want* to love you. And I do.' Miranda brushed tears off her cheeks.

'It's not always enough,' Cole almost whispered, still looking into the valley.

'It can be.'

'It won't be when I turn into the kind of person my brother was, or my father is.' His eyes met hers as his voice cracked. For the first time Miranda noticed the tape recorder sitting in the grass. She knew then he'd listened to the tape.

Miranda took his face in her hands. 'You won't ever be that kind of person. Ever. Look, your father is not an evil man. I think if the circumstances of his life had been different he would have been a different man. He really loved your mother and thought he could live with the concept of raising another man's child. But it began to eat at him – consume him – until he became a steel-hearted tyrant. He still has feelings, for you and your mother, but he's forgotten what he's supposed to do with them.

'As for Crayne, he was only your half-brother. Who knows what genes this Gunther handed down to him? My God, he was a double agent. The kind of work he was in validated a violent lifestyle. What's more, your father's abuse of Crayne may have developed tendencies that might have never surfaced had he not been a victim. It was just a bad combination. And don't forget Sable. She zeroed in on his weaknesses and manipulated them for her own purposes.'

'Yeah,' Cole put in acidly. 'And she's a woman I spent three years of my life with. What does that say about me?'

'I don't know,' Miranda breathed, as she let her hand slip from his jaw. 'Did you love her?'

'No. I didn't even know her,' Cole answered without hesitation. 'That's why I decided to break it off. Before I met you.'

Miranda let out the breath she had been holding. 'We've

384

both made mistakes. Look at me. I spent years with Rick.'

Cole's eyes searched hers. 'Did you love him?'

'No. I thought I did for a while,' Miranda admitted, the honesty difficult. 'But I didn't know what love is. Now I do.'

'It's hell,' Cole observed drily. But Miranda could see the dancing light returning to his eyes.

'And heaven.' She reminded him with a small telling smile. His eyes warmed then burned into hers as he pulled her into his arms. This wasn't a sweet kiss like the night before, when he was trying to say goodbye. Their mouths and bodies met with a passion so strong they both struggled to meet the power of it. Desire collided with emotions deeper than either had experienced before. They weren't aware of the individual movements of their hands, fingers, tongues, just the sensations each touch unleashed.

Miranda didn't feel the hard ground or the cool wind on her bare body. She only felt him with her, in her . . .

Cole forgot his doubts and surrendered to becoming one with Miranda . . .

The sun rushed the treetops before they spoke again.

'Why did you think to look for me here?' Cole asked softly, his hands caressing her hair.

'Because this peak is "our place",' Miranda said as if the answer were obvious.

'It is?' Cole's brows rose as he gently mocked her.

'Well, why did you come here?' she questioned pointedly.

Cole laughed in surrender. 'Are our disagreements always going to end this way? With you skillfully trapping me into the truth?'

'Of course.'

'I give up, since you know me better than I know myself.'

'You betcha Buster,' Miranda kissed him on the nose. 'That's why I'm never giving up on you, even if you give up on yourself.'

'You know, after what we've been through, those

arguments over carpet color and babies' names won't be so bad.'

Miranda sat up and looked hard at Cole. 'Are you trying to ask me something, Cole Taylor?'

Cole's eyes twinkled. 'Since you know me so well, thought you would've answered before I ever asked the question.'

She smiled. 'I still want to hear the question.'

Cole, barefoot and barechested, with only blue jeans zipped but not buttoned, got down in front of her on one knee. He ran his hand through his hair as he cleared his throat. Miranda suppressed a smile at his familiar habit.

'Miranda Randolph, will you marry me?'

Her eyes traveled the length of him, then rose back to his eyes. 'I think you hold an unfair advantage, asking me while looking like that.'

'I'm not above coercion,' he admitted slyly.

Her index finger went to the indentation that ran between the muscles of his stomach. She trailed it down to his jeans and followed it back up his chest. 'And if I say no?'

His hand removed her finger. 'Then no more of that.'

Miranda pouted. 'Well, I guess I have only one answer for you.'

Cole couldn't believe his heart stopped waiting for her answer, but it did. Until she finally whispered, 'Yes.'

Laughing, they fell into each other's arms, and looked out on the valley.

'It seems a shame to save this view only for rides,' Miranda said thoughtfully.

'Well, we will need a bigger house. I guess we could build up here,' Cole said. 'But what would I do with the cabin?'

'Burn it down,' Miranda said in a monotone.

Cole looked at her sharply. Then he gently turned her to face him. 'Did he hurt you there?'

Tears burned behind Miranda's eyes. 'No, I hurt him. And I don't ever want to think about it again.'

'Okay. It gets torched. But it's gonna cost a lot of money to build this far off the road. And you're not marrying a rich man.' He paused. The planes on his face hardened before he continued. 'I refuse to take any of my father's money.'

'Money won't be a problem,' Miranda said with a sly smile.

Cole's left eyebrow arched. 'Oh? Why is that?'

'Because I am marrying a man who is going to be both rich and famous.'

'It's great that you believe in me, but I'm just not commercial enough. I don't want to prostitute my music for –'

She put her finger on his lips. 'You won't have to. You got a record deal.'

His face recorded a rainbow of emotions – disbelief, shock, elation. As she explained Jared Williams's visit, he rained kisses on her nose, ears and neck.

Suddenly, he stopped and drew back. Miranda let her monologue fade away as she studied his eyes.

'Would you have accepted my proposal without the impending fame and fortune?'

Cole's tone was teasing but Miranda could detect just a hint of seriousness. She wondered if he would ever regain the cocksure attitude she'd fallen in love with from the first moment she'd seen him.

'Why don't you turn the record deal down and find out?'

'Hell, no,' Cole blurted out.

Their laughter floated down to the canyon below. And as the sun slipped behind the trees, casting a tangerine glow on the wispy clouds in the purpling sky, Miranda and Cole planned their future. Together.

THE EXCITING NEW NAME
IN WOMEN'S FICTION!

PLEASE HELP ME TO HELP YOU!

Dear *Scarlet* Reader,

As Editor of *Scarlet* Books I want to make sure that the
books I offer you every month are up to the high standards
Scarlet readers expect. And to do that I need to know a
little more about you and your reading likes and dislikes. So
please spare a few minutes to fill in the short questionnaire
on the following pages and send it to me. I'll send *you* a
surprise gift as a thank you!*

Looking forward to hearing from you,

Sally Cooper

Editor-in-Chief, *Scarlet*

*Offer applies only in the UK, only one offer per household.

QUESTIONNAIRE

Please tick the appropriate boxes to indicate your answers

1 Where did you get this Scarlet title?
Bought in supermarket ☐
Bought at my local bookstore ☐ Bought at chain bookstore ☐
Bought at book exchange or used bookstore ☐
Borrowed from a friend ☐
Other (please indicate) _____

2 Did you enjoy reading it?
A lot ☐   A little ☐   Not at all ☐

3 What did you particularly like about this book?
Believable characters ☐   Easy to read ☐
Good value for money ☐   Enjoyable locations ☐
Interesting story ☐   Modern setting ☐
Other _____

4 What did you particularly dislike about this book?
_____

5 Would you buy another Scarlet book?
Yes ☐   No ☐

6 What other kinds of book do you enjoy reading?
Horror ☐   Puzzle books ☐   Historical fiction ☐
General fiction ☐   Crime/Detective ☐   Cookery ☐
Other (please indicate) _____

7 Which magazines do you enjoy reading?
1. _____
2. _____
3. _____

And now a little about you –
8 How old are you?
Under 25 ☐   25–34 ☐   35–44 ☐
45–54 ☐   55–64 ☐   over 65 ☐

cont.